MMXVII

THE WHITE REVIEW
243 Knightsbridge
London, SW7 1DN
United Kingdom

ISBN 978-0-995743-71-7

Design by Ray O'Meara
Typeset in Joyous
Printed and bound by TJ International

Supported using public funding by
ARTS COUNCIL
ENGLAND
LOTTERY FUNDED

THE WHITE REVIEW
ANTHOLOGY

CONTENTS

CONTENTS

VALENTINE'S DAY 2010, BROOKLYN: an intern at the *PARIS REVIEW*
skips his shift as an undocumented worker at an Upper East Side restaurant
to have drinks with a BBC journalist and art critic visiting New York. *THE
WHITE REVIEW* is born, or at least the drunken idea of it.

A year later we launched the first print issue at Daunt Books in London's
Cheapside. An unholy coalition between the Conservatives and Liberal
Democrats had recently formed a government, promptly tripling tuition fees
and sparking protests. The first shots in the Arab Spring had been fired;
anti-austerity protests in Greece exposed cracks in the façade of European
solidarity that would swiftly widen; Donald Trump was briefly a frontrunner
for the Republican candidacy, though his eventual decision not to stand still
felt then like the inevitable triumph of sanity over satire. Meanwhile, print
journalism and book publishing were dying a slow death – remember the
digital revolution? – and we intended to do something about it, though we
didn't know quite what.

The desire to launch a magazine was born out of our respective frustra-
tions at the state of contemporary publishing in London, and indeed cultural
and political commentary in the United Kingdom. Where could an aspiring
writer–critic–editor (whatever it was we were back then) hope to get published? The established literary magazines at home seemed to be closed shops,
conservative either in their politics or their tastes. (There were exceptions,
we discovered retrospectively, among them the poetry journals *CLINIC* and
POPSHOT.) We lamented the decline of cultural criticism and essay-length
journalism, forms which seemed increasingly in danger of confinement to the
ivory tower. We were exasperated that the visual arts, so central to London's
culture, were so often made inaccessible to audiences without the theoretical
training demanded by gatekeepers determined to protect their own territory. So, inspired by the success of little magazines in New York – the *PARIS
REVIEW, N+1, BOMB*, to name a few – we set out to create a new platform for
writers, poets, critics and artists who might not otherwise find a place in the
publishing landscape.

We didn't much know what we were doing, in truth. We borrowed a name
from *LA REVUE BLANCHE*, a publication edited by the bomb-throwing anarchist art critic Félix Fénéon which took up many of the principles we sought to
appropriate for ourselves – to publish ambitious, innovative writing; to bring
art and literature together; to publish a new generation of writers; to engage
with the world around us. There was even a manifesto, which will never
again see the light of day. Buried in the grandiosity was sincerity: we wanted

to offer emerging writers an opportunity to test the limits of their talents with the support of conscientious and committed (if inexperienced) editors, and to produce a magazine that had as its first aim to promote their achievements.

We wrote solicitous emails to writers we admired but didn't know, and to people we knew who wrote. It helped that Tom McCarthy, firmly in the former camp, agreed to an interview in the first print issue (the generosity of writers and artists whom we admire has been an essential, and heartening, feature of our seven years). We published a piece about a dead person (Primo Levi), even some poetry by a dead person (Charles Cros, translated by Sophie Lewis). Soon enough we decided no more dead people − we were to be a contemporary magazine − though we have made exceptions for Edouard Levé and Christoph Schlingensief, notably.

That first issue shaped our editorial policy − a commitment to translation, and to emerging writers alongside established − and gave us a structure for the print edition that has endured through the years. Each issue features two or three interviews with established writers and artists, around which we publish two or three pieces of fiction; a similar number of essays; at least two sections dedicated to the work of a single poet; three series of artworks, typically one in black and white and two in colour; and a different artist on the cover of each issue. We learned about the slush pile; we learned how to say no; how to commission; how to work with writers; we became editors.

We raised the start-up capital − £7,000 − through friends and family and through the crowdfunding website WeFund (the list of 'friends' at the back of each magazine is testament to the number of small donations that allowed us to get off the ground). This allowed us to build a website and produce our first print issue, which sold well enough that we could afford a second. (It has been hand to mouth ever since.) We later applied for, and were awarded, Arts Council funding, which made it possible for us to pay contributors to both the print and online editions of the magazine. We remain eternally grateful to the Arts Council, and to a system of state funding which still (despite drastic cuts) makes it possible for charitable organisations such as THE WHITE REVIEW to pursue its enshrined commitment to 'promoting the arts and literature for the benefit of the public'.

In 2010 we met Ray O'Meara, who became the magazine's designer and art director. We had meetings. He showed us some typefaces he'd been working on. It turned out that we had similar ideas of what a magazine could be at a time when people were saying the last rites over print publishing. As Anne Carson would state in a later interview with the magazine, 'Reading and thinking are physical operations. So you can affect both of them by order-ing the text as a visual, aural, tactile, choreographic, dynamic event.' Only in print is this possible. Ray designed a typeface and produced an object which, while beautiful in itself, served to complement and perhaps even elevate the writing it contained (writing, not merely 'content'). We learned about 'kern-ing', 'orphans', 'widows' – and how painstaking and time-consuming it is to produce a book. Ray's bold design also bought the magazine time, as the first three issues sold to a predominantly design-oriented readership while we sought out the literary and artistic audiences who would become the commu-nity we had so longed for.

We brought this community together through an extensive programme of events. These performances, film screenings, panel debates, readings and interventions quickly became a central part of our mission as a small insti-tution, and in the seven years since our first we have hosted over a hundred events across the UK, Europe and the United States. The vast majority of these have been free to attend. A tip to aspiring publishers: free drinks go a long way to getting crowds out, whether in a greenhouse in Wapping, a car park in Peckham, a bookshop in Berlin, a gallery in Bristol, or an artist's studio in Hackney Wick. Yet in all of these instances, only once has a mem-ber of the audience purposefully set his girlfriend's hair on fire. No lasting damage was done.

Alongside the print issue of the magazine we launched an online platform which we hoped would complement and support it. Besides making it possi-ble for us to reach an infinitely wider audience than would have been possible through the distribution of the print magazine, the website has also allowed us to experiment with the new possibilities offered by online publishing, and to consider how the two formats can work effectively together. In that spirit we launched an important collaboration with the independent commission-ing body Film and Video Umbrella. 'White Screen' commissioned writers including Hannah Black, Juliet Jacques and Mark von Schlegel to respond to artists' films from the twenty-five year FVU archive. The films and their written complements were published on a dedicated website (http://www.thewhitereview.org/white-screen/). That commitment to finding new audi-ences has led to a number of other offshoots to our central programme of publishing and events over the years. We have run a series of radio shows broadcast by Resonance FM, produced by Bella Marrin, and showcasing our doubtful ability as radio presenters. There was a film series at the Institute for Contemporary Art, London, for which we invited writers and artists including Will Self and Ed Atkins to select and introduce a film of their choice. In 2013, with the support of the Jerwood Foundation, we launched The White Review Short Story Prize, which helped in the first years to supplement our revenue as well as helping to identify some of the most startling talents in British and Irish fiction.

At the time of writing, we have published twenty print issues and sixty-four online issues. This book collects some of the best fiction and essays we have published over the course of that time. Among the emerging talents featured here, Jack Cox, Evan Harris, Jesse Loncraine and Patrick Langley made their print debuts in the magazine. Alexander Christie-Miller had written plenty in print, mainly for the Times, but never at such length. His piece 'Forgotten Sea' charts the long decline of falconry in Turkey's Pontos region. Claire-Louise Bennett, winner of the inaugural White Review Short Story Prize in 2013 for 'The Lady of the House', has gone on to become one of the most exciting writers today. To be able to publish these writers alongside new work by the likes of Anne Carson, Chris Kraus, Deborah Levy and China Miéville, all included here, has been one of the greatest thrills of publishing *THE WHITE REVIEW*. Another has been the opportunity to juxtapose their writing with the work of artists we admire, represented here by two historic contributors: Camille Henrot, whose drawings adorn the cover, and JH Engström, who contributes a series of photographs. Their inclusion is a nod to the series of artworks and visual essays directed by Ray O'Meara since the first issue, a key feature of the magazine.

Political writing, however obliquely one defines it, has never been far from our preoccupations. Lawrence Abu Hamdan's piece 'Listening to Yourself' offers a verbatim transcription of an interview undertaken by a refugee in application for asylum. With 'Debt', Natasha Soobramanien and Luke Williams demonstrate that fiction can be political, and collaborative. Evan Lavender-Smith's Bernhardian fiction 'A Vicious Cycle' reads eerily premonitory post-Trump and post-truth. The inclusion of pieces by Álvaro Enrigue (tr. Rahul Bery), Samanta Schweblin (tr. Brendan Lactot) and Gabriela Weiner (tr. Lucy Greaves) are testament to our history of publishing works in translation.

We have consistently sought to situate culture within the wider social and historical circumstances of its production. To this end, Rosanna Mclaughlin untangles the networks of money and influence that define the practice, exhibition and sale of contemporary art, while Lauren Elkin examines the place of women's writing today, finding its roots in the *écriture féminine* of Hélène

Cixous, Luce Irigaray and Julia Kristeva. Also in the literary critical vein, Jennifer Hodgson and Patricia Waugh expound on the perceived decline of British fiction, while Lars Iyer puts forward a manifesto for literature after the death of literature, presumably written in the nude, in his hot tub, which argues for a new writing 'at the wake'. We hope you enjoy the party.

BEN EASTHAM & JACQUES TESTARD

NUDE IN YOUR HOT TUB, FACING THE ABYSS (A LITERARY MANIFESTO AFTER THE END OF LITERATURE AND MANIFESTOS) BY LARS IYER

I. DOWN FROM THE MOUNTAIN

Once upon a time, writers were like gods, and lived in the mountains. They were either destitute hermits or aristocratic lunatics, and they wrote only to communicate with the already dead or the unborn, or for no one at all. They had never heard of the marketplace, they were arcane and antisocial. Though they might have lamented their lives – which were marked by solitude and sadness – they lived and breathed in the sacred realm of Literature. They wrote Drama and Poetry and Philosophy and Tragedy, and each form was more devastating than the last. Their books, when they wrote them, reached their audience posthumously and by the most tortuous of routes. Their thoughts and stories were terrible to look upon, like the bones of animals that had ceased to exist.

Later, there came another wave of writers, who lived in the forests below the mountains, and while they still dreamt of the heights, they needed to live closer to the towns at the edge of the forest, into which they ventured every now and again to do a turn in the public square. They gathered crowds and excited minds and caused scandals and partook in politics and engaged in duels and instigated revolutions. At times, they left for prolonged trips back to the mountains, and when they returned, the people trembled at their new pronouncements. The writers had become heroes, gilded, bold and pompous. And some of the loiterers around the public square started to think: I quite like that! I have half a notion to try that myself.

Soon, writers began to take flats in the town, and took jobs – indeed, whole cities were settled and occupied by writers. They pontificated on every subject under the sun, granted interviews, and published in the local press, St Mountain Books. Some even made a living from their sales, and, when those sales dwindled, they taught about writing at Olympia City College, and when the college stopped hiring in the humanities, they wrote memoirs about 'mountain living'. They became savvy in publicity, because it became evident that the publishing industry was an arm of the publicity industry, and the smart ones worked first in advertising, which was a good place to hone the craft. And the writers began to outnumber their public, and, it became apparent, the public was only a hallucination after all, just as the importance of writing was mostly a hallucination.

Now you sit at your desk, dreaming of Literature, skimming the Wikipedia page about the 'Novel' as you snack on salty treats and watch cat and dog videos on your phone. You post to your blog, and you tweet the most profound things you can think to tweet, you labour over a comment about a trending topic, trying to make it meaningful. You whisper the names like a devotional, *Kafka, Lautréamont, Bataille, Duras,* hoping to conjure the ghost of something you scarcely understand, something preposterous and obsolete that nevertheless preoccupies your every living day. And you find yourself laughing in spite of yourself, laughing helplessly at yourself, laughing to the verge of tears. You click 'new document' and sit there, shaking, staring at your computer screen, and you wonder what in the world you can possibly write now.

II. THE PUPPET CORPSE

To say that Literature is dead is both empirically false and intuitively true. By most statistical indicators, the prognosis is good. There are more readers and writers than ever before. The rise of the internet marks the rise, in some senses, of a deeply literate culture. We are more likely to text each other than to talk. More than ever before, we are likely to comment or write than to watch or listen. The oft quoted fact: there are more graduates of writing pro-grammes than there were people alive in Shakespeare's London. As Gabriel Zaid writes in *So Many Books*, the exponential proliferation of authorship means that the number of published books will soon eclipse the human pop-ulation, soon there will be more books than people who have ever lived. We have libraries on our phones, books (in or out of print) available at a touch of the finger. The mighty Amazon, the infinite Feed, the endless Aggregation, the Wikiwisdom, the Recommendations, Likes, Lists, Criticism, Commen-tary. We live in an unprecedented age of words.

And yet... In another sense, by a different standard, Literature is a corpse and cold at that. Intuitively we know this to be the case, we sense, suspect, fear, and acknowledge it. The *dream* has faded, our *faith* and *awe* have fled, our *belief* in Literature has collapsed. Sometime in the 1960s, the great river of Culture, the Literary Tradition, the Canon of Lofty Works began to braid and break into a myriad distributaries, turning sluggish on the plains of the cultural delta. In a culture without verticality, Literature survives as a refer-ence primer on the *reality effect*, or as a minor degree in the newly privatised university. What *was* Literature? It was the literature of Diderot, Rimbaud, Walser, Gogol, Hamsun, Bataille and most of all Kafka: revolutionary and tragic, prophetic and solitary, posthumous, incompatible, radical and paradoxical, a dwelling for oracles and outsiders, it was defiant and pathetic, it sought to break and alter, to describe, yes, but in describing, shatter, it was outside the culture looking in, and inside the culture looking out. Works of this nature, works in this *spirit*, no longer exist. Or rather, they still exist, but only as a parody of past forms. Literature has become a pantomime of itself, and cultural significance has undergone a hyperinflation, its infinitesimal units bought and sold like penny stocks.

What caused this great decline? We can point to the disappearances of older class and power structures. The decline of the Church, the aristocracy, the bourgeoisie – those great foils of Modernist energies – have dissolved. Like Kant's dove in free flight cutting through the air, the writer needs to feel a kind of *resistance* on the part of Literature, needs to work *against* something even as it struggles *for* something. And what is there to work against when there's no one left to antagonise? We could speak of *globalisation*, of the incorporation of the whole planet into the world market, which has the effect of weakening of past cultural forms and national literatures. We notice the ascension of the *individual* to a place where idiosyncrasy itself becomes commonplace, where the self, the soul, the heart, and the mind are demographic jargon. There is little sense of a tradition to wrestle with – no *agon* of authorship that we associate with the writers of the past. We could point to the *populism* of contemporary culture, to the dissolution of older boundaries between high and low art, and to a weakening of our suspicions about the market. Writers now work in concert with capitalism, rather than setting themselves against it. You're nothing unless you sell, unless your name is known, unless scores of admirers turn up at your book signings. We could also point to the banality of liberal democracies: by tolerating everything, by incorporating everything, our political system licenses nothing. Art was once oppositional, but now it is consumed by the cultural apparatus, and seriousness itself reduces into a kind of kitsch for generations X, Y and Z. We have not run out of things to be serious about – our atmosphere boils, our reservoirs of water go dry, our political dynamic dares our ingenuity to permit catastrophe – but the literary means to *register* tragedy have exhausted themselves. Globalisation has flattened Literature into a million niche markets, and prose has become another product: pleasurable, notable, exquisite, laborious, respected, but always small. No poem will ferment revolution, no novel challenges reality, not anymore.

The history of Literature is like a sound in an echo chamber, growing fainter with each reiteration. Or, to use another metaphor, it could be said that Literature was, after all, a finite resource – like oil, like water – that was tapped and burned away by each explosive new manifestation. If the history of Literature is a history of new ideas about what Literature can be, then we have reached a place where modernism and postmodernism have drunk the well dry. Postmodernism, which was surely just modernism by a more desperate name, brought us to our endgame: everything is available and nothing is surprising. In the past, each great sentence contained a manifesto and every literary life proposed an unorthodoxy, but now all is Xerox, footnote, playacting. Even originality itself no longer has the ability to surprise us. We have witnessed so many stylistic and formal gambits that even something original in all its constituent parts contains the meta–quality of newness, and so, paradoxically, is instantly recognisable.

Some sound the old clarion, call for a return to the old ways, demanding that Culture return on its chariot and restore the significance of literary authorship, but their grandiose demands are noted with doubt, derision, or not at all. The 'classics', from antiquity to the present, are all repertory routines, like THE NUTCRACKER at Christmas. Literary prestige exists only in a liturgical fashion, as quaint as a nun on the metro. Who but the most pompous of the third wave of writers can take themselves seriously as an Author? Who could dream of archiving their emails and tweets for a grateful posterity? The seclusion of Blanchot has become impossible, as has the exile of Rimbaud, the youthful death of Radiguet. No one is rejected or ignored anymore, not when everyone is published instantly, without effort or forethought. Authorship has evaporated, replaced by a legion of keystroke labourers, shoulder to shoulder with the admen and app developers.

One could argue that we ought to be grateful for this new order. Isn't it nice, after all, to emerge from your hobby shed as a fledgling novelist? So others might read you: what a surprise! That people read fiction at all any more: likewise, a surprise. Your friends and family think it's nice, too. So you've published a novel! Do people still read them? Well, fancy that! For your circle of friends, the fact of having published a novel trumps anything it might contain. The fact that your name will come up on a Google search with something more than nude pictures of you in a hot tub is already something. And so the prestige of authorship gives way to the prestige of an ephemeral kind of literary careerism, one which is quickly forgotten.

What, then, is so terrible? The stalls of the marketplace provide a fascinating babble, a white noise for a well–adjusted lifetime. Let a thousand flowers bloom, etc. Perhaps the demise of Literature marks the end of a certain need. Perhaps we should give up the ghost. To what end do we *require* the pantomimic wraith of the *poète maudit*, the leering shade of Rimbaud or Lautréamont with its bottle of absinthe and its bloodshot eyes? For the pragmatic among us, the end of Literature is merely the end of a melodramatic model, a false hope that has gone the way of psychoanalysis, Marxism, punk rock and philosophy. But for the less pragmatic among us, we realise – we experience – what has been lost. Without Literature we lose Tragedy and Revolution both, and these are the two last best modalities of Hope. And when Tragedy disappears, we sink down into a gloom, a life whose vast sadness is that it is less than tragic. We crave tragedy, but where can we get it when tragedy has given way to farce? Shame and scorn are the only response now at literary readings to literary manifestos. All efforts are belated now, all attempts are impostures. We know what we want to say and to hear, but our new instruments cannot hold the tune. We cannot *do it again* nor *make it new* since both of those actions have telescoped to equivalence – we are like circus clowns who cannot squeeze into their car. The words of Pessoa ring in our ears: 'Since we are unable to extract beauty from life, we attempt at least to extract it from our incapacity to extract beauty from life.' This is the task given us, our last, best chance.

III. SICK OF LITERATURE

'Whoever writes is exiled from writing, which is the country – his own – where he is not a prophet.'
—— Maurice Blanchot

As in any death, any calamity, our first, perverse reaction is denial. We loved our literary geniuses too much to admit their days are done. We dance around the Bloomsday maypole and taste the word Camus on our tongues like the Eucharist. With pomp and circumstance, the award ceremonies vainly bestow medals of greatness on novels that vaguely mime our fading memory of masterpiece. The prestige, the debris, the body of Literature remains even as the spirit has fled. Only a very few writers have grasped the dire nature of our current literary moment. Only a few writers write truthfully about the state we are in and the obstacles set against us. Their work is sickly and cannibalistic, preposterous and desperate, but it is also, paradoxically, joyous and rings with truth. There is a terrible honesty in this work that sets us free.

These are the writers who show us how, perhaps, we can proceed.

Before we can be healed, we must begin with the diagnosis. The narrator of Enrique Vila-Matas's *MONTANO'S MALADY* suffers from a kind of 'literary sickness', wherein he experiences the world only in terms of the books he has read by the great names of literary history. He is condemned to understand himself and everything around him in terms of the lives and works of the authors who obsess him. His motive for writing *MONTANO'S MALADY*, is to find a cure – to leave Literature by way of literature.

In the first section of the book, a freestanding novella, Montano visits Nantes to free himself of his literary sickness, but finds himself more deeply mired in it. The city itself can only remind him of Jacques Vaché, the legendary proto-surrealist known only through his letters to Breton, who was born there and took his life there – as well as of Breton himself, for whom Nantes was second only to his beloved Paris as a source of inspiration. And when Montano visits his son in that same city, he can only see himself as the ghostly father of a Hamlet who, like Shakespeare's character, pretends to be stark raving mad.

Montano is trapped by literature. Deciding to leave the city in desperation, catching the first train out of the city, Montano admits 'this is a very literary thing to do, I also know that trains are very literary' – modes of transport, too, have become infested with his sickness. A subsequent trip to Chile provides no relief – flying in a small plane, he can think only of Antoine de Saint-Exupéry, who delivered mail over the same mountains. Montano evokes countless other authors on the way: Danilo Kiš, Pablo Neruda, Alejandra Pizarnik and so on.

Montano suffers. He is pressed up too close to literature. The world itself seems to be a system of literary tropes, literary associations. Montano can't even dream of suicide, about putting it all to an end, since death is 'precisely what literature talks about most'. There is no way out – there's no course of action he can follow that does not risk becoming thereby some kind of literary cliché, literary kitsch. For Montano's predicament is not only that he is trapped in Literature, it is that Literature itself appears like a tawdry stage set.

Montano's infection has its roots in Kafka (indeed, what problems of the last hundred years have not been anticipated by Kafka?). Montano writes that there's no one more 'literature-sick' than the Prague-born author. 'I am made of literature', Kafka says, but Kafka managed to make a literature out of this sickness. *THE CASTLE* might, as the narrator of *MONTANO'S MALADY* suggests, allegorise the impossibility of exchanging exegesis for reality, of escaping sickness for health. But the very act of creating allegory out of his illness becomes a kind of literature. Kafka, in other words, can still write Literature, and so his literary sickness is, for a time, assuaged.

Vila–Matas's narrator has even fewer options available to him than Kafka. The structures of religion had collapsed for Kafka, leaving him in the realm of allegory, but for Vila–Matas, even the structures of allegory have collapsed, even the structure of narrative itself have fallen into ruin. Even Kafka could tell a *story*, but this is beyond Vila–Matas's narrator. Whereas Kafka was born too late for religion, we are all born too late for Literature. As the narrator of MONTANO'S MALADY replays the lives and works of literary legends, he shows only how remote these figures have become for us, these writers who Literature itself already seemed to keep at a distance. Literature is moving away from us just as it was moving away from our literary prede-cessors – from diarists like Gide, who, as described in MONTANO'S MALADY, is forever dreaming of writing a Masterpiece. For the idea of a Masterpiece – or even *dreaming of writing a Masterpiece* – is itself part of literary kitsch. This is what the narrator means when he claims that *literature itself* suffers from Montano's malady: Montano's sickness – seeing the world in terms of Literature – is also Literature's, a mirror that can no longer reflect the world.

'Don Quixote represents a civilisation's youth: he *made up* events; and we don't know how to escape those besetting us', writes E. M. Cioran. To make up events, even to allegorise them, doesn't seem possible anymore. As when we spit into the wind, our slightest literary gesture flies back to stick to us. This, as in the virtuosic brilliance of the first part of MONTANO'S MALADY, can be funny. But in the end, it's exhausting: as one reviewer claims 'the jokes start wearing thin' and the book becomes 'tortured'. It is difficult not to agree that the narrator seems 'to have lost the plot – not that there ever was one – entirely'. And yet, and yet, despite the awful impasse, Vila-Matas ends on a note of surprising defiance, even hope: the narrator and Robert Musil kneel before a great abyss, surrounded by the pompous, self-satisfied writers ('en-emies of the literary') who congratulate each other at a grotesque literary festival. 'It is the air of the time,' says the narrator with regret, 'the spirit is threatened.' But Musil contradicts him: 'Prague is untouchable... it's a magic circle. Prague has always been too much for them. And it always will be.' For a book whose purpose is to identify the terminal sickness of Literature, MONTANO'S MALADY ends by insisting that something yet remains, that there is some resolute, secret quality that cannot be undone even by times like ours.

We turn to Thomas Bernhard, another sufferer from Montano's malady.

ESSAY

Nothing to be done, no way out, nothing left to do except to mark the fact that there is nothing to be done, and no way out. The same story told over and again – the attempt to find time and space to complete a summa, some great compendious saying-it-all work on a particular topic, be it the nature of hearing, or the music of Mendelssohn, in which the narrator's report of the insurmountable problems facing this project become the story itself. Bernhard develops his topics – the resentments and frustrated desires of would-be intellectual life, the guilt and suffering of living after the total compromise of Austrian authority, the moral abomination and aftermath of Nazism – through a cacophonous theme and variation of prose. His great iterative loops of consciousness stretch to the breaking point, spiral into a hurricane of rage and frustration. His books turn like whirlwinds, gathering all and everything in their path: hyperbolic profundities fly alongside pitiful mundanities, Old World aphorisms collide with scatterbrained peevishness, grand denunciations fold into banal distractions. The value of a suitcase, the value of a life, how pet dogs sabotage all intellectual thought, how breakfast is a kind of assault. His sentences, always on the brink of falling apart, seek not simply to represent life – the ordinary, tedious life of failed philosophers, failed scientists, failed musicians, and failed literary writers living under tainted regimes – but to enact the forces that comprise it.

The unceasing forward momentum of his prose speaks to a complete intolerance of failure, of compromise, and of a hatred of the strutting imposture of those who do not understand their own failure and compromise. By declaring war on themselves, Bernhard's frustrated narrators, never able to find time and space in which, finally, to write – in which to imitate their masters, be it Schopenhauer or Novalis, Kleist or Goethe – declare war on a culture in which such imitation has become impossible. Bernhard is a name for a plughole around which all of older Culture, all of Literature and Philosophy, seems to swirl and drain away. He mourns, aghast, the suicide of Culture even as he spews bile upon the remaining 'enemies of the literary': the state-sponsored artists, actors, writers and composers of the insufferable dinner party of *Woodcutters*. He is caught in a kind of hateful reverie of the non-literary life, as embodied in the socialite businesswoman sister in *Concrete*, even as, in *The Loser*, he postulates that the only possible outcomes of an artistic endeavour are suicide, madness, and abject failure.

Of course, the irony of Bernhard is that while his narrators fail again and again even to begin, Bernhard himself *has* found a form and a way to speak. His musicians may have forsaken music and his musical scholars cannot write a single sentence about music, but Bernhard has made a music for himself. It is a grotesque symphony perhaps, a farcical, laughable, ludicrous, black hearted waltz, but there is something thrilling, dare we say beautiful, in its song of abnegation. Once again, as in the work of Vila–Matas, only at the very edge of the abyss can we remember what is untouchable.

A final example of literature that faces its own demise and survives: Bolaño's *The Savage Detectives* is a book about an attempt to create a literary vanguard in 1975, written after the conditions for vanguardist practice had collapsed. It is a book about political revolution written in a period after the inevitable failures of such revolutions have revealed themselves. It is a novel about a literary avant–garde and yet the novel itself resists the conceptualisation and stylisation that a literary avant–garde requires. It is an ecstatic, passionate novel – Bolaño himself describes it as a 'love letter to my generation' – that plays out as a parody of the desires for Literature and Revolution. It is a novel, like all recent novels, that comes too late, but unlike most others it finds a way to address this lateness. In doing so, *The Savage Detectives* provides another model for how all would–be authors can appropriately speak about our anachronistic dreams.

The supposed heroes of the book, Ulises Lima and Arturo Belano, leaders of the literary 'gang' called the Visceral Realists, are rarely on stage in the novel for very long. For the most part, we hear of them only at a remove, through the disparate narrators Bolaño calls forward to tell their tale. And the verdict on them is mixed – they have an admirer in gauche and excitable law student Madero, whose brilliantly funny diaries bookend *The Savage Detectives*, but they have their detractors, too. 'Belano and Lima weren't revolutionaries. They weren't writers. Sometimes they wrote poetry, but I don't think they were poets, either. They sold drugs,' says one of Bolaño's narrators. 'The whole visceral realism thing was... the demented strutting of a dumb bird in the moonlight, something essentially cheap and meaningless,' says another. In the end they head towards 'catastrophe or the abyss', as they wander the world, still attempting to strike literary and political poses when the time for Literature and Politics has gone. 'We fought for parties that, had they emerged victorious, would have immediately sent us into a forced labour camp', Bolaño writes of his generation. 'We fought and poured all our generosity into an ideal that had been dead for over fifty years'.

To knowingly pour yourself into a dead ideal – this is the quality that permeates *The Savage Detectives*. Bolaño's insight, and it is both unsettling and unshackling, is that the only subject left to write about is the *epilogue* of Literature: the story of the people who pursue Literature, scratching on their knees for the traces of its passing. This is no mere meta-gamesmanship or solipsism; this is looking things in the face. We live in a culture where a million writers mimic the great literary forms they adore, only vaguely aware how they regurgitate kitsch. We all know Franzen's *FREEDOM* cannot be Flaubert, and yet we cannot quite comprehend why that door is closed to us. On a yearly basis we see dead styles – realisms, modernisms, new-journalisms, playful postmodernisms – presented as the latest fad, as retro as the plague. It's time for literature to acknowledge its own demise rather than playing puppet with the corpse. We must talk directly about the farce of a culture that dreams of things it cannot possibly create, because this farce is our tragedy. We must face the gloom and bitter humour of our situation. Why else does one of Bolaño's narrators draw dwarves with giant cocks as he waits out his time in an Israeli prison cell, or Madero make his companions play guessing game over the cartoons reproduced on the last pages of *THE SAVAGE DETECTIVES* as they near the end of their quest for Cesárea Tinajero? These are the behaviours of people living after Literature. Once again, as in Cervantes, the most compelling narrative is that of Literature's role in our lives, except in our contemporary setting, the role is of a will-o'-the-wisp above the quagmire, a ghost shaking its chains, a vanquished entity who hypnotises a legion of idiots: the would-be novelists, the would-be revolutionaries, the critics, philosophy lecturers, lit-blog editors, magazine subscribers, and would-be intellectuals – all of us.

IV. WHAT TO WRITE AT THE WAKE

'There is plenty of hope, infinite hope, but not for us.'
—— Franz Kafka

So here we are, on this side of the mountain, nostalgic for the great storm-struck plateaus where our writer-ancestors once worked their magic, but knowing that we live on the lowlands. Here we are at the end of Literature and Culture, stripped, bereft, embarrassed. We are children tromping in old boots. Perhaps even Bernhard and Bolaño are too grand for us to imitate! We should study the perverse doodlers, David Shrigley and Ivan Brunetti. Their very choice of medium shows how they have embraced their doom.

We should disconnect our computers and put the books out on the stoop and forget we ever learned to read or care. But for those of us who cannot escape the need to scribble and type, here are a few pointers.

Use an unliterary *plainness*. It knows the game is up, that it's all finished. The style of THE SAVAGE DETECTIVES is notably *un*literary, almost inelegant, for all the virtuosic restlessness of its narrative voices. It has 'a choking directness'. Even Bernhard, for all his grammatical convolutions, writes, finally, with a kind of pathetic obviousness, he does not gussy or adorn, but spews instead the stuff of his complaint. The abyss needs the clear steadiness of a testimony, it needs the day-after sobriety of a witness-report to remember what went before. Literature is no longer the Thing Itself, but about the vanished Thing.

Resist closed forms, resist masterpieces. The urge to create masterpieces is a kind of necrophilia. Writing must be open on all sides so that the draft of real life – gloomy, farcical life – can pass through it, rifling its pages. Vila-Matas says that he feels it is necessary for whoever writes a fictional text to show his hand, to allow an image of himself to appear. But it is an image of *farcical life* that shows its hand in that literature which comes after Literature. The author must give up on aping genius. Rather show the author as ape, the author as idiot. Don't have the hubris of being the comedian. You are the straight man in this farce; the universe is the funny man. So don't be silly, cute, crack jokes, or play coy, but allow hilarity, a cleansing painful laughter that splits your sides and your heart. Follow your own foolishness like tracks upon the sand.

Write about *this* world, whatever else you're writing about, a world dominated by dead dreams. Mark the absence of Hope, of Belief, of Commitments, of high-flown Seriousness. Mark the past from which we are broken and the future that will destroy us. Write about a kind of hope that was once possible as Literature, as Politics, as Life, but that is no longer possible for *us*.

Mark your *sense of imposture*. You're not an Author, not in the old sense. You haven't really written a Book, not a Real Book. You're part of no tradition, no movement, no vanguard. There's nothing at stake for you in Literature, not really, for all your demented strutting. In addition, *very few people are actually reading*: mark that fact, too. *No one's reading, idiot!* There are more novelists than readers. There are *so many books...*

Mark your gloom. Mark the fact that the end is nigh. The party's over. The stars are going out, and the black sky is indifferent to you and your stupidities. You're with Bolaño's characters at the end of the quest, lost in the Sonora

Desert, and at the end of all quests. You're drawing stupid cartoons to pass the
time in the desert. That's it, the whole of your oeuvre: the drawing of stupid
cartoons to pass the time in the desert.

Don't be generous and don't be kind. Ridicule yourself and what you do.
Savage art, like the cannibal you are. Remember, only when the thing is dead,
picked at by a million years of crows, gnawed at by jackals, spat upon and
forgotten, can we discover that last inviolate bit of bone.

ESSAY

THE FISHERMEN
BY JACK COX

THE DAY HE ARRIVED IN ROME Milan bought a newspaper for the classifieds and some oranges from a vendor at the train terminal whose eyes went from the money to the coat it came from in one doubtful curve. It was not a very cool morning but aside from the new things he tucked under his arm as he ran for a passing bus, everything that Milan owned was in his coat.

He got down from the bus before it crossed over the Tiber to the Borghi and followed a flight of marble steps to the riverbank. With the newspaper spread before him he circled openings for all kinds of work and if his pencil came down and stayed he took a dictionary from his pocket and propped it open on his knee. He peeled an orange with his free hand, threw the skin on the garbage caught between the rocks beneath his feet and spat the pips into the river.

As the day got warmer he made a pillow with the coat and stretched out on the stone. The slow white clouds throbbed in his eyes. He was tired after the hours spent cooped in the trains and was beginning to drift asleep when two boys came scampering over the rocks with a fishing line strung between their hands. Milan watched as they lifted the line over and over until a fish flapped sparkling up from the river. It was long as their brown arms, a gasping relic. One worked the hook from its mouth as the other took a plastic bag from between the rocks and they wrapped it.

Milan called to them. He wanted to know where did they sleep. They slept on the riverbank. He couldn't sleep with them but he could sleep on the riverbank: the weather was mild, some sick Americans were doing it. Milan pointed to the fish rolling in the bag. What would they do with that. Sell it to a restaurant. He asked if they thought he could get work at one of the restaurants but they made a fuss and waved him down and after that he couldn't get them to pay him any more attention.

The first night on the riverbank was very uncomfortable. Back from the cold marble slab he felt the pulse of his blood flowing as the river flowed past his padded ear without returning. From out of the dark it spun brass beneath Castel Sant'Angelo and rushed over the weir in ghostly haste. Dawn broke before he could hold his eyes shut.

¶ He worked on a building site, emptying garbage, as a waiter taking trays up and down the street and between tables. He worried about the police. He had no permit to work and he knew if they caught him they would put him on a train and fifteen hours from any given moment it would be grief, ancestry and a dry cunt all over again. Milan took precautions to blend in.

He dressed down but nicely and he learned a lot of bad words and how to truncate his sentences slightly in the right places and he worked on those felt Roman vowels that are not the shrill silver of Florence or Venetian swindle or the rich buckshot of Sicily. He learned to be haughty and very polite, and he stayed out of trouble.

The bar where he worked was in a courtyard in Trastevere and it was busy at most hours. In the evening the lights that ran in and out of its fretted awning like a vine came on and their reflection scattered over the cobblestones as Milan approached, lurching a little with the phantom weight of concrete sacks and humming the bits of foreign music that had, years ago, returning to a radio hidden under his sheets, slipped down to reside with the habit of breath. He stopped and looked up.

Tomaso was standing in the doorway of the bar watching him. Ahó, che contempli le stelle, tu?

Milan dropped his head and hurried on. He shrugged as he passed his boss in the doorway. È bella.

E tu come sei bello, eppure te pago.

Though Tomaso was apparently from an old Roman family the bar was his idea and he ran it for himself. He treated his employees well and ran a clean, safe kitchen. Milan started out washing dishes but Tomaso saw the profit in putting a suit on him and sending him out to wait tables and he was right and Milan was a success with the customers. He never asked Milan what his plans were and Milan suspected he thought he was earning money to send home.

He undressed in the bathroom and washed the last slats of dust from his armpits and from between his buttocks with his wet shirt. When he was in his uniform he rubbed a soapy thumb over his teeth then rinsed his mouth out.

From the coffee counter Tomaso pointed to a table at which a man and a woman and child had just sat down. Sarebbero der tu' paese. Nun so se pàrleno l'itajano.

Milan welcomed them and asked for their order. The man, who was extremely well dressed and whose hands moved in slim arcs as he spoke, pointed to a wine on the menu and ordered coffee and a glass of lemonade in broken Italian. The woman didn't look at either of them. She had fixed her eyes out the window and as they spoke she opened her mouth slightly without turning. The boy's chin came just above the tablecloth and his dark hair fell plumb to his eyebrows and he also stared away but it seemed to Milan to no purpose. He supposed he was their son though the man was blonde and the woman was platinum blonde.

He took them their drinks. Her lids dropped as he leaned to place the glass of lemonade before her son. She thanked him and he caught her eyes in his and nodded. Someone had crumbled a piece of bread on the tablecloth but all related hands were still as he put the drinks down. They didn't stay to finish the wine.

When Milan returned to the counter Tomaso wanted to know if he had been mistaken. Milan nodded. Sono ungheresi.

Tomaso unlocked the cash register and shook his head. He said the Eastern Europeans thought Rome was America. Pènzeno che ce farano 'n be' futuro. He pursed his lips. Hai vist'i 'sti schifosi n'i giardini, sott'i ponti. Ecco 'ndó càpiteno. Ma che futuro! Me fa sta' male 'a Roma der futuro.

Milan said that family had money.

Tomaso shrugged. E va be', nun è 'a stessa cosa.

¶ The woman and her son came back to the bar the following day. It was Sunday and Milan was working the afternoon. She smiled at him and said good afternoon with a good accent. Milan said hello to the boy but he didn't seem to hear. She asked Milan how long he had been working in Rome. Milan told her. Did he like it. No he didn't like to work much but he liked it here.

She was wearing a long burgundy cardigan despite the sun falling right into the courtyard. A thin gilt chain dipped and rose over her collarbone. She ordered ice cream. When Milan brought her the bill she asked if he would be free later to take the two of them around. They had not been in town very long. It was a nice day.

He said he would be. He met them at five o'clock on Ponte Garibaldi. The boy was wearing an old-fashioned straw hat and she had left her cardigan behind. She shielded her eyes against the sun and waved. Milan was surprised to see a pair of white canvas shoes below her dress. The two had walked out to the middle of the bridge to watch a boat passing underneath and they turned and covered half the distance as Milan approached, she leading her son by the hand, his eyes lost in his private bar of shade.

Milan took them to the Campidoglio and if she had been already she didn't say so. She said it was very beautiful.

They talked and walked too fast and in the museum Milan thought he might break something. The boy lagged further behind her outstretched arm as they descended the wide equestrian stairs of the Campidoglio in the bright evening.

They walked beside the gliding river and Milan kissed her and she told him she would like to take him to a hotel and he said he agreed to everything. Her name was Magda. He followed her into the lobby of a large hotel in Prati. The concierge nodded when he saw them and took down a key from the false onyx panel behind him. The lights of the low–slung chandeliers rippled in its black sheen. Milan hesitated. She leaned and spoke into his ear, non preoccuparti. Her husband had gone home for business. He wouldn't be back for a week.

They took the elevator and all the way she spoke to her son about the horse they had seen on the Campidoglio. It seemed he liked horses but he didn't respond. It was not a real horse. Milan thought maybe he only liked real horses.

They left him in the sitting room by the window. In the bedroom they didn't draw the curtains. She sat at a commode by the bed and unlaced her shoes. Milan was undressed first and he leaned over her and gently pulled her dress over her head. Her breasts fell in two shallow sways across her chest. Milan stood alone and groaned and surprised them both. And there was the colour of her son's hair.

Her throat and her mouth were warm and sweat shone in the small curves. Her smell filled his mouth. He thought he pulled her down around his hips and he thought it was triumph but she took pleasure in his fast writhing and his wet blue eyes and the blind hug of his hands on her buttocks and when he came it was a gift.

¶ She watched him through her eyelashes as he picked his clothes off the floor. They had slept a little and the sun had gone down and now the lights of the city wavered through the smog the length of the window. His body gleamed in the dark from that borrowed light. The traffic hummed on the glass.

He saw her watching him and smiled. She realised that where she lay she was better illuminated than he was and the knowledge made her shut her eyes. Then he was touching some part of him to her knee and barely singing Wagon Wheel and his fingers were on her eyelids. Quanti hanni hai?

Vent'uno.

Sei sposato?

Sì.

They made love once more then he got dressed. She pulled on a robe and saw him to the door but he asked her to dinner and she said, why don't you have dinner here and stay the night. But he couldn't, he had to be at a building site early Monday, so they kissed and said goodbye. When he was gone she went over to Viktor and spoke to him and took off his straw hat and laid it on the couch.

In the morning she was up and waiting when the maid came to put a tray with their breakfast in the sitting room. She woke her son and helped him to clean and dress, then she spread jam on a piece of toast and poured him half a cup of coffee and they ate in silence. They made plans to visit a gallery but threw them up and went walking.

When they got back to the hotel there was a note at the desk from Milan. He asked her to meet him outside the lobby that evening. She paid a maid to sit with Viktor and she put her hair up with an old silver clasp that had belonged to her mother and she went down and waited by the water.

He was late. He came running in new blue jeans. He kissed her where her hair scuffed over her cheek in the wind that blew up from the river. They bought two paper cups of crushed ice and walked close together. Andiamo da te.

No, c'è la cameriera. Sta con Viktor.

He took her down some steps to the riverbank. It was cooler there and her skin thrilled. They came to a deep recess in the stone wall but she didn't want to go in. She couldn't see well but it smelled inhabited. He told her not to mind and led her with the tips of his fingers into the shadow. The sun was beginning to set over the opposite bank but it was still higher than the mouth of the cave and her eyes were sunk in darkness. She felt his lips brush her ear, her cheek. He lifted her dress and her breath shot down her throat. Still he had not gone into her. She reached out and immediately her hand found his, open as if it were begging, and the lowering sun flooded the cave with light and when she jerked her head at the opening she was blinded. She blinked back in the cave.

He was hopping on bowed legs and pulling at the buttons of his new jeans and there were pots and pans hanging on the wall and rugs rolled in the corner. He grinned but he was furious. She bent deftly and slipped her knickers from her ankle and pushed them into his pocket and they left.

Chi vive là?

Gli zingari.

Sarebbero arrabbiati se lo sapessero.

Sì.

Sei maleducato.

There was cement dust on his forearms. He held a hand to her hip and her dress sliding under it where an elastic had been made her long for him with infinite patience. He asked about her son. She told him about her son and her husband. He told her about the village he left and about his wife who had been old family business and much younger than him. Magda thought perhaps he was cruel to his wife. She asked him how long he planned to stay in Rome and he said forever. He said he wanted her, he wanted her to stay with him in Rome. She said that was crazy. He said he loved her and he wanted her to stay with him.

She said she had a son. They walked in silence along the riverbank until it got dark and the path filled with an electric light that cut out new shadows for them. He told her he wanted her to stay. She knew his insistence came in part from the pressure in his body and she took her hand from his and stroked the small of his back with her fingers. He could not live illegally in Rome forever.

Vero. He could take her back home. Having a wife was not such an obstacle. He could get work in the city and they would rent a flat and later buy it. He would give her a child.

They walked up onto the street and she refused to take him back to the hotel. She had left her son long enough. He told her to promise that she would see him again. She promised. Promise to let him make love to her again. She laughed in surprise and said she promised. They were tender when they said goodbye and when she looked back he was waiting.

¶ Magda's husband had returned early. She and Viktor came back to the hotel one afternoon and he was sitting in the lobby reading the newspapers. He touched Viktor on the head and kissed her.

In their room he took off his jacket and called for a bottle of whisky and one of Fanta. He talked to his son about his trip and asked after what he had seen, had he seen the Colosseum, the Forum, Neptune driving his horses over loose change. He was gentle and courteous with Viktor. Knowing what she did about his upbringing she thought he would have beaten him sometimes but he was always gentle. She sat on the couch and pushed her shoes off with her toes and tucked her legs up.

The maid came with the drinks. He filled a glass with ice and poured one for Magda. She held the glass in her lap and closed her eyes. Viktor slurped through his straw. She looked at her husband, at the fair hair swept back and the bright, elegant folds of his shirt, and felt she had almost forgotten him but looking at him could see nothing in need of remembering.

He suggested they take a stroll and choose a place to eat. At first she said she was tired, then agreed anyway. She changed into slacks and a new blouse while he shaved with the door open.

He found a bow tie in the bathroom. He stood in the doorway with half the lather scraped from his jaw and the bow tie in his hand and his braces hanging loose on his hips and looked at her. This is an old comedy thought Magda and was afraid because they had never been here before and she didn't know all the things he was capable of doing. At first they didn't speak. He was an oppressive husband but at last he said it was worth having a real holiday and went on shaving.

She knew then that he had been with other women and was surprised not to have thought of it before, and perhaps there were many other women and perhaps other children. He hadn't let his semen into her since Viktor. She felt dizzy in her guts and it was the thought she could be pregnant.

They walked, the three of them, by the river. Magda had been raised in Budapest like her husband and they had met at university. They were sweethearts for a long time before they married. He was a nice dancer and he knew Hungarian folk songs and sang them to her when they were younger. They made familiar jokes as they walked through the streets to Trastevere and Viktor laughed a beat behind with the hollow stammer of a spirit who laughs with no one.

After the others had gone to bed Magda went down to the lobby and called the number Milan had left her when they last parted. She didn't know what kind of a place the number was for. After a while a voice answered and she asked to speak to him. She heard a relay of voices then and someone else got on the phone and told her Milan wasn't there, did she want to leave a message.

The following day her husband took care of Viktor and Magda went out alone. She spent the morning in the galleries of the Villa Borghese but she was distracted and couldn't look at anything for long so she walked in the park back the way she'd come. She lingered under the trees and watched other people pass. She stopped by a fountain and leaned with one hand on the smooth pocked marble and cupped the other for the water. The sun on the broken surface dazzled her.

In the park she felt she was being followed. For some reason the concierge had warned her about the place so she left. Just outside the park she thought she saw Milan at a bus stop but when she turned back to check he was gone. There was only a man waiting with his cap pulled down over one ear and his hands in his pockets. Later, as she made her way along Via del Tritone, she thought she saw Milan reflected before her in the glass door of a wine cellar. He wasn't there when she turned. She turned again and he wasn't there. She walked all the way to the river.

Police cars were parked around the entrance to Ponte Vittorio Emanuele II and people had gathered to look. She joined them in peering over the bridge. It seemed a gypsy had fallen in a whirlpool and drowned. Some of his people, family perhaps, stood below them on the bank talking to a police officer. They nodded and pointed tacitly. Magda heard a woman beside her say he was a good swimmer but he fell in the wrong place and they hadn't found his body. Maybe it would turn up at sea. The river swept under them in fast green curls.

Magda glanced at the faces around her and moved on. At the end of the bridge a young punk held out a rattling tin and his mutt tangled harmlessly in her legs. She dropped him fifty cents and turned towards the boulevard to San Pietro. All along the footpath tourists waited in line for the basilica and merchants sat at easels making little paintings of the view at sunset. The bells rang out for mass. Magda was hungry and wanted to find a place to stop and eat but she moved in spurts. By now she was convinced that he was following her and she turned at every corner but it was no good, the city was full of handsome unwashed boys and they all looked back. She pushed her hands through her hair. Right out of the blue sky it began to weep, and the painters packed up and ran for cover.

WEEPING MACHINES
BY DEBORAH LEVY

THAT SPRING I SEEMED TO CRY most on escalators at train stations. Going down them was fine but there was something about standing still and being carried upwards that did it. From apparently nowhere tears poured out of me and by the time I got to the top and felt the wind rushing in, it took all my effort to stop myself from sobbing. Even the heroin addicts who stood outside the station begging for used travel cards didn't bother to approach me. It was as if the momentum of the escalator carrying me forwards and upwards was a physical expression of a conversation I was having with myself but I wasn't really sure what I was thinking about. Escalators, which in the early days of their invention used to be called 'a travelling staircase' or 'a magic stairway', had mysteriously become a danger zone.

I made sure I had lots to read on train journeys. This was the first time in my life I had ever been pleased to read newspaper columns about the things that happened to the writer's lawnmower. When I wasn't absorbed in this kind of thing (which I experienced as being shot with a tranquilliser dart) the book I read most was Gabriel Garcia Marquez's short novel OF LOVE AND OTHER DEMONS. Out of all the loved and loveless characters dreaming and scheming in hammocks under the blue Caribbean sky, the only one that really interested me was Bernarda Cabrera, the dissolute wife of a Marquis who has given up on life and on his marriage. To escape from her own life Bernarda Cabrera is introduced to 'magic chocolate' from Oaxaca by her slave lover and starts to live in a state of delirium. Addicted to sacks of cacao and fermented honey, she spends most of the day lying naked on her bedroom floor 'enveloped in the glow of her lethal gases'. By the time I got off the train and started to weep on the escalator that apparently was inviting me to read my mind (at a time in my life when I preferred to read other things) I began to regard Bernarda as a role model.

I knew things had to change when I found myself staring intently for a week at a poster in my bathroom titled 'The Skeletal System'. This featured a human skeleton with its inner organs and bones labelled in Latin and which I constantly misread as 'The Societal System'.

I made a decision. If escalators had become machines with torrid emotionality, a system that transported me to places I did not want to go, why not book a flight to somewhere I actually did want to go?

Three days later, I zipped up my brand new laptop and found myself sitting in aisle seat 22C heading for Palma, Majorca. As the plane took off I realised that being stranded between the earth and the sky was a bit like being on an escalator. The man unlucky enough to be sitting next to a weeping woman looked like he had once been in the army and now spent his life lying on a beach. I was pleased my cheap airline buddy was a tough guy with hard square shoulders and jagged welts of sunburn striping his thick neck. I did not want anyone to attempt to comfort me. If anything my tears seemed to send him into a tantric shopping coma because he called for the air hostess and ordered two cans of beer, a vodka and coke, an extra coke, a tube of Pringles, a scratch card, a teddy bear stuffed with mini chocolate bars, a Swiss watch on special offer, and asked the crew if the airline had one of those questionnaires to fill in where you get a free holiday if it's drawn out of the hat.

When the plane landed in Palma at 11 p.m., the only taxi driver prepared to drive me up the steep mountain roads might have been blind because he had white clouds floating across both of his eyes. No one in the queue wanted to admit they were anxious he would crash the car and avoided him when he pulled up at the taxi rank. After we negotiated the price, he managed to drive without apparently looking at the road and instead had his fingers on the dial of the radio while staring at his feet. An hour later he began to manoeuvre his Mercedes up a narrow road lined with pine trees that I knew went on for a deceptively long time. He managed to get halfway up and then suddenly shouted NO NO NO and abruptly stopped the car. For the first time all spring I wanted to laugh. We both sat in the dark, a rabbit running through the grass, neither of us knowing what to do next. In the end I gave him a generous tip for driving so dangerously and started the long walk up the dark path that I vaguely remembered led to the hotel.

The smell of wood fires in the stone houses below and the bells on sheep grazing in the mountains and the strange silence that happens in between the bells chiming suddenly made me want to smoke. I had long given up smoking but at the airport I had bought a packet of Spanish cigarettes, fully intending to start again. I sat down on a damp rock under a tree that was a little way off the path, pushed my laptop between my shins and lit up under the stars.

Smoking cheap Spanish filthy sock tobacco under a pine tree was so much better than trying to hold it together on escalators. There was something comforting about being literally lost when I was lost in every other way and just as I was thinking I might have to sleep on the mountain that night, I heard someone shout my name. A number of things happened at once. I heard the sound of someone on the path and then I saw the feet of a woman in red leather shoes making her way towards me. She shouted my name again but for some reason I was unable to attach the name she was shouting to myself. Suddenly a torch was being shone in my face and when she saw me sitting on a rock under a tree smoking a cigarette, the woman said, 'Ah there you are. '

I saw the woman's face was shockingly pale and I wondered if she was mad. But then I remembered I was the mad one because she was trying to get me off my rock on the edge of a mountain dressed for the beach on a night when the temperature had fallen to below freezing.

'I saw you walking past the hotel. I think you are lost eh?'

I nodded, but must have looked confused because she said,

'I am Maria.'

Maria was the owner of the hotel and she looked much older and sadder than the last time we met. She probably thought the same about me.

'Hello Maria.'

I stood up, 'Thank you for coming to find me.'

We walked in silence back to the hotel and she pointed with her torch to the turning where I had missed the path, as if she was a detective gathering evidence for something neither of us could fathom.

The terrace at the front of the house with its tables and chairs placed under the olive trees looked exactly the same as it did when I last stayed here. Everything was the same. The ornate tiled floor. The heavy wooden doors that opened out onto the ancient palm tree in the courtyard. The polished grand piano that stood majestically in the hallway. My room was exactly the same too, except this time when I opened the doors of the worm-eaten wardrobe and saw the same four bent wire clothes hangers on the rail, they seemed to mimic the shape of forlorn human shoulders.

The next morning I decided to visit the village shop to look for the pure chocolate that had so intoxicated Bernarda Cabrera. The strange thing was I found it. There in front of me, lying with the other bars of more familiar confectionery was a bar of Chocolate Negro Extrafino: Cacao 99%. Ingredientes: cacao, azucar. It even had a warning on the wrapper telling me this chocolate was 'intensidad'. The owner of the grocery store was a distinguished Chinese man originally from Shanghai. For as long as I had known him he was always reading books behind the counter, tortoiseshell spectacles perched half way down his nose. His black hair was now streaked with silver as we exchanged superficial greetings: how are you, yes not many tourists at this time of year, yes it is very cold, the forecast said it might even snow, how was I going to spend my day?

I told him I was about to walk to the next village to see the monastery where George Sand and Frederick Chopin stayed during the winter of 1838.

He smiled but it was a more of a grimace. Ah yes. Jorge Sand. The Majorcans did not like her. She dressed in men's clothing and she said Majorcans preferred their pigs to people. No. Jorge Sand was not a woman he would like to share a bottle of wine with. When I laughed I was not really sure what I was laughing about or who I was laughing at. I paid him for the chocolate, and then as a second thought bought an extra bar of the 99% cacao for Maria.

George Sand (who was really Baroness Amantine Aurore Lucile Dupin) smoked large cigars to get through her day. She would have needed them living in the gloomy Carthusian monastery of Jesus the Nazarene. With its withered flowers and suffering wooden saints lurking in the alcoves, it seemed a sinister place to live with children and to have a love affair. The guidebook told me that she had no choice but to rent rooms here, because no one dared offer accommodation to Chopin who had been diagnosed with tuberculosis. I had only ever read half of one of her books, but I admired her for trying to keep cheerful for her children and writing at her desk wearing Chopin's trousers instead of wasting her life weeping about her circumstances. With this in mind I briskly walked out of the monastery and made my way through the almond trees towards the silver sea, fierce and roaring beyond the cliffs.

As the waves crashed on the rocks and the wind numbed my fingers, I waited for something to happen. I think I was waiting for a revelation, something big and profound that would shake me to the core. Nothing happened. Nothing happened at all. And then what came to mind was the poster in my bathroom called 'The Skeletal System' which I had misread as 'The Societal System'. I thought about all the things I had hoped for and I laughed. The sound of my own cruel laughter made me want to die.

❡ Later that evening, when I asked Maria's belligerent brother for an extra blanket to get me through another night in freezing Majorca, he pretended not to understand me. I could smell wood smoke all over the valley and it was obvious to me that every house had a fire going. Sure enough the one restaurant open out of season had a log fire burning at the back of the room and I made my way towards it. When the waitress came to tell me that noooo waaaay could I sit alone at a table laid for three, I took a tip from Maria's brother and pretended not to understand her. This prompted the German couple sitting nearby wearing identical hats, coats and walking boots, to translate what she was saying into German, then Portuguese, and finally a language that sounded like Russian. I concentrated on the menu with incredible focus, nodding annoyingly at the furious waitress and earnest linguists, until I noticed the Chinese shop owner was sitting at the bar. He waved and walked over to my table for three.

So, he asked me, did I still think the Majorcans were lucky to meet a lewd and discourteous woman like Jorge Sand?

I told him, yes, they were very lucky to meet her and I was very lucky to meet him too because I was just about to be dragged away from my table. He sat down and explained that even though she came from the sophisticated cuisine of France where everyone cooked with butter, it is not right to mock peasants for cooking in cheap oil, as she did. His accent became more Chinese than Spanish when he said that. It was as if his voice had suddenly dropped from one altitude to another, like turbulence on an aeroplane. I invited him to share a bottle of wine at my table for three.

At first we talked about soup. He told me he had more or less forgotten how to make CHINESE soup. Many years ago he had left Shanghai aged 19 on a ship heading for Paris, where he worked in a fish shop. His bedsit in the 13th arrondissement always smelled of the crab and shrimp he cooked most days. This perplexed his landlord who said the room usually smelled of urine – as if that was what was required in Paris. Europe was mysterious and crazed. He had to learn a new language and earn his rent, but it was the start of another way of living and he was excited every day. Now he sold calzone and bratwurst to tourists and he was richer, but he wondered what else there was to look forward to? I think he was asking me a question but I did not want to answer it. He took a small sip of wine and placed his glass neatly, almost surgically on the table. And then he lifted up his hand, and with his two fingers outstretched, briskly tapped my arm. I decided I had nothing to lose by telling him about crying on escalators at train stations. He leaned forward to listen because I was speaking quite softly. His eyes were clear and kind.

The palm trees outside the restaurant were covered in snow by the time we finished our bottle of wine. Neither of us had noticed. The German couple were now pointing at their boots, congratulating each other (in English) for having had the foresight to bring arctic clothing to Majorca in spring. My companion nudged me and I saw Maria had just walked in to the restaurant. She looked surprisingly tall in a heavy coat trimmed with fur as she made her way to my table for three. She was carrying a small suitcase.

'My brother told me you were cold.'

'Yes.'

'I have made you a fire. There are blankets on your bed.'

'Thank you.'

There was an awkward silence.

'Are you going somewhere Maria?'

It was as if I was a detective gathering evidence for some thing neither of us could fathom.

'Yes.'

Maria did not want to talk. Not at all. I opened my bag and gave her the chocolate with the big 99% on it. And then I counted out the rent for my hotel room, four nights in cash because I thought she might need it for whatever she had to do next.

Returning from Palma to Gatwick I did not weep when the plane took off and found its equilibrium in the sky. And when I stood on the escalator that carried me up to Baggage Reclaim, I realised the momentum of being carried upwards while standing still somehow suggested Hope and The Future. Es-calators had become angels, their steel wings spread between the past (going down) and the future (going up), eternally journeying between the two. I now understood what had made the tears spill out of me as the wind rushed in through the Exit at train stations. The future is always where the wind is blowing. Stepping into the future means leaving people behind. The escalator had become a machine on which I was breaking a story, a story about loss. I knew this because the Chinese shopkeeper whose father was a steel worker had told me that escalators, or the 'revolving staircase', patented in 1859 by Nathan Ames of Massachusetts and then redesigned by the engineer Jesse Reno, were first described to the modern world as 'endless conveyors'.

TOPSOIL
BY JESSE LONCRAINE

THE EVENING HAD SPRING IN IT. Faintly sweet and peppery. To disturb a small tree sent birds chattering skyward. Weeks before there had been no birds anywhere. Hector watched them scatter like shrapnel. Whatever colour they were, the birds looked black against the purple sky. He drove a shovel into the marked patch of ground with the heel of his boot. Levered the blade backwards and forwards, grinding his way into the thawing earth.

A youngish woman watched him from the driver's seat of a 4x4 parked at the edge of the field. The vehicle was the only one in sight. They were far from the main road.

Hector dropped to his knees and turned a grabbing of topsoil in his hand. He said a prayer and crossed himself – forehead to chest, right shoulder to left.

The woman in the car honked the horn and he felt the sound in the earth.

'Damn you, Martha,' he said, 'I'm coming.'

He rose and made his way back through the field to the car where Martha was tapping a beat on the steering wheel. She ran her fingers through cropped hair, and turned the key in the ignition.

'Well?' she asked over the sound of the engine.

'We start tomorrow.'

'I knew it. What did I tell you? Spring.'

'Yes.'

'About time.'

'Come on,' said Hector, 'let's go.'

¶ Hector arrived home and sat with his wife, Jelena, while she cooked their dinner. She uncapped a bottle of Tuborg and poured it into a glass which she placed in front of him on the dining table. He thanked her and gulped down the cold beer.

'I was working in the garden today while you were gone. The ground has finally softened.'

'You're right, it has.'

'Will you start digging soon then?'

'Tomorrow.'

'Tomorrow? As soon as that?'

Jelena placed a bowl of vegetable soup in front of her husband and a basket of sliced white bread in the centre of the table. Hector took a piece of the bread and dipped it into the steaming bowl of soup. He watched intently as the liquid crept up the length of the bread. Jelena brought her own bowl to the table and sat down opposite him.

'Tell me what you're thinking.'

Hector raised his eyes to meet his wife's. He smiled and popped the soggy bread into his mouth and sucked out the broth. The bread formed a sweet dumpling in the shape of the roof of his mouth.

'I'm thinking we deserve a holiday.'

'*Ho-li-day*. The word sounds vaguely familiar.'

'Once I finish my work, I promise.'

'You know I'm only teasing.'

Hector took a sip of the soup and pushed his bowl to one side. Jelena watched him. She frowned at the unfinished meal.

'I'm sorry. It's delicious. I'm just not hungry tonight.'

'You should eat.'

Hector shrugged. He waited for his wife to finish her soup before lighting a cigarette. Jelena took her own packet of cigarettes from a pocket in her apron and lit up, too. They breathed smoke out the side of their mouths and Jelena stroked her husband's leg beneath the table. She knew what he was thinking.

After smoking, Jelena stood and cleared their plates. She poured Hector's soup back into the pot and left the bowls in the sink to wash up later.

'How about something sweet? Will you eat some chocolate?'

'Thank you, darling. Nothing. I'll eat in the morning. I'll have a stomach for it then.'

He got up from the table and stooped to kiss Jelena on the forehead. She had married a giant, almost seven feet tall. Many women were scared by Hector's height, but Jelena found it attractive. When they slept, she pulled one of his heavy limbs on top of her and passed the night almost crushed under its weight. That was how she liked to sleep, with her husband's immense body burying her. But Hector's body was consuming itself of late. He ate less and less, and only then when she badgered him. His hands and feet and head were starting to look unbalanced, comical, as the muscle slipped away from the bones. Jelena said nothing about his drinking because she knew the beer gave him much-needed calories. She added extra cream and butter to their meals wherever she could, but it only seemed to make her grow fatter.

¶ In the living room, they sat together on the couch with Jelena's legs resting on her husband's lap. Hector read over his notes while Jelena watched an old cartoon on the television with the sound muted.

'Tomorrow, maybe I'll come with you.'

Hector tipped his glasses and looked at his wife.

'Come with me where?'

'On the dig.'

He rested his notes on her legs and laid his hand on her hip.

'What's brought this on?'

'I've been having nightmares. My imagination's been running wild lately. Today, in the garden, I thought that maybe coming with you would help soothe my mind.'

'Nightmares? About what?'

'About what's beneath us, in the ground.'

'We know what's there. It's simply a matter of finding it.'

Jelena turned back to the television. She felt his eyes on the side of her face. A cartoon mouse peered out of a hole in the wall, surveying the room for danger. The shadow of a cat tiptoed across the wall and the mouse retreated back inside his hole.

'So, will you let me come with you?'

'I don't think it's a good idea.'

'Maybe not. But still, I'd like to come this once.'

'Very well. Martha is collecting me at five.'

'I'll be ready.'

Strewn about the coffee table were Jelena's books of sheet music. Hector moved a pile carefully to one side and put his feet up.

'How's your composition going?' Hector asked.

'I haven't played once in four days. I can't seem to concentrate. Perhaps it's the changing of seasons. I don't know. I remember even when I was a child I found the melting snow extremely depressing. Other children were excited because it meant summer was on its way, but I was always sad when winter ended.'

'My melancholy crocus,' he said, and lifted her legs off his lap and folded his glasses into his shirt pocket. 'I'm going to bed. Are you coming?'

'I'll be up soon. I just want to clear up a little.'

Jelena rose from the sofa and went to the kitchen to wash the dishes and cover the soup. Standing at the sink, she looked out into the garden, still bare from the long winter. There was a moon and hardly any stars. If she squinted, she could just make out the mounds of disturbed soil where she had dug the holes that morning. Perhaps she'd known she would find nothing, but it helped to know that she was looking too, that she was helping Hector with his work.

¶ A cold mud swallowed her bare feet as she trudged through the open field. It had rained and her dress grew heavy at the back where it trailed along the ground, collecting the grey mud. She was glad to be there, in spite of the biting air. Towards the middle of the field, she could see Hector and his team, busy working, digging in the white halogen glare of their spotlights, their shovels seeming like mechanical arms, rhythmically snatching at the earth and depositing it in mounds at their feet.

A generator hummed nearby. She admired the beauty of their efficient labouring, like some socialist mural of the country at work.

Suddenly she was naked and cold. Her clothes lay discarded behind her in the muddy field. The wind blew her hair into her mouth and eyes. It stung her nipples.

She knelt down and plastered her breasts in a layer of mud then spread her knees and took another handful and ran the mud between her legs, covering herself. The wetted soil clung to her pubic hair, forming into thick, stalactitic clumps. A plane roared overhead and when she looked up she could just make out her name on the undercarriage in iridescent lettering. She watched as it dwindled to a speck in the sky, until all that was left was a slowly evaporating vapour trail.

Lifting her legs grew harder as she walked. Each step caked her feet in new layers of mud, making her legs feel unnaturally heavy. Soon the mud rose around her ankles and her feet sank further into the ground. She gripped her right leg at the knee and pulled her foot free, planting it a step in front. She did the same with her left leg and proceeded like that for a few metres – prizing one leg free and then the other. Finally the effort was too much and she gave in and just stood there, planted in the ground up to her calves, feeling herself not so slowly sinking. Within minutes her knees had disappeared, and soon the mud held her upper thighs like tight-fitting stockings. She splayed her buttocks with her hands and let the mud slip between them. Her body was suddenly hot and feverish. As she sunk below her navel, her breath quickened. she raised her arms and allowed her stomach and chest to sink into the clinging earth.

¶ Jelena's eyes shot open and the pain of Hector inside her ripped through her body as if she had been staked alive. She writhed beneath his weight and screamed at him:

'Get off me. Get off me.'

Hector pulled himself out of her and rolled away, a look of confusion and fear on his face.

'What's wrong? What did I do?'

'What were you *doing* to me?'

'What was I doing?'

'You were, you were in my –'

'It wasn't me. You put it there.'

'I put it there? Are you fucking crazy, Hector?'

'Jesus, Jelena, calm down. Were you asleep?'

'Of course I was asleep. What did you do to me?'

'I didn't do anything. You rolled over and rubbed yourself against me until I was awake and then you took me with your hand and put me inside you, in there.'

She scanned her husband's face in the half-light and then got out of bed and stormed to the bathroom. She locked the door. Hector called after her:

'Jelena, come back. Are you okay?'

He could hear her crying through the door as he wrestled with the handle.

'Let me in.'

'Go away.'

'Please, Jelena. Let me in. Are you hurt?'

'No. Leave me alone.'

Hector retreated to the bed and switched on a lamp. The clock showed 3.50 a.m., just over an hour until Martha came to collect him. He pulled back the bed covers. There were spots of blood on the sheets.

'Jelena,' he called, 'are you okay?'

'I'm fine. Leave. Me. Alone.'

He pulled on some underwear and went downstairs. In the kitchen he went over in his mind what had happened – just as he had told her. He hadn't done anything wrong. He hadn't initiated anything. Still, the thought of his wife upstairs alone, crying, bleeding, made him nauseous. He lit a cigarette to calm his nerves.

Jelena sat on the toilet bent forward with her arms wrapped around her stomach. She tore some sheets of paper from the roll and used them to touch herself gently where it stung. She winced from the pain, took in short, sharp breaths. When she looked at the paper it was red. The pain was interior too, dull and throbbing. She sat on the toilet for ten minutes willing herself not to cry. Eventually she stood and turned on the shower and waited for the water to run as hot as it would go. The almost scalding heat of the water on her neck and back. Once the shock had mostly subsided, Jelena felt her nerves

calming. Slowly, her thoughts shifted to Hector downstairs, and to his empty
stomach. She finished showering, dried off, and placed a sanitary towel in the
seat of her knickers. back in their bedroom she pulled on some jeans and a
loose-fitting shirt and fixed her hair in the mirror – a simple bun on top of
her head. Before going downstairs she made the bed.

'Will you eat some eggs?' she asked.

'There's no need. I can make something.'

'Will you eat eggs, or won't you?'

'Jelena, I'm sorry.'

'Forget about it.'

'Are you okay?'

'I'm fine.'

'You promise?'

'Martha will be here soon. Go get dressed. I'll make us some breakfast.'

¶ It was about an hour's drive to the site. They passed early commuters en
route to the factories outside of town with their heads bowed low and hooded
against the cold. Some of the men held out their thumbs in hope of a lift. They
gave the impression of being devout men on some pilgrimage to who knew
where.

Jelena was drifting off to sleep when Martha swerved to avoid a drunk who
lurched into the road, suddenly and with intent. She leant out the window and
shouted a string of foreign curses. Jelena turned in her seat and watched the
drunk man as he chicken-danced behind them in the dark.

'So Jelena, how do you like it, living here?' asked Martha.

'I like it fine. It's a good place to write.'

'Why's that?'

'There are very few distractions.'

'It's boring as hell, in other words.'

Jelena smiled. It was not exactly what she meant.

'Personally, I can't wait to get out of here. The food stinks and the men are
all miserable drunks, aren't they, Hector?'

He nodded that they were.

From the backseat, Jelena noticed the bald patch on her husband's head,
a new part of him unknown to his former lovers. She reached forward and
squeezed his shoulder as Martha signalled right and slowed down. They
turned off the tarmac and onto an unpaved road, lined on either side by naked
trees – the forest the last remaining sanctuary of winter. After a mile they

arrived at a simple wooden gate manned by two soldiers. Martha brought the vehicle to a crawl and flashed an ID card. The soldiers greeted them with frosty breaths and waved on the 4x4. Jelena caught Hector's eye in the rear-view mirror – his thick eyebrows pinched together in a slight frown. She could tell that the soldiers made him uneasy. They drove on. The road climbing steadily.

'We're nearly there,' said Hector.

'It's chilling to think they came along this road,' said Jelena. Hector nodded, but as Jelena spoke the words she knew they sounded forced, out of place. She wished she'd said nothing.

They rounded a bend and the trees gave way to a large open field. It was not as she'd imagined. There were several other cars with their engines running, and Hector's men trekked back and forth with heavy equipment, shouting to each other, laughing. Rusted farm tools and old water containers lay strewn about in ugly heaps. A faint daylight was beginning to show the contours of the land. The field was mounded and irregular, the soil untilled for years.

'Don't get in the way,' said Hector, jumping out of the car before it had even stopped.

'Ignore him,' said Martha, turning back to Jelena, 'he gets like this out here.'

Jelena got out of the car and watched Hector giving orders, impressed by the way her husband moved around, directing his team without hesitation. Looking at him radiating energy in that bleak place, Jelena found him intensely attractive. She imagined herself lying down with him there, in the field, beneath him, between him and the ground.

Hector's men pulled white jumpsuits over their clothes and measured out a twelve by twelve square beside a crooked tree in the northwest corner of the field. They marked the four corners with wooden stakes and joined them together with lengths of string, setting the perimeter in place. Then they began to dig, methodically, a foot deep across the entire square, depositing the earth on blue tarpaulin sheets. A second team sifted through the excavated mounds with hand trowels, creating smaller subdivided piles of rocks and wood and filtered soil. Martha circled the scene with a digital camera, taking photos and making notes in a small leather-bound book. Hector checked his watch and the rising sun.

Jelena went and stood beside her husband. She offered him a cigarette.

'No, thank you.'

'Do you mind if I have one?'

'No, go ahead.'

'Why do you think they chose this place?'

'Most likely because of the tree. This corner of the field wouldn't have been farmed. That makes it much less likely to be discovered.'

'But there's a whole forest. Why would they come out here, in the open?'

'The root systems are too dense in the forest. It's harder to dig.'

The men had stopped. Hector moved away from his wife and conferred with a man in a white paisley bandana. She watched them take handfuls of soil and feel its texture between their fingers as they talked. Hector made some motion towards the square and the man in the bandana nodded. Hector patted him on the shoulder and soon the men were digging again. Another foot of soil was removed, the process of sifting repeated. A measuring stick was driven into the ground as they dug further down. They worked in near silence, only a young woman listening to music and humming a barely audible melody as she trowelled the mounded earth.

'What were you talking about, just then, with –'

'Alberto. I was asking his opinion on the subsoil. He can tell from the density if it's been dug up before.'

'What did he say?'

'He said it has.'

'That's a good thing?'

'It means we're in the right place, yes.'

As absentmindedly as if they were in bed, Jelena reached for her husband's hand.

He turned to her:

'What is it?'

'I'm sorry. Nothing. I wasn't thinking.'

Jelena drew her hand away. She guessed that he was angry with her for coming, but she didn't care. She needed to be there. Her presence was something Hector would simply have to abide.

The first rays of sun warmed the back of Jelena's neck, and her body and the tree cast a shadow over the deepening pit. Two of the men drew sunglasses from their breast pockets, which seemed strange in the soft morning light and the shadows. The woman with the headphones raised her hand and Martha jogged two sides of the square and knelt down beside her. She quickly signalled for Hector to join them. The others had stopped digging and were watching Martha.

'A baby's shoe?' said Martha, placing the scrap of leather in Hector's palm.

'You're sure it's a shoe?' he asked.

'That's what it looks like.'

Hector's jaw stiffened and his eyes narrowed to a concentrated stare.

'May I see it?' asked Jelena.

Hector handed her the earth-filled shoe, little bigger than a packet of cigarettes. Jelena turned it over in her hand, traced her fingers along the sole, and over the brittle tongue. Time and the elements had turned the leather hard.

'She's right.'

'Please, everyone,' said Hector, 'keep digging. Martha, bag this.'

Hector returned to his spot beneath the tree, crouched on his knees and scratched his beard. He barely seemed to notice Jelena, still at his side.

'Hector, are there children here?'

'Must you keep asking so many questions? Didn't I tell you not to get in the way?'

'I'm sorry. It's just, I thought you said it was only men.'

'The shoe, if that's even what it is, could be from anywhere. It was in topsoil. Topsoil changes over time. It lies. Animals come from the forest and dig around looking for food. The rains drag soil from further uphill. It was probably left here by some family picnicking in the shade. You can't trust what you find until you get further down.'

Beads of sweat glistened on Alberto's tanned forehead. Every few minutes he rested his shovel against the side of the pit and wiped his brow with a corner of cloth from his breast pocket. Jelena had met him once before, at a dinner for Hector's team back in the autumn. Alberto had praised her cooking. She smiled at him now, and he nodded. His overalls were unzipped and tied at the waist. He wore a T-shirt on which a dark grey lake of perspiration was spreading outwards from the centre of his back. When his men were chest-deep, Alberto called for the buckets to be lowered into the pit to carry the soil up to ground level. He looked up at Hector and shrugged. Still nothing.

Martha wandered over and stood beside Hector and sighed. 'We're at four feet, Hec.'

'Never mind that. Alberto said—'

'I know what Alberto said. I'm just saying we should be prepared for the possibility that this isn't what we were expecting.'

It seemed to Jelena like sound advice, but Hector waved it away with a hand in front of his face, swiping at an imaginary fly.

'This is the place.'

'How can you be sure?' Jelena asked, but Hector only stared into the pit in silence. The morning drew on without discovery.

¶ At the first glimpse of bone, Alberto replaced the shovels with more precise tools and Hector clambered down into the grave and dusted the earth from an adult male skull. He inspected it quietly, peering into the cavities and turning it carefully in his hands. The others watched as he re-enacted the execution – placing a finger on the base of Alberto's skull – demonstrating how the bullet entered through a small hole in the back of the cranium, and exploded out the front, just above the eyes, leaving a three-inch exit wound with its sharp, fragmented edges.

The skull was passed around in a sort of ritual. Each member of the team held it for a moment, some raised it slightly into the sun like the passing of a sporting trophy. When the skull reached Martha, she placed it on a numbered tray and photographed it from several angles. The men returned to the pit where the bones appeared now like eagerly sprouting bulbs woken by the changing season. They came up from the ground one after another for the next four hours: femur, clavicle, tibia, ribs, humerus. Efforts were made to keep the skeletons intact, but the bodies had fallen into the pit one on top of another, and with the decaying of the flesh the bones had mingled, without their soft exteriors to define them, so that each corpse was indiscernible from the next: scapula, sternum, sacrum – a continuous chain of human remains and two gold molars glinting from jaws smiling at the midday sun.

The final skull count was seventeen when Alberto hit rock and the grave was declared exhumed. All the victims were grown males. Several bullet casings were recovered among the bodies. No clothes were found – the men had been buried naked. No engraved wedding rings, no stopped watches, no dog tags, only a single glass eye, with an iris that polished sky-blue. Boxes were brought from the trucks at the edge of the field and the bones carefully labelled.

Hector was the last to emerge from the grave. Jelena stood at ground level and looked down at her husband, sitting with his back against the wall of the pit. His eyes were closed and she could see that he was talking to himself or perhaps saying a prayer.

'Hector.'

He opened his eyes and looked up at Jelena, silhouetted against the afternoon sky.

'I'm coming down.'

'Don't bother. There's nothing to see. I'm coming up now anyway. It's cold and damp down here.'

Hector climbed out of the pit using a rope ladder tied to the trunk of the tree. He kissed his wife on the forehead, gathered his things from a pile at the edge of the pit and headed towards the cars.

'Hector, wait.'

'What is it?'

'Do you think they were brought here naked?'

'It's unlikely. They came here alive, were stripped, and made to stand at the edge of the pit, where you're standing now. All the wounds are the same. One by one, they were killed with a single bullet to the back of the head, and they fell directly into the pit.'

'What do you think in that moment when you're standing in the cold, naked, waiting to be executed?'

'Most people cover their private parts. They feel humiliated, even though they know they're about to die.'

'...'

'Let's go. Martha's waiting.'

Hector and Jelena crossed the field in silence. Halfway back to the cars, Jelena stopped and turned around.

'What is it?' Hector asked.

'Nothing, go on. There's something I want to see. wait for me in the car. I won't be long.'

Before Hector could object, Jelena set off running back across the field. Her bun slipped out as she ran and her hair danced red on her shoulders. At the tree, she reached out her hand and bent forward, catching her breath a moment. She looked back at him briefly and then Hector watched as she climbed down the rope ladder and disappeared from sight. He turned to see if his team was watching, but they were busy loading the equipment into the vehicles and hadn't noticed. Only Martha was looking, and he wasn't concerned if she saw Jelena's strange behaviour. He often confided to Martha about the problems in his marriage. Hector wondered if he should go and fetch his wife, but returning to the grave might draw the attention of his crew. He remained where he was, waiting for her to reappear. Hector grew more restless with each passing minute. A flock of geese soared overhead.

Three minutes passed. His restlessness changed to concern when it occurred to him that in her haste Jelena might have fallen from the rope ladder and broken her ankle, or worse. Martha had lost interest and put her seat back so that all he could see was her hand draped casually out the driver's side window, a cigarette between her mannish fingers.

He checked his watch, as if that might hurry Jelena along. The strange night, their somnambulistic sexual encounter, which had drifted from his thoughts over the course of the day, returned to him. His pulse quickened and he had a sudden feeling that Jelena wanted him to follow her – that she was waiting for him at the bottom of the pit. The men were still busy. He pictured Jelena sprawled naked in the dirt. Had she not undone her hair with a flick of her wrist as she ran? He took a stride towards the tree. Another. His feet felt heavy, as if they were reluctant to follow. He prized each foot from the ground. A determination to love his wife, to fuck her, welled up like something fermenting in his gut. And then Jelena's head appeared above ground. She hoisted herself out of the pit and retied the thick mane of hair above her head. Hector stopped. He watched her come towards him. When she reached him, she kept walking.

'I told you to wait in the car,' she said.

'What were you doing?'

'I just wanted to see what it was like down there.'

On the drive home Jelena lay across the back seats of the 4x4 and slept. She heard Martha and Hector talking in the front, but nothing of what they said, only the sound of their voices and the rise and fall of the road as they drove through the hills.

¶ Anna could see them walking around up there, above her – no way that they could see or hear her buried so deep underground. She opened her mouth to call out to them but bits of earth fell onto her tongue and into the back of her throat and choked her. An earthworm worked its way into her nose and she could feel it, like thick snot, curl itself around her uvula as she gagged. She watched them passing over her with their digging tools and felt the vibrations in the earth as they broke ground near to where she was buried. Not near enough and they would miss her and she would be left there to rot.

It began to rain and she could feel the rain seeping down through the soil and wetting her skin, and soon the weeds were pushing their way out of her pores and out of the ground and uncurling into small flowers that the men trampled with their work boots. She cried out for them to stop treading on her, but they still couldn't hear.

Bits of her were bone – her feet and ribs and skull, and bits were flesh –

her breasts and hips and buttocks. An assembly of body parts decaying, each in their own time. Her eyelids opening and closing. Her heart still beating strongly inside her muddied ribcage. The men were above her now, coming directly down with the bladed edges of their shovels, slicing the earth apart like meatloaf, severing tough tree roots with single strikes.

How will they know to stop when they reach me, she wondered.

They did not. Hector struck first. His shovel cleaved off her right hand at the wrist and she felt the metal against her bone and her fingers curling around a rock in their last-ditch effort to reach for something and hold it. Hector shovelled out her dismembered hand and showed it to the other men. One of the men used her hand to feel and prod the groin of another and everyone laughed.

¶ Hector woke up drenched in sweat and alone in the bed. Light showed through the crack beneath the bathroom door. He pulled his sodden T-shirt over his head, and slipped out of his shorts, and sat there naked with his feet on the floor, panting in the dark. He recalled the early days of their love affair, long before Jelena, when he lived in New York and she had just published her book. The launch in Midtown where his friend introduced them:

'Anna, meet Hector. A fellow exile.'

She shook his hand. 'It's a pleasure to meet you, Hector.'

'Likewise.'

'Hector digs up bones,' said his friend.

'A palaeontologist?'

'Forensics,' Hector corrected. 'What is your book about?' he asked.

'It's a history. Please, help yourself to a copy. They're over there on that table.'

They got drunk at the event and he invited her back to his apartment. They seemed to fuck forever. She felt so tiny next to him, like a stuffed animal, or a doll, in his bed.

'I came inside you,' he said.

'It's okay,' she said. 'I'm on the pill.'

He pulled her close to him and they fell asleep entwined, and when he woke in the morning she was gone, but she had left her phone number on a pad by the side of his bed. A week later, he called her and she came over and they repeated the sex. By the third or fourth week they had decided to move back home, against the advice of their friends. The night before she disappeared she asked him if he thought they would both survive the war.

'Of course,' he said.

'How can you be so sure?' she asked.

Hector got out of bed, pulled on a fresh pair of shorts and went downstairs. The house was silent. He looked at the clock on the wall above the refrigerator. An hour until Martha picked him up. He opened the fridge and looked for something to eat, but he wasn't hungry so he sat at the kitchen table and smoked a cigarette. He heard the padding of Jelena's feet on the stairs and then he felt her hands on his shoulders, rubbing them.

'Let me make you something to eat,' she said.

'You're too good to me,' said Hector.

'Yes,' she said, 'you're probably right,' and patted the bald spot on the top of his head.

He ate the eggs she placed in front of him dutifully, though they tasted mainly of butter and were too rich for him. When Martha pulled into their driveway and beeped her horn, Hector was still at the table in his underwear.

'Please tell her I'll be out in a minute,' he said as he raised himself up off the chair and left the room to get ready.

ON THE EXAGGERATED REPORTS OF THE DECLINE IN BRITISH FICTION
BY JENNIFER HODGSON & PATRICIA WAUGH

'THE SPECIAL FATE OF THE NOVEL,' Frank Kermode has written, 'is always to be dying.' In Britain, the terminal state seems indigenous to the culture. Beating our chests about the lassitude of novel writing appears to be a critical tradition in its own right. Our last literary season has long passed, it's generally agreed. Whatever happened to the British novel? Well, according to folklore it succumbed to the inclement weather of later consumer culture, or the New Philistinism, or the dumbing down of a compromised welfare consensus, or the paralysing legacies of modernism or a post-imperial loss of status. These days, we might lay the blame for the troubled fate of the British novel with the publishers, the prize culture and, latterly, what is being euphemised as the 'Amazon problem'. But we somehow suspect that these are only the tokens of a more intractable and elusive national malady. That there's something rotten about British culture that somehow fails to nourish the writing and reading of new fiction.

See, for example, the response of one writer, currently fêted in academic Europhile circles, who we voxpopped about new British fiction for this piece: 'I'm not sure I have anything to say. I didn't know there was any.' Disingenuous hauteur or self-possessed national self-dispossession? Is this now ritualised disavowal of the new in British fiction merely an empty but unexamined myth ripe for explosion, or are there real but more obstinate problems in nurturing innovative fictional writing in Britain? If so, do the problems lie with the writing, the perception of the writing, or with the national culture that frames production and reception of the writing? Or do the problems begin somewhere else altogether? Our refusenik jabbed his index finger at the problem and then shrugged his shoulders and walked away. Did he wish to deny his own status as an innovator, or his identity as British, or is he the self-styled exception that proves the rule?

In a culture where all too often literary 'innovation' is read as 'degeneration', where the experimental novelist is viewed as a case of narcissistic personality disorder, and where the new is identified with a 'creeping' cosmopolitanism that dilutes the local produce, the very idea of British innovative fiction comes to sound like an *oxymoronic* supplement – a kind of pharmakon – to the idea of the *moronic* inferno. Though postmodernism only ever reared its head disguised as a kind of indigenous contested empiricism – like arguments for the existence of the Loch Ness monster or Tony Blair's sincerity – its spectral afterlife is now source for lingering embarrassment within literary academia: pomo sold out, went commercial, went moronic, got down with the dodgier intimates of the inferno.

Academic literary critics attempting to push the case for a rejuvenated new British novel tend to sidestep the problem of the oxy and are anxious to avoid being tarred by the moronic. So they reframe the new in the terms of someplace or sometime or something else, most often the 'neo-modern' or the 'late modern' or the 'anxiously modern'. Or they have a field day with riffs on the 'new realism': hysterical, hyper-, contested, problematised, paranoid and dirty – but hardly ever *contemporary*. Peter Ackroyd wrote in 2001 about the way in which British novelists were now beginning to present reality as 'uncomfortable, as being demanding ... less open to conventional habits of narration and description' and about how we are 'continually being made aware of the oddness of the ordinary, the menace and brutality which is behind the conventional political and social worlds'. Groping for a suitable nomenclature to append to the new writing, however, he ends lamely, albeit with characteristic disavowal of ownership: 'You might, I suppose, call it the new realism – paranoid realism.'

Soft-centred liberals all, we British seem shackled either to the safety of the readymade category, or the already canonised, or to the comfortably quotidian. Our peculiar creed is mortally suspicious of untrammelled aestheticism, endlessly asserting the primacy of content over form. In accounts of British writing, even now – long after such a thing could be anything other than a rather quaint anachronism of an old culture war – the avant-garde features as a kind of bogeyman. One whose dandified aestheticism belies a questionable politics, a moral compass gone awry; who must be beaten back by decency and common sense. Literary experiment still tends to be perceived as a pernicious form of French 'flu: of course we should still be *bloody grateful* for the English Channel, separating, as it does, steady, dependable old Blighty from *that kind of thing.*

A new, more 'patriotic' British citizenship test requires those seeking permanent residency in Britain to answer examination questions on Shakespeare, Dickens and Hardy. Without intending to revive that old chestnut of the British cultural studies of the eighties – all those debates about the national culture and the avowed 'greatness' of Shakespeare, Dickens and Hardy as Arnoldian touchstones of value – we still feel a kind of weary bafflement that official sanction should once again be given to the idea that learning a soundbite Shakespearian chakra might offer a quick route to cultural assimilation, or to what is considered most vigorous and most valuable about living in a new as well as an old country. Is this really the best they can do? A mercantilist visionary, a nineteenth-century Christian humanist, an agrarian *fin-de-siècle* melancholic?

But we no longer live even in an age of mechanical reproduction. We live in a post-industrial, neo-corporate, trans-national world of globalised forces where locating yourself in the particularities of a specific time and place requires more than rote-learning the decontextualised soundbites of English literary tradition. Contemporary Britain, like the United States and the nations of Europe and Asia, is now a country with complex interconnections across the globe, through the circuits of international finance, the networks of the new corporate governance and management, and the social networks of the new media. Some of our newest fiction negotiates a path through this entanglement of the local and the global with exuberant style and an almost forensic eye for the way in which the experiential nuances of imagination, perception, memory and dream are all shaped by a culture, a place, a moment and memory. Shakespeare is not the only British inventor of New Worlds. If you were looking for the 'state of the nation' in British writing, you might put down *HENRY V* and set aside for a moment *TESS OF THE D'URBERVILLES*. You might, admittedly, linger over *HARD TIMES*, but you'd be better advised to turn to the occult histories of David Peace, for example, for their reflection of a nation struggling to come to terms with the very worst of its recent past, or to Nicola Barker, whose salty, Rabelaisian *bizarrerie* offers a truly democratic, and ordinarily strange, picture of Britain.

The British writer-critic James Wood, now distinguished Harvard professor and unacknowledged legislator of the fiefdom of contemporary fiction, has done much to consolidate the history of British literary fictional decline. Initially drawing useful ballast from Hugh Kenner's lament for a 'sinking island' after the demise of literary modernism, his transatlantic prognostications drew further scaffolding from postcolonial critics' version of the great Aetiolation. Jed Esty has written the best-known account, but in framing it as yet another Empire Writes Back story, tethering the scope and preoccupations of the novel to shrinking Britain's post-imperial context, he places any reader in the inevitably compromised position of seeming, churlishly, to write back to an Empire That is Writing Back, and seeming, therefore, to collude with Empire. One of the official histories of the retreat from heroic, British ocean-going ambition, the Imperialist triumphalism anatomised in Conrad's *HEART OF DARKNESS*, Esty's account sees imperial greatness now stranded in a stagnant backwater, a kind of Kenneth Grahame messing about on the river, with Ratty, Badger and Mole, dabbling with the ducks in the safe rivulets of *English* pastoral. In this account, Forsterian lyrical realism established itself as *the* British Way of Fiction by turning British into English. Though Forster may have barely registered the sinking and the shrinkage of the nation in 1910, he noted all too well that its hub, its capital, floated vertiginously on a 'sea of porridge' thickened with foreign capital. Forster's answer was to exchange the hub for the heart and to recommend a quiet nativist retreat to the English Country House, the village pageant, with a dash of Pagan or Gothic mystery, and the occasional hint of German Romanticism.

Zadie Smith, kicking her heels on her way across the Atlantic, recently paid homage to the vision in her transatlantic novel *ON BEAUTY* (2005), with its hard-won humanism and its belief in the redemptive power of art. A caricature, of course. Yet the Kenner-Wood-Esty case is curiously borne out in unlikely places. There is abundant evidence that our innovative writers – in a softer version of Eliotic European-Christian-Greco-Buddhist re-fashioning – have collaborated with it, seeming to need psychologically to eschew the allegiances and associations of 'Britishness' or 'Englishness' and to assert the innovator aspect of their identities through self-conscious association with the Continental or the Transatlantic: one thinks here not only of Eliot's editorship of *THE CRITERION*, but of Murdoch's homage to Queneau and Beckett in her first novel; Trocchi and Brooke-Rose's love affair with French intellectual culture; Spark's with the Catholicism of Maritain rather than Newman; A. S. Byatt's avowal of herself as a European; Martin Amis's love-hate relationship with America and American writers such as Bellow and Roth; Zadie Smith's aforementioned looking back through the lens of all things cross-Atlantic (hip-hop and David Foster Wallace). Similar tendencies are evident in some of the most interesting and vigorous new writers such as Tom McCarthy, whose novels resonate with the Beckettian, the phenomenological and the existential, or in Alan Hollinghurst and Adam Thirlwell, who embrace an aristocratic, Euro-transatlantic lineage of James and Nabokov, Edmund White and Milan Kundera. Without exception, of course, all these self-avowedly 'cosmopolitan' writers marry with and promiscuously blend the foreign with the indigenous, the international with the demotic – but what seems to fix their identity in their own eyes and ours is their avowed association with cultures and traditions that are not British.

Some British writers seem to be getting over the hang up: they borrow and read and allude with ease to what Rushdie refers to as the 'sea of stories' and they write happily of the Isle of Dogs, of Shepperton, of Luton, the London Orbital, the East End, the lowlands and blackened wastelands of the industrialised Midlands, lives lived in back-to-back streets, on New Build Infotechland estates, remote Scottish islands, and the endless out-of-town shopping malls of the New Britain. This is a marked change from our parochial literary past. Take for example Kazuo Ishiguro's oft-pronounced sense of the difficulties of escaping the provincialism of British fiction in the seventies, the feeling of Britain's increasing marginalisation in world politics, a geographic isolationism so evident that it seemed impossible to imagine that literary value could not be part of the general 'shrinkage'. British writers felt that the Big Events were happening elsewhere; interesting fiction was bound to follow; the balance of powers was shifting.

His own novel *The Unconsoled* of 1996 was a brilliant rendition of the dangers and seductions of 'going International' as a way of escaping this threat of parochialism (interestingly also the theme of Adam Thirlwell's more recent novel of that name). Ishiguro's *The Unconsoled* is a psychomachia of the newly professionalised cosmopolitan artist struggling to maintain a fierce public relations 'schedule' with pressures on him to perform his art and exercise a telescopic ambassadorial philanthropy. On yet another tour, he finds himself in a strange space of nowhere, an international hotel, in an unnamed place, at an unnamed time, somewhere in the middle of Europe. He wrestles too with a landscape awash with material projections of his own autobiographical memories, fantasies, dreams and fears. Surely a figure for the new professionalised and internationalised writer, Ryder bumps up against the ghosts of his past and the buried and split-off alters of himself, in a landscape built out of hints and glimpses of *The Waste Land*, Ariadne on Naxos, Escher's drawings, the films of Bergman and the Coen brothers, German Romanticism, Nietzsche and Freud, the traditions of the Mittel-European volk.

Similarly, literary modernism, which for so many years was the straw man of a British distrust of intellectualism, has in recent times seen its stock rise. On the publication of *Umbrella* in 2012, Will Self confessed that for all his previous excursions into the demotic and the grotesque, he'd really always been a closet modernist. *Umbrella*, he says, with its four hundred pages of unbroken stream of consciousness, is the book he wanted to write all along. Self's belated coming out is a measure of the extent to which the prejudices that were rife amongst modernism's first- and second-generation legatees – C. P. Snow, Kingsley Amis, The Movement poets et al. – had persisted well into the closing decades of the twentieth century. That stereotype of modernism as a toothless old crone comfortably installed, decades before, at the centre of Establishment good taste and none-too-threatening when busied with manifesting fevered daydreams of some prelapsarian Edwardian past – but all too susceptible to fifth columnist tendencies – was not easily shifted. As late as 1992, John Carey's THE INTELLECTUALS AND THE MASSES conspiracy-theorised the modern's apparent systematic and pre-meditated attack on mass culture.

Now, after the fag end of pomo, modernism seems to be having a moment. As the early years of the twenty-first century categorically fail to deliver anything like the extraordinary flowering of artistic energies that emerged during the first decades of the twentieth, writers and critics (and publishers, with all the entrepreneurial spirit of the original Moderns) are beginning to reinvest in modernism's achievements. In some cases, it's being reinvented anew on the same terms as the old prejudices, welcomed back as modernism-without-the-menaces, thoroughly domesticised and with the sting of literary experimentation removed – Smith's ON BEAUTY we've already mentioned, but see also Alan Hollinghurst's THE LINE OF BEAUTY. Ian McEwan famously declared against the 'dead hand of modernism', in fear, presumably, of that avant-garde bogeyman, as if, as China Miéville has commented, 'the dominant literary mode in postwar England was Steinian experimentation or some Albion Oulipo'. But even McEwan has written a 'modernist' novel, ATONEMENT – if only to indict and rewrite modernism for its dereliction of duty.

For others, however, it's being returned to as an unfinished project, as a fundamental turning point that British culture, ostrich-like as ever, seems to have missed. Gabriel Josipovici's recent kulturpessimismus polemic, WHAT EVER HAPPENED TO MODERNISM? (2010) condemns a buttoned-up Englishry that he sees as dreary and anecdotal, unable to distinguish between reality and l'effet de réel; one that has consistently misunderstood the modernist project. To ignore the avant-garde, says Tom McCarthy, whose own critical success as a novelist is testament to a renewed appetite for modernism, 'is the equivalent of ignoring Darwin'. But about the novels yielded by this twenty-first-century modernist impulse – Self's UMBRELLA and McCarthy's own C, for example, which have been breathlessly heralded as a kind of modernism après la lettre – there is something of the Sealed Knot. These are, inevitably, not modernist novels as such (and how could they be?) but novels about modernism. Ones that adopt its pre-existing codes, tropes and conventions for the sake of nostalgia – which, it bears repeating, doth not modernism make. The category of modernism, ever loose to the point of unwieldy, increasingly seems to mean a 'better class' (read: borrowed from the -isms of the European avant-garde) of literary allusion. Or it is deployed merely to denote a sense of solidity, of seriousness, of authenticity, or of difficulty.

For Josipovici, what has been crucially ignored by British book culture is the ways in which modernism represents the 'coming into awareness by art of its precarious status and responsibilities' and will therefore 'from now on, always be with us'. Thing is, to a certain extent, it always has. Josipovici, McCarthy and Co. seem to be relying upon the same bowdlerised version of British literary history as their adversaries. In fact, part of the problem for the serious literary novelist in Britain has actually often been the difficulty of getting over modernism. Not just as a problem of production, but one of reception too. The new experimental writer was once almost inevitably going to be dubbed the new Beckett or Kafka or Joyce. Once modernism was set up as introspective and concerned with the 'dark places of psychology', to use Woolf's description, writers of the forties like Green, Bowen and Compton-Burnett saw the challenge as finding a way to eschew the assumed 'inward turn' in order to create worlds through dialogue, expressionist rendition, behaviourist technique and phenomenologies of perception that blurred memory and perception, inner and outer voices, hierarchies of narration.

Crucial to this was the intuitive novelistic recognition (spelt out later, philosophically, by both Sartre and Merleau-Ponty) already powerful in Bowen and Green, that feeling is not always, most often not in fact, felt; feeling is most often experienced as the feeling-tone or mood that seems more the attribute of a world or a scene: the vibrancy of backlighting, shadows, edges, colours, the rhythm and pace of a world made in words. Perception is style, as Martin Amis has insisted, but perception is also style that unconceals, tacitly and obliquely, a world and, through a process of reverse introjection, a self. That the world exists for me as my world and that I exist for myself, is what Sartre refers to as *ipseity*. The feeling that I don't exist, the loss of a tacit sense of self-presence, that I don't inhabit my body or the world, is the feeling-tone pervasive in fiction since the seventies but first captured as part of a new inhospitable and corporate world in Camus' THE STRANGER. Meursault cannot feel at all, but his world is conveyed through one of the most powerful and distinctive 'feeling-tones' in modern fiction (Amis, incidentally, uses the word in TIME'S ARROW in a similar attempt to write the Nazi soul). This mode of disconnection in its blank, or hyper-reflexive, or comically disjunctive form – that begins with Dostoevsky, Kafka, Musil and Beckett – has been a major orientation of twentieth-century literary fiction in Britain, but is barely remarked upon in the general preoccupation with making fine discriminations between realism and modernism and late modernism and postmodernism.

It is the very self-consciously executed *modus vivendi* of McCarthy's *REMAINDER*. Take the *WATT*-like scene with the carrot in the physiotherapy clinic:

> I closed my fingers round the carrot. It felt – well, it felt; that was enough to start short-circuiting the operation. It had texture; it had mass. The whole week I'd been gearing up to lift it, I'd thought of my hands, my fingers, my rerouted brain as active agents, and the carrot as a nothing – a hollow, a carved space for me to grasp and move. This carrot though, was more active than me: the way it bumped and wrinkled; how it crawled with grit.

Like Ryder, this protagonist is another who conceives of himself as an artist; this novel too – like Ishiguro's *NEVER LET ME GO* or Hilary Mantel's *BEYOND BLACK* or Hollinghurst's less overtly experimental *THE LINE OF BEAUTY* or Smith's *ON BEAUTY* – is a disquisition on the place of art in a commodified world.

Here a Platonic intentionality – but it could as well be romantic – attempts to materialise its vision through various corporate networks of facilitation and, in the process, exposes the dangerous and mechanistic splitting of mind, body and world that lurks in the Platonic and the Cartesian and is now generalised over Britain in the corporate world of reality management. McCarthy's twenty-first century Frankenstein inhabits and acts out a hyper-reflexive world of 'cool' where money is able to hire an army of networked agents, project managers and special-effects workers specialised in the materialisation of corporate 'vision' as the already confabulated memories viewed as the remaining source of the idea of a soul. Like Ishiguro's, McCarthy's novel too is also about fiction as compensation – a settlement – that undoes itself as it points up all those losses and holes in the real. It is a world where performance is all, and weariness, the weariness of the self, has long set in; where a Beckettian akrasia is now a circuit-disconnect between wiring and neurotransmission in the brain and wiring and neurotransmission to the muscles of the body. It is a world where the pre-reflexive has been almost entirely replaced by the management of the event and the orchestrated confabulation of the 'real' as memory, dream and perception.

REMAINDER has made its mark, perhaps, because it so exquisitely connects the metafictional with the neo-corporate with our revived interest in the phenomenology of perception and imagination and feeling. How does a novelist preserve the anagnosia that is at the heart of practical daily living, the tacit knowing that eludes language? How do you do it in words? And how do you use those words to expose a world where words have been betrayed into the service of a coercive management and production of a kind of emptied out real: the new management protocols of event production, performance monitoring and the corporate scripting of the real as 'cool'? Perhaps the really new realism is that we turn to fiction to experience the feeling of the real. Maybe it's to this that James Wood refers when he defines 'novelistic intelligence' as the capacity to invoke the 'reachably real'. Maybe he's not just propounding the rightful function of the novel as merely fictional shadow-play. but somehow we doubt it. Nonetheless, this takes us somehow beyond the postmodern.

In our obsessions with modernism, postmodernism, realism, neo-modernism, late modernism, the hysterical, the paranoid, the hyper- and the ever 'new' realism, perhaps we have forgotten that a major strength of the British novel has always lain in this kind of phenomenological, often semi-expressionist rendition and self-conscious rehearsal of the building and dismantling of imaginary worlds and the fabulation of a sense of the real. It is there in Sterne's ironic laying bare of the sentimentalist claims for the novel at the beginning of the era of political economy, or in Woolf's dissemination of mind through the complex representation of phenomenologies of perception, memory and imagination, or in Muriel Spark's wicked way of estranging us from our lived and assumed modes of estrangement as she takes a willed detour round the sentimental to restore us to a proper empathy with the poor, the marginalised and excluded.

Without this altered perception of literary history, the fifties will continue to be written up as a disappointing and unambitious return to or collapse back into middle-of-the-road social realism: ignoring the surrealism of A. L. Barker, the comic and haunting expressionism of late Green, the hyper-reflexive strangeness of Rex Warner's THE AERODROME, the Tourettish and grotesque mimicry that makes up much of Amis's LUCKY JIM, the Wittgensteinian reflection on and enaction of solipsism that is William Golding's PINCHER MARTIN, the dispersed, disconnected consciousness that engages the experience of factory life in Sillitoe's SATURDAY NIGHT AND SUNDAY MORNING, or the comic suburban grotesque of William Sansom's brilliant novel THE BODY. Writers such as Beryl Bainbridge, Doris Lessing, early McEwan, Murdoch, Spark, Ballard, Kelman, Burgess, all cut their teeth as part of this trajectory; the legacy extends to McCarthy, Barker, Peace, Self and many others.

To accept this alternative picture is surely to take on board the possibility that there are outward-looking but native traditions of experiment that exceed the usual accounts of the so-called inward turn of modernism, or the turning inside out of fictional convention in the postmodern, or the insider-outsider, Empire Writes Back, double perspectivism of the postcolonial. There is a native version of phenomenology and it flourishes in our fiction; surrealism, expressionism and blankness rub along with comic extravagance, linguistic exuberance and a Todorovian kind of fantastic, happily mingling natural with supernatural and the spiritual and transcendental with the weird and wacky. A kind of British *bizarrerie*.

Yet, the story of the decline of the nation tacked onto the fortunes of the novel, the academic obsession with historical and stylistic placing and categorisation, even a kind of lingering Leavisism that sees art primarily as a guide to the moral or the good life, all create problems for the perception, reception and encouragement of aesthetic newness in Britain. The self-induced dispossession of national identity so marked in our literary culture seems, well, *British*. And it often feels remarkably difficult to avoid the self-fulfilling pressure of the stereotype. Turn to the American writer Jonathan Franzen's recent apologia for his own style of autobiographical fiction, for example, and there's no hint of such identity problems: 'When I write,' he says, 'I don't feel like a craftsman influenced by earlier craftsmen who were themselves influenced by earlier craftsmen. I feel like a member of a single, large virtual community in which I have dynamic relationships with other members of the community, most of whom are no longer living. As in any other community, I have my friends and I have my enemies. I find my way to the corners of the world of fiction where I feel most at home, most securely but also provocatively among my friends.' Franzen's place is comfortably globetrotting round the worlds of fiction in his head: the world of fiction as a world of story-worlds and not promotional tours, publicity launches and national book culture.

But a question remains, perhaps, whether there was actually a falling off during many and various periods which commentators have identified as their literary *annus horribilis*. In a now-infamous 1993 editorial to the literary magazine GRANTA, Bill Buford blamed the word 'British' itself for poisoning the wells of talent: 'a grey, unsatisfactory, bad-weather kind of word, a piece of linguistic compromise'. In a landscape (then) beginning to seem more refreshed by the voices of the transnational, the migrant and the diasporic, the idea of 'British', however, for Buford, seemed to hang in the air like a toxic miasma, stymieing progress and the cultivation of the new. 'British' was a bad spell; no longer a description of the real. 'I still don't know anyone who is British. I know people who are English or Scottish or Northern Irish (not to mention born in Nigeria but living here or born-in-London of Pakistani parents and living here... or born-in-Nigeria-but-living-here-Nigerian-English).' but Buford too (also an American) now seems strangely hung up on the Kenner account, convinced that the only means of renewal still depended on Imperial powers, now in reverse as the Empire Wrote Back.

Though there is no necessary connection between the luminosity of events in history and the significance and value of artistic representation, literary critics seem curiously attached to this view of things. They are driven perhaps by different concerns than writers themselves, concerns to do with historical placing, cultural trajectories, political interventions, real or imagined, and less so with the nitty-gritty of that incredibly difficult task of imagining and making a world. If we literary critics thought more like novelists and less like historians or sociologists, perhaps we might begin to see that the fifties consisted of more than Angry Young Men or deferential genuflections in bicycle clips. Perhaps we might begin to do justice to the immensely variegated and innovatory work of that decade and perhaps we might see the fifties is a good place to begin to explode the Kenner and co. myth of inevitable decline? Similarly, perhaps, the 1980s had more on offer than a political imagination fired up by Margaret Thatcher or the Empire Writing Back or Lyotard's critique of metanarratives. Perhaps even the 1970s, as the Age of No Style, had styles that awaited a hermeneutic imagination more attuned to factories than flares, ghosts than governments, Granny rock than Glam rock (Beryl Bainbridge's THE BOTTLE FACTORY OUTING perhaps as against Martin Amis's THE PREGNANT WIDOW).

Writers are freer than critics to ignore the strictures of periodisation, the interminable debates about location and positioning. They can stick their necks out more freely – aren't they meant to? – without alienating an 'interpretive community' or being excluded from the academic Research Exercise – the six-yearly cull of academic 'research' imposed by a national government stingy on higher education funding but generous to the point of silliness with the provision of League Tables:

I've never understood the categorisation of postcolonial writing. I've been sent papers where I'm talked about as a postcolonial novelist, but I'm never sure about the definition. Does "postcolonial" mean writing that came out in the postcolonial era? Or does it have to come from a country that used to be part of an empire, and which, after the colonies started to devolve, changed into an independent state? Or does it mean writing by people who don't have white skins... Whether somebody is postcolonial seems to be defined by the writer's biography rather than by their writing, and that's what makes me very suspicious of postcolonial writing as a category.

Ishiguro voices something often obscurely felt but ne'er so well expressed – or, more likely, ne'er dared to be expressed, at least by academic critics forced to keep one eye on political and the other on professional correctness. What if novels are primarily now read as ways out of loneliness, as Jonathan Franzen has recently averred? Does that make them less difficult to write? Or less political? Doesn't that entail trying to understand and find ways to represent, analyse and imaginatively transform the sources of our sense of contemporary disaffection or lack of or skewed affect? Historicisation in fiction is rooted in the singularity of a story world, created through a process of formal imagination and craft. If we make fiction 'piggyback' too much on history, as Ishiguro suggests later in the same interview (2012), 'it leads to the preservation of mediocre books whilst some brilliant books are forgotten because they don't fit the clear historical model.' We've persisted in drawing upon a textbook version of literary history, at the expense of engaging fully with the realities of literary practice. And in so far as such a model ever could anywhere, the one that bisects the twentieth century more-or-less down the middle, dividing its paper assets between the categories of modernism and postmodernism – drawing a discreet veil over a mid-century 'return to realism' which we prefer not to talk about – has never comfortably applied here. sometimes new mutations, hopeful monsters, struggling to push their way out of blighted soil are trodden over by the love affair with historical frames or correctness.

Yet, despite the successive incursions of threads, pockets and outcroppings of the experimental and the reality of a more variegated literary history than 'official' accounts almost always offer, the mainstream picture of the British novel is still dominated by the idea of a time-worn 'English style'. Colm Tóibín recently characterised the 'quintessential English novel of our age' as 'well made, low on ambition and filled with restraint, taking its bearings from a world that Philip Larkin made in his own image'. Zadie Smith, in her essay 'Two Paths for the Novel', speculates on the future of fiction in English by way of reviews of novels by latter-day realist Joseph O'Neill, and of Tom McCarthy as the great hope for British avant-garde writing. She finds O'Neill's is the road most travelled. His 'breed of lyrical realism' (there we go again) has 'had the freedom of the highway for some time now, with most other exits blocked'. Although Smith specifies the Anglophone novel, her view seems more narrowly applicable to fiction in Britain. At the Edinburgh Writers' Conference last year, China Miéville spoke of the English novel's 'remorseless prioritisation... of recognition over estrangement'. The timeliness of Ali Smith's revival of the old literary chestnut of style versus content at the same event is perhaps testament to the paucity of our thinking about what novels are and what they can do.

We've had the good grace to export this ethic in the views of James Wood, 'the finest literary critic writing in English today' (as is customary to append). His pleas for reason and decency against a pervasive American fetish for vulgar stylistics, for those 'very "brilliant" books which know a thousand things but do not know a single human being', issue weekly from the pages of the NEW YORKER. for in Britain, where, as we've seen, the state of the novel is more likely to be closely pegged to the state of the nation, fiction has been obliged to provide a repository for stable truths and social order. 'Englishness' (very rarely 'Britishness') has remained a major preoccupation in our fictions. Novels have long been burdened with providing the sense of spiritual coherence that social commentators insist we so sorely lack despite, or in fact because of, an increasingly dispersed and devolved national culture.

Last year, the summer of the British monarch's Diamond Jubilee and the London Olympics tested an uneasy, class-conscious, and ambivalent relationship with a nationalism reinterpreted as national pride and belonging that many British people are still loathe to admit. Those celebrations followed on from the previous summer's outbreak of violence, raids, looting and riots that saw major areas of the city of London in flames. Interspersed with BBC coverage of Wimbledon, a new Shakespeare season and pictures of the Olympic torch on its progress round the towns of Britain were documentaries and narratives of the mostly 16-24 year-old rioters now released from prison and facing life with disabling criminal convictions. As for nationalism, as Stefan Collini writes, we seem always to have insisted that such a primitive – and historically troublesome – impulse is something that happens elsewhere. The issue has long been a vexed one here. The World War II-era injunction to 'Keep Calm and Carry On' has become the atavistic mantra of Recession Britain visible everywhere from towels to teacups. It appeals to our mythic image of ourselves; the 'blitz spirit' with which we might weather this new Age of Austerity. But as our 'collective symbol', the Union Jack has an uncomfortable double existence. It is similarly, 'harmless' pageantry, a Little England party favour, but it is also historically loaded and queasily evocative, making us instinctively – and often unquestioningly – uneasy.

We have not lost our mania for manifesting the particularity (and the peculiarity) of being English. The metaphysics of Eliot and Leavis might have gone lukewarm for many and stone cold for most, but we still continue to attempt to conjure a coherent whole from less than the sum of its parts. But the smoggy mill towns, red pillar boxes and fried breakfasts of an English particularist like Orwell have, however, given way to rather more ersatz assemblages. The cover of last year's Britain-themed issue of GRANTA depicts a chipped bone china teacup with its handle wrenched off. This, neatly, is the 'Broken Britain' of tabloid and Tory parlance. The nation recorded within is peopled with desperate pen-pushers, small-time dealers of recreational pharmaceuticals, missing children, Eastern European lap dancers and timorous lower-league footballers with Lady Chatterley-esque designs upon the groundsman. It's an urban-pastoral hinterland, hung with a murder-scene gloaming of incipient menace. Abandoned old-New Towns and sink estates, the condemned edifices of post-war utopian dreaming – and of local government corruption – feature heavily. So, too, does a British state of mind governed by shame, repression and lassitude and given to random and not-so-random acts of violence.

Yet it is with these ingredients, the poet and novelist John Burnside argues, that we might put Britain, like Humpty Dumpty, back together again. '[H]ome, or identity,' he suggests, 'can be found in cultural ruins.' Britain might be, as self-styled alternative poet laureate Simon Armitage has it, reduced to a 'shipwreck's carcass' and 'down to its bare bones', but with the loss of 'old certainties' comes the loosening of the old hierarchies too, and with it the possibility for remodelling Britain along more democratic, more egalitarian lines. This, for Burnside, is cause for a 'tender, if guarded, celebration':

> To recognise the new values that emerge from the makeshift is to discover the earliest traces of a new direction, the first tentative steps in a spontaneous remaking of ourselves, the hazy outline of a democratising order that imagination finds in the unlikeliest of places.

But is this really the cause for (albeit cautious) jubilation? Should a 'sense of identity' really come at such a cost? And is celebration really the most appropriate response? GRANTA's picture of Britain is not, as it purports to be, an unflinchingly democratic picture of a diverse society, but the finessing of a poverty of many kinds into the picturesque; the requisite local colour now provided by all those on–the–bones–of–their–arse Britons.

Burnside seems at once to under– and over–estimate what art can do. We might now be rather more sceptical about the real–world capabilities of the artistic imagination to ameliorate social injustice. And we might question how effective a model of egalitarianism narrative fiction can be. The iconography of this 'Broken Britain' is well on its way to becoming a collection of clichés of 'Englishness' that is just as politically malign, cosy and self–satisfied than the old one. Burnside's is, at least, a very British sentiment: It might be *crap* but at least it's *ours*. For Martin Amis, on the other hand, the appropriate response to a country he recently declaimed for its 'moral decrepitude' is satire. 2012's 'State of England' novel, LIONEL ASBO, is a parting shot as Amis absconds for America. 'Who let the dogs in?' the epigraph asks, in the first of many woefully misjudged (and woefully out–of–date) pop culture references. In the novel, Amis romances Britain's underclass into a coterie of grotesques that are at once Jerry Springer–generic and farcically bizarre: the single mothers, illiterate bruisers and petty criminals are joined by a glamour model–slash–aspiring poetess, pitbulls raised on Tabasco. The response has been almost unanimously negative; unsurprising since, as one reviewer commented, Amis's novel amounts to little more than narrative–as–trolling.

Fellow novelist Nicola Barker has been a rare voice in defence of LIONEL ASBO, arguing, in her review, that 'maybe modern England needs offending'. She maintains that thin–skinned Britons might well need this kind of baiting to shake them from their cosy, tea–and–biscuits slumber. Surprising, this, from Barker, since although she was recently puffed as the 'female Martin Amis', her own novels engage with the 'reality' of living in Britain (*whatever that might mean*, her fictions always insist on appending) with an authenticity and a sensitivity rarely seen in Amis's. Far from proffering a searing critique of the state of the nation, Barker's so–called progenitor appears to be in cahoots with a culture that is, in terms of its cruelty and vacuity, already way beyond the poison of his pen. See, for example, the ritualised humiliations of über–franchised reality television or even more so our government, whose economic policymaking in the face of the global economic recession evinces a level of care and sympathy more often seen in the S&M parlour, or indeed, in the public school fagging system with which Prime Minister David Cameron is so familiar. 'We' (who, *us*?) have been decadent, chastise the swingeing cuts initiated by the coalition government, and now, inevitably, *we must be punished*.

It is customary, at this juncture, to segue effortlessly into tentative optimism. To defer to the 'complexity' of the situation. To issue disclaimers about the partial view of our presentism. To talk of 'green shoots' and 'possibilities'. This piece, in a sense, is no exception. We suggest that what afflicts the British novel might not be as elusive as it seems. That the problem, in fact, might lie closer to home.

Literary criticism, once envisioned by F. R. Leavis as the 'humane centre' of British culture, long since split into the factions of Grub Street and Ivory Tower, and there has been little love lost between the two since Leavis's heyday. Reacting against this ethical burden, the British literary academy was a keen late adapter to continental theory. Over-eager, in fact; for it was soon accused by novelists of having all but abandoned the novel, having thrown the baby out with the bath water of Leavis and the New Criticism. This caricature of academe is, at least in part, the product of a long-standing British mistrust of 'Theory'. Yet who could blame literary academics for sexing up the British novel with liberal applications of cool, continental philosophy on hot topics like death and desire; or those who manage to divine an encounter with the Lacanian Real in the po-faced sex-farce (sometimes labelled 'neo-Victorian') of Ian McEwan's *On Chesil Beach*? But in this era of impact-assessment and quota-fulfilment, the academy's attempts to grapple with the British contemporary novel have often felt like a will-this-do concession to relevance. Perhaps it would be better advised to modify its attempts to validate its objects of study by overburdening them with demands for relevance to political or government correctness and simply try to lift the longstanding taboo on aesthetic evaluation that might lend its weight to, well, better novels.

The literary press in Britain has eagerly taken up the Leavisite slack, moonlighting as the moral advocate of the self-consciously middlebrow. It exists as the heavily subsidised, loss-making adjuncts and supplements to newspapers, with the exception of the *London Review of Books*, funded by its editor's family trust. Perhaps because of this, as with so much cultural life in Britain, our literary press is all too aware of a public service remit, but is by no means sure of whom its audience might comprise. It addresses an Ideal Reader that is both unapologetically philistine and impossibly highfalutin'. That likes its books 'serious' and 'weighty', but not 'dry' or 'obscure' and certainly never to 'lack heart'. That wants its ethical heuristics trussed up in majestically lyrical prose.

Whilst British literary critics are reverential about the innate value of the (definite article, capital letter) Novel, they remain wholly unconvinced about the broader possibilities of fictional narrative. See, for example, Liam McIlvanney and Ray Ryan's take on the 'novelness' of novels in THE GOOD OF THE NOVEL (2011):

> One can say, for one thing, that the truth of novels cannot be rendered in any other form; it cannot be abstracted or codified, turned into thesis or proposition. Novelistic truth is not data, not reportage, not documentary, not philosophical tenet, not political slogan. Novelistic truth is dramatic, which means above all it has to do with character... In exploring character, the novel's key strength is the disclosure of human interiority. To the question, what does the novel do?, we might most pertinently answer: the novel does character, and the novel does interiority.

Character and interiority; no mention here of the novel's capacity not just to 'disclose' but to expand the remit of human experience, for instance, to offer temporary access to other ways of perceiving. Or of the novel as thought experiment, as a viable form of knowledge all of its own – let alone as a ticket to peak experience at the limits of language. Here – where novels are breathlessly praised for their skilful navigation of our twenty-first century dilemmas and for the delicate craft of their storytelling – lies what used to be called literary fiction in Britain. E. M. Forster need not have worried about the fate of his 'little society' – it is alive and well, at least in the pages of the literary press.

Until the 1970s, new and innovative British fiction could at least count upon its allies in publishing. back then, 'good' books were safeguarded by the support and patronage of swashbuckling, semi-mythical publishing mavericks like John Calder, Marion Boyars and Tom Maschler. Now, in these dark days for the book industry, as the novelist Deborah Levy has commented, 'There is no way you can send a fierce, exotic and brutally truthful hothead novel out into the British rain in a recession and expect a deal to be on the table with scones, tea and the DAILY MAIL.' New books are subject to the bottom line of multinational publishing conglomerates which are rationalising and prioritising as never before. Even the braver editors have the jitters, unwilling to take a punt on those books deemed untested and unmarketable. To emerge from the slush pile now, novels must meet cynical editorial policies which attempt to second guess, on the one hand, the whims of the market by trying to appease some phantasmic lowest common denominator and, on the other, the vagaries of literary prize culture by seeking to appeal to some gold standard of literary 'good taste'. And, overall, insist on radically underestimating the appetites of the British reading public. This, then, is the British literary establishment. The perfect pricks, so to speak, to kick against. Or, so you might think. But, in fact, a book counterculture in Britain has been slow to emerge. There are exceptions, without doubt: this very magazine, of course, the newish press And Other Stories, for example, who enjoyed early success with Levy's *Swimming Home*, the imprint Faber Finds, which is making efforts to put right the wrongs of literary history, and others. But still the little magazines, periodicals and presses of other cultures do not exist in such significant numbers here. Tellingly, when the *Observer* recently profiled the thriving lit mag scene, it looked to New York and to *n+1*, *Triple Canopy* and the *New Inquiry*.

In fact, in Britain, increasingly there's the sense that new and innovative fiction is beginning to abscond from the realm of the strictly 'literary' altogether, and is making for the sunnier and more welcoming climes of the art world. See, for example, the Semina series of experimental texts edited by writer and artist Stewart Home, published by Bookworks, an independent art publisher. Or Visual Editions, which seeks to draw together the art book and the literary text to publish what they call 'visual writing' like Adam Thirlwell's *Kapow!* and Jonathan Safran Foer's *Tree of Codes*, alongside a new edition of what is perhaps the ur-text of the experimental novel, *Tristram Shandy*. Will the art world, then, provide a place for innovative writing to flourish in Britain? Can a home be found for this ailing medium in a milieu that is less hamstrung by misplaced moral and ethical obligations and the strictures of the marketplace (both real and imaginary) and, significantly, is better funded?

And where might this leave British book culture? Despite their differences, writer, critic and academic alike find themselves under threat and compromised – economically and existentially – by the restructuring and redevelopment of the new globalised neo-corporatisms, with their token nods to green recycling and New Age recovery, and their sinister and often systematic appropriations of everything from art to the social network to the 'event'. The work of art exists no longer in a romantic–modernist age of mechanical reproduction but in the disseminated and pervasive global networks of the neo-corporate and the new knowledge economy. Being 'local' is unavoidably a way of being 'global'; getting inside the singular consciousness may be less a business of flowing along a stream of consciousness than evoking a structure of feeling of a world that, as Musil discerned long ago, is filling up with men without qualities, men incorporated into the neo-corporate spaces of the new knowledge economy. If postmodernism was a lament for depths lost to late consumer capital, it was always easy prey to charges of mendacious and slippery complicity with the enemy. If we are currently now officially in an 'interregnum', past the post and into a new age of 're' – redevelopment, recycling, restructuring, reparation, reconciliation, residue, remainder, remembrance, recession – trying to rebuild foundations, recover roots and reimagine a future reconnected with a revisioned past, we are also being forced to acknowledge how far past the post we are in other ways too – poised uncertainly but apocalyptically on the brink of environmental disaster and economic collapse. Artistically and imaginatively, though British and stranded on a sinking island, we too inhabit the new world of the globalised and the neo-corporate frozen style that deploys its resources in the professional management and production of the real. There is, quite discernibly, a new climate of seriousness, a sense of 'growing up' from postmodernism, but the abatement of fears about the death of the author by no means presents new death threats to the artistic imagination. Innovative and ambitious novels certainly continue to be written in Britain; there might be more of them, and those that there are might be better known, if only there was someone to vouch for them.

ESTATE
BY CHINA MIÉVILLE

TWO NIGHTS RUNNING I WOKE UP with my heart going crazy. The first time, as I lay there in the dark, I heard a group of guys outside. They were running, shouting 'Hurry!' and 'We'll miss it!' I wondered if I should do something, but I couldn't hear any fighting or smashing glass. I got up when they were all gone. I kept my light off and parted my blind to look down.

There was rubbish under the streetlamps. There was a big rectangular bin, its lid open, and all around it was a rim of paper and plastic and leaves.

It was August. The slats of the blind left black dust on my hand.

The next night foxes woke me. I knew their swallowed barks but I'd never heard a racket like that before. One night when I was really young, before we moved to the estate, our cat was in heat – my mother explained it to me carefully – and as I was closing my bedroom curtains I saw that the tree at the bottom of our yard was full of cats. They were switching their tails as the light went down. They were all staring, it seemed to me, at me. They started up these boylike horny tom cries.

I listened to the fox calls and wondered if that was the sort of thing going on. If they were courting, in a city tree, or on the roof of a corrugated shed.

There's a park near my flat with a little playground in it, populated by friendly plastic animals. One's a fox, with bright red fur and a blue cap. I imagined a bunch of real foxes circling that cartoony figure in the dark.

I went and stood outside. It was much colder than it should have been, like winter. The foxes shut up. Under a lamp was a noticeboard for the tenants' association. A torn sign about a coffee morning. Recycling. A meeting called by a social capital group called OBYOSS, about regeneration. The name of one of their organisers was familiar.

The playground wasn't far. I went past closed shops and into unlit rows. There's a robin next to the fox. It's about the size of a 3–year–old, and dressed like a pirate. There's a badger and a pig. They're the same size: they aren't to scale.

A few cars passed, streets away. There was no rain but the air felt wet. I heard percussion. A knock–knock–knock. Hooves.

The sounds echoed between the damp walls. I thought I could smell pollen. Light was coming up from an unkempt side street. Something glowing. The hooves got louder.

The air was full of dust and little leaves. I had to squint to see.

There was a guttering noise. The shadows of street trees jumped madly. Wavering light reflected in the windows of a shop, in the fronts of the machines that, for a few coins, would spit out toys and sweets.

The light flared and rolled and went out. When I reached the side street I stood with the wind shoving at me. I smelt smoke but there was no fire anywhere. There was no sound.

❡ I went back the next day. A group of kids were circling a puddle on their bicycles. Two older men struggled with shopping. There were scorch marks high up a lamp post. In front of one small house a young family giggled at their fussing baby. It grizzled but they seemed delighted.

'Can you believe it?' its mother said. 'You were so ill last night, you little terror! Now look at you!' The baby burped and everybody laughed.

Their garden was thick with some flowering bush. I doubt it was ever healthy, but to me it looked freshly ripped, missing foliage. I tugged at one of the broken branches, as if my hand was something grazing as it passed.

❡ Back at the estate, people were clustered in little groups between the blocks. There was a woman there who lives close to me and likes me because I made faces for her toddler one time.

'You were at my school, yeah?' she said. I hadn't realised until that moment. 'Did you know Dan Loch?'

'Yes,' I said. I was startled. 'I knew who he was, anyway.'

'He's back.'

'Right,' I said. 'I think I saw his name on something.'

'Don't pretend like you don't care.' She smiled as if we were conspirators.

When Dan was expelled from our school he and his family had left the estate altogether. I was one of the kids who watched him go.

The Lochs lived in a stretch of flats by outbuildings full of maintenance stuff, where addicts would take drugs. We climbed up onto the roofs and lay on our stomachs to watch Dan's family.

His mum was hauling his younger sister over her shoulder, their crying faces close together. His dad shuffled behind them, a suitcase in each hand. In front of them all was Dan, sniffing the air as if that would decide him which way to go.

We made no effort to hide. It was all a bit solemn. Dan looked up and acknowledged us with raised eyebrows. He looked at the sun, paused, beckoned, and turned into the city, his family behind him.

'He was in Paris and South Africa,' the woman said. 'Now he's back.'

'This the welcoming committee?' I said.

The police hovered at the edges of the square but there was no trouble.

¶ We stayed into the night. A lot of the people there I didn't recognise. That's surprising when you've been in the estate as long as I have. Some wore country clothes, and sounded like they came from posher areas than ours.

When it got dark people got more raucous. They listened to music on their phones, and some were even dancing, joke-dancing to show they weren't taking it seriously. It drizzled.

A little after ten o'clock I heard a clacking. There was a brief cheer.

People came from behind one of the towers. Eight or nine of them, in overalls, with sports bags over their shoulders. Each carried a pointed stick, speared litter they shoved into black rubbish bags. They knocked their sticks together rhythmically. There was a woman who couldn't have been older than 19. A man in his 60s, waving like a celebrity. In front of them all was Dan. I wouldn't have known him if my neighbour hadn't put him in my mind.

They conferred. They whispered, pointed in various directions, down passageways and under concrete. They slapped hands at last in a complicated salute and went separate ways. We all picked one of them to go after.

I followed Dan. I said his name. He glanced. It took him a moment but I could see he knew me.

'Yeah,' he said. 'You alright?' He touched his finger to his forehead and twirled his litter-stick. He was elegant.

I said 'Dan,' again, but he was gone. A group of teenagers passed me. 'Shut up,' one said. 'Man's focusing.'

Dan fingered walls and bollards. He passed a knocked-over bin and knelt to examine it. We hung back. I felt like I was seeing him leave home again.

By a concrete ramp and a commercial space that had never been let, the wall was blackened. Dan began to run.

He was taking us down routes I'd never seen. Behind those blocks the only noises we made were those of our feet and bikes. The bases of the brown towers ran up to the surrounding streets, which were not deserted. Cars crossed the bridge over the canal.

Dan stopped suddenly in the light of late-night shops and we all stopped with him and he stared into shadows and bike sheds, derelict, their doors permanently open. He waved at us to stay still. Very slowly, he put his stick and sack down. He took the bag from his shoulders and opened it.

Firelight flared. There was a roar of burning. A stag walked out of the dark.

It shone. Its antlers were on fire.

The stag was huge. It regarded us without fear. The antlers were like the branches of a great tree. They rushed with flame. They sent up oily smoke, lit the cars and the lots and the pedestrians. The antlers spat.

The stag swung its brawny neck. It walked towards us with forest calm. It paused and lowered its head and lapped at a gutter.

We didn't move. It went on at last towards the road. I heard screaming. Two men came out of a late-night shop, stared and ran. One fell backwards and kept scooting along the pavement on his arse. The other yelled his name and came back for him.

There was a horrible series of thuds as a car swerved and hit another, and then as a third hit them. Fire spread along the animal's tines.

Dan was clicking something together. A rifle. One of the boys on bikes whooped and Dan shouted 'E! Nuff!' without looking round and made the kid freeze.

Clots of stuff fell from the stag's head and made its pelt smoulder. It crossed the road close to us. I smelt the burning hair. The animal was twitching.

Dan sighted. His quarry staggered. It hesitated, it swayed. The fire was accelerating, crawling down the antlers. The stag blinked.

Dan fired.

The stag spasmed and buckled and bowed.

There were whoops. But Dan cursed and did something to his weapon. It wasn't his bullet that had done this. The flames began to take the stag's big head.

Dan took aim again. Another car careered across the road. The deer was too lost, shaking too hard to look, if it even had eyes still and they weren't burnt up. The car slammed into its kneeling body.

Glass exploded. The burning animal flew so hard into the railing on the bridge I felt the impact in the air. Its antlers splintered, leaving stumps in the head-shaped fire.

'Jesus Christ!' I shouted. A man fell out of the car holding a bloody wound.

'Fuck,' Dan said.

The deer was half off the bridge, fitting. You could see its teeth through the fire pulling back its lips. It lolled. Its weight shifted and it tipped and we shouted 'No!' as if that might stop it falling but it didn't. It plummeted out of sight. We heard it hit the water.

'What does that mean?' someone said at last. 'Did it work?'

'You can't tell straight away.'

'What do you think?'

Dan was disassembling his rifle. He saw me looking and rolled his eyes at me in an *Ah well* way. Gave me a wave and swung the bag back over his shoulder. I think I was the only one who saw him walk quickly away, back into the estate, into the dark under the towers. Everyone else was by the railings, watching the smoking carcass bob rump-up in the canal.

¶ The council got it out with a crane. They used one from the building site on the other side of the water. They didn't even have to reposition it. The operator just turned it round and dropped the hook and fished the stag expertly out.

It dangled, all ruined, dropping bits into the water as it rose in chains.

There was a public meeting organised by locals. I heard it was confused. No one was sure why they were there. You heard a lot about the stag in the estate those days, of course. But no one knew anything. Only a few people, if the topic came up, would get a faraway look, and maybe tap their noses or something, like bullshitters.

So I thought that would be the end of it, but it wasn't. About a month later, the office of the government's head vet, or something like that, held a press conference. They wanted to discuss the results of the post-mortem.

The undersides of the stag's hooves, they said, had been coated with an epoxy like dense rubber. The antlers had been saturated in something bituminous, long- and slow-burning. Except where they protruded from the skull and skin: there they'd been treated with retardant, to slow the downward creep of fire.

The animal's blood was full of a ketamine derivative of unknown sort, cut or altered in ways the scientists didn't fully understand. But they were confident it closed down pain sensors, numbed flight-fight instincts.

It had been made into a deer unconcerned that its antlers were on fire.

It had been dying the whole time we followed it, in a poisoned stupor, burning alive.

∴

The OBYOSS posters promising urban renewal faded. No one took them down. I looked for Dan in the flat that had been his family's. It had been empty for years. 'He's gone back to Cornwall,' my neighbour said. 'That's what I heard.' I walked past a launderette and a teenage boy opened the door and came out in a fug of dryer smell and said, 'I seen you was looking for the Dan man. I've got something for you.'

'You want this?' he said. 'You want this yes or no? It's a hundred.'

He had a short length of blackened antler. It smelt of burn. 'Put that in your garden, it makes your plants grow. Put it in your house, it gives you money.' He gave me more reasons I should buy it and I did. It was surprisingly light. I put it on top of my TV, as he also suggested. 'Makes your reception perfect,' he said. 'Check Channel 4 tonight.'

The footage was of the rolling of the fiery barrel or whatever, some harvest festival in a market town. 'Look at you,' I said, as if the man onscreen could hear me, as if the footage weren't months old.

It was Dan. He was one of those hoisting a burning thing onto his shoulders, carrying whatever it was, wherever.

¶ There's been very little regeneration on the estate. Two months after Dan disappeared, in Birmingham and then in Glasgow, burning-antlered stags sauntered down main streets as long as the drugs held. In Birmingham, someone in the crowd shot the deer with a bow, then a gun. The arrow hit its left leg, the bullet killed it and the crowd dispersed. The one in Glasgow died all by itself.

A huge albino animal, its head under a corona of fire, went walking in a run-down neighbourhood of Montreal, to be put down by terrified cops. A stag set off in a Parisian *banlieue* street at midnight followed by awe-struck youth but something was wrong with its preparation and it collapsed and started dying almost immediately.

No one's ever been caught preparing or releasing any of the beasts.

In New York two days ago, someone let scores of hares loose on Roosevelt Island. They went racing everywhere, jumping, feverish, boxing each other, all sinewy and pugnacious in the waste-ground. There was something glinty and wrong with their ears. I saw it on YouTube. Within a few minutes they started to die. They weren't afraid of the locals who tried to grab them, and sometimes, disastrously, succeeded.

Running the length of each of the hares' ears was a knife. They slashed people's hands. They were like straight razors, one end driven through the fur into the hares' skulls. The blades protruded, sutured to the ears with fishing wire. Mostly, the clots and bloodstains resulting from these alterations had been wiped away or bleached invisible, but if you held the dying things carefully and looked closely you could see the joins.

They're building a new playground. I looked at the plans: it's going to be much better. I saw diggers and men in overalls getting ready to uproot the plastic fox and all the others. 'What'll happen to them?' I asked, but the land-

scapers shrugged. I keep imagining those garish animals in a landfill, under
the earth.

BARKING FROM THE MARGINS: ON ÉCRITURE FÉMININE BY LAUREN ELKIN

I. TWO MOMENTS IN MAY

2 May 2011. The novelists Siri Hustvedt and Céline Curiol are giving a talk at Shakespeare and Company in Paris. The shop is filled to bursting, and the audience spills onto the sidewalk outside. The topic of their discussion, they announce, is the 'strange bias against fiction in general and fiction by women in particular'. Men don't read books by women, they lament; women's writing seems only to appeal to other women. 'Would you have written the same book if you were a man?' Curiol reports having been asked on numerous occasions. The question, she implies, has become so banal as hardly to be worth answering: 'Yes, no, maybe,' she says. Both authors dismiss the idea that men write as men, and women write as women. 'Novels do not have a gender,' says Curiol. One audience member, an emissary from the French feminist group La Barbe ('The Beard') berates them, quite aggressively, for turning literature into a battlefield. Hustvedt protests: 'You've misunderstood entirely what we were trying to say.' Meanwhile the bookshop's owner, Sylvia Whitman, shakes her head in bafflement as she's asked to account for the actual ratio of male to female authors on the shop's shelves.

20 May 2011. I'm at an academic conference in Paris. A graduate student gives a paper on a novel about partition by the Pakistani writer Bapsi Sidhwa, making what seems to me to be an innocuous yet perceptive argument on the vexing ways in which gender and colonialism intersect in the novel. During the discussion period, the student is dressed down by the two (female) faculty members chairing the panel. 'Do you really think Sidhwa has anything to say about partition that's different from Salman Rushdie just because she's a woman?' The student is silent. 'Don't work only on women's writing,' one professor, a placid blonde with an immobile page boy haircut counsels her. 'That goes for all of you,' she says. 'It's been done, and by people much older than you. It's over. Find something else to work on.'

I'm gobsmacked. I've just defended my Ph.D. on British women's writing of the 1930s.

My advisor, Jane Marcus, helped found feminist literary criticism in the US. Neither she nor any other feminist scholar I've encountered has ever said to me *Our work is done; why don't you work on something else*? I'm suddenly terrified that I've been pouring my heart and soul and all my time for nearly a decade into a field that is considered wrong-headed and irrelevant by the rest of the academy. By concentrating on women's writing, had I effectively locked myself up in a room of my own, out of touch with the world?

For years I accepted unquestioningly the value of what I was doing. I had gone to a women's college, found an abundance of feminist professors with whom to work in graduate school, and was awash in secondary source material on subjects like mine. But in those first few months after I received my degree, I began to seriously think about whether or not it was worthwhile to study women's writing for its own sake, or whether the concept of 'women's writing' was still useful and important. I found myself uncomfortably nostalgic for a time when feminism was unquestionably useful. Today, especially in the supposedly enlightened groves of academe and the literary world, many people are complacent about gender and inequality; they think that at least in North America and Western Europe those questions have been answered, that to prolong a discussion would be to split hairs, that a prize for women's writing is pointless (or, hilariously, sexist).

I thought of a passage in the prominent feminist critic Rachel Blau DuPlessis's book *BLUE STUDIOS: POETRY AND ITS CULTURAL WORK*:

> In 1971 it washed over me... that all of culture from the very beginning would have to be re-seen with feminist eyes. Everything would have to be remade – all cultural products, all fields – name them! In a millisecond, far beyond drowning in the enormous sea of this, I lifted up as on a gigantic green-blue-gray wave. Riding the "second wave"? A long march through texts and institutions is more like it. Everything! Remade! Ever since, I have been doing what I could. It's not euphoria or fashionableness. It's more like Conviction.

I admired DuPlessis's Conviction, but my own was shaken. How valid *is* it to keep trying to re-see through feminist eyes?

II. WRITERS, PURE AND SIMPLE

Women's writing is a subject that really gets people riled up – see the brouhaha in early 2013 over the all-girl Costa Prize shortlist, the ongoing debate over whether the Orange should still exist (it doesn't, Orange having withdrawn its funding; in 2013 it was awarded as the privately-funded 'Women's Prize for Fiction'; the liqueur producer Baileys has now stepped in to lend its name to the prize), the statistics revealed by the VIDA count (which year after year shows a disturbing imbalance in favour of male reviewers and authors amongst many prominent magazines and newspapers), or 2010's *Affaire*

Franzenfreude (that is, 'taking pain in the multiple and copious reviews being showered on Jonathan Franzen' in the wake of the publication of his novel *FREEDOM*). Writing by women simply isn't read, received, or written about in the way writing by men is.

It's also a subject that gets very knotty very quickly – are we talking about writing by women writers for women readers, writing by either sex that is written for women readers, or anything written by women? 'Women's fiction' tends to signify not only low literary standards, but small domestic subjects, or as Virginia Woolf put it:

> Speaking crudely, football and sport are "important"; the worship of fashion, the buying of clothes, "trivial". ... This is an important book, the critic assumes, because it deals with war. This is an insignificant book because it deals with the feelings of women in a drawing-room.

FREEDOM was billed as the Great American Novel, while similarly ambitious novels, like Jennifer Egan's *A VISIT FROM THE GOON SQUAD*, were considered really good books – she beat Franzen to the Pulitzer – but not revelations of who and what Americans are. Never mind that in an overlarge, diverse country like the US, the idea that one novel could speak for a quintessential 'American' experience is totally devoid of meaning; no, Franzen's novel did not speak for us all. 'It takes the authority of a male voice to write from the centre of culture,' Hustvedt said in Paris that night in May. 'As women, we're just barking from the margins.'

This may partly account for why many women writers have argued, like Hustvedt and Curiol, that writing does not have a gender: they are attempting to claim universality for their novels. In her 1998 article 'Scent of a Woman's Ink', Francine Prose wondered at the fact that although women helm top magazines and publishing houses, publish serious fiction, and are read by serious male writers, the prizes that year 'had the aura of literary High Noons, publicised shoot-outs among the guys: Don DeLillo, Philip Roth, Thomas Pynchon, and Charles Frazier'. Some feminists, she wrote,

> Can't help noting how comparatively rarely stories by women seem to appear in the few major magazines that publish fiction, how rarely fiction by women is reviewed in serious literary journals, and how rarely work by women dominates short lists and year-end ten best lists.

Prose's idea of a defence of women writers is to say that it is impossible to tell a woman's writing from a man's writing. She's bothered by 'how quick men are to identify female emotion with "fey" sentimentality, and how often certain sorts of macho sentimentality go unrecognised as sentimental,' and goes on to demonstrate that counter to received wisdom, some men do write sentimental fiction about domestic subjects (she cites Hemingway and Frederick Exley), and some women can write ambitious, toughminded books about war and evil (Prose calls on Flannery O'Connor and Deborah Eisenberg). '[T]here is no male or female language,' she concludes, 'only the truthful or fake, the precise or vague, the inspired or the pedestrian.' This may be true, but Prose's defensive/offensive strategy casts the discussion of what women's writing might be in a negative light, restricting it to questions of content and tone rather than form and – yes – language.

In February 2010, Claire Messud (the author, notably, of THE WOMEN UPSTAIRS, a novel about an angry woman who can't keep quiet any longer) guest-edited an issue of GUERNICA devoted entirely to women's writing, despite arguing that women are 'writers, pure and simple'. Gender is 'an irrelevant fact of birth', she said that she believed when she first got the job, and that she thought to base an issue around it was as absurd a prospect as 'organis[ing] a fiction section comprised of blue-eyed Capricorns from Atlanta'. And yet, she writes, because of their gender, women 'are too often overlooked by the silly popularity contests that are juries and boards and lists'. This is due to the 'cultural expectation that male writers are somehow more serious, more literary, or more interesting'.

To sum up the problem: Messud is right to identify the fact – and it is a fact – that the media and culture machine greets work by men with a greater respect, and is more prepared to offer accolades to books about war than to books about a family. Given this state of affairs, women writers too often play by these rules, instead of writing their own. If the male viewpoint is thought to be the universal viewpoint, it's understandable that women writers would want to slip into it unannounced, as if by insisting on their difference, they might not make it in the door. To say 'we, too, can write like Pynchon' means we're not writing like ourselves. It is to accept the hegemony of the masculine postmodern canon.

What kind of writing might women do, then, when they're not playing by the rules? And when did we get to be such rules-followers, anyway? It was a long haul to get to the point where we could read and write what we liked. Whereas at one time, Father's library of novels would be hidden from curious young women for their own moral protection, now we account for 8o per cent of the fiction-buying public. We're no longer hiding our manuscripts under our needlepoint. So why, then, would we want to erase our gender as writers? Why, like Prose, do we need to point out how we can write like the boys? What's wrong with writing like girls?

III. THE DIFFERENCE OF VIEW

Hustvedt, Curiol, Messud, and Prose's arguments advance a literary variant of equality feminism, which holds that there is, or should be, no difference between men and women. This is in contrast to difference feminism, which is based on the assumption that women experience the world in a fundamentally different way from men and any equality between them must account for these differences. This divide has riven feminist literary criticism, and is often, problematically, thought of with Anglo–American equality feminists on one side, who tend to be interested in literary and material history, and so-called French feminists on the other, whose philosophies of difference emerged from post-structuralism (vive la *différance*!). These two ways of thinking about difference yielded two main strands of feminist criticism: gynocriticism and gynesis.[1]

In her 1979 article 'Toward a Feminist Poetics', Elaine Showalter identified gynocriticism, or female-centred criticism, as a programme that aims to construct a female framework for the analysis of women's literature, and to develop new models based on the study of female experience. Gynocriticism begins at the point when we free ourselves from the linear absolutes of male literary history, stop trying to insert women into the lines of the male tradition, and focus instead on the newly visible world of female culture. Although it does consist largely of re-evaluating and recuperating works by women that have fallen out of favour or been misread over the centuries, gynocriticism also examines the way a given author's relationship to history, society, and culture is activated within the text. A gynocritic would assert that – as Messud discovered – gender does condition our experience of the world. Recent scholarly work on the twentieth-century poet Muriel Rukeyser's 'lost'

---

1. Over time, the two ways of reading have more or less blended. (These terms, however, have fallen out of favour, doubtless in part due to their unfortunate names.)

first novel *SAVAGE COAST*, based on her eyewitness account of the Spanish Civil War, indicated that the book was refused by one publisher in 1937 for overreaching while that publisher jumped at the chance to publish Rukeyser's more appropriately feminine lyric poetry on more 'domestic' subjects than war. The novel manuscript sat in an unmarked file in the Library of Congress until this year, when it was published by the Feminist Press at the City University of New York. The writer's gender does partly influence whether or not what she or he writes will see the light of publication, and will also influence how the book is marketed.

Gynesis, on the other hand, looks at the discursive effects of femininity which can allegedly be found (or which desire to be found) in the texts of some authors, not all of whom are women. Gynesis is interested in, as Mary Jacobus put it, 'not the sexuality of the text but the textuality of sex,' or the ways in which sexuality takes textual form. With its sensitive, nerve-based approach to language, it's a more interesting way of reading than gynocriticism; it looks at 'a kind of writing which is not specifically gendered but disrupts fixed meaning and encourages textual free play beyond authorial or critical control'. Gynesis is related to the French concept of *écriture féminine*, which is generally referred to in French because its English translation – feminine writing – is too literal a rendering. Disruptive writing might be better, but you lose the association with gender. *Tant pis*: we're stuck with the untranslated *écriture féminine*.

No one really uses these terms anymore, but they are useful in cutting a path through the weedy overgrowth of the 'women's writing' discussion. The critiques launched by the publication of the VIDA statistics, by Franzenfreude, etc., belong to the realm of gynocriticism. But in their haste to respond to these perceived slights, writers like Hustvedt, Curiol, Messud and Prose deny the possibilities opened by reading the feminine as 'a discursive effect that disrupts the master narratives of Western culture' (as Susan Stanford Friedman put it). In *A ROOM OF ONE'S OWN* Virginia Woolf builds a genealogy of women's writing, from Sappho to Lady Murasaki to Aphra Behn to George Eliot, and argues that women writers must remake the 'masculine' sentence for their own use, creating a 'woman's phrase to hold back the male flood'. Yet she also wrote that 'it is fatal for anyone who writes to think of their sex... It is fatal for a woman to lay the least stress on any grievance,' and lambasted Charlotte Brontë for allowing her anger to distract her from her story. This is a paradox that many a feminist critic has been forced to contemplate, if not to reconcile; the kind of contradiction that might lead you, like that French professor, to throw in the towel altogether. But perhaps we ought to leave the ambiguity unresolved. The key to more comfortably dwelling in this uncertainty, it seems to me, lies in Woolf's essay 'Women and Fiction'. A woman writer may write about different subjects from men, or not. But, Woolf says, she writes with a different perspective: the 'difference of view'.

This difference of view is the basis of *écriture féminine*, the 1970s feminist movement that called for writing that refused the patriarchal constraints of language, grammar, and syntax, one that would be rooted in difference – and différance. Much of the literature produced by *écriture féminine* does nothing but think of its sex. Women, write your bodies, Hélène Cixous and Catherine Clément encouraged in *LA JEUNE NÉE*, the 1975 book translated as *THE NEWLY BORN WOMAN*, calling on the subversive power of the marginal, the archaic, the savage, and casting it – or recasting it with a difference – as feminine.

Throughout history 'woman' has appeared as the sorceress and the hysteric, figures which have been both exoticised by society and purged from it. Cixous and Clément celebrate these figures – witches and thieves and dancers and midwives – and proclaim that the woman who can harness their power is 'pure desire, frenzied desire, immediately outside all law'. *LA JEUNE NÉE* is a wild text, composed of alternating (and occasionally duelling) essays by Cixous and Clément. It lashes out at 'systems', most notably the hierarchical binaries that have organised the world, keeping the feminine on the side of the dark and mysterious, of the irrational and the undisciplined (as opposed to enlightened, rational masculinity). Once these concepts have been reinvested with value, Cixous claims, woman will be able to write herself, freed from that which is:

> always reserved for her (guilty of everything, every time: of having desires, of not having any; of being "frigid", of being "too" hot; of not being both at once; of being too much of a mother and not enough; of nurturing and of not nurturing...).

In her landmark essay 'The Laugh of the Medusa' (1975), Cixous proclaimed that for women, writing must come from the physical specificity of their experience of the world. Woman (for she writes mainly in the singular) 'must write about women and bring women to writing, from which they have been driven away as violently as from their bodies... Woman must put herself into the text.' While 'it is impossible to define a feminine practice of writing,' and while 'this practice can never be theorised, enclosed, coded,' this doesn't mean that it doesn't exist.

ESSAY

Here, too, the ambiguity is deliberate. *Écriture féminine* is a form of writing that contests fixed meanings, opens up a range of possible interpretations that are always in play, and encourages a disruption of the dominant (phallocentric) discourse. The 'Holy Trinity' of so-called 'French Feminism' – Cixous, Luce Irigaray and Julia Kristeva – think of the maternal as a crucial aspect of writing the body: writing must originate from our bodies; we must write 'with white ink', as Cixous proposes. The *féminine* in *écriture féminine* is meant to be understood not literally as the female body, but as a metaphor for a libidinal economy which Cixous thinks of as 'the effect of desire, of love'. It's not a question of content as much as it is one of form: 'Feminine' writing is not necessarily writing about women, but rather writing that is '(re)productive, giving life to new possibilities for imagining and so living women's bodies and desires', as the scholar Kari Weil puts it.

Cixous reclaims hysteria (from the Greek *hyster*, meaning womb) as a creative force. On the other hand, Hustvedt, in her memoir *THE SHAKING WOMAN: A HISTORY OF MY NERVES*, writes about this long tradition of confusing women's health issues with their wombs and refuses to continue the association. For Cixous this is productive, and for Hustvedt limiting:

> From ancient times through the eighteenth century, hysteria was regarded as a convulsive illness that originated somewhere in the body – in the uterus or the brain or a limb – and the people suffering from it weren't considered insane. It is safe to say that if any one of the doctors above had witnessed my convulsive speech, he might have diagnosed me with hysteria. My higher functions weren't interrupted; I remembered everything about my fit; and, of course, I was a woman with a potentially vaporous or disturbed uterus.

Écriture féminine, Cixous says, is about making language visceral, so that we literally shake with it:

> Listen to woman speak in a gathering (if she is not painfully out of breath): she doesn't 'speak'; she throws her trembling body into the air, she lets herself go, she flies, she goes completely into her voice, she vitally defends the 'logic' of her discourse with her body; her flesh speaks true. She exposes herself. Really she makes what she thinks materialise carnally, she conveys meaning with her body. She inscribes what she is saying because she does not deny unconscious drives the unmanageable part they play in speech.

Hustvedt's 'disturbed uterus' belongs to a Western tradition that uses women's bodies against themselves – a form of equality feminism that works to recuperate women's histories from the prejudices of history. But *écriture féminine* comes under the heading of difference feminism, as it urges women to enjoy the ways in which they are different from men, by nature as well as nurture: Cixous would dance her vaporous and disturbed uterus.

And how's this for subversive – *écriture féminine* doesn't even need to be written by women. According to Cixous and Kristeva, Proust, Joyce, Mallarmé, Lautréamont: all were versatile masters of *écriture féminine*, which Kristeva calls 'Menippean language', after the Greek parodist and satirist. 'Masculine' language, within Cixous's schema, can be thought to represent writing that reproduces a patriarchal, status-quo vision of the world, and 'feminine' writing a mode which challenges that. 'Women's writing,' then, comes to be redefined as revolutionary, paradigm-shattering work, whether or not it's actually written by women.

Alas, *écriture féminine* frequently gave birth to a lot of bad writing, much of it by Irigaray and Cixous themselves. By 'bad' I mean not difficult or anti-syntactical, but awkward, heavy-handed, ponderous, dwelling, as it does, halfway between theory and fiction. One of its primary characteristics (is) a lot of unnecessary/sub/versive punc/tuation. For example, an author might notice that the word 'mother' contains the word 'other'. You can do a lot of nice visual things with that. M/other. (M)other. M.Other. Mother/Other. (*Écriture féminine* and psychoanalysis keep good company.)

Much of the work produced in this spirit is gnomic, ludic, irreverent. A typical move of *écriture féminine* is to look for the words contained in the words we use as a matter of course; this kind of wordplay is typical of French literature (sometimes known as *calembours*). Cixous and Clément love it when you can find subversive ideas caught in the *calembour*: 'La jeune née' gives you *là je nais* ('there I am being born') *l'age né* ('the born age'), *la jeu né* ('the born game' – the gender of the article's wrong but that's part of the fun) and 'La Genet, a feminine writing outlaw', a tribute to the poet-thief Jean Genet. Sartre's 'Saint Genet' is the patron saint of *écriture féminine*, and one of Cixous's favourite figures, since he is the hero of the delinquent, the self-disenfranchised, the alienated, the rebellious.

Here is a typical example, from Cixous's *VIVRE L'ORANGE*:

> To all of my *amies* for whom loving the moment is a necessity, saving the moment is
> such a difficult thing, and we never have the necessary time, the slow, sanguineous
> time, that is the condition of this love, the pensive, tranquil time that has the cour-

age to let last, I dedicate the three gifts: slowness which is the essence of tenderness; a cup of passion-fruits whose flesh presents in its heart filaments comparable to the styles that poetry bears, and the *spelaïon* as it is in itself a gourd full of voices, an enchanted ear, the instrument of a continuous music, an open, bottomless species of orange.

The *spelaïon* is a gourd full of voices? What does that even mean? And yet in an orthodox reading of *écriture féminine*, to demand logical meaning is *to be a dupe of the patriarchy*. We are not here to mean. We are here to be 'singers of spending and waste, against conservative narcissism', as Cixous writes (*PRÉNOMS DE PERSONNE*, 1974). Cixous, as Verena Andermatt Conley writes, 'considers poetry – defined not in opposition to prose but as the subversion of coded, clichéd, ordinary language – necessary to social transformation'. Cixous believes in the political impact of poetry to 'displace the operating concepts of femininity in major discourses governing (Western) society'. Cixous's poets, then, far from being the unacknowledged legislators of the world, are more accurately the anarchists storming the gates.

Écriture féminine is a key component of what Anglo-American critics tend to think of as 'French feminism', a term which was invented by non-French feminists to give a name to what they saw as the commonalities across the work of female scholars and writers like Cixous, Kristeva, Irigaray, and Monique Wittig. Yet in France, 'French feminism' has little meaning. 'Figures like Hélène Cixous are not really recognised in France,' Elsa Dorlin, a professor at the Sorbonne, told Zoe Williams in the *GUARDIAN*. 'In civil society, there is a hugely anti-feminist mentality.' *LA JEUNE NÉE* has been out of print since 1998. If you want to look at a copy of it at the Bibliothèque Nationale de France, you must view it on microfiche – their sole copy has gone missing.

If *écriture féminine* has today fallen out of favour both in France and beyond, the reasons for this may have something to do with the hyperbole of the movement. The canonical writing of écriture féminine is distinctly embarrassing. You try teaching Luce Irigaray's *THE SEX WHICH IS NOT ONE* in an undergraduate seminar, as a friend of mine does (at a women's college, no less). An oft-quoted passage argues that women experience their sexuality differently to men, in a way that makes her students want to slink under the table:

A woman touches herself by and within herself directly, without mediation, and before any distinction between activity and passivity is possible. A woman "touches herself" constantly without anyone being able to forbid her to do so, for her sex is composed of two lips which embrace continually. Thus, within herself she is already two – but not divisible into ones – who stimulate each other.

'The students are so relieved,' my friend told me, 'when they come to class the day we discuss it, to find that I'm not asking them to take it really seriously.' Perhaps Irigaray's kinky improvisations are intended to be read with one eyebrow firmly raised.

But *écriture féminine* was a product of the 1970s, that era of intense feminist intervention and inflamed rhetoric. All those sorceresses and nature goddesses and breast milk – there's very little irony there, little in the way of self-mocking distance, the kind which would accompany this kind of argument today. This is why we cringe: these women are unabashed. Think of Agnès Varda's feminist musical *L'UNE CHANTE, L'AUTRE PAS*, a film about two women who militate for women's rights, one by running a family planning clinic, the other by singing avant-garde feminist songs in public squares around France. In one song, a celebration of the physical experience of pregnancy, a character called Pomme sings of herself as 'une belle ovule/une fabrique de cellules' ('a beautiful ovary/a factory for cells'). 'I want to say what I feel through women's images,' Pomme explains. Such feminist flourishes seem heavy-handed and, occasionally, combative: key terms of the movement like 'patriarchy' and 'oppression' have today become instant conversation-killers. We avoid them at all costs so as to be taken more seriously: a kind of collusion with our censors.

Still. Gourds and *spelaïons* aren't the best we can do, are they? More important to retain from *écriture féminine* is not its overblown rhetoric, but the way it treats femininity as *jouissance*. One of the key values of post-structuralist theory as well as *écriture féminine, jouissance* is about the pleasure taken in language. *Jouissance* is a disruptive force, employed by *écriture féminine* in order to cause trouble – an idea borrowed from the Russian literary critic Mikhail Bakhtin, who coined the term 'carnivalesque' to describe the disruptive power of laughter in the public gatherings one finds in Rabelais. Constantly calling attention to the ways in which language jokes with itself, revelling in puns that even your dad would be embarrassed to make, and in the endless multiplication of signifiers, as if language on its own were not sufficiently slippery, *jouissance* delights in the liberating potential of language turned against itself. 'I laugh because of words,' Cixous writes in her Prix Médicis-winning novel *DEDANS*. If we occasionally laugh at 'The Laugh of the Medusa', it's safe to say it's laughing at itself.

Of course to generalise about 'woman' as Cixous so often does is problematic, reductive, possibly essentialising. These critiques have been made, and made, and made. Critics like Barbara Smith, Deborah McDowell, and Barbara Christian accused Cixous and Irigaray of assimilating 'woman' to some kind of faux universal ideal that very often turned out to be upper middle class, white, and Western. 'Woman is not a monolith,' said a recent contributor to the GUARDIAN in an odd critique of Cixous that accused her of espousing ideas no different than those found in the pages of COSMO. But somewhere in here, there is a message that continues to be relevant. Cixous and Varda urge women to speak up as women, regardless of whatever combination of class and race and sexuality and geopolitical/religious/social nexus produced them. Cixous and Varda urge women not to write to please.

IV. WE NEED WASTE

The thrust of the movement (so to speak) comes from its modernist embrace of fragmentation and disruption. While the modernists found they could no longer write in the old ways, the followers of *écriture féminine* wrote in protest of prose which reinforced conventional ways of seeing the world. This is a message that recurs in two important books by women that have been published recently: HEROINES by Kate Zambreno and UNMASTERED: A BOOK ON DESIRE, MOST DIFFICULT TO TELL, by Katherine Angel. Both books work in autobiographical modes; Zambreno's book blends literary criticism and biography, while Angel verges toward social commentary and philosophy. Both authors are white, comparatively privileged, address heterosexual partnerships, and are in their 30s. Both texts are fragmentary, eschewing narrative and argument in favour of accumulation and juxtaposition, full of digressions and parentheticals and meaningful line breaks. There's nothing particularly new about these techniques, but in the joining of form to content they revive the concerns of *écriture féminine* for a contemporary readership.

Zambreno's book aggregates bits and pieces of the novels, diaries, letters, biographies, and autobiographies of what she calls the 'mad wives of modernism': Zelda Fitzgerald, Vivienne Eliot, Jane Bowles, Virginia Woolf, Jean Rhys; those women writers whom history pathologises as crazy, excessive, messy, whose husbands, in some cases, stymied their creative output (not permitting them, in some cases − for their own good − to write, for fear of over-excitement), who as often as not ended up in institutions or in prison. 'Who gets to say what's pathological?' Zambreno asks, interweaving these fragments (shored against their husbands) through a series of reflections on her own choices as a would-be writer. Following her librarian husband across the US and to the UK as he moves from job to job, Zambreno becomes less and less comfortable with the role of the 'wife', refusing the passivity it confers. At faculty parties, she is introduced as the 'wife of'. She is asked to accept that her husband's tenure-track job offers determine where they live, and how; she must follow patiently, taking what adjunct teaching work she can ('Adjunct, adjunctive.').

HEROINES tears a gash across the neat tableau of the adjunct wife, even if her husband's job security does afford her the time to write, and a place to do it in. '[A] room of one's own can feel like a prison if there's no reason to leave it,' she notes. She describes yelling, screaming, clawing at her husband when he leaves for work in the morning. 'I AM THE ARTIST,' Lucia Joyce screamed at her father as she hurled a chair across the room. Zambreno turns to these 'mad wives' for comfort but also to lash out at the powers that keep women silent, letting other people speak for them.

UNMASTERED takes up language's inadequacy to express our sexual desires, even when we are invited to share them: there are no controlling husbands here, and yet there is silencing in the form of self-censoring. Through a sparse chain of notes, anecdotes, and quotations, Angel questions the nature of her desires: is there something un-feminist in liking pornography, or in wanting to be dominated? If not, where do we draw the line? How do we ask for what we want while negotiating the gender roles we and our partners seem to slip into involuntarily? The book is told in brief statements, each statement numbered and on its own page, rarely taking up much of it. These spaces in the text allow things to unfurl in silence, in the gaps in discourse. 'I like something to be suggested to me, and then to run with it myself, in the wide open spaces of my mind, my body.' The gaps could be (and have been) read as writerly passivity, but they are a profound statement on women's self-silencing. Cixous notes, in LA JEUNE NÉE: 'Woman is always associated with passivity in philosophy... Either woman is passive or she does not exist. What is left of her is unthinkable, unthought.' In return, Angel posits that this passivity is a kind of activity, actively wanting to receive, in ways that are by turn serious, needy, ludic.

Angel muses on the limits of words, on what we call on words to do. She runs over the gaps between lovers, lays bare the failures of language to narrow those distances. We do other things with language than communicate: we protect, we stimulate, we caress, we bring in all sorts of issues from outside the bedroom. UNMASTERED attempts to speak the things that are hard to say, or things that cannot be said, or things we've said too many times. 'I am tired of this voice, of my voice, of your voice.' All the spaces and blanks in the book take on an amazing tension in this context, flat only on the surface, deceptively simple. We hold back what we want – even the merest unformed suggestion of what we might want – out of fear of what it might reveal about us. We have no control over how our words, our desires, are taken. The gap is too wide; the space where translation takes place, between enunciation and understanding, is too wild. So we bring in metaphors to try to define that terrain, to tame it, to draw a map of it.

Zambreno was attacked in the autumn 2012 issue of BOOKFORUM, where Jessica Winter encouraged her to pick up a newspaper and remember that some people are just trying to pay the rent, but this is an intellectually dishonest response; Zambreno's concerns are not less pressing because they belong to someone who is fortunate enough not to have to worry more than the next person where the rent is coming from. Also in BOOKFORUM, Cristina Nehring took Angel to task for her 'postfeminist mumbo jumbo, adolescent narcissism, excruciating erotic overshares, pseudopoetry, pretentious academic jargon'. In a kinder review in the GUARDIAN, Talitha Stevenson reproached Angel for rewriting Robert Frost without being sufficiently famous:

> Angel also takes diaristic liberties. The one-pager "These woods are lovely dark and deep. / Lovely. Lovely. Dark and deep" is a deliberate misquotation from Robert Frost's poem 'Stopping by Woods on a Snowy Evening'. The presumption here is that a reader will experience a sufficient degree of fascination with Angel's subjective reading of the poem. This might have been justified by stardom or at least a recognised body of work, or, had it occurred in the context of fiction, by a narrator's self-importance. But none of these conditions applies. We all ought to know that only people who love us wish to listen to our dreams.

This slap on the wrist seems misguided: are we more interested in hearing Carol Ann Duffy's dreams than Katherine Angel's? The aim of écriture féminine was to break the 'expected sequence,' as Woolf put it. Angel's text does just this. The function of the critic ought not to be to rein in what we're allowed, as writers, to do; but the best writing will always transgress the boundaries of acceptability.

Whatever you may think of Zambreno's prose, her anger, or her political engagements (and I was frequently frustrated while reading), the very point of *HEROINES* is to highlight the ways in which women writers are perennially asked to scale it back. Be less. Take up less space. And, as Angel writes – as if responding to Zambreno's book – we comply. We want to be good, we want to be liked. 'Let the boy win at tennis!' she parrots. In one section Zambreno writes of a fling she had with another young writer. They compare notes on their novels:

> He tells me his is a ONE THOUSAND PAGE novel. Mine is a slim nervous no-vella, a grotesque homage to *MRS DALLOWAY*, and an exorcism of my toxic–girl past, published by an experimental feminist press.

> He tells me his work will be the longest first–person novel EVER. We discuss the respective length of *TRISTRAM SHANDY*, *ULYSSES*, *INFINITE JEST*, *WAR AND PEACE*, etc. He is pulling out his cock and comparing it with those writers with whom he will be compared. (I will be compared to nobody, I think. I am sent into an existen-tial crisis when I get home, and for weeks afterwards.)

It's an incredibly sensitive person who can be depressed for weeks because of a stray comment like that, but this is Zambreno's point. Think of her as the canary in the coal mine of the literary gender wars: she may be more sensitive than most, but that doesn't make her wrong. A man gives his novel a sweeping title like *FREEDOM*, and is hailed as the voice of his generation. A young woman on a television show announces to her parents that she is the voice of her generation and quickly corrects herself: 'or a voice... of a gener-ation'. Both Zambreno and Angel deal with the issue of excess, of being *too much* – a familiar trope in confessional feminist writing. We trim ourselves down, we try not to take up too much room. In Angel's text this translates, for her male lover, into fears of inadequacy: 'When the thing is dominated by speaking, when there are too many words words words, it is because, in fact, you are somehow not enough. By which I mean that you do not feel yourself to be enough; and that feeling makes you shrink, in your eyes and mine.' We do everything we can to keep others from feeling diminished, including diminishing ourselves.

Angel's book operates in a mode which Zambreno once described as 'an-orexic'; writing on her blog, Zambreno differentiated between 'slim, disci-plined' texts like Clarice Lispector's *THE HOUR OF THE STAR*, as opposed to 'bulimic' works like her own, inspired in part by Dodie Bellamy's *BARF MAN-IFESTO*, attempts 'to reclaim feminine writing, or radical writing by women, or feminist writing, from asceticism, from anorexia'. Bulimic writing takes in everything, and lets it all out again, indiscriminately. '[It] could be read as more feminist, perhaps, the idea that we as women are supposed to be slim, careful, poetic, and this is a way to write rage and messiness and chaos.' (Lest we begin to think Zambreno is validating these serious illnesses, she jokes, 'I am going to reclaim all modes of feminine self-destruction as aesthetic strategies!')

The recurrence of the term 'slim' is telling – isn't that how Zambreno referred to her own novel, 'slim and nervous' as opposed to her ex-fling's log-orrheic (bulimic?) doorstop. But of course the digestive process would be different for a man, secure in his place in literary culture, than for a woman. I am being only somewhat facetious, as, I imagine, is Zambreno. She concedes that 'anorexic' texts can be feminist as well, in their reactions to 'the big bloated tomes of patriarchal "geniuses", ... these works are challenging what a traditional novel or book is, a fuck-you to the market-driven world of plot and character and traditional narrative.'[2] And *HEROINES*, then, can be read as a purposeful move away from the 'slim' nervousness of Zambreno's earlier work towards a kind of women's writing that has relaxed, stopped dieting, stopped worrying about trying to please men.

However, as useful as they may be, we ought not to treat these two categories too schematically; there can be much overlap between them. It's a mistake to oppose these veins of composition to each other, to valorise one over the other, as Emily Cooke supposes Zambreno does in her essay for *THE NEW INQUIRY*, 'The Semiautobiographers': 'Which has the greater claim to liveliness, reality, truth? The "disorderly" narrative or the "highly toned

---

2. Which recalls Sheila Heti's *HOW SHOULD A PERSON BE?*, bulimic in its polyvocal assortment of narrative, stage dialogue, emails, its blend of invented characters and real people: 'One good thing about being a woman is we haven't too many examples of what a genius looks like. It could be me. There's no ideal model for how my mind should be. For men, it's pretty clear. That's the reason you see them trying to talk themselves up all the time. I laugh when they won't say what they mean so the academies will study them forever. I'm thinking of you, Mark Z., and you, Christian B. You just keep peddling your phony-baloney crap, while I'm up giving blow-jobs in heaven.'

artificial" one?'³ The problem with the bulimic/anorexic model of women's writing is that it isn't a true dichotomy; neither has more of a purchase on 'truth'; both are attempts to reroute the sentence, either by omission, by cutting, by oversharing.

As Cixous writes in *LA JEUNE NÉE*, 'there is waste in what we say. We need waste. To write is always to break the exchange value which keeps the word in its rail, to give its savage part of abundance, to uselessness.' Zambreno provides the waste; Angel gestures at it. I might prefer Angel's as the more unified, elegant text, but Zambreno's defiant disordering, its stream of consciousness, observations and notes argue no coherent central argument, but taken together form a mountain of testimony that demands to be addressed.

What we may retain of Cixous's efforts is to bring her ideals to bear on contemporary writing, and ask, as readers: to what extent does this text challenge hierarchies, and to what extent does it reproduce them? If there is anything to learn from the excesses of *écriture féminine*, it is this. Cixous's urging women to write their bodies and desires and thereby 'unleash their power' is essentially a message of empowerment to all writers, regardless of gender.

Zadie Smith wanders into Cixousian territory in her famous essay for the *NEW YORK REVIEW OF BOOKS*, 'Two Paths for the Novel', in which she considers the routinised lyrical realism of Joseph O'Neill's *NETHERLAND* against the more purposeful language of Tom McCarthy's *REMAINDER*, which she calls 'one of the great English novels of the past ten years'. There is, indeed, a kind of deranged *jouissance* with which McCarthy's narrator carries out his increasingly dangerous game of reproducing the traumatic events he's lived through. A particular kind of need to understand our post-capitalist technology- and service-mad society emerges from the compulsion to repeat: what do the patterns mean, what is happening behind them, what exactly fell out of the sky onto the main character's head and where are all these coffee-chain loyalty cards leading us?

Smith argues that 'most avant-garde challenges to Realism concentrate on voice, on where this "I" is coming from, this mysterious third person,' and McCarthy's clearly unreliable first-person narrator is curiously able to adopt

---

3. There was something very strange about a female critic writing such a mannered, well-argued essay treating a book whose *raison d'être* is to protest the ways in which women writers have been policed, managed, and ordered to behave themselves. *Il n'y a pas de hors-texte*. We are not exempt from these behavioural demands, merely because we write about them.

a universal viewpoint precisely because he is so much in the dark. Woolf, I think, would agree that this use of voice is the source of the needed disruption, the disruption women's writing must stage to break out of the conventions that keep it in second place. Finally, the legacy of *écriture féminine* is not a question of women's writing or men's writing, but of the ways in which a text gleefully troubles convention, and, even if it can't speak truth to power, at least addresses insistent questions to it. *Écriture féminine*, as we have inherited it, is a means of writing with an awareness of the tradition we write into, and a commitment to adopting whatever techniques are necessary to write our way out of it. Woolf decried the deeply flawed 'women's novels' written by women who 'altered [their] values in deference to the opinion of others'. Women writers must be urged to speak their own values in their own voices, and we need a reading practice, and a literary culture, that will be attentive to that attempt.

I eventually got over my crisis of faith in feminist criticism, and continue to champion both women writers and 'disruptive' writing by writers of either gender, as a literary journalist and scholar. Too often I'm appalled by the frat boy culture of the mainstream literary world, bros bigging up bros, girls up for whatever the boys decide ('put his favourite perfume on / Go play a video game'). This is what, it seems to me, lies behind the mean-girl reviews of *HEROINES* and *UNMASTERED*: a reprimand that feminism's tone has to avoid excess in order for its points to be heard. *Don't embarrass us, girls, or the men will think we're silly!* A little less self-censoring; a little more Conviction, please.

In reviews of Zambreno's and Angel's books, both authors have been told to 'check their privilege', as the saying goes, to consider the many women who are worse off than they, as if any feminist intervention (or any 'serious women's novel') ought to centre on issues like abortion, childcare, income disparity, domestic abuse or it ceases to be valid. But that's just it: surely it's the more insidious inequalities, the ones that are more difficult to put your finger on, that require the kind of subtle reasoning characteristic of, say, literature. What Bapsi Sidhwa has to say about partition from her woman's perspective may not be radically different from what Salman Rushdie has to say, but if we don't ask the question, we'll never know.

THE LADY OF THE HOUSE
BY
CLAIRE-LOUISE BENNETT

WOW IT'S SO STILL. Isn't it eerie. Oh yes. So calm. Everything's still. That's right. Look at the rowers – look at how fast the rowers are going. Ominous – yes, like the calm before the storm. If you like. Look at the rowers! Two long boats and bodies – rowers – like rungs or something. Like notches or rungs – or struts or bolts – something. The sound of the machine drying the bathmat behind me in front of you, very low – a good machine. Time to leave you to it pretty much. Handwriting, here and there – little notes, as you go along, things not to forget. They move me actually. Along with the photo on your travel pass, they move me.

I didn't put on my hat even though it's as cold as forever and the hat's right there in my bag at the bottom. My mascara came away in the night and for that hat to look any good requires a little recent eye adornment – I realise that. And I didn't say anything, not a word, about the creature beneath the water. No mention of the monster. The flowers are lovely instead, especially the roses. Oh yes, you say. They're high enough that I don't see Mary getting out of her car. I don't have to see her any more, walking by and going into her house – it's nice actually.

Would it be a scaly monster with a tremendous tail I wonder, or something wraithlike with straggly wings? Will it, in other words, be something dredged or something fallen? A decision doesn't fix because the day is actually more nuanced than at first appeared – and anyway I don't know where exactly but there is something shifting and suddenly the whole scene is quite altered. And yet, for all the world, it appears perfectly composed. As if hovering in fact. The whole vista hovers.

Some kind of trick obviously. I could remain like this all day I expect and not get any closer to working it out.

It wouldn't be a big deal – the monster's coming up from beneath wouldn't be a big show. If it went on behind anyone as they walked along the river bank for example they might not even turn around. They could easily carry on walking in the direction of home and miss the whole thing. Actually for all they know this kind of thing is going on all the time just behind them without them noticing – though in some area of themselves they are aware, naturally, of what is going on – and this is why, from time to time, they behave in a way that, in the normal scheme of things, seems utterly irrational and unprovoked – because of this chimerically transcribed influence that they have zero conscious knowledge of. That could happen a lot I should think.

Up it would come, from beneath the water, of this you can be sure, without any ripple or wave. Just a little white showing. Air. Air tipping over in linked white collections.

I get so violently upset often. But now, look at this, not any more! This morning everything is fine with me. I even stay after eating some toast, which broke up pretty badly into very unequal pieces when you tried to apply some cold butter to it.

There.

And without looking at me you put the knife down onto the draining board sort of immediately and you scooted off along the worktop to where the kettle is. I would have been exactly the same. I would have done exactly the same thing and in just the same way. I hate Mary's car by the way. I hate the cars your neighbours drive. All of them. What the fuck is it they are thinking of? Exactly? You have things like kitchen towel and coasters, and cats that aren't yours. One of the cats walks with you up and down the drive – if the weather is good enough in the afternoon you walk up and down the drive. And you've got an electric blanket.

It had never before occurred to me that anyone might ever be afraid of me. And now, when I must accept that that is something somebody might in fact feel, I find it difficult to take seriously. For now it is all I can do to acknowledge the possibility – giving it credence is something that may or may not develop later. It's not angry I feel. I am not angry. It's easier for me to take a shower at home – which is still the case even when the immersion hasn't been switched on since yesterday morning so that the water won't be anywhere near warm enough for an hour at least. Maybe when I get home I won't have a shower anyhow. It doesn't bother me either way because I self-clean very well. As such, I don't know why, when I went into your bathroom to put my tights and knickers back on, I turned the knickers inside out. That's a new and very strange thing to do – I thought it at the time actually, as I was doing it, but I carried on anyway because perhaps I found it interesting or something. Perhaps I thought this deviation contained some sort of judicious insight. It seemed natural to go along with it – to not resist it, so, understandably, I wondered if it might lead to something – evolutionary passages have strange methods of harnessing palpability after all.

Nothing, anyway. Just an uncomfortable sense that my smell was being worn on the outside and smothered by tights. I look at but don't touch the earrings on the windowsill above the toilet cistern because I think maybe it will be nice if I leave them for you to notice later on, when you get back from shopping perhaps, or in the night, when you have got up to take a wee. What about this monster? Nothing more spectacular than a big bad-ass pike if you want to know. Shunting back and forth beneath the rowers, doing that shark thing with its eyes. That shark thing it learnt off the shark in the cartoon. So, in the end, here's a pike that imagines it's a shark. Leave it. I hate the colours of things today – the lack of deportment to be more accurate. Everything looks pissed upon. Like cats everywhere have just been endlessly pissing on everything all night. Drenching all the grasses and stone tracks and the leaves from every year that lie about. I hate cats if you want to know. I hate coming across photographic records of putatively outlandish cat be-haviour and I hate hearing about cats. I hate hearing about how the cat walks with you, up and down the drive in the afternoons, when the weather is good enough – often the weather is not good enough. I sit in my place and look out at the weather and weigh it up too – and that's not as straightforward actually as might be supposed. Some days I think, no way, there'll be no walking up and down the driveway today – and then there comes a little light maybe, or, more likely, some sound, such as cows or birds – something really nice and uplifting, some indication that the world is really getting going again, despite the impression it tends to give. I don't mind the impression it ordinarily dis-seminates for the reason that I understand it – then again this is a somewhat curtailed claim because truth be told there does come a point when I hate its ongoing despondency so much. It's as if the sky some days is just hanging around. Moping – just moping. Moping and slouching and indolently seeth-ing. I'd like to shake it hard. Fuck you. Fuck you too. Man alive. Anyway, it was just a little idea, this monster. And now when I consider it that was the mistake, because if you want to know it started as an involuntary image – that was all. Just one of those visions that occur without prompting when your mind has retracted and is alert, or – the other way – when it spreads out and is almost completely oblivious. I can't be sure which state it was my mind was at when the monster came about – if I say the first I immediately know it is the other and then if I say the other it is obvious that in fact it was after all the first. What a lot of nonsense really, but then why on earth not spend some time in the evening this time of year trying to recover the landscape of some substratal figments? If you must know when we're side by side he and I rarely exchange any affiliated comments pertaining to our immediate surround-ings. About what is actually right there in front of us – no, I don't suppose we ever occupy the same place at all. Side-by-side we're in completely different worlds. This then was a rare thing. To establish by empirical increments a shared perspective was a rare thing. So of course, when the monster came, all by itself, I almost shot a finger out excitedly towards it. Because, naturally, it seemed entirely possible – logical, actually – that the monster, in a different incarnation notwithstanding, had happened to him too.

Later on I cycle to the out-of-town supermarket and as I get onto the second road I notice that both cars which pass me in opposite directions have their lights switched on to the max. It seems darker here than it did two minutes ago outside my house when I was putting on my gloves and then sort of swiped at the bicycle saddle with my left elbow to make it dry. I have no other choice but to turn around and go back for my body lights. It's a load of shit that I didn't bring them with me – I even took them out of my rucksack to make more room for the groceries I was heading off to buy – what a load of shit. Where is my fucking sense of eventuality exactly? When I get out onto the second road a second time it's really obvious how quickly the last bit of light is getting used up, and of course there is so much rubbish all over the small fields I pedal alongside of. Entire household sacks filled completely up and knotted tightly and stowed into the back of the car just so and driven here. Not exactly spur of the minute then – but there's very little difficulty in rationalising the implementation of even very appalling activities. That's just something anyone can do very effectively and on the spot in fact. I notice the fullness of the moon when I come out of the supermarket – it's right there in front of me when the automatic doors retreat. The sky isn't yet black so the moon has a sovereignty it doesn't often possess – but in a way it looks as if it is coping with stage fright. Yes, it is as if the curtains have just opened on it! And so low is it that it seems only natural and forthright to reach out to the cowering moon. Pssst, take it easy, fix your gaze on something and get your balance babyface – that's right, I'm bucking up the moon of all things – and yes, look, it's as if in fact the moon has closed its eyes and is taking a slow inhalation.

A deep breath before the rise and shine. I really want to communicate all of that, to tell you about the moon and its dithering autonomy and how I encourage it to get a grip and shape up, but I've already put my gloves back on and so I leave it, as inflexible as that seems, and when I get home, even though I take my gloves off right away, I don't text you immediately about the moon – I hang up some coats that were looking very untidy on the back of the armchairs and I light the fire and I take a bin liner from beneath the sink and dispose of some perishables that were left on the worktop and I go back outside to take the main shopping bag off of the back bike rack, and I think I also eat some cheese before I text you about the moon. As it turns out you're in the cinema so empathising with the moon's wincing fullness isn't on the cards for you at all right now. The moon of course will still be there, or thereabouts, when the movie has finished and you leave the cinema – but naturally I can't vouch for what condition it'll be in by then. The sky by then you see will undoubtedly be absolutely black – and a bit avuncular too I expect. It could actually get a little camp tonight if you ask me. Keeping the moon up with its camp and conspiratorial antics. Keeping the moon up all night long! Look at that, look at the moon yawning its head off all night long! You're not enjoying the film, in fact it's terrible, and I have a hunch which film it is and you ask me how I knew and I say I was talking about it in the week with a friend – which is true but doesn't answer your question – and I add that despite wearing gloves my hands got really cold while I cycled back from the supermarket. I was surprised actually, at just how cold my hands got, given that I was wearing gloves, and a little bit later on, while talking on the phone to my friend who lives nearby, I mentioned to him how cold my hands had been, despite my wearing gloves, and I asked him about a pair of thermal gloves a friend of ours had lent me and which I'd subsequently lent to him one evening. We'd made jokes about those gloves the evening I lent them to my friend for the reason that they are the sort of gloves you'd wear in Siberia and wasn't it just like our friend to have the sort of gloves you wear in Siberia, but now, since the wind is supposed to be coming more or less directly from Siberia, they are not quite so funny anymore.

I also watched a really terrible film, yet there was something so kindly about it that it was a while before I could admit how awful it was, by which time its awfulness was somehow indivisible from its kindness, so I carried on with it, right up until the end – which of course I do not recall. Now and then throughout each thing that passes I see something like a lopsided Godzilla sticking up through the water – it's so revolting, the way my mind keeps on turning it over, trying to substantiate it. I must have really needed an idea to get hold of. I must have been really desperate to have something relatable to work with. Something with girth! Not a metaphor, nothing like that – I've never wanted the monster to stand for something, that's for sure. At the very most I would have maybe said something about the house nearby, which, by the way, did seem a bit susceptible. Just having it in my field of vision felt uncomfortable if you want to know, as if I was a pent-up pervert in fact. Even looking away was calculated. Even looking away was looking. The first time I got home I turned on the immersion just like I knew I would, but I didn't take a shower, and even though I took my tango dress off and dropped it into the laundry basket I did not remove my undergarments so if you must know I'm still wearing tights and my knickers inside out. The smell of me like a young mouth to a compound fence. It's better anyhow to leave things alone. I've decided that once and for all. I don't want to be in the business of turning things into other things, it feels fatal for one reason. As if making the world smaller because of all the intact explanations that need to occur in order for one thing to become another thing. Secretly, deep inside, I accept I've no option but to retire from a vocation I've never achieved any success from and my plan now is to really throw in the towel and go to Brazilmysorebalimontanatrondheimnyonsbristol, as soon as my lease is up. And there's no fear of my lease being renewed by the way because my landlady has had to put all three cottages on the market.

She's more or less been forced to if you want to know. When she came around to tell me she was with her sister who was wearing a very peculiar hat with a wide furry brim which I couldn't deduce the point of at all. I hated the hat to be perfectly blunt, and I also hated, maybe even more so than the hat, the pale frosty lipstick she had selected to wear. Whatever was the point of all that? Exactly? She kept looking down at some metal things I have resting near my door and then back up at me as if all of this was a question I would feel pressed to answer, but I easily ignored her and asked my landlady how she felt about having to sell. I could sense her response was regrettably hampered by the presence of her sister and the impatient brim of her peculiar furry hat, which took up a lot of space actually so that it was quite a job for the pair of them to stand side-by-side in my doorway. She said it would be ages yet before anything happened and in any case they'd have to give me two months notice because of how long I'd been here and I said that was just fine. As a matter of fact I've been thinking about taking off somewhere I said. Is that right, she said, anywhere in mind? Oh, Brazil, I said. Brazil, she said. My landlady's hands were very apparent for some reason and in order to stop looking at her fingers especially I found I looked down at my own hands, which upset me very much actually, so I said that's fine again and keep me posted then I went into the kitchen, and not long after, while I stood by the kitchen sink swilling out the teapot, two men arrived who I presume were estate agents because of the kind of folders they waved about and did nothing with.

It's a devil to know what to take seriously.

I don't know why it was I got talking about Martin's Hill like that – I don't know what exactly I was getting at with that little reverie on the arm of the armchair this morning. Has it really become an inclination of mine to reminisce in such a gratuitous way? And since when? Because if you must know

I don't recall ever regarding anything I may remember from my past as being particularly interesting or poignant, or even especially reliable actually. On account of my radical immaturity – characterised by a persistent lack of ambition – real events don't make much difference to me, as such the impact they have upon my mind is either zilch or blistering, and so, naturally, I have to question my facility to form memories that have any congruity at all with what in fact took place – landmark events and so on included. Having said that my dreams demonstrate a rather impressive mnemonic flair – I don't dream about the past, not the outside past, but quite often I will dream about, for example, daydreams I had when I was much younger – beside trees, behind curtains, that kind of thing. You see? Even so – despite my generally dubious mode of relation – I seemed rather determined to make something out of Martin's Hill.

It might be the case that I thought my somewhat poeticised rendering of its central catastrophe made me sound perspicacious and grown-up, and very aware of how one's life develops according to the uncanny notation of subtle kairotic moments. As a rule of thumb I don't have much enthusiasm for inventorial reflection, however, on this occasion I transgressed my thumb multiple times – I even went so far as to say we had chicken. Now, I can't be sure at all that we had chicken. It's very likely we had chicken because it happened in the mid-90s and everyone knows that a staple component of an English picnic in the mid-90s was cold roasted chicken, along with some sort of pasta salad, and French bread and satsumas, and a six-pack of chocolate mini-rolls. Martin's Hill of all things! Oh yes, I really went into some detail and highlighted quite the prelapsarian scene this morning after broken toast while prodding the arm of the armchair with my pernickety sit bones his head more or less beneath my chin both looking out right across everything. The lake, the river, the ruined castle, the shrubs, the tall trees, the dismal clouds, the pissed-upon reeds, the rowers and their boats, the monster, the house nearby, the children, their mother, the garage, the garden tools, the drying clods, the hallway, the stairs, the doors, the keyholes, the bed, the underneath, the terror, the cold floor, the ankle-straps, the perpetuating dust. And one side of Martin's Hill was very steep, I explained – I think I may have used the word gradient if you want to know – and I think my brother's ball must have rolled down it you see, there must have been something anyway that lured him to that side of the hill because you wouldn't normally go that side ever – it was very steep you see, and overgrown – steep, uneven, and rough. Orange. Blue. Orange. Blue. Orange. And he was alright for the first few steps, then he couldn't keep pace – he lost control and he fell actually. Fell all the way down to the bottom of Martin's Hill. All on his own with me just looking, and there was the proof I suppose that I was older at last.

I hated feeling that actually yet it was sort of attenuated by the anticipation I had towards the evening to come and didn't those two sensations, first loss and high hopes, combine to produce possibly my initial experience of melancholia. And didn't I immediately discover that melancholia brought something out in me that felt more authentic and effortless than anything I'd previously alchemised.

Look here, it's perfectly obvious by now to anyone that my head is turned by imagined elsewheres and hardly at all by present circumstances – even so no one can know what trip is going on and on in anyone else's mind and so, for that reason solely perhaps, the way I go about my business, such at is, can be very confusing, bewildering, unaccountable – even, actually, offensive sometimes. It's easy to be suspicious of a drifter like me and it frequently happens that I am accused of all sorts of impertinence. This time last year for example someone I know in a sort of professional way arranged to meet me in a hotel conservatory around lunchtime purely for the purpose of relaying an unflattering compendium of controvertible opinions pertaining to my character and outlook – an apocryphal catalogue of puerile anecdotes, which, by the way, he'd quite obviously had some assistance piecing together – and all this for my own good apparently! Well let me tell you I found the whole ordeal very off-putting and I had no instinctive way of responding to it – it was just about beyond me. We'd ordered buns and the buns were on the coffee table and there were those stupid cartons of vapid jam I hate so much next to the buns. I tried to be gracious, be gracious I thought, but that was a confounding prescription for the reason that I could not at all determine who out of the two of us I should be gracious to.

It was very disturbing actually and it wasn't until after I'd talked it over with a friend in her car on my driveway a few times that I felt sure enough of myself to not give two hoots about it any more. It's all by-the-by now. Under the bridge and so on. Since we are going on a two-day outing tomorrow I brought the phone down to the garden after lunch and called him so we could discuss arrangements. He was eating soup if you want to know. Tomato soup with a drop of milk stirred in. He asked me right at the start of the phone call if I'd mind him eating his soup while we talked and I said I didn't know, maybe I would mind, it depended on how much noise he made. I was teasing, of course, that had been the intention anyhow, but as it turned out there was also a trace of sincerity in my voice, which took me by surprise actually – I quickly counteracted this unattractive flash of knee-jerk resistance by laughing a little, which was very relaxing of course, and then I invited him to go right ahead and eat the soup.

Because it had been established he was eating soup we talked for a little while about soup – he eats soup almost every day whereas I seldom bother with it and it was actually as if he needed to somehow reconcile this difference, or at least understand it better. When he surmises that I don't like soup I find I'm reluctant to agree – I do like soup very much in fact, but I don't enjoy the process of eating it – all that lifting and lowering of the spoon over and over, it soon gets very tedious, so mechanical – no, it's the dismal activity of eating soup that turns me off, not the taste. I'm rolling about on my sleeping bag near the washing line while these disparities are addressed – the weather has been so good the last two days I took the opportunity to wash blankets and cushion covers and small rugs. I tell him about the cycle I went for last night, how beautiful it was because of the way the lanes were moonlit. I told him I got upset and pissed off because of a dog that ran out at me and went on barking at my ankles even as my legs lost density and the pedals spun uselessly beneath their sudden cascade. He told me I should bring a stick with me so in future I can belt dogs like that across the head and I point out that it might be difficult to take a stick on a bike and he says I'd figure it out. You need it, he says. Your shirts dried nicely I say, I'll iron them a bit later – do you want me to bring both tomorrow? Yes, he says, bring them both. You'll need another one, I say. Yes, he says, the one I'm wearing. Which one is that, I ask. I don't know yet, he says. Oh, I say, you mean the one you'll be wearing tomorrow – not now. Why don't you wear the blue linen one, I say. The one with spots on, he says. Yes, I say – even though they're not spots, they're very small flowers. Okay, he says, I'll wear it with the navy jumper. You look nice in that, I say. Then, at the end of the phone call, he reveals that he's been holding the soup bowl and drinking from it with one hand and holding his mobile and talking to me with the other the whole time.

You know, he says, if you were to drink soup like I'm doing now you wouldn't have to worry about a spoon and you could enjoy it better.

To be honest, I think I may have already experimented with taking soup directly from the bowl but as it turned out it wasn't a practice I was particularly comfortable with adopting for the reason that it felt actually as if I were pretending to be from somewhere I'm not – I don't know where, another continent, another epoch possibly – it hardly matters – it's the sensation that's relevant and the sensation, above all else, was one of displacement. Strange really. Besides which I often drink coffee from a small noodle-bowl and that just suits me fine if you want to know. I've four small noodle-bowls and it works out well with each, the terracotta one especially. And the green of course. I struggle to drink tea out of anything that isn't white and chipped in the right place – and that's still unwavering even though I drink it black now. When I was at school I was friends with a girl whose mother had no idea really when it came to housekeeping, the kitchen was especially unpleasant – deathly in fact. She had some pretty morbid ideas you see, such as storing teddy bears and owls in the freezer chest. Can you imagine? Fascinating really. From time to time she made efforts to introduce some warmth to the place, efforts that were so negligible that there was often something very untoward about the incongruous items they found expression through – embossed handtowels for one, and patterned mugs for another. Now, I'd already come across patterned mugs and as such was quite familiar with the concept – and although not preferable very occasionally they are perfectly passable. Nothing like these though – these were quite shuddersome on account of the pattern not being limited to the outside of the mug – as incredible as it sounds a single motif was discoverable on the inside of the mug too. She thought that was great, I remember very well her making a point of showing it to me. Do you think your mother would like these, she asked me, and of course I said yes even though she absolutely would not. In the same way, when he recommended drinking soup from the bowl there was really nothing else for me to say than that I would of course give it a go sometime.

Sometime! Never say sometime, for the reason that, unfortunately, with each day that passes that I don't drink soup from the bowl I feel terribly remiss, as if I am spurning him in fact, which is, naturally, an awful way for me to go on feeling. He was pleased with the suggestion you see, I could tell. I could tell it had been coming together in his mind throughout our conversation. He'd solved the problem you see – and that's the way some people are. They are ceaselessly finding ways of getting to grips with the world, of surmounting certain antipathies so as to apply themselves to it that little bit more. It's quite admirable really, how they refuse to let anything come between them and the rest of it – Oh, the rest of it! Sort of there, sort of hovering there all the time. Different ideas come to me now and again – strategies I suppose that might inculcate a little more compatibility. I just don't know if I'll ever get the hang of it if you want to know – as a matter of fact I think I've left it a little too late to cultivate the necessary outlook.

And the outlook, it seems, is everything. It's very difficult for anything to mean anything without that because without an outlook there is, obviously, no point of view. I open out the ironing board for the first time ever and set it up right by the window even though it's more or less completely dark outside by now. I find his two shirts in the laundry basket and decide I'll iron the darker one first – why a decision such as this came about at all I don't know, since both shirts would surely be ironed, and yet, inexplicably, it must have seemed as if one ought to be done before the other because when I laid both shirts across the ironing board I stood looking at them for a while trying to figure out which one that was. And actually I think the right choice was made because it wasn't long after I got started on the darker shirt that I began to feel very happy indeed and if you must know I was soon wishing there were more shirts of his for me to iron. I stood at the window ironing his two shirts for tomorrow, the darker one first, and I knew damn well how easily I could be seen. I don't know what's out there – I never could quite work it out – and all that time I spent behind the green curtains in the dining room at home, not getting any closer to it. And why shouldn't I stand at the window like this? Why shouldn't I be seen? I'm not afraid. Not afraid of any monster. Let it stand in the moonlit lane and watch me. It's been watching me all along, all my life, coming and going – and I don't know what it sees as it stands there, I don't know that it is not in fact becoming a little afraid of me – and I have to be doubly careful I think, not to frighten it away, because between you and me I can't be at all sure where it is I'd be without it.

ORDINARY VOIDS
BY PATRICK LANGLEY

I AM STANDING IN A PARALLELOGRAM of shrubbery outside London City Airport. Ed is twisting a dial on his Mamiya RZ67 and squinting into its viewfinder. He is wearing a Berghaus anorak, as standard, with a beanie hat, hiking boots and a flannel shirt. His breath is clouding up around his face. The camera's lens is pointing at a factory in the distance, a complex heap of blocks and towers known locally as Sugar Mountain, officially as Tate & Lyle. It rises abruptly at the end of the residential street, a gargantuan prison-like structure that might have functioned as a set for the film adaptation of *1984* had they not used the ruinous Beckton Gas Works a few miles east of here. It is an architecturally hermetic building, anxious to preserve the final vestige of industrial productivity in an otherwise idle landscape. Directly in front of us is a two-lane arterial road. Cars zip past like urgent telegrams. Every surface has been designed to enclose, repel or separate. There are wooden fences embedded in concrete troughs. There are concrete bridges and glass walls. There are barriers, railings and painted lines —

'*Excuse* me? You're not allowed to take *pictures* here!'

We turn to see a man in a hi-vis vest. His nylon shirt is of that municipal non-colour that sits somewhere between turquoise and grey. An ID card hangs from a branded lanyard at his neck.

The best thing to do in situations like these is ignore the non-threats, take the photograph you've come to take and defend that tiny patch of civil freedom from the powers that seek to invade. The official seems reluctant to break the invisible screen that separates the designated walking space from the decorative shrubs in which we stand. It isn't long before he strides forth, stepping through the plants in standard-issue boots, to reiterate his demands.

¶ Consciously structured to minimise friction, slowness and delay, airports are places of social and spatial control. Their architecture tends towards the abstraction of geometry, lines, planes, parabolas and arcs; grids across which the traveller moves like a mathematical function. Passengers are screened and processed: those who fail to meet standards are incarcerated or rebuffed, and the rest are funnelled through the airport's branching architecture and up into the sky. Rather than inhabiting a particular point in space, with all its social, geographical and historical specificity, it feels as though we're caught in an intersection of extended lines: flows that move from Lisbon to London to Luxembourg, from Beckton to Canning Town. Most of the people who use this airport are business class human beings. There's an abundance of men and women in suits, pinstripe and plain, tugging those tiny one-night travel bags with the plastic wheels and the telescopic handles, with broadsheets tucked beneath their arms. The workers who comprise the airport's staff are differently choreographed, slower and more intimately linked to their surroundings. They empty bins, fix broken light fittings and direct baffled passengers towards the lavishly signposted check-in desks. Two policemen sit outside the entrance in an unmarked 4x4, peering through the windscreen as they slurp their paper cups of post-mix Diet Coke. Pale clouds above, pallid concrete below. It is cold, not yet the brutal X-ray cold of the coming winter, but a crisp and vivid chill that pulls all edges into focus.

¶ 'It's actually illegal what you're doing. If you don't stop taking pictures I'm going to have to involve the police. I don't want to have to do that, you know, I don't want to, but I will, because you're not allowed to take pictures here, it's as simple as that.'

And so on.

The Mamiya RZ67 is a medium format camera. It's roughly a foot long and distinctly unwieldy, with its bellows-mounted lens and periscope viewfinder. You don't carry so much as lug it around, like a bag of bricks or a sleeping child. Add the fact that the camera is generally used with a tripod, and the result is among the most conspicuous 'I AM A CAMERA!'-style cameras in the game. It's unlikely we're doing anything suspicious. If we were, we'd be using iPhones.

We aren't living through this moment so much as playing our part in a choreographed scene, a diorama of urban trespass. What's doubly absurd about the situation is that the photograph just taken is, admittedly, boring. Once Ed has developed the film in his bathtub a few days from now, this black-and-white landscape will faithfully convey the sprawling blandness of the scene, its generically urban bleakness. Photographers are not a common sight around these parts, which might partly explain the disproportionate paranoia. What puzzles me is the demonstrable fact that we aren't interested in the airport itself: the lens is pointing the other way, and so is our attention. The official continually threatens to call the police but the theft, if that is what this is, has already taken place. Ed pulls the image into focus and clicks the trigger: light enters the chamber and exposes the film.

We walk off, nipping through gaps in the passing cars, and the official watches us leave. The way the sun slopes in at a mid-October angle, barely high enough to scrape the tops of the local factories, makes the airport glow like a pyre.

∴

Silvertown in London's Docklands, east of the Isle of Dogs, west of Beckton and north of the Millennium Dome, is custom built for post-apocalyptic fantasies. It's the kind of landscape you'd glimpse through a train window and quickly forget, a featureless portal to other, more interesting places. It is the antithesis of spectacular London; of skyscrapers named after kitchen utensils; of the Olympics. Once a busy stretch of smokestacks, mills and quays, Silvertown feels today like the site of a mass evacuation. (During the Blitz, it was precisely that.) It came into being almost overnight, in a flurry of industrial speculation during the mid-nineteenth century, and collapsed a little over a century later. The haste of its construction matched the speed with which it was later abandoned. Silvertown is a synecdoche of post-industrial Britain. It came from humble origins, ascended an apex of power and pride, then fortune struck it low and now it languishes in obsolescence, waiting to be digested by the future that consumed it.

❡ In 1844, Silvertown did not exist. Seven feet below the water level, these acres of marsh were dotted with patches of quicksand and sunk in floodwater each spring. Cattle grazed, reeds grew, Viking, Dane, Saxon and Roman relics slowly petrified in alluvial mud, but hardly anything settled here – why would it? This is how London looked before London existed: a wet and windswept fenland, its soft topology contoured by the creep and suck of tidal fluid.

The River Lea marks the border between London and Essex – although, as Dickens opined, 'there is no limit to London' – and thus the area fell outside the capital's municipal purview. This hinterland status had been with it for centuries. During the 1300s the Sherriff of Kent renamed the area Wicklands, 'Between-Lands'. And it might have stayed like that, an overlooked stretch of empty, sunken marsh, were it not for the Metropolitan Buildings Act, newly introduced in 1844, which banished harmful industries like animal rendering, printing, and chemical manufacture from the capital.

Enter the historical personage of Samuel Silver. By all accounts, of which there are few, he was an archetypal Victorian tycoon. Driven from the capital by the Act, he set his eye on a muddy stretch of river. In 1852, he opened a rubber factory which produced waterproof clothing, belts for machinery, telegraph cables and ebonite, a form of vulcanised rubber. Silver's factory was the only building for miles; but factories create jobs, and jobs attract people, and soon the building began to send out feelers, terraced tenements where workers lived within spitting distance of their jobs. A shipbuilders and ironworks sprang up on nearby land; soon two sugar moguls, Mr Tate and Mr Lyle, established factories here too. Reed-green was steadily smothered by concrete-grey. The industrial outposts started to link and mesh as roads and housing grew, like isolated cells expanding and connecting into a tissue, hardening the land to industrial use. This stretch of the Plaistow Marshes, once a blank on a map, is named in honour of its founder: Silver's Town.

¶ A trio of interlinked water trenches forms the hollow core around which Silvertown is oriented. Built between 1855 and 1921, the Royal Docks were the largest in the world, deep enough to accommodate the hulking steam ships that hove in, pregnant with wares, from British colonies in Africa, India and the Middle East. These massive ships weighed around 30,000 tonnes – which goes some way to explain the vast scale of the docks, and the weight of mourning their abandonment implies – and linked the city to other merchant cities around the globe. What happened next is typical, not just of the Docklands, but of all commercial ports. From the 1950s onwards containerised shipping became increasingly common and the docks weren't able to service the much larger ships, nor were they designed to handle the new standardised steel containers. The docks at Tilbury in Essex took up the slack, and Silvertown's quaysides steadily emptied. Thousands of jobs, most of which were casual, poorly paid and in constantly short supply, were lost; dock companies folded, warehouses shut down and the local communities dissipated. Since then, not much has changed. Silvertown is ripe for redevelopment, but such alchemical transformation has yet to take place. Decommissioned factories, apartment complexes, building sites, waste grounds and public parks are thrown together without purpose or plan, a midden of industrial offcuts and reject space. Canary Wharf was redeveloped and so was Beckton, but Silvertown has yet to be invaded and transformed.

¶ Riding the DLR from Shadwell, stocked up on croissants, crisps and bottled water, Ed and I ventured east and the city thinned. We walked and talked and skulked at the side of the road, and Ed took photographs while I tried to 'soak it all in'. Ed was principally interested in the formal qualities inherent to this largely infrastructural space, the patterns produced by plant life and concrete. My attentions were focused instead upon that impalpable substance certain places produce, which can't be measured or contained but can be approximated through writing. Living in cities comes naturally – I've been doing it all my life – but writing about cities is a whole other problem.

This was partly due to the nature of the area, and one of its paradoxical attractions: we wanted to act like tourists in a place where there was nothing to see. There were no moments of jolting discovery, just the atmospheric oddness of an urban backwater, where a house clad in beams of wood shares a street with an active chemical refinery, and where the terraced roofs are brushed by the landing gear of incoming air traffic. Everywhere we turned we were met by absence. The acres of vacant spaces, the disused offices and factories were the result of an economic emptying, whose ravages proved more damaging to the area than Luftwaffe bombs.

❡ In recent years the 'non-place', which emerged as an object of academic study before filtering through the worlds of art and cultural journalism, has gained widespread attention. The anthropologist Marc Augé popularised the term 'non-places' in his 1995 book, in which he claims that 'the extreme flexibility of the global system... is extraordinarily adept at appropriating all declarations of independence and every attempt at originality.' Augé cites the proliferation of airports, stations and supermarkets as evidence – any place that facilitates transport and transaction to a vaguely defined 'elsewhere' while suppressing an identity of its own. The theory of non-places enables us to analyse the creeping doppelgänger effect of contemporary urban environments, with their copy-pasted high streets and déjà-vu malls. Rather than producing variation and discovery, non-places render travel, and travel writing, obsolete.

Augé argues that 'supermodernity' – an accelerated and technologically determined form of capitalism – has become the dominant global force, subsuming local character into an ever-more homogenised environment geared towards a growing need for international transit. To follow this argument to its absurd extreme, the world will one day resemble the city of Trude in Italo Calvino's INVISIBLE CITIES: 'The world is covered by a sole Trude, which does not begin and does not end. Only the name of the airport changes.'

∴

❡ A wasteland, a chair, evening. The foreground figure is lit side-on, tanned by the photographer's lamps. The smell of fibrous weed-stems rises up through the humid dusk. Looking like a sailor on shore leave in his heavy coat and white hat, he sits on a director's chair, twisted round to the camera with one arm over the stretched canvas back, a half-smile on his solemn, still-boyish face. Loosely gripped in his hand, like a toy handgun, is a Super 8 camera. In spite of the transparent staging there's a casualness to the way he sits, his posture slouched, his face relaxed, as if this is what he does every evening: make films in darkling plots. A broad beige edifice fills the background of the image. Although it is clearly industrial, the structure has the forbidding grandeur of a fascist palace: white letters ten feet tall proclaim it to be the Millennium Mills.

In a 1987 interview for the *Observer* magazine, conducted during the promotional drive for *The Last of England*, Derek Jarman said: 'Sometimes I look out the window and think we're dead already, that the bomb has already dropped in our minds.' The notebooks he kept leading up to and during the film's production, now housed in the BFI archives, record the titles which Jarman flirted with: The Art of Mirrors, Night Life, Xenophobia, G.B.H., Bliss, The World's End, Deathwatch. Jarman wrote in them with a quill, and they are as much a collage as the film itself. Notes, poems, photographs, newspaper cuttings, diary entries and pressed flowers make the pages warp and bulge. At one stage he transcribes Matthew Arnold's 'Dover Beach' by hand and makes several references to the 'dead sea of industrial decline' whose 'stagnant waters erode the crumbling cities'.

This sombre conjunction of images – the sea, the ruins of industry – frequently recurs in Jarman's notes as a symbol of decay and departure, and Silvertown went some way to literalise it. Scattered with the empty shells of failed industry, it is also home to the Thames Barrier: a line of tide defences rising from the water, silver cladding shining in the sun. This is where the estuary begins, where the river broadens out towards the sea beneath the 'luminous space' described by Conrad in the opening pages of *Heart of Darkness*. (Conrad lived in the town of Stanford-le-Hope in Essex, a few miles east of the docks at Tilbury where, centuries previous, Queen Elizabeth gave a rousing speech to her troops on the eve of the Spanish Armada. Jarman's female leads often bear a striking resemblance to that pale-skinned monarch, and she's a central character in *Jubilee*.)

Jarman didn't need to build a film set, which was useful since he couldn't afford to. Silvertown, its mill in particular, was everything he needed, both

studio and muse. Only a few miles east of the building site which would become Canary Wharf, Silvertown was beholden to different rules. An outsider mentality could flourish here: nonconformist, queer, avant-garde, and in its own way opportunist – one of Jarman's aims was to 'exploit and make palatable the wasteland'. In Jarman's hands Silvertown became symbolic of national malaise, but in practical terms it afforded immense artistic freedom. 'We have found a perfect location near the gasworks down the road,' he writes in the notebooks, phrasing film production as a skirmish and a salvage operation. 'Day by day the victorian [sic] terrace houses are bulldozed and as we have no money to start the film we decide to film for one day over the Whit weekend before these streets disappear for ever.'

¶ A collage of Super 8 home movies and documentary footage interspersed with wordless vignettes and impressionistic set-pieces, THE LAST OF ENGLAND is among the most overtly arthouse of Jarman's films, a punkish swansong for the death of England's soul. It sits somewhere between the anarchic, countercultural social vision of JUBILEE and the morbid introspection of BLUE, looking outwards at the country gone to the dogs and inwards at a cave of fading memories. THE LAST OF ENGLAND is a meditation on the combustible blend of sadness and rage, self-reflection and fury, inspired in Jarman by the dying of the light – his own as well as England's. (He discovered he was HIV positive shortly after filming began.) Set in the future, infused with the past, it is an indictment of Jarman's present.

¶ In THE EMPTY SPACE, the theatre director Peter Brook writes: 'I can take any empty space and call it a bare stage. A man walks across this empty space whilst someone else is watching him, and this is all that is needed for an act of theatre to be engaged.' For Brook, as for Jarman, empty spaces are rich with potential. They are the actual backdrops across which virtual dramas unfold. Silvertown has the feel of a film set minus the camera crews and lighting rigs, less a historical place than the location of an as-yet unrealised fiction. What's surprising about THE LAST OF ENGLAND is how much it differs from the kind of film you might expect this place to inspire.

Silvertown would be the perfect setting for a 'gritty' Guy Ritchie gangster film in which a quartet of mockney wideboys get in over their heads with a drug cartel from Eastern Europe: cars would chase each other down the long grey empty roads; an MDMA factory would be secreted in a cavernous warehouse; a torture scene would take place in a building site after dark;

and bare-knuckle fights would break out in the courtyards of dilapidated factories. Jarman's film, however, eschews such urban nastiness, aspiring instead towards elegy. It is steeped in Romantic and modernist poetry, melodrama, arthouse erotica and touches of queer cabaret, none of which seem linked with the understatement and inertia of the place itself; rather, the film suggests how national legacies, particularly the financial systems, now failed, upon which our modern economy was founded, might provide symbolic fodder for art. If the film has relevance to us today, then this is where to find it: not the mournfulness of its content, but the ambition of its form.

¶ Silvertown provided substance for Jarman's Super 8 cells. It was equally a blank screen upon which to project. In 1988, two years after Jarman filmed here, this is what the Millennium Mills became, when Jean-Michel Jarre descended on the Royal Docks. For two nights he performed his opus *DESTINATION DOCKLANDS*, a spectacle of industrial light and magic. Tens of thousands of people lined the desolate quays, enhancing the building's fascist air with the suggestion of a mass rally. The blank face of the disused mills was lit up by projections and light shows, while the onstage band wore an incongruous array of outfits, long black trench coats, pillbox hats and ethnic capes. Jarre's title choices, including a suite called *INDUSTRIAL REVOLUTION*, point towards his kitsch assimilation of the post-industrial sublime – factory music for people who've never worked in one.

¶ I do lots of research on foot, as so many urban writers seem to do, and when I get home I start googling. This is how I first hear the echo of Jarman's presence: not by glimpsing a ghost at a window, but by typing 'millennium mills' into the search box and reading the top result, a Wikipedia entry. I order *THE LAST OF ENGLAND* from Amazon. The effortlessly smooth process takes a matter of minutes. It does not require that I leave my room. I watch the DVD as soon as it arrives. That flicker of a red against a concrete wall, that quayside edged by giant cranes – just as Jarman processed Silvertown, I find myself processing Jarman. Returning to Silvertown on foot, his film folds itself into my reading of the landscape, and vice versa, like a pair of mirrors.

¶ Ed and I wander down the North Woolwich road. The air tastes of dust. Our legs grow heavy with walking. When people aren't ignoring us, they view us with gentle suspicion; apart from the encounter at the airport, no one seems to care where we walk. Fences topple and nobody comes by to fix them. Security guards sit lonely in one-man Portakabins, failing to care as we slip through unlocked gates and past decades-old 'no entry' signs.

This is not to say that Silvertown is a free-range territory. There are fenced-off wastelands and tensely guarded building sites, and they are occupied by absent powers. The largest of these runs alongside the North Woolwich road. We climb up from the pavement and find a path that runs alongside the slatted wooden fence; behind this is a fifty-acre plot of disused space. Recently attempts to turn this stretch of concrete and weeds to profit have met with disaster, struck down by the Silvertown curse: the white tents of an eerie and abortive London Pleasure Gardens linger on behind the gates. At the centre of this waste ground is the building Jarman filmed in.

¶ Built in 1905, Millennium Mills pumped out a hundred sacks of white 'Millennium Flour' every hour. The building's pale-brown outer walls are striped with concrete columns thrusting skyward like the searchlights deployed by Speer in his Cathedral of Light; its windows conceal a warren of stark, eviscerated rooms, titanic in their scale. I've never been inside the building, it's too heavily guarded now, but a number of self-described 'urban explorers' managed to break in before the security lockdown. The photo-essays which result, posted on blogs and online forums, reveal the complexly ruined texture of the building's interior: giant threshing machines patterned with rust, screw-like chutes that spiral down several floors, walls which crackle with flaking paint.

In Jarman's film this picturesque decay is harnessed to social critique. The mill's roof becomes the stage for a series of executions by firing squad. Refugees sit in huddles on the quay surrounded by fascist militants, their balaclavas and snug machine guns evoking the IRA. (The IRA bombed Canary Wharf in 1996, ending a seventeen-month ceasefire.) In the film's most visually ravishing scene, which takes place on the quay beside a blazing bonfire, Tilda Swinton rips off her bridal dress in a swirl of silk and tailor's shears.

¶ THE LAST OF ENGLAND is not a polemic. It muddles distinctions between private sorrow and social collapse and despite its aesthetic radicalism draws on a traditional, even conservative, set of cultural references. As Jarman himself noted in one of his journals, later published in book form as MODERN NATURE: 'Shakespeare, the Sonnets, Caravaggio, Britten's Requiem, what more traditional subject matter could a filmmaker take on?' Alienated by postmodernism, which treated the past not as a hallowed realm of inviolable forms but as a scrapbook of outdated attitudes, Jarman remained stubbornly anachronistic. His was a paradoxical rebellion. In order to position himself against the conservative social environment he felt surrounded by, he sought refuge in an idealised cultural past – one that, with its virgin queens and faded empires, can come depressingly close to a *DAILY MAIL* vision of England.

¶ Rather than Jarman's 'dead sea of industrial decline', Britain was plunging deeper into a different kind of liquidity. 1986 saw the 'Big Bang' of financial deregulation, a cornerstone of Thatcher's economic policy: out with the red tape and burdensome taxes, in with the virile flexibility of a free market; the chummy old broking firms of the City were swallowed up by much larger and more competitive multinational outfits such as Goldman Sachs and Lehman Brothers. The Big Bang revived the City's international standing, made some people astronomically rich, and ultimately paved the way for the worst recession in a century just over thirty years later. So it's appropriate that we find ourselves in Silvertown as the delayed effects of that shift continue to shape our present moment.

Silvertown is the stage upon which a new redevelopment will shortly commence; a return to the top–down, neoliberal mega–schemes that endowed the Docklands with its flagship spectacle, Canary Wharf. The fifty–acre quayside that Jarman once filmed in will soon be redeveloped as part of a £1.5 billion project into a 'new innovation quarter and destination for global brands'. There will be the usual 'mixed use' development, a Ballardian ziggurat stuffed with offices, shopping centres, luxury apartments, gyms, cafés, galleries, restaurants, landscaped semi–public gardens and a series of 'brand pavilions' in which 'top brands will be able to showcase their latest products and interact with customers in an entirely new way'.

Buildings such as the Millennium Mills were once considered the apex of architectural aspiration. They were megastructures, symbolic of Britain's industrial might, but the paradigm has shifted from concrete to glass, production to consumption: Millennium Mills must go. (Rather than be redeveloped in the manner of Butler's Wharf, by Tower Bridge, where Jarman briefly lived and worked during the 1970s.) The building has an implacable appearance, more of a rock formation than a building. Its architectural resilience is in ironic counterpoint to the fragility of the economic model upon which it was founded: it will take a huge amount of dynamite to bring the building to its knees, but the shipping industry that once sustained it collapsed without the aid of explosives.

⁙

Charlie lives in a tent inside a hut. The hut is made from plywood planks and strips of wood and is protected by blue tarpaulin lashed with rope and weighed down with rocks. Outside the tent he has a small front garden. The mossy ground is heaped with triangular paving stones which he's dug up from the soil and used to border a path. At the centre of the path, a stack of the stones has been arranged in a basin. This is where he tends his fire: hearth, boiler, radiator and stove. Every time we've visited, flames have been quietly chewing through coal, dry branches and planks of salvaged MDF.

We first met Charlie because of the fire, or rather smoke. We'd dawdled around the Shopping Park for a few stupefied hours, trying to locate traces of the Beckton Gas Works where Stanley Kubrick filmed *FULL METAL JACKET* in 1986, the same year Jarman was making *THE LAST OF ENGLAND* just a few miles upriver. The Gas Works covered an area larger than the City of London but had been disused since 1967. We found a few fat silver pipes arcing out of the ground, cylindrical frames of dead gas towers and some A-frame concrete supports you can glimpse in the movie's imagined Vietnam, but no real sense that a famous film was shot here. I don't know what else we'd been expecting.

¶ 'There's nothing here now apart from ground. It's been reduced to ground level.' Charlie's accent is hard to place. A Yorkshire burr, a cockney twang. He later tells us he's from Plymouth. 'They had large buildings all over the place. Furnaces, tower blocks, even an underground railway, like a train to shift the coal from one place to another, underground tunnels. All that's disappeared. It's all been levelled off and the land reclaimed, put to different use. Which is a pity really as that was a really good landmark. The Beckton Gas Works. It was well known.'

Charlie's descriptions of the Gas Works conjure an Atlantis of smog and concrete. There were dozens of crumbling, reinforced concrete blocks, craters, hills and ditches. Other people lived rough and made their living off the land, stripping back pipes to uncover the lead, collecting sheets of scrap they loaded onto shopping carts and wheeled to scrap yards in Canning Town. The so-called Beckton Alps weren't far away: great hills of rubble and waste materials that were later converted into artificial ski slopes. When we tell Charlie about our project, he says: 'You should have come twenty years ago. You'd have had a project then.'

¶ Stanley Kubrick's aim with FULL METAL JACKET was to make a war movie that didn't celebrate or denigrate war but simply 'showed it like it is'. Whether or not it's possible to depict violence without inspiring violence is moot (Kubrick pulled A CLOCKWORK ORANGE from the cinemas after a series of death threats and copycat crimes), but the film succeeds in capturing something of the arbitrary nature of war and in exploring, as Joker puts it in a pivotal scene, 'the duality of man'. Matthew Modine's Joker is the film's main character, in so far as it has one, but he is less an agent of the action than a lens; the filmic focal point. Too passive to be classified a hero, he looks upon the devastation ironically. A peace symbol badge is pinned to his jacket but 'BORN TO KILL' is scrawled on his helmet. Peace is an abstract ideal (a logo; a Logos) which our intrinsically violent species can strive for but never attain.

Joker is a ludic trickster who dances round the rules, immunised against the horror that surrounds him by his playful mocking of it. Humour is a prophylactic for the manifold insanities of war. (The other, as demonstrated by Private Pyle in the first half of the film, is suicide.) Alive to the absurdity of conflict, Joker carries the wry flame of satirical farce that Kubrick kindled in DR. STRANGELOVE. Joker's refusal to take the war seriously is the most serious thing about the film.

¶ Kubrick was fascinated by collapse. Almost all his films explore what happens when the systems that surround us begin to break down. A CLOCKWORK ORANGE was filmed mostly on the Thamesmead estate, a then-new social housing scheme a few miles downriver from Silvertown on the opposite side of the Thames. Intended as a panacea to London's inner city overcrowding, Thamesmead quickly plunged to sink estate status. Its buildings began to leak and crumble almost immediately, and its terraced, tunnelled architecture made it an ideal location for muggings. Kubrick seems to have intuited this bleak future from the estate's inception (the first tenants arrived in 1968, and three years later Kubrick's film was in the cinemas). The concrete terraces and flat canals, bespeaking the modernist faith that good design makes better people, become the sets for an antic ballet of recreational violence. At a time of optimistic, even utopian thinking about the future of urban environments, Kubrick prophesied doom.

❡ Where Jarman's films posit the Docklands as a breeding ground of resistance, a marginal space where marginalised people could organise themselves in opposition to the establishment, for Kubrick it signalled a different kind of conflict. This is unsurprising, given their sharply contrasting temperaments: Jarman the spontaneous poet who once described his films as an excuse to have fun with his friends; Kubrick reputed to be a compulsive micromanager who inspected every atom of his films. For both, however, the Docklands was a stage, an opportunity to realise filmic fantasies of imagined worlds, and the atmosphere of the area at that particular mid-eighties moment is both amplified and overwritten by their films. THE LAST OF ENGLAND metonymically suggests that the whole of Britain is equally ruinous and desolate: that the industrial endgame of the Docklands represented the decline of the entire country. It's very much a State of England film, but it is equally a State of Jarman film; exploring the collision of past and present through the prism of individual memory. Kubrick was drawn to the otherness of the Docklands, the bleakness and dereliction that make it seem totally extrinsic to the city, somewhere else. He also hated travelling. Filming abroad was out of the question, and besides, he had his ready-made dystopia.

❡ The Stanley Kubrick Archives hold the photographs Kubrick used to dress the Beckton set. I come here after visiting Silvertown and sit between the glass partitions and beneath the illuminated white ceiling panels – some designer's wry nod to *2001* – filtering through those famed grey archive boxes using purple rubber gloves. Chunks of concrete are caught in the wire webs. Every window gapes, blown out. The concrete structures are tall, hollow, stilted, arched, their sheer sides bursting into tufts and spillages of demolition and decay. Grass is everywhere, the same reedy, stubborn stuff Ed photographed in Silvertown. Bombweed. Rubble forms haphazard dunes and hills between the buildings. Some of the photographs are scrawled with biro: 'Can we demolish this?' and 'long lens pan'. Others are covered with sheets of cellophane across which palm trees, wicker fences and oil barrels have been drawn in hasty squiggles, cartoonish impositions on the photographs. These doctored pictures point to the surprising ease with which an East London gasworks was transported halfway round the planet and two decades back in time into the war-torn city of Hue.

❡ Susan Sontag writes in *ON PHOTOGRAPHY* that, 'Bleak factory buildings look as beautiful, through the camera's eye, as churches and pastoral landscapes.

More beautiful, by modern taste.' Beckton suited Kubrick's needs, fulfilled a function. But there are uncanny echoes of the work of Bernd and Hilla Becher, the German artists who documented the structures of Germany's rapidly vanishing industrial landscapes. Kubrick's production team used similar large format film stock and their images, taken in a similar full-frontal fashion, have the same bleak beauty that Sontag identifies. Again and again, however, the artful abstraction is compromised by the presence of a figure. In one shot, a man in a short-sleeved shirt holding a shopping bag gazes up at the side of towering silo as if contemplating its hugeness. Another shows a man atop a fallen wall. The concrete has attained a soft, marshmallowy appearance in its collapse, the dislocated chunks held together quilt-like by an endoskeletal grid of metal wires. The man's hands are in his pockets: a casual, smiling pose like a hunter's trophy photo after a large kill. Seen through these images, the whole of the Beckton Gas Works has the feel of a Kraken's corpse.

❡ Several of the *FULL METAL JACKET* photographs feature the film's production designer, Anton Furst, holding a striped measuring pole twice his height. On one level his job was to recreate Vietnam, on another to create a nightmare vision of eternal conflict. Furst told one interviewer: 'If the sun came out, Stanley didn't shoot. It was supposed to be the image of hell.' Furst cuts an exquisitely morose figure, shoulders hunched against the cold, never looking into the camera but at some unseen point in the distance. Sometimes he is close enough that you can count the creases on his face, other times he's a far-off figure, a doll. Often he isn't in the pictures at all. Although he is part of the image, he is also a ghost, not really part of the landscape at all. It isn't hard to read the Beckton landscapes as essentially psychological; a state of mind solidified, just as Millennium Mills was for Jarman.

❡ I don't know how old Charlie is, I've never asked, but I would guess he's around 75. His face is deeply creased and darkened with grime. His eyes are folded deep in the sunken sockets. More than 'dirty', the impression he gives is 'weathered'. His hands are very firm and have the engorged, muscular appearance of a farmer's hands, work-hands puffed and burnished by the elements. The back of his neck is even more deeply creased than his face and the creases, again, are etched with grime. Yet the dirt seems less a substance imposed on the skin than a feature of the skin itself. He is part of the ground; it is part of him.

Charlie swears he was one of the extras for FULL METAL JACKET (uncredited, of course). A few weeks after Christmas, I conduct a 'formal' interview with him on our third visit to his home. I use a borrowed Zoom H4n digital recorder, a handheld plastic box which has two silver, pincer-like mics at the front. It resembles a taser or sci-fi torture device, but Charlie isn't fazed. There is even a hint of professionalism to his interview technique, as if he's been briefed already, knows the drill. Just before I click Record, he offers us both a glass of port.

¶ The garden surrounding Charlie's hut has the peculiar neatness of a lovingly furnished fishbowl, but this ecosystem grew of its own accord. I ask where the limits of his dwelling are, expecting him to point towards the grassy verge that shields him from the gaze of passing cars; instead, he pulls out his Freedom Pass and holds it an inch from my eyes. I'm unsure about the precise significance of the gesture, but perhaps what he means is that his garden goes with him. It is able to roam, as he can, and is therefore potentially endless. There is, however, rich specificity here. These plants speak an indigenous dialect. They breathe the same traffic fumes. Their roots have sucked this scrim of mud for its limited nutrients, which have stained their leaves the same wan green. Only weeds, and not much to look at, but their presence is in quiet contrast to the air of human rootlessness so potently felt in Silvertown. I picture the plants growing downwards, fixing the loose mud the way certain beach reeds stabilise sand dunes, and in time become soft-floored forests – but this is too easy a metaphor, and there are limits to this kind of growth. Ringed by a motorway, a DLR depot and a sprawling shopping centre, the sky scored by endless aeroplanes, the ground veined by hidden pipes, Charlie's garden is incongruously still. Its location renders it typical of contemporary non-places, in which architectures of movement have supplanted those of dwelling, but if this isn't a home then I don't know what is. Trapped somewhere between town and country (the concrete has morphed into moss), we might refer to Charlie's garden as an edgeland, an interzone, a liminal realm or a new wilderness. We might turn from Marc Augé to Zygmut Bauman, who speaks of the 'empty spaces' left over 'after the job of structuration has been performed on such spaces as really matter'. The proliferation of such theories points to a crisis, not only in our encounters with urban space, but in our need to conceptualise those encounters through writing. Peripheries have taken centre stage. Alienation is mainstream. Yet none of these thoughts seem remotely relevant here as we crest the verge one afternoon to see Charlie bent forward with a pick-axe in his raised hand. He is gouging holes in the shallow earth and plucking out the coals which riddle the soil like black potatoes. This, after all, was once a dumping ground. All the vegetation here has gathered over the forty-odd years since it was decommissioned: dig a few feet deep and you hit paving. There are species I've never seen before and cannot name, such as the bush with papery lantern-leaves, and the sprouting triffid whose thickly padded leaves are covered in suede-like fur. All the trees are of the van Gogh variety, their branches crazily kinked. The chemical traces of the old Gas Works must have warped their DNA, contorting them into these precious, blown-glass shapes. Correspondence between Kubrick and North Thames Gas, who owned the site, includes several references to contaminated soil and the 'oxide waste dump' to the north. Clause 33 of the rental contract Kubrick signed states: 'Many areas of the site contain toxic waste with hazardous chemical content including oxides, phenol, arsenic and other known carcinogens.' The soil is not simply hostile to life but actively toxic. The presence of life of any kind would therefore seem miraculous. 'You've got a lot of vegetation which don't give a damn about humanity,' says Charlie. 'If it wants to grow here it will grow here, and that's it.'

MORÄN
BY JH ENGSTRÖM

TO KILL A DOG
BY SAMANTA SCHWEBLIN

tr. BRENDAN LANCTOT

THE MOLE SAYS: NAME, AND I ANSWER. I waited for him at the indicated location and he picked me up in the Peugeot that I'm now driving. We've just met. He doesn't look at me, they say he never looks anyone in the eyes. Age, he says, 42 I say, and when he says that I'm old I think that he's definitely older. He wears little black sunglasses and this must be why they call him the Mole. He tells me to drive to the closest square, settles into his seat and relaxes. The test is easy but it's very important to pass and for this reason I'm nervous. If I don't do a good job, I'm not in, and if I'm not in there's no money, there's no other reason to join. Beating a dog to death in the port of Buenos Aires is the test to find out whether you're willing to do something worse. They say: something worse, and look away, as if we, those on the outside, don't know that it's worse to kill a person, to beat a person to death.

When the avenue splits into two streets I choose the less busy one. A line of stoplights changes from red to green, one after another, and lets us advance quickly until a dark, green space emerges from between the buildings. I think that maybe there are no dogs in this square, and the Mole orders me to stop. You didn't bring a club, he says. No, I say. But you're not going to beat a dog to death if you don't have anything to beat it with. I look at him but don't answer, I know he's going to say something, because now I know him, it's easy to figure him out. But he enjoys the silence, he enjoys thinking that each word that he says is a point against me. Then he gulps and seems to think: he's not going to kill anyone. And finally he says: today there's a shovel in the trunk, you can use it. And no doubt, behind those sunglasses, his eyes twinkle with pleasure.

Several dogs are asleep around the fountain in the centre of the square. The shovel firm in my hands—the moment to strike can occur at any time—I move closer. A few of the dogs start to wake up. They yawn, take to their feet, look at one another, look at me, growl, and as I get closer they move aside. Killing someone, someone in particular, is easy. But having to choose who ought to die takes time and experience. The oldest or youngest or the most aggressive dog. I must choose. Surely the Mole is watching from the car and smiling. He must think that anyone that who is not like them is incapable of killing.

They surround me and sniff, a few move away because they don't want to be bothered, and go back to sleep, forgetting about me. For the Mole, through the dark windows of the car, and the dark lenses of his sunglasses, I must be small and ridiculous, clutching the shovel and surrounded by dogs that are now going back to sleep. A white one with spots growls at a black dog, and when the black one snaps at the white one a third dog approaches, barks, and shows his teeth. Then the white dog bites the black dog and the black one sinks his sharp teeth into his neck and shakes him. I lift the shovel and the blow strikes the back of the white dog with spots, who falls to the ground howling. He's still, it's going to be easy to carry him, but when I take him by the feet he reacts and bites my arm, which immediately begins to bleed. I pick up the shovel once more and give him a blow to the head. The dog falls again and looks at me from the ground; he wheezes but is otherwise motionless.

Slowly at first and then with increasing confidence I grab him by the feet again and carry him towards the car. Between the trees a shadow moves, a drunkard approaches me and says, you can't do that sort of thing, the dogs know who the guilty one is and will get even. They know, he says, don't you get it?, he sits on a bench and looks at me nervously. As I reach the car, I see the Mole in his seat, waiting for me in the same position that he was in before, but I realise that the trunk of the Peugeot is open. The dog falls like a dead weight and looks at me when I close the trunk. In the car, the Mole says: if you left him on the ground, he would have got up and left. Yes, I say. No, he says, you should have opened the trunk before. Yes, I say. No, you should have done it but you didn't, he says. Yes, I say, and I regret saying it at once, but the Mole does not reply, he looks at my hands instead. He looks at my hands, he looks at the steering wheel, and I see that everything is covered in blood, there's blood on my pants and blood on the floor mat. You should have used gloves, he says. The bite hurts. You come to kill a dog and you don't bring gloves. Yes, I say. No, he says. I know, I say and shut up. I prefer to say nothing about the pain. I start the engine and the car pulls smoothly away.

I try to concentrate, to discover which of all the streets that appear could lead me to the port without the Mole having to say anything. I can't afford to make another mistake. Maybe it would be a good idea to stop at a pharmacy and buy a pair of gloves, but those kinds of gloves won't do and at this hour the hardware shops are closed. A nylon bag won't do any good either. I can take off my jacket, wrap it around my hand and use it as a glove. Yes, I'm go-ing to have to get the job done that way. I think about what I said: get the job done, I like to know that I can talk like them. I take Caseros, I think it goes to the port. The Mole doesn't look at me, doesn't talk to me, doesn't move, keeps looking ahead and breathing steady. I think they call him the Mole because beneath his sunglasses he has little eyes.

After a few blocks, Caseros intersects with Chacabuco. Next is Brasil, which goes out to the port. I turn the wheel abruptly and take the curve with the car leaning to the side. In the trunk, the body bumps against something and I hear noises, as if the dog was still trying to get up. The Mole, I think surprised by the strength of the animal, smiles and points to the right. Braking as I turn on to Brasil, the wheels screech and with the car tipping over again there's a noise in the trunk, the dog trying to pick himself up from between the shovel and other stuff in the back. The Mole says: brake. I brake. He says: accelerate. He smiles, I accelerate. Faster, he says, go faster. Then he says brake and I brake. Now that the dog has got knocked around, the Mole relaxes and says: drive on, and doesn't say anything else. I drive on. The street that I'm on doesn't have traffic lights or white lines, and the buildings are getting older and older. Any minute now we'll be at the port.

The Mole points to the right. He tells me to go for three more blocks and take a left, towards the river. I obey. We're already at the port, and I stop the car in a parking lot filled with rows of containers. I look at the Mole but he doesn't look at me. Without wasting time, I get out of the car and open the trunk. I didn't put my coat around my arm but I don't need gloves any more, it's all done, I need to finish quickly so we can get out of here. I can only make out some yellow lights in the distance from the empty port, lights that illuminate a couple of boats weakly. Maybe the dog is already dead, that would be best, I think, I should have hit him harder the first time; but he's definitely dead now. Less work, less time in the Mole's company. I would have killed him right away, but this is how the Mole does business. They're whims, bringing a half-dead dog to the port doesn't make anyone braver. Killing him in front of all those other dogs would have been much harder.

When I touch him, when I grab him by the feet to lift him out of the car, he opens his eyes and looks at me. I let him go and he falls back into the trunk. With his front paw he scratches the bloodstained mat, he tries to get up and his back legs tremble. He's still breathing but pants heavily. The Mole must be counting the minutes. I pick the dog up again and something must hurt him because he moans, though he's no longer moving. I set him on the ground and drag him away from the car. When I go back to the trunk to look for the shovel the Mole gets out. Now he's beside the dog, looking at him. I approach with the shovel, I see the Mole's back and behind him, on the ground, the dog. If no one learns that I killed a dog, nothing will be found out. The Mole doesn't turn around to say anything to me. I raise the shovel. Now, I think. But I don't bring it down. Now, says the Mole. I don't bring it down on either the back of the Mole or on the dog.Now, he says, and then the shovel slices the air and strikes the head of the dog, who, on the ground, howls, quivers for a moment, and then everything's quiet.

I start the engine. Now the Mole will tell me who I'll work for, what my name will be, and how much cash is involved, which is the most important part. Take Huerga and then turn on Carlos Calvo, he says.

I've been driving for a while. The Mole says: at the next street pull over to the right. I obey and for the first time the Mole looks at me. Get out, he says. I get out and he moves to the driver's seat. I stick my head through the window and ask what's going to happen now. Nothing, he says. You hesitated. He starts the engine and the Peugeot pulls away in silence. When I look around I realise that he's left me in the square. In the same square. From the centre, near the fountain, a bunch of dogs start to get up, little by little, and look at me.

FORGOTTEN SEA:
THE FALCONERS OF THE
EASTERN PONTOS
BY ALEXANDER
CHRISTIE-MILLER

I.

As I stood on the flanks of the Kaçkar Mountains where they slope into the Black Sea near the town of Arhavi, the placid horizon of water struck me with a sense of fear. It was the same feeling many people get when swimming in the open ocean: you imagine the emptiness stretching for hundreds of metres beneath your kicking legs and experience a kind of vertigo; the blackness below assumes a hostile presence, and you wonder what it might conceal, and shudder at the loneliness of sinking into it.

I was visiting the northeast corner of Turkey – a region once known as the Pontos – in pursuit of sparrowhawks. I had heard about a local falconry tradition that seemed so unusual as to be scarcely credible. As I became more interested in the region, however, and the falconers and their dying pastime, I became ever more fascinated by the Black Sea itself. If the Mediterranean has been a canvas for human history, a teeming petri dish in which Western culture evolved, the Black Sea has had a more diffident relationship with the people surrounding it. Apart from in the north, the flat curves of its coast are largely bereft of the islands, peninsulas, and natural harbours that have fold-ed the Mediterranean so snugly into the societies that fringe it. Before they strung their colonies along its southern shores 2,500 years ago, the Greeks called it *Axeinos* – the Inhospitable Sea.

Perhaps I felt this fear because of what I had read about the flood. During the last ice age, when global sea levels were more than 100 metres lower than they are today, the Black Sea was a freshwater lake disconnected from the Mediterranean. As the ice melted and the sea level rose, it remained as much as 90 metres lower than the neighbouring sea, which was separated from it by the sill of land on which Istanbul now lies. In 1997, American scientists Walter Pittman and William Ryan published a theory claiming that the wa-ters of the Mediterranean spilled over this sill 7,500 years ago in a cataclysmic flood. A surge of water 400 times greater than the Niagara Falls plunged through the channel now known as the Bosphorus with a roar that would have shaken the ground like an earthquake. In roughly two years, 60,000 square miles of land were flooded as the level of the Black Sea equalised with that of the Mediterranean. In the north, the deluge created the Sea of Azov and the Crimean Peninsula. Pittman and Ryan provocatively claimed that the calamity was of such a scale as to impress itself on human mythology ever since, as the Flood. Not everyone accepts their theory, and some scientists argue that the rebalancing of the two seas was more gradual, and the original difference in levels smaller than they have suggested, although corroborating evidence has been found recently in the form of underwater canyons at the Bosphorus mouth that show signs of catastrophic erosion consistent with that caused by a giant cataract.

It was not only this ancient rumour of disaster that impressed me that late summer day: I was also thinking about the anoxic zone. Beneath the Black Sea's surface lies the world's largest basin of dead water. From a depth of around 150 metres to the bottom, some two kilometres below, the sea is without oxygen, and thus without life. Most bodies of water, from ponds to oceans, undergo a natural process known as turnover, whereby deep water depleted of oxygen by organic processes rises to be replaced by water from closer to the surface. Due to the unusual hydrological system in the Black Sea created by its disproportionately large fresh watershed, and constricted access to the neighbouring Mediterranean, this process has not occurred there for thousands of years. In its depths, bacteria have stripped the oxygen from organic sulphates to form hydrogen sulphide, which is dissolved in the water and turns it acidic. During the First World War the British tested the noxious, combustible gas as a weapon.

Scientists and archaeologists who have ventured into the anoxic zone describe a void, in which even the seabed seems to lack substance and solidity. It is coated in a black, fluffy sludge: the sapropels, an untouched feast of organic matter that accumulates in these conditions. 'It's a very quiet world that we don't see any place else,' says William Ryan. 'There is nothing crawling on it, nothing burrowing in it, no fish diving for food.' Submarines that venture down there return to the surface gleaming, purged of rust. The acidic water eats metal, but organic remains decay at a rate slower than they would in oxic conditions. The only things on which the eye may gain purchase are the dead fish or debris that fall onto the seabed and lie there, abstracted in the blackness.

As I read about these things, and about the processes of cultural and environmental destruction that overwhelmed the Pontos in the past century, the Black Sea seemed to be a kind of guilty conscience, a repository for all that has been thrown away. In April 1982, the military junta that ruled Turkey issued a directive ordering that state documents older than twenty years be destroyed or recycled as part of a 'housecleaning' operation to free up new storage space. In the city of Trabzon this was taken to include the Ottoman provincial archive, much of which was duly dumped in the sea: tonnes of documents stretching back 500 years to Mehmet the Conqueror's seizure of the city from the Comnenes. The incident is cited by historian Taner Akçam in his book examining the deportation and annihilation of most of Anatolia's Armenians between 1915 and 1919, and is among many examples illustrating the Turkish state's pathological indifference to its own past. 'This pattern of wholesale disregard for its own posterity is characteristic of an authoritarian institutional culture that tends to evaluate history and historical documents as potential "threats" that may, in some cases, need to be destroyed,' wrote Akçam. 'Finding no inherent value in preserving its own past, Turkish officialdom prefers to get rid of it.'

The dumping of the archives echoes a more brutal event that occurred in the same place seven decades earlier. When Trabzon's Armenian population was deported and massacred, 3,000 orphans remaining in the city were killed in a variety of ways, but mostly through mass drowning operations in the Black Sea. Among the eyewitness testimonies concerning these events given by Turkish officials and foreign diplomats, Oscar Heiser, the American consul to the city, reported that boats 'were loaded with people at different times [with the result that] a number of bodies of women and children have lately been thrown up by the sea upon the sandy beach below the walls of the Italian monastery here in Trabzon and were buried by Greek women in the sand where they were found'.

II.

Each autumn as the cold spreads across Russia and Eastern Europe it sets in train a vast migration of birds of prey. Passing through the Caucasus and entering Anatolia, eagles, kites, harriers, buzzards and hawks gather in the thousands where they travel through narrow bottlenecks formed by the passes of the Kaçkar Mountains.

A few months before I witnessed this spectacle myself, I had met a Turkish conservationist who described a tradition connected with it. As the migration reaches its peak in September, the men of the region send their children to hunt for an insect, a large burrowing cricket. This is placed alive inside a trap where it acts as bait for a bird, the red-backed shrike. Once the shrike is caught it is tethered to a long pole, which, after two or three days, it becomes accustomed to using as a perch. Equipped with these aerial rods, the men take to the mountains to fish the skies for sparrowhawks. Attracted by the fluttering of the shrike, the hawks plunge into nets. From that moment, the men keep the birds with them almost constantly, and within only a few hours a hawk has forgotten its wildness to the point that it is content to eat from a man's fist. Within as little as a week, it may trust its new keeper so completely that it will fall asleep on his hand. When the birds are thoroughly tame, usually within ten days, they are taken out to the cornfields to hunt quail, which pass through the region on a parallel migration. The hawk is held in the palm of the hand and cast like a winged javelin at its quarry. If properly trained, the bird will remain with its kill until its captor comes to retrieve it. After about a month and a half of hunting in this way, when the quail season ends, the hawks are released back into the wild to complete their migration, bound for North Africa or the Mediterranean.

The Turkish for *Accipiter nisus*, the Eurasian Sparrowhawk, is *atmaca* ('atmaja'), which takes as its root the Turkish word *atmak*, to throw, in reference to the action used to cast the bird at its prey. The tradition itself is called *atmacacılık* ('atmajajerluk'), and the man who does it (for they are all men) is called an *atmacacı*.

As throughout Europe and the Middle East, falconry was a prominent part of the culture of the Ottoman Empire. At one point the Sultan kept a team of 3,000 falconers, who were exempt from taxation. Street names here and there in Istanbul retain references to this past. *Doğancılar Parkı*, Falconers' Park in Istanbul's Üsküdar district, was where the royal falconers were quartered. Turkish surnames abound with variations on *Doğan* (falcon) and *Şahin* (hawk). Falconry, however, has almost entirely disappeared in modern Turkey. Most vestiges of it were swept away along with other trappings of the Empire when it collapsed in the wake of the First World War. Its decline in Europe and elsewhere happened through the course of the seventeenth to nineteenth centuries and was linked to the rise of the firearm, industrialisation, and the collapse of the feudal societies with which its practice was tightly bound. In the twentieth century, the transmission of falconry knowledge has depended on a relatively small pool of dedicated practitioners. Yet here and there, in regions sheltered to some degree from the transforming currents of modernisation, falconry has survived into the second half of the twentieth century as part of the fabric of everyday life.

The men who practise *atmacacılık* are mainly Laz, an ethnic minority of some 50,000 or so people living in the provinces of Rize and Artvin to the east of Trabzon, and who speak in their homes a language related to Georgian. The history of *atmacacılık* remains fairly obscure. The earliest possible reference I have found comes from Johan Schiltberger's *BONDAGE AND TRAVELS*, an account of the author's odyssey through Anatolia, Russia, and the Middle East around the turn of the fifteenth century, when the region then known as the Pontos was loosely controlled by the Grand Comnenian

Empire. Schiltberger, a German fighting in the army of King Sigismund of Hungary, was captured by the forces of Ottoman Sultan Beyazit I, for whom he then served as a runner and visited much of Anatolia. He describes a legend encountered when travelling in the Kaçkars, of a castle in which a beautiful virgin is guarded by a sparrowhawk on a perch. To whoever sits outside her chamber for three days and three nights without sleeping, the virgin grants a single wish. If the wish contains any trace of pride, impudence, or avarice, the supplicant will be cursed. The legend seems to refer in a garbled way to the medieval practice known as 'the watch', by which a falconer would sit with a newly acquired hawk for three days and nights, allowing neither himself nor the bird to sleep. After a while the hawk, in its tired state, would simply forget to be scared of the man, and accept its human perch.

I flew to Trabzon in early September, where I was met by Doğan Smith, Turan Basri and Louis Smulders. Turan and Louis were both falconers, British and Dutch respectively. Doğan, an American biologist who has dedicated himself to the study of the tradition, was our guide. In the string of towns along the E70 coastal highway, you can tell the falconers by the crisscrossed scabs and scratches on their hands: they do not use gloves. We were standing outside the falconers' café in Pazar; a group looked on, hawks on fists, cigarettes in mouths, as Metin Yoğurtcu shook a quail carcass before his bird then tossed it a few feet across the car park. Drawn by its eyes, the hawk slid from his arm and unfurled its wings into a diagonal fall; it levelled – breaking with a flutter – grasped forward with its talons and alighted on its prize before casting its eyes about as if searching for challengers, then fussily refolded its wings. Little by little, he was teaching the bird to hunt from his hand, or rather to hunt irrespective of his presence, and to allow him to approach and retrieve the kill. Metin, early 40s with a square jaw, blue eyes and hair a premature white, eased the bird back onto his fist and raised it to his eye, stroking his hand along its neck and back and looking at it with an air of rapt, guileless pride. The hawk, ignoring him, darted its head this way and that, indifferent to his touch. Above them the traffic of the coast road rumbled on.

I don't know where I had imagined these men before I met them, but it was not here, not in the urban sprawl of these coastal towns. In Pazar, the falconers' club was tucked beneath an overpass of the E70; in another town, behind a run-down bus station. Moonlighting as *atmacacılar* for two months of the year, the rest of the time they were janitors, grocers, pharmacists, or electricians. A more likely setting might have been the one for which this region is best known in Turkey: plunging wooded valleys, pristine mountain pastures, tea terraces, and scattered villages of timber houses. Though I had never set foot in it, this landscape was familiar from the photographic murals that jump from the walls of regional restaurants in improbable, overpowering greens.

III.

When I was first told about *atmacacılık*, I knew little about falconry, but what I did know mingled with my greater ignorance to make the tradition (the capture of a sparrowhawk, its training in a week, its release) seem almost mythical. As a teenager, I had harboured a brief fantasy of becoming a falconer, and had read about it for a week or two before realising that the commitment, hard work and patience it required were beyond me. I knew it was a delicate and time-consuming practice, and that of all the raptors the sparrowhawk was among the most notoriously difficult. It seemed almost impossible that a man could train a bird plucked from the wild in so little time. My amazement increased when I learned that the *atmacacılar* handled them with none of the usual paraphernalia. They did not use hoods, which are often put on a hawk's head in order to shield it from alarm during transport. They did not even use scales to weigh their birds, usually considered crucial in the case of the sparrowhawk, which due to its small size is acutely sensitive to either under- or over-feeding.

Unlike humans or dogs, most species of raptor are not social animals and are incapable of forming dominant or submissive relationships. They have never been domesticated, in that we have never influenced their evolution for our own ends. They are iron-willed, driven by inflexible passions of fear and hunger; a falconer's task is to eliminate the first and manipulate the second. If mishandled, the bird will remain in permanent rebellion until it dies of stress or exhaustion. It is sensitive to the subtlest of new experiences, and accepts the falconer's presence only when it stops viewing him as a source of danger. The falconer must come to share this sensitivity and moderate even his most trivial actions. Coughing or blowing one's nose, for example, may cause deep anxiety. Jack Mavrogordato, in *A HAWK FOR THE BUSH*, an authoritative work on the training of sparrowhawks, advised falconers to breathe softly around a newly acquired hawk, avoid staring at it, and wear dark glasses to hide their alarming human eyes.

Should a bird of prey escape even for a few hours, it will swiftly revert to its wild state. Habits that run counter to its nature – trust in humans, for example – will quickly fade if not constantly reinforced. Upsetting or traumatic incidents, meanwhile, sear themselves indelibly on their minds. A falconer

cannot lose his temper with his bird, ever. Victories in the 'manning' process – days of calm in which the hawk slowly feels itself more comfortable in
human company – are only ever provisional, but defeats are often final. In
falconry, perhaps more than in any other of the alliances we force on animals,
it is the human that must bend his life around the hawk. The bird transforms
only subtly, and only in so far as the human is transformed in its own eyes.

Raptors radiate an air of savage intelligence. When one thinks of 'bird-
brained', one imagines the prey species, pigeons and so on. In fact, the reasons
for us assuming their stupidity are quite shallow. Their eyes are monocular,
placed either side of the head, unable to consider one object together. When
a pigeon twists its head from side to side, it creates the impression, to human
eyes, of a creature with a limited perception of the world around it. The eyes
of a predatory bird are binocular, like our own. When its face is turned towards you, you have no doubt that it is considering you. The psychotic yellow
of a sparrowhawk's eye, the permanent scowl of its brow, its head endlessly
and minutely adjusting its gaze, convey the impression of a mind both acute
and imperious, in which humans are merely threatening objects to be tracked
and avoided.

The visual world *Accipiter nisus* inhabits is far richer and more spacious
than our own. Its eyeballs, only about 10 per cent of the surface of which are
visible in the face, are so large that they touch together in the middle of its
skull, and are nearly the same size as its brain. Its vision is similar to other
birds of prey: a highly flexible lens allows it to scrutinise objects 500 yards
away as easily as those a foot away; its retina receives a broader range of light
than our own, edging into ultraviolet, and in a resolution eight times higher.
Like those of all birds, its eyes are immobile, and to gain a better view of an
object the entire head must be rotated, lending it an expressive air of inquisi-
tiveness. Often when studying an object it will crane its whole body forward
and down, perhaps because its twin foveæ – the parts of the retina with the
greatest acuity – are located on the lower half of its eyeball. When a hawk
studies its handler in this way it looks almost as if it is bowing, creating a false
impression of submissiveness.

The sparrowhawk is a prolific killer of small birds. In a single year in the
wild, a successful breeding pair and their chicks will consume a weight of
flesh equivalent to 2,200 house sparrows or 600 wood pigeons. It is among
the family of raptors known as the short-winged hawks, so called because
they are adapted for flight in woodlands. Long tails and a narrow wingspan
make them more manoeuvrable than the falcons, their long-winged cousins

that are adapted for soaring in the open sky. The sparrowhawk is a creature of stealth, of lethal ambushes and camouflaged pursuits through the undergrowth. Many birds of prey happily eat a variety of meals, but the sparrowhawk's diet is unvariegated: it feeds exclusively on small birds. This means that even in comparison to other predators, its life is geared uniquely around the mania of hunting. Unlike falcons and eagles, which usually kill their prey instantly through force of impact, a sparrowhawk will grip its victim, clenching and unclenching its talons until it is so thoroughly perforated as to be immobile. It does not particularly care about killing it, so long as it is still enough for the hawk to begin eating. A sparrowhawk that cannot kill twice a day, every day, is unlikely to survive long, and in this battle to feed themselves the majority quickly fail. Of those that successfully fledge, as many as two thirds of all males and half of all females die in their first year, principally of starvation. They are creatures balanced between their own death and that of their prey, crafted by the constant pressure to kill.

Along with their larger cousin the goshawk, they are often seen as the crude butchers of the raptor world. People who have observed them closely, however, believe individuals develop sophisticated hunting techniques, learning for example to imitate the flight of harmless birds in order to fool their prey. They are experts at using cover – tree trunks, hedges, garden fences, parked cars – in order to maximise the element of surprise. Their hunting is practical, unglamorous, but effective. Falcons and eagles are showmen by comparison. A falcon will ascend into an amphitheatre of sky before folding its wings and diving on its prey: a stooping peregrine is the fastest creature on the planet. The suspense is greater, the outcome less certain. This translates into eagles and falcons being considered the more prestigious birds. Of the two short-wings, it is generally the goshawk that is the more popular: it is larger, easier to handle, and can take a wider variety of prey. In northeast Turkey, it is impractical to fly falcons and eagles in the enclosed landscape of thickly wooded mountains, valleys, and small fields, and there is little game large enough for a goshawk. The target is quail, and the only hawk adept at taking it is the sparrowhawk.

IV.

We traded the grey congestion of the coast for the uplands above Arhavi, where narrow valleys cast shade over steep terraces of tea and stands of hazel, and homesteads smattered the slopes. Further up, this gave way to woods of chestnut and hornbeam, as we drove up a track cut by the parks commission to fight forest fires. We had with us the shrikes, which had little bowls of meat or egg fixed to their poles for sustenance. The birds, mainly females with plain brown backs and whitish breasts, radiated an intense, miniaturised energy: hopping up and down the length of their sticks, sampling their food, studying and working with their beaks at the strings tethering their legs. The birds are fitted with blinkers that allow them to see only downward, intended to prevent them panicking at an approaching hawk. In the old days these were made using a quarter of a hazelnut shell, stuck on with pine resin. Today they are usually a semicircle of leather, warped using a lighter flame and stuck on with superglue. The men insist that these simply fall off after a couple of weeks without causing any lasting injury.

The sea, a primary blue, was stretched smooth as a platter beneath the sky, and the green mountains piled hazily into the distance as the coast curved away into Georgia. Beneath the migration route, the trappers had set up hides covered with brush with narrow eye slits facing eastward, towards the oncoming migration. Above us flowed an unending procession of birds of prey. There were hundreds, probably thousands; steppe buzzards and honey buzzards, red kites, hen harriers, Montagu's harriers, pallid harriers, a range of eagles: imperial, Bonelli's, and others I could not distinguish. In places they gathered in eddies, towering upwards on thermals until they were mere specks in the blue. The men ignored this spectacle; sparrowhawks fly low, close to the treeline, easy to miss. Next to the hides were a series of nets, loosely pegged to a semicircle of hazel rods. When a sparrowhawk approaches, the shrike is stuck out and the pole waved so that it flutters above it. The hawk dives at the shrike but hits the net. The shrike generally survives the encounter, although I was told there are occasional casualties: a clever hawk will see the trap and attack from the other side.

I had not seen it approach, but one was suddenly thrashing in the net. It was retrieved and tightly bound in a handkerchief, and left on a table, where it lay like a cob of corn with a livid, staring head; this was the start of the training process. A hawk, if it must be physically constricted, should be constricted entirely. If it is able to struggle even slightly, its agitation will increase, but if it is unable to move at all it will grow calm. After a while the captured hawk was equipped with jesses – leather straps fastened round the legs to secure it to a tether – and moved to a perch beside the hut, where it sat, wings drooping and mouth agape. If I approached even within a few metres it would bate wildly from the perch, but within an hour or two it began to calm.

The trappers claim they can catch as many as twenty sparrowhawks a

day in this way. Most are immediately released, since the falconers use only newly fledged females; sparrowhawks being the most sexually dimorphic of raptors, and the males are too small to reliably hunt quail. The females are so much larger – almost double the weight – that they are known to hunt and kill the males. Raptors caught on their first migration, known as passagers, were once the birds of choice for falconers everywhere. They have the advantage over eyasses – birds taken as chicks from the nest or reared from eggs – of already knowing how to hunt, making the falconer's job easier. Haggards, older birds caught on their second migration or later, are more hardened in their fear of man and therefore more testing. The most dependably human-bonded birds are imprints, eyasses reared by hand that believe the falconer to be their mother. These also harbour negative traits: they will often scream for food and their lack of wariness around humans can make them unusually aggressive.

When raptor populations plunged worldwide in the 1960s, due mainly to the use of the pesticide DDT in agriculture, the trapping of wild hawks was tightly regulated or banned in many countries, and captive breeding programmes began. In Turkey, legislation banning *atmacacılık* was passed in 1984, but the tradition continued much as it always had. After lobbying from falconers, it was re-legalised in 2002. Today falconers must be licensed, and are only allowed to trap sparrowhawks, and only a certain number each year.

While sparrowhawks are among the world's most abundant birds of prey, the practice remains controversial, and is despised by Turkey's environmental and animal rights lobby. The falconers argue their tradition has a positive effect on the population. They take hawks at a time in their life cycle when the natural mortality rate is highest – around 50 per cent – and claim to release them well-fed and in peak condition. Conservationists on the other hand say that the birds' survival chances may be damaged by their captivity, and by the consequent delay in their migration. Since no scientific data has been gathered on the subject it is hard to say more. A very feasible study could be done in which trackers are fitted to sparrowhawks used in *atmacacılık* and those released immediately on capture in order to compare their fate once returned to the wild.

In recent years, another criterion for the selection of sparrowhawks has become increasingly important: the colouring. Doğan has recorded at least sixteen subtly differentiated hues recognised by the falconers, from *kara* (black), to *kızılçam* (red pine) and *beyaz* (white), and which category a bird falls into is the subject of frequent and heated teahouse debate. The birds vary in their juvenile plumage: they are pale breasted with darker backs, ranging from brownish-slate to shades of buff or ochre. Most prized and rare is the white sparrowhawk, fading pictures of which usually adorn the walls of the falconers' cafés. One old man pulled a wallet from his pocket and showed me with relish at least a dozen creased photographs of bygone hawks as if they were old sweethearts. In recent years the obsession of some *atmacacılar* with this purely cosmetic quality has been taken by more serious practitioners as the sign of a general malaise. 'In earlier times it was only important that it was a good hunter because it had to catch quail. The colour didn't matter,' said one falconer. A growing number of *atmacacılar* are interested solely in trapping the hawks for fun, or having a fine-looking bird to take to the teahouse. 'I only do it to be out in the mountains, in the fresh air and the joy of having the contest between the small bird and the large bird,' said one. 'The moment it is in the net I'm not interested anymore. Unless it is an exceptional bird I release it straight away. If it is a very beautiful bird I take it to the café and show it off.'

V.

Once a year on 23 June, the eve of the feast day of Trabzon's patron Saint Eugenios, the women of the city would bathe in the Black Sea. This tradition persisted among the Muslim population long after the Christians, among whom it presumably originated, had left the city, and was witnessed by the historian David Winfield in the summer of 1960 as he was supervising the restoration of the frescoes at the city's Hagia Sophia. It continues to this day in towns along the coast in the form of local marine festivals, known as *aladurbiya*.

During the course of that work Winfield met Anthony Bryer, with whom he was later to write THE BYZANTINE MONUMENTS AND TOPOGRAPHY OF THE PONTOS. The product of four decades of research and scholarship, this forensic work quarters every valley and town of the region, delving into the roots of their names, the legends and traditions of their people and plumbing 2,500 years of historical literature.

It is also an epitaph. The Pontos – a region of the Black Sea coast stretching from the west of Trabzon to the Georgian border in the east, bound by the Kaçkar Mountains – had ceased to exist as a cultural region by the time their work was published in 1985, and had become a purely historical thing. It was the victim of a century-long process of cultural, ethnic, historical and environmental destruction. In the years since Bryer and Winfield first met, 'the Pontos has suffered a greater physical transformation than in its entire previous history,' they wrote in their preface. 'We believe these decades are the last in which our work would have been possible.' William Hale, a retired professor of the School of Oriental and African Studies in London, who worked on the Hagia Sophia restoration with Bryer and Winfield, recalls that in those days tobacco fields and grazing cows stretched to the beach where the women held their ritual bath.

Today, an artificial embankment of freshly-blasted boulders makes up the entirety of the Pontic coast. In the past fifteen years, 250 miles of coves, rocky outcrops, shingle beaches, old piers and town waterfronts have disappeared beneath the asphalt of the E70 highway. On a grey afternoon in Trabzon I negotiated with difficulty the four-lane cordon that now severs land from sea. I watched some coots bob in the black water as a thin drizzle flecked the rocks near to where a huge stone visage of Suleiman the Magnificent glowers down on an empty park. I tried with mixed luck to piece together a sense of the old city from the modern one that has engulfed it. I found what had been the nineteenth century Armenian cathedral, its dark stones disassembled and reconstituted into the blockish headquarters of a state bank. In some places, the riddled and half-inhabited remains of the city walls looked romantic. I saw the Hagia Sophia standing alone on a rubble-strewn hill. It was soon to be reconverted into a mosque. Regrettably I did not make it to the citadel, where Rose Macauley's heroine in THE TOWERS OF TREBIZOND painted the city from the ruins of the imperial palace, while imagining the intrigues of the Comnenian court.

I have come to see the E70 not only as the literal link between the towns of the falconers, but as a thread that connects the various kinds of transformation and destruction wrought on the Pontos over the past hundred years. The more organic forces of economic development are now concluding what began in the early twentieth century with ethnic upheaval and forced cultural assimilation. The coast road was the final and dramatic solution to what had been one of the defining traits of the Pontos: its inaccessibility. The region had little in the way of coastal lowlands. The wooded mountains, with their steep river-strung valleys, plunged straight into the sea. For centuries most transport was by boat, despite the poor harbourage. When Mustafa Kemal first surveyed the region as Turkey's leader in 1924, he was rowed ashore from his ship because the town of Rize had no jetty that could accommodate it. In the 1950s young men leaving to perform their military service were picked up from the beach in a rowing boat that ferried them to a waiting vessel. Before a tunnel was blasted through a shoulder of mountain near Arhavi in 1960, the 100-mile journey from the Georgian border to Trabzon could take six or seven hours. The idea of a coast road had been discussed for years, but work began fitfully in 1987. It then progressed at speed after the election of the current Justice and Development Party government in 2002, which enacted a nationwide infrastructure development programme on the back of an economic boom and was completed in 2007. Today nearly every beach as far west as Samsun lies under asphalt. People sometimes joke that where they once lived on the sea, they now live on the highway.

After the Greeks had yoked the Black Sea's shores with their trading colonies and started to exploit its riches, its name was inverted from *Axeinos* to *Pontos Euxeinos*, the 'Hospitable Sea'. The Pontos was once so closely associated with the sea that it took its name from it. It was a place at once worldly and arcane. In the same way that far-flung islands beget unusual flora and fauna, its thickly wooded mountains and deep valleys made it a haven for the survival and elaboration of obscure cultures; and yet its position at a terminus of the Silk Road, and the sea-spanning trade network of its Greek population, also made it a place distinguished by its cosmopolitanism and tolerance. When the Byzantine Empire collapsed following the sack of Constantinople by the Fourth Crusade in 1204, an unusual Pontic splinter state emerged: the tiny but bombastically named Grand Comnenian Empire. For 250 years the Comnenes – a deposed Byzantine dynasty – governed over a kind of relict, freighted with the obsolescent pomp of Rome. Its rulers styled themselves 'Emperors of All the East, the Iberians, and the Overseas Lands', and its opulence amazed European envoys sent there. It retained its improbable sovereignty through its rulers' deft diplomacy, and the advantageous marrying of princesses to the neighbouring Georgians and the various Muslim rulers surrounding it.

The Pontos remained a place apart long after Trebizond fell to the Ottomans in 1461. Turks settled in the region in greater numbers, but a large Greek contingent persisted, comprising about a quarter of the total population as late as 1910. Trebizond thrived fitfully as a trading port, foreign powers posted consuls there, and Greek and Armenian merchants and bankers rubbed along with the growing Muslim populace in a harmony unmatched in most other parts of Anatolia. Language, religion and tradition bled into one another.

This world collapsed at the start of the twentieth century, when the fabric of the Ottoman Empire was torn apart by the competing nationalisms of Turks and Greeks and the machinations of the imperial powers, culminating in a bloody sifting of its ethnic and religious constituents around the years of the First World War. After the purging of the Armenians in 1915, the Greeks were evicted in 1922 as part of a forced population exchange negotiated between Athens and Ankara. The Greek merchants left, taking their trade network with them, and the Communist regimes that later arose on the Black Sea's farther shores offered no outlet for it to be revived. The people of the Pontos had their gaze torn inland, towards the new Turkish capital Ankara. In the territories of Anatolia Mustafa Kemal Atatürk set in train a state-building enterprise that was antithetical to everything that had hitherto defined the Pontos. The new nation was to be homogenous, inward looking, and avowedly hostile to the region's non-Turkish past.

VI.

Over the coming decades, its architectural history was destroyed, vandalised or left to decay. Of the roughly seventy buildings that were once churches in Trabzon in 1915, only ten survive today. Many were dismantled following the departure of the Greeks and Armenians, but what began as an assault on Christian heritage evolved into a more widespread revolt against the past. As the drab modern city expanded, historic mosques were demolished, including one of the oldest, the Tabakhane. Nationally, Ottoman–Arabic script was scrapped in favour of Latin characters and Turkish was stripped of its Arabic and Persian words, meaning that in time historical documents and inscriptions became indecipherable to all but scholars. The campaign of Turkification was most pronounced in the purging of the millennia-old toponyms of towns and villages. The current names of the towns of the falconers – Pazar ('Market'), Çayeli ('Teatown'), Fındıklı ('Hazeltown') – are bland creations of bureaucrats, imposed over older ones whose roots went twenty centuries deep. Pazar, for example, had been Atina, whose provenance was first discussed by the historian Arrian 1,900 years ago; he suggested it was a place sacred to Athena. In fact, Winfield and Bryer argue, it may have been older still, a Hellenised version of a Lazuri word meaning 'the place where there is shade'.

Not everything was swept away. Hidden in the steep valleys of the Pontos were communities that seemed to defy the rigid categorisation imposed by the new national identity, but which remained in place due to having embraced Islam, often centuries before. Around the town of Of, east of Trabzon, live the Oflu, several thousand of whom still speak in their homes a Pontic Greek dialect that is considered the closest living relation to ancient Greek. Back in the mountains further east are the Hemşin, who speak a kind of Armenian and, unlike their kinsmen, traded the cross for the crescent some five centuries ago. The most numerous, however, are the Laz, perhaps the region's most ancient inhabitants. They are associated with the Kingdom of Colchis, centred around present-day Batumi, from where Jason and the Argonauts won the Golden Fleece.

The Lazuri language is most closely related to Mingrelian, a member of the Georgian language family. It has survived, in the words of the writer Neil Ascherson, 'like some ancestral wedding dress that is of no use to anyone outside the family'. Today, these old identities are worn lightly, in jest, or not at all. 'In the past, some of those people living close to the coast were Greeks and those living closer to the mountains were Armenians, but neither of them accept that identity today,' one falconer told me. 'They say it to each other as a joke.' An insult sometimes aimed at the Hemşin by the Laz is *dönmüş Ermeni* – 'converted Armenian' – to which the Hemşin can respond with *dönmüş Meğrel* – 'converted Mingrelian'.

Today, the Eastern Black Sea Region, as the former Pontos is now known in Turkey, is renowned as a hotbed of conservatism and ultra-nationalism. 'If people from around here are ever stopped by police anywhere in the country, they let us go as soon as they hear our accent,' said one Laz falconer. 'Everyone knows that the people from around here are loyal.' Trabzon itself is an inversion of the vibrant and tolerant city that preceded it. The young killers of Hrant Dink, a Turkish-Armenian journalist murdered in 2007, were recruited from the city, a fact that is sometimes touted as a source of pride. In the summer of 2013, as a mass protest movement gripped the country, a popular act of dissent was to paint street stairways in the colours of the rainbow. One group made a contrasting statement, however, painting a stairway near the Istanbul street where Dink was gunned down the colours blue and red: those of Trabzon's football club.

In the past two decades a movement has emerged to assert Laz cultural and language rights, but it has more support among the diaspora in Istanbul than in the northeast, where such things are seen as echoing Kurdish separatist aspirations. Some of the Laz I spoke to about it expressed a wistful regret at the slow death of their language. 'The older generation wanted their children to learn proper Turkish and not a dialect,' said one falconer in Pazar. 'I'm sorry I didn't teach my children the language, and now they are asking me why I didn't.'

As we sat in a falconer's hide looking out over the expanse of the Black Sea, a golden light flared in the distance as the afternoon sun caught the face of a skyscraper in Batumi, on a faraway headland. Any cross-border cultural ties were effectively cut during the Communist era, and the fall of the Iron Curtain has done little to restore them. The early 1990s saw a horde of impoverished traders from the former Soviet bloc who flooded Turkish towns and were chiefly known for the shoddiness of the goods they peddled, which threw on its head Turks' notion of their inferiority to the great powers, and led many to take a prouder view of the country's place in the world. 'Natashas' – prostitutes from the former Soviet Union – set up shop in local hotels, becoming the means by which many local men ruined their families and finances, indirectly boosting religious political parties through a surge in support from outraged wives. Today the situation has settled, but Georgia is still regarded by many with some contempt, as a place of hedonistic escape, and a source of cheap smartphones. Batumi, said one falconer, was a place of 'gambling, entertainment, and sex. That's all.'

VII.

The arrival of an unusual bird brought tension to the falconers' teahouse in Çayeli, dividing those in the courtyard of the pine-panelled café between fascination and sour disinterest. A young man had entered with a female goshawk on his arm. He had caught it about a week before, but was showing it in public for the first time. Beak aghast, the bird jerked its head at the panorama of threat around it, bating powerfully from its keeper's fist. A knot of men had formed and was inspecting the hawk, but others remained on their stools, muttering disapproval. In this region there is no game large enough to be caught by a goshawk; the only reason to have one on your fist is to show it off. The serious falconers often complained that many of those catching and keeping hawks had no intention of ever hunting with them. They cared only for the fineness of the plumage – what one called 'the coffee house criteria'. 'It is like going to a party with a beautiful girl on your arm,' one said. 'A real hawker will spend his days catching quail.'

The young man was obviously besotted with the bird. It had a martial look, and was three times the size of the sparrowhawks around it, which cowered when it was brought close to them. Its breast was cream, tinged with russet, and irregularly flecked with dark vertical brushstrokes. Its eyes were almost white, with only a faint greenish wash, and as it gradually calmed, it cocked its head upwards and scanned the sky as if contemplating escape. The young man said he would train it and hunt with it. A little while later another falconer invited us to his home to see his birds. Our own presence in the café had caused excitement, and the young man had sought advice from Louis on how to care for the hawk, and asked to join us. He got in the front passenger seat, the goshawk still on his fist. As he pulled the door to, the bird bated in alarm, and the door slammed shut on its unfurled wing. He opened it again; the wing fell limply to the bird's side, a patch of blood clotting the feathers where the bone broke the skin.

The thin sobs of the goshawk – an unexpectedly feeble sound, helpless and self-pitying – rendered silent the other commotion that erupted in those first few seconds. We immediately set off for a vet. The young man's face was heavy with dejection: he seemed close to tears, and there was an air of grief in the car. On the way we talked uselessly over the circumstances of the disaster, trying to rationalise and explain it, our efforts punctuated with awkward silences filled by the bird's faltering cries. It was the young man's fault. He had never taken the hawk in a car before, a new and frightening experience to which it should have been introduced with care. He also made a basic mistake by holding it on his right fist – the door side – rather than on his left. We talked about what would happen next. No one thought the vet would be of much help. Louis believed the kindest thing was to kill the bird: the break meant it would never fly again, or at least not well enough to survive in the wild, and it would be miserable kept in captivity and unable to hunt. The young man said he didn't care; he would keep it as a pet. The vet turned us away, saying there wasn't a person in the whole country who could help. We went on to the falconer's house, and Louis took the hawk and bound its wing to its breast, in a position he said might allow the bone to mend. He recommended putting it in a dark, quiet place. They took it to a shed, and I didn't see it again.

I saw the boy again when we returned to Çayeli a few days later. When I asked him about the bird, he showed no flicker of his former distress. He said he had shown it to an older falconer who had immediately wrung its neck, telling him it was *bozuk* – broken.

VIII.

'When I was a child there were 5,000 falconers here. Now there are 300,' said Kemal Özbayraktar, head of the falconry association in Arhavi. 'Our culture is dying.' Kemal is a tall man in his early seventies with silver hair, a polished Istanbul accent, and an air of dignified severity. We visited the home his father built in the hills high above the town, where his elder brother now lives. Up the steeply twisting lane to the house, a medley of the exotic and the familiar glowed in the afternoon sun: kiwis and chestnut, hazel, hornbeam and tangerine, banks of faded papery hydrangeas, and below, pillows of tea rippling down the hillside to the town, where the slender minarets and smokestacks of the tea factories merged with the gathering dusk.

More than anything, it was the arrival of tea that marked the fall of *atmacacılık*. In the early years of the Turkish Republic, the provinces of Rize and Artvin were among the poorest and least developed in Turkey; the people were mainly farmers, living on maize and rice. Falconry had long been a part of this subsistence lifestyle. The oldest falconers still remember the women of the household plucking quail and pressing them into huge clay pots where they were salted and stored, then consumed through the winter. Hızır Yoğurtçu, an 80-year-old with limpid blue eyes, recalled the limitless bounty of the days when farmland covered the coastal strip and ran up the river valleys.

'Once I went out with my father, and by the end of the day we had ninety-nine quail,' he had told me at the Pazar Hunting and Falconry Club, where he held court. 'My father said we should have a hundred. Just as he said it the hundredth got up, just next to us. And then we had another, so it was a hundred and one in a day. That was fifty years ago by the Fırtına River.'

The new regime was looking for ways to drag the northeast out of its penury and isolation. The state had made fitful efforts to encourage the cultivation of tea in the area around Rize since shortly before the Ottoman collapse, and these continued in the 1930s. Regulations were drafted for the industry but it was only later, when the Democratic Party came to power in 1950, that a plan emerged to put tea at the heart of the regional economy. The state created an entire industry from scratch: it built factories, trained workers, subsidised plantings, created the market and bought the crop. Hitherto Turks had largely been coffee drinkers. Coffee had to be imported, however, so new tariffs on foreign coffee and tea effectively excluded any competition.

It was a spectacular success. The product of the eastern Black Sea coast flowed to every corner of the country, turning Turks into a nation of tea drinkers almost overnight. In those early years, people in the northeast called their new crop the 'green gold'. When he was a child, Kemal remembered, a kilo of tea was the same price as a kilo of olives or sugar. The government paid an incentive to plant it, and every family cleared every patch of soil they could put a spade in to make way for it. 'We lost the hazelnut woods, we lost the corn and we lost the rice. The whole region changed,' said Kemal.

Men worked in the factories, women in the tea fields. The verdant plantations were a desert to the creatures that once thrived on the corn and rice, however, including the quail that would hole up in them during migration. 'Where tea is planted, not even grass grows below it. There's nothing left for quail to eat,' said Kemal. Not that it mattered. With the salaries they now earned, people no longer needed to produce their own food. In less than a decade, the northeast changed from being a place which people left to seek their fortunes into a magnet for migrant workers. The benefits trickled through the whole economy: local hauliers were contracted to transport the harvest, a construction boom created work for builders, furniture makers, plumbers, and so on. People left their villages and moved into houses and apartments in the coastal towns, such that today, the entire strip from Trabzon to the Georgian border is an almost unbroken stretch of conurbation. The pressures and responsibilities of modern life left little space for something as time–consuming and suddenly obsolete as falconry. 'In the past, a wife would say to a lazy husband, "At least you could go out and get a hawk and catch some quail,"' said Kemal. Now the popular stereotype is the reverse: where once a wife would berate her spouse for not hawking, she now berates him for doing it. 'All women hate it,' pronounced one falconer. Falconry had become *boş işi* – 'pointless work'.

Whatever nostalgia there is for the past, however, is overridden by a sense of the enormous material progress the tea brought. The misgivings most people express about the industry has more to do with the bust that hit it in the 1980s, and which has dimmed its lustre. In today's neoliberal Turkey, the tea industry is a relic of the past: still mostly in public hands, with the government company, Çaykur, setting a fixed annual purchase price for the harvest. Turkish tea is dependent on protectionism, since it could never compete on an open market with tea from India or China in quality and production cost. Nonetheless, as Turks now routinely rank among the top tea consumers in the world, it has become the product by which the northeast proudly defines itself, and the mainstay of its economy. In the centre of Arhavi, a statue has been erected showing a man and a woman clasping hands, each thrusting their free arm up into the air. They brandish the twin symbols of the town: the woman a sprig of tea leaves, the man a sparrowhawk. Positioned almost back–to–back, they seem to be walking in mid–stride, as if pulling each other apart.

IX.
During the few days I spent in Kemal's company he was rarely without a

hawk. It was usually on his fist, or on the hand rest between the driver and front passenger seat in his car, or on the long bar perch in the restaurant at his cultural centre. He had even constructed a perch in the street outside the pharmacy he ran with his wife. Like most of the more serious falconers, he would have one or two exceptional birds which he would keep permanently – another falconer had one that was now 10 years old – and perhaps two or three others that he would capture, train, hunt, and release in the traditional way over the course of a season. Mavrogordato wrote that a falconer should be 'something of a thought reader, consciously if somewhat surreptitiously watching his hawk and taking note of its passing moods'. The falconers seemed acutely aware of their birds' moods, even if they appeared to be ignoring them. They would sit, one hand stroking its back and neck, raising or lowering the bird or shifting its position, all the while deep in conversation with their friends. This stroking was constant, and is one of the key tools of manning: in time the hawk ignores the physical contact altogether. If the bird was alarmed, signified by an open mouth or drooped wings, it would be held aloft slightly so it could look down on its captor and feel itself more secure. Eventually it would grow calmer, shift its tongue in its mouth, scan the room, and concentrate on an object other than its human keeper. When a bird is truly relaxed, Kemal explained, it will sit on one claw, with the other curled up into its feathers. The ultimate sign of trust is if the bird falls asleep on the fist: 'This makes me happier than I can say. It is like when a small child falls asleep on his chair and you carry him up to bed.'

At the cultural centre that Kemal runs in Arhavi he explained the principles of manning a hawk. From the moment of its capture, he said, a good bird can be trained in a week, but more typically ten days to two weeks. 'When they train dancing bears, they heat the ground beneath their feet, and the heat makes them lift them – it's done with force. You cannot do that with a bird. The important thing is the love you have for it... There has to be a feeling that the owner loves the bird and it will trust him to protect it.'

In modern falconry the question of how much time to keep a bird on the fist is much discussed, and yet Kemal and the other falconers I met were not vexed by it. Most would keep a bird on their fists for short stretches of perhaps forty minutes or so at a time depending on its mood, sometimes with almost constant bating. It would erupt into the air and then plunge down and hang – wings open, head to the ground – and be lifted back into place only to do the same again and again. It was good for the hawks to be together, Kemal said, because they would relax quicker in each other's company. Sometimes these sessions, generally in the teahouses, would continue late into the evening. When a bird is truly accustomed to human company 'it does not matter if it sits on your fist or on a wooden post.'

Food is the most vital tool in training, and a hawk is made to feed from the hand on its first day of captivity. Generally its first meal is egg, which will form a staple of its diet in captivity. The bird is tricked into eating by being encouraged to peck at a fist holding the food. It is generally on the second day that it is introduced to company for the first time, being taken to the teahouse, ideally with dogs around as well. When the hawk is sufficiently comfortable the falconer may begin to throw it a dead quail on a lure. After about a week to ten days, or whenever the bird is judged to be familiar enough with people, it is taken out into a field or woods where there is a lot of wildlife; if it shows the proper keenness, such as bating at passing birds, it is generally judged ready. The first quail it is flown at is normally captive bred and released from the hand on a creance – a light, long line that hawks are flown on during train-ing. The field is tilted in the hawk's favour because if it fails to make a kill on this first attempt the experience can be psychologically damaging; it will not believe it is possible to hunt in conjunction with man, and may refuse to do so in future. When birds are lost, it is almost always after an unsuccessful hunt. If the hawk makes a kill it will generally stay with it and allow the falconer to approach. If it fails to strike however, it will likely go to a tree and continue to hunt alone. Every minute it is gone, its connection to its keeper weakens, its wildness returns. Passagers and haggards of most raptor species – even those kept in captivity for years – are usually able to integrate back into the wild.

Mavrogordato noted that passage sparrowhawks could sometimes be 'curiously and unexpectedly amenable to the discipline of training', and the question of how the *atmacacılar* manned their birds in such a short space of time had ceased to seem so mysterious. Kemal estimated that he had handled some 2,000 sparrowhawks over the course of his life; catching several in a day, he was able to sense very quickly which birds might be most amenable to man, even from the way they approached the net. 'There are smart ones and stupid ones. The ones that see you from far away and attack anyway are stu-pid, the ones that circle the net and find the best approach are clever... There are some that are so afraid of people that you cannot train them. But there are some that already hunt quail, and if you find one of those then you are very lucky.' He reckoned he had had only five such birds in his lifetime.

Also, the falconers do lose their birds, often. Kemal said he had lost maybe 20 per cent of those he had flown. Sparrowhawks are easily obtained, and the falconers will often have two or three at a time. If one disappears, another can quickly be procured. This means that *atmacacılar* tend to take more risks in flying a hawk that may not be perfectly manned. Often they are not trained to fly to the fist, which is important if one wishes to retrieve a bird from a tree. Generally they rely on the fact that a hawk will seldom miss its target, and so will not often have cause to escape.

At Kemal's cultural centre in a huge darkened room full of chairs and tables, we watched a documentary about falconry featuring a younger Kemal. In grainy washed-out colour it took us through the stages of sparrowhawking, from the catching of the cricket to the bird's release. Kemal told the interviewer how he had moved back to Arhavi to pursue his love of falconry. In the final scene, Kemal stood on a rocky sea wall, in a raincoat, hood up. He held the bird and gently kissed its back, before releasing it dovelike into the air in jerky slow motion, waving it goodbye.

X.

I took the bus to Istanbul's Atatürk Airport, where I hired a car and struck out along the shore of the Sea of Marmara towards the countryside beyond the town of Silivri, to meet Salih Doğrusadık.

Through the city suburbs I passed the lagoons, pale and insipid in the dirty morning light, before making my way down a series of forking lanes until I arrived, miraculously, at the small camp Salih and his friends had built in a hollow between some fields. Autumn was greying without the graceful hues commonly ascribed to the season. The landscape was rolling and enclosed in an English way, with pillows of woodland and the kind of sad, feral feel one often gets on the verges of cities. Speculators owned it, perhaps, or people who knew better than to care too much.

On a long perch fixed between the branches of a tree were tethered two sparrowhawks. *Karakız* – 'Black Girl' – had been caught about a month earlier, and was '70 per cent trained', Salih said. We sat and drank tea in the square wooden shelter he and his friends had erected. Salih was a mechanical engineer, 50, balding with a wide warm face. Every year he took a month's holiday, and he spent all that time here, hawking. Once a week he would go to get supplies and see his family at his home in Ümraniye on the other side of Istanbul. The trip between Silivri and Ümraniye would take him across the length of the metropolis, some forty miles as the crow flies, a drive of four hours, in bad traffic, through a nearly unbroken sprawl of city. Around this time a documentary came out called *EKÜMENOPOLIS*, about urban overdevelopment in Istanbul. It took its title from a theory originated by the Greek city planner Constantinos Doxiadis, who argued that, based on current models of urban development, a time will come when all the world's cities will fuse together into a single urban sprawl, the 'ecumenopolis', encompassing the entire globe. The idea was rhetorical, of course, but the kind of growth it was criticising pertains in Istanbul, where the construction industry is used to lubricate a system of political patronage and where forests of skyscrapers proliferate on the city's fringes in soulless half-empty wastelands.

Atmacacılık arrived in Istanbul in the 1940s when people moved there from the Black Sea coast. Like Rize and Artvin, the city lies on a major bird migration route, and they found that on the wooded hills around Beykoz and Sultanbeyli they could trap hawks in the same way they had back home. Salih was 17 when he moved from Çayeli to study machine engineering at Istanbul's Yildiz Technical University, and he never returned. He was already a keen falconer when he came to the city. 'I started playing with birds as soon as I could walk. My father wanted me to be a falconer and I was more interested in birds than my brothers.' When I asked him about how he remembered Çayeli, about how it has changed, he said that in his childhood you could count the number of people in the neighbourhood who didn't have sparrowhawks. 'We were hunting so many quail that we could use them as meat through the whole winter.'

Today, among the Black Sea community in Ümraniye, he is one of the youngest falconers. 'I miss the old days when all of us were doing it... *Atmacacılık* is a culture that passes from father to son. In Turkey you don't pick up a hobby when you're old, you have to grow up with it.' Like most of the falconers I had spoken to, Salih used the word 'hobby' – a direct loan from English – with slight reticence. It is a recent concept in Turkish, and implies both a lack of seriousness and also a certain irresponsible disregard for more weighty matters, such as work and family. What about his own children? He has one son, now 16. Salih's wife had made him agree not to pressure the boy into taking up *atmacacılık*. He painted a familiar picture of the wife and hawk at odds. 'Falconers have to walk a tightrope when it comes to their wives. Sometimes it's harder to hold this balance with our wives than it is to train the birds.' He said he would still have taken his son out hawking if he'd expressed an interest, but he never has. 'He doesn't know anything about *atmacacılık* and he doesn't know much about Çayeli.' He will graduate high school next year, and plans to study computer engineering at university. 'I understand why my son won't get involved. I'm sad but I understand it. We want our son to grow up and be a man, and by that we mean to have a good education, a religious education, get a wife and give us grandchildren. That is when you reach a point of happiness, I suppose.'

We went over to the birds and saw that Karakız was keen and ready to hunt. Salih walked through the field, holding her aloft in his crooked arm like a soldier one sees in the war scenes on Greek vases. When the chase occurred it was both slower and faster than I had imagined. The quail had erupted from the grass, a compact whirring of wings. The hawk loosed from Salih's hand floated behind it, so smooth and silent she seemed suspended in the air. It closed on the quail and the two birds merged and sunk to the ground together. It was over in perhaps five seconds. The hawk sat on its prize with an air of defiance, surveying the weedy ground around it. Sinking to his knees Salih crept forward on all fours and for a moment the two seemed to eye each other in standoff. The hawk did as she was trained, however. She looked about herself with haughty indifference as Salih's hands reached for the quail. She watched his fingers as he parted the feathers on its head, and presented her with the exposed pink skin of the crown; the hawk pried its beak through the skull and tasted the brain.

Heading back along the Marmara, dozens of boats were scattered at the mouth of the Bosphorus: rusting hulks from the former Soviet bloc, oil tankers, vast Chinese container ships. These sometimes wait for weeks to pass through the congested channel, and dot the horizon of the Marmara, lights glinting in the evening, like an armada of floating cities. Again I imagined the flood, and pictured all the boats in the tug of a fearful current, drifting in eerie unison towards the mouth of the strait. I thought of the people of the Pontos thousands of years ago; to them, the flood would have seemed like a slow, ceaseless tide. On that precipitous coastline, the waters ultimately advanced only a few hundred metres. At a certain point, however, they must have feared it would never stop. It is a natural human reflex to imagine the frightening forces of one's day pursued to their most disastrous conclusion. Fleeing over the Kaçkars, they would have looked back with dread at the thought of the water beyond creeping higher, imagining the day when it would crash over the peaks and inundate the entire world.

RESISTANCE
BY CHRIS KRAUS

31 Standish Ave.,
Rosedale, Toronto 5
7 February, 1963

Dear Mr and Mrs Tuck, -

Thank you for your nice Christmas card which arrived well before Christmas. I wish you could have seen the seventy-two cards I had on display in our living room, and among them was the one from you. Christmas is a busy time, but interesting. My Christmas Day was a lonely one until I left the house at 4:30 in the afternoon to go downtown to have my supper in a restaurant. Following that, I went to my cousin's home to spend the evening. I was back home at 11 o'clock, and was soon off to bed. However, there was one 'bright spot' while I was alone - it was Her Majesty's Christmas Message. I'm sure you heard it too.

I was glad to get your letter early in December, and to know the calendar arrived safely. You said you had not been well, but was feeling better. You also said that Mrs. Tuck had high blood pressure, and was not feeling well. I do hope she is much improved. Do take good care of yourselves – both of you. Good health is our greatest asset.

I do part-time work, so keep plenty busy. This house seems to require quite a lot of my time. In a house there is always something requiring to be done, and I do all my own work. Even though I live alone, I find plenty to do. It is quite a responsibility, as well as expense, but I have to live somewhere, and apartments, too, are expensive. I much prefer one's own home, to an apartment, so I will carry on here as long as I can do so.

I think I told you that John and his wife were going to California for Christmas. John enjoyed himself, and said the time was too short.

We have had a good share of cold weather, but as yet not much snow. Winter is getting by, and we will all welcome spring. Can you notice the daylight stretching out? It is quite noticeable here, and I always watch this with interest.

You said you and Mrs Tuck would see what this coming summer would bring forth, and perhaps you could both make a trip up here. That would be very nice, and this home will make you welcome, should you wish to stay here – will cost you nothing. You will not see Mother, but I will take care of you both as best I can.

This is all for this time. Write when you can. Your letters are welcome.

Sincerely,
Bertha Lowe

¶ I found this letter in a disused Anglican school building in Pouch Cove, a town fifteen miles north of St John's, Newfoundland. The letter was typed and tacked onto a board in one of the bathrooms. In its last incarnation, the school had been used by a foundation to house visiting artists from all over the world. One of the artists must have scavenged it out of the pile of debris in the mouldering building, which had been red-tagged last summer during a drawn-out dispute between the foundation director and the Pouch Cove Building and Safety Department. The letter was touching in its archaism. Beyond its literal obsolescence – who, who isn't trying to be quaint or cute, writes letters anymore? – it reflected certain lost cultural values: an absence of high expectations, a stoic acceptance of loneliness. It reminded me of my parents. I copied it into my notebook.

¶ During the past several years I've chosen to live somewhat nomadically, accepting various invitations from cultural institutions like the one in Pouch Cove. I have a house that I'm rarely in near downtown Los Angeles. The house has a value – although not to me, since I'm usually travelling – so I often loan it to friends, friends-of-friends, family members, even passing acquaintances met during these travels. (During the past several years I've noticed the fierce desire that once pre-empted rational choice evaporating. Slightly confused, I concluded the best course to follow was: if I don't actively want something and someone else does, just let them have it. This applied to my house.)

Last August, when I arrived at the house in LA en route to Pouch Cove after spending the summer in Mexico, I noticed several small, insignificant things misplaced or missing. The front door key (redundant, since I leave the house open) was gone; also, the TV remote and the black plastic scoop used to measure espresso-ground coffee. I asked Justin and Karen and Bob and Jerome and Rose and Samantha and Joan – all of whom used the place briefly during my absence – about these things, but no one knew anything. Nothing major was missing and the house was left clean. There was no one to blame, certainly nothing to rage about – but the losses were very unsettling. Each of these things was part of my LA routine, which, I liked to think, resembled the life of a Seventies sitcom air hostess.

What bothered me most was the loss of the black plastic scoop. Made of hard shiny plastic, it came with the Bodum French Press-style coffee pot sold at Starbucks for $34.95. I'd encountered a similar problem two years ago, when houseguests Charlie and Billy and Jane accidentally broke the glass flask. They left a nice note and ten dollars. Theoretically the flask was replaceable for $10.95, but the Silverlake Starbucks (a thirty-minute round trip from my house) was out of stock on this item. Faced with the choice of driving to Glendale, Pasadena or Burbank on one of my three days back in LA in the hope that one of those stores would have the replacement, or simply buying the whole thing again, I surrendered my credit card... though not without airing my views on softly enforced consumption to the barista; a rant as wasted as the use of air-quotes around phrases like 'choose to service my own account' to call centre workers in prison, or India.

But the 'challenges' posed by the loss of the black plastic scoop during the summer proved insurmountable. (I'd just 'concluded' six months of therapy, after concluding that the seventy-five minute round trip drive to an inconvenient Westside location to discuss my resistance just wasn't worth it. It occurs to me now, as I think of the black plastic scoop, this fact might be relevant.) Because the black plastic scoop had never been sold as a separate component of the Bodum French Press, at Starbucks or anywhere, and moreover I learned, after driving to the Silverlake Starbucks, the entire chain has stopped selling these coffee pots, replaced them with travel mugs.

Where do you find a black plastic scoop? I tried searching the web, but no luck. Jerome, my ex-husband, was empathetic. (He and his girlfriend Rose were among those using the house.) 'I am aware of the plastic scoop and its fragile existence,' he said. This show of support nearly moved me to tears. Jerome understood. And I wondered: just how much time and care should a person spend in the attempt to replace a fetishised object? Or rather – a commonplace object that, in its absence and newly unattainable state, becomes fetishised? Although Jerome was helpfully quick to point out that this desire, transferred onto an object, in fact defines the term 'fetish'. But was this correct? There was no Freudian guesswork involved in my need for the black plastic scoop, no magical thinking. I'd already had a black plastic scoop. I simply wanted it back.

Still, at a certain point, one must ask: At what point is it better to devote one's mental focus to simply getting over the plastic scoop, and, as they say, 'moving on'? Asking yourself this question is like asking what's real. Can you notice the daylight stretching out? How do we accommodate loss, how do we live alongside it?

¶ When Walter Benjamin travelled to Moscow in the winter of 1926, he kept a diary. He was not a habitual diarist. He was funding the trip by writing articles for magazines back in Berlin, and took notes to make his job easier. He travelled to Moscow because he wanted to see for himself what life in a realised communist culture was like. He also travelled to Moscow because he wanted to see a woman he loved, Asja Lācis.

He and Lācis had met two years before in Capri. At that time, he was married and she already had two other lovers, but they embarked on an intellectual/erotic romance which included the writing of manifestos and, presumably, some kind of sexual congress. They met up in Berlin the next year, and then once again, in Riga. Lācis, a Lithuanian actress, lived in Moscow with her companion, the theatre director Bernhard Reich. She was a communist; a colleague of Meyerhold, Brecht. In Berlin, a few months before, Benjamin wrote: 'This street is named Asja Lācis Street, who laid it through the author,' a pretty sexual dedication to ONE WAY STREET, the book he'd just finished.

When Benjamin arrived in Moscow, Lācis was hospitalised in a sanatorium with a mysterious illness. Presumably Benjamin knew of her attachment to Reich; in fact, he found Reich 'a fabulous guy', and during his trip, the three spent most of their evenings together... at Asja's bedside playing dominoes and eating halvah; attending concerts and plays; meeting most of Moscow's cultural innovators. Sometimes Benjamin goes out alone with Reich. Sometimes Benjamin goes out with Asja, although he laments that they're 'rarely alone'.

What's astonishing about Benjamin's MOSCOW DIARY is that while his longing for Lācis pulses through his descriptions of Moscow, it does not overwhelm them. The trip is not about their doomed love; doomed love doesn't even necessarily inform all of his Moscow experience. The diary is a portrait of the most enviable, ultimate form of urbanity where grief exists and can be sampled, like some exquisitely potent local intoxicant. On 15 December he records that Lācis 'never turned up' for their date... and goes on to describe St Basil's Cathedral, Moscow arcades, wooden toys, the political histories of some acquaintances, and the 'beautiful view of the long string of lights' on Tverskoi Boulevard.

On New Year's Eve, the snow 'had the sparkle of stars... When we arrived in front of her house, I asked her, more out of defiance and more to test her than out of any real feeling, for one last kiss in the old year. She wouldn't give me one. I turned back, it was now almost New Year's, certainly alone but not all that sad. After all, I knew that Asja, too, was alone.'

Benjamin's closest friend Gershom Scholem was not buying any of it. 'The diary is desperate in its outright urgency... [it] leaves us without insight into or understanding of this intellectual dimension of the woman he loved... The times he waits in vain for Asja, her continual rejections, and finally even the erotic cynicism that she displays to no uncertain extent... makes the absence of any convincing evocation of her intellectual profile doubly enigmatic... Everybody was bewildered by these two lovers who did nothing but quarrel.' And: 'the theme of their relationship', Gary Smith writes in the afterword, 'drawn as an erotic red thread... is one of obsession and denial'. Harvard University Press reduces this further on their back–jacket copy to 'the account of his masochistic love affair with this elusive – and rather unsympathetic – object of desire.'

These interpretations of Benjamin's experience – clearly stated by him, in his own words, in his own diary – remind me of psychotherapy.

At the end of his trip, Benjamin lost sight of Lācis as his sleigh left the hotel, and rode to the train station in tears. Nine years later, Bernhard Reich – together with all Jewish German émigrés – was banished from Moscow, then jailed. Lācis was interned for more than a decade in Kazakhstan, after the first Stalinist purge.

Who defines happiness? And is it a goal? We have had a good share of cold weather, but as yet not much snow. Is my need to recover the black plastic scoop masochistic, or is it more like – 'I know what I want' – a self-affirmation?

This is all for this time. Write when you can. Your letters are welcome.

A WEEKEND WITH
MY OWN DEATH
BY GABRIELA WIENER

tr. LUCY GREAVES

WE ALL HAVE TOMBS FROM WHICH WE TRAVEL. To reach mine I have to get a lift with some strangers to a place in the Catalan Coastal Range. I'll be spending the weekend taking part in a workshop called 'Live your Death'. The main challenge of this adventure will be to relate my death in the first person, without really dying, I hope. In the brochure they talk about us facing things very similar to NDEs (near death experiences), watching the film of our lives, glimpsing the light at the end of the tunnel, having out-of-body experiences and seeing languid and distant little men calling us affectionately from the threshold where it all ends. It's also possible, I think, that I'll be put on a plane and taken to an island where weird things happen. In the meantime I'm getting to know some of my fellow passengers.

'Did we meet at "Recycling Ourselves"?' asks the man.

'No, it was at "My Place in the Universe",' she replies.

'Oh yeah... and have you found it?'

'Not yet...'

'After all these workshops you still haven't found it?'

'I'm working on it.'

'What you need is a clear objective,' says the man, who despite all the money he's spent on self-help workshops seems not to have grasped certain basic principles. For example, that you don't greet a woman by asking her if she's figured out what to do with her shitty life yet. I can think of various things to say to them both to solve their problems and earn myself some cash: that he try closing his mouth every now and again and that she tell guys who reckon they know more about her than she does where to go.

'Well, girls, are you ready?' This is the man's second time at the death workshop and he claims to know what he's talking about.

'You have to take your clothes off, yeah? Get naked, yes siree.'

The woman and I look at each other. The man turns around and just speaks to me this time:

'You must have good lungs because you're from over there, down south, people have good lungs there. You're going to need them. I don't want to give too much away, but we're going to grab you by the hair and drown you a bit...'

Even though it's clear he's having us on, the woman, who says her brother persuaded her to come – 'after one of these workshops he left his difficult girlfriend and his horrible job at the bank and became a better person' – is shocked and throws me another pleasantly questioning look.

'Heey, girl, uncross your legs, you'll stop the energy flowing!' says the man.

I do what he says. We're almost there.

¶ The workshop centre is a big house in the hills. It's surrounded by trees and has views of the Mediterranean. The huge swimming pool is empty. There are different existential workshops with other groups and topics running at the same time. Emotional education is a luxury item, but some of us can afford it. At reception, next to the herb tea table, I pay the bill and feel a bit dirty, like when you pay for drugs, which is something I don't like doing either. Or when you transfer money to your psychoanalyst.

Paying for spiritual well-being doesn't seem normal to me. Nor does paying for a lung operation, but that's the way things are.

I settle into the small room I'll be sharing with two other people. I put my four changes of comfortable clothes in the wardrobe, my wash bag in the bathroom and, what the hell, I go out to socialise. Apparently one of the aims of the workshop is to find oneself fully with other human beings, something normal people only do after four drinks. A girl sits down next to me.

'"Death"?'

'Yes,' I say. 'You...?'

'I'm in "Death" too. The word already seems a bit less scary, right?'

'Uh... I guess so.' I ask her who the women dressed in white are.

'They're from "Apologise to your Mother". Is it your first time?'

'Yes.'

'Lucky you! It's going to be one of the most important experiences of your life. This is my fourth time.'

People reoffend, and this, depending on how you look at it, could either be a very good or very bad sign. A bell rings and we go into the main room, which has huge windows looking out over the sea. There are more than thirty of us in 'Live your Death' and none of us are wearing shoes. The workshop leader asks us to introduce ourselves and say why we've come. He looks at me and says 'You start', so I have no other choice:

'My name's Gabriela. I'm Peruvian, but I've been living in Barcelona for eight years. I've come because... I'm afraid of death, more so recently, and because I feel disconnected...'

I say all this because it's the truth. There are other truths, but we've been asked to keep it brief.

Before coming, all the participants signed a document in which we promised not to disclose anything that happens here. That's why I've deliberately changed the name of the workshop and I won't use any proper names, not even the workshop leader's, a famous intellectual in Catalonia. I also had to complete a psychological test, one of the ones used to detect your weaknesses.

You have to put a series of ideas in order from from 1 to 18 and from best to worst. For example, I gave slavery a 15; blowing up an aeroplane full of passengers, a 16; burning a heretic alive, a 17; and torturing someone, an 18.

These are honest answers. I suppose I am a good person, after all.

One by one the others share their reasons, all of which have to do with finding themselves.

The workshop leader explains that this is not therapy. He says it's a time within time. Four days in which we'll experience more than in four months. An experience of dissolving the ego which is, in the end, what death is. A rite of initiation and catharsis to kill the selfish child we all still carry inside, to find our place in a cosmic, social and familial framework. The fear of death is a fear of life.

All that said there's little more to add, except that the workshop entails confronting something as terrifying as 'impermanence'. The idea is that we're going to lovingly discover the greatness of dying and help someone to die, because we'll be expected to play both roles.

In this context, those of us taking part have to find the problems that limit our lives. The technique to achieve this: a kind of consciousness-altering rhythmic breathing in time with music and sounds, all of which will help us to reach a psychic representation of death, heal wounds, and find the cause of our blockages.

Symptoms that indicate the proximity of death and which we'll experience during the workshop while either dying or assisting: dry mouth; dehydration of the skin; use of strange language; the need to return home and reconcile oneself with someone or something; weight loss; feebleness; fragile bones; vomiting; the desire to defecate and expel everything alien to us; death rattles; involuntary movements; glassy eyes.

The workshop is to death what a simulation is to an earthquake. Except, perhaps, for the minor detail that no one will escape death.

Before going to bed we have another task: to draw a self-portrait at tables covered with coloured pencils; I scribble a monstrosity à la Frida Kahlo with a spiny heart and a computer mouse chained to my wrist. Inside my stomach I've drawn a Gabriela with two heads: one is smiling and the other is crying. A typical drawing to impress a psychologist, I think. When I get into bed I start to feel the first effects of the workshop: I can't help remembering the fucking awful bedsores on my grandmother Victoria's body. Bedsores are dead skin, the war wounds of sick people: lying in bed for a decade can be more damaging than battle. Unable to communicate, unable to recognise us, I find it hard to believe she was able to say goodbye or see any kind of beautiful light before she went. I think, too, about the last time I saw my grandmother Elena alive; she had been blind from diabetes for several years, and was on a trolley in the corridor of a public hospital waiting for a bed. She asked me for water, she was really thirsty, so I gave her a sip from a plastic cup. She said: 'I'm going to die, love, take me home, I don't want to die here.' I lied to her: 'You're not going to die, Granny.' I kissed her on the forehead and left. She died an hour later in that same corridor.

¶ I haven't been to the doctor for five years. Not even for a miserable check-up. Ever since I gave birth I've felt immortal, or I've forced myself to feel immortal. I try only to get ill with things I can cure with a simple visit to the pharmacy. That said, I've been feeling strange for a while now. I don't know how to explain it, I just don't feel well. One day I finally decide to make an appointment with my GP, who in turn books me in with the nurse for a general check-up. He also orders a blood test to see what's going on. I have to wait two weeks for the results. The nurse weighs and measures me and takes my blood pressure. There's nothing wrong with me, of course, doctors have always thought I'm a shambles. It's ridiculous, but every time I leave a consulting room I'm sort of disappointed that I'm not really ill. I don't want to be ill, of course, but for some reason my ego can't handle being so insignificant in any context, even in a hospital. So, when the nurse takes my blood pressure and says 'It's really high,' someone inside me smiles. The devil, perhaps. It's an impulsive, unhealthy delight, revenge for all these years of perfect health. '150/109,' says the nurse. 139/89 is normal.

I'm 35 years old. I'm a woman. In other words, I'm young and up to my eyeballs in progesterone. These two factors are arguably better than a life insurance policy worth a million euros. That's two weighty reasons, I tell myself. 2–0. I win. But it turns out I don't. I haven't got a simple increase in blood pressure because for the whole of the next week I don't eat salt and stuff myself with vegetables and go back to see the nurse and it's 158/110. She takes my blood pressure in my right arm and my left, three times in each. Finally his scientific eminence – my condition merits the presence of the doctor himself – comes out and starts whispering with the nurses.

During these minutes of uncertainty, my blood pressure goes through the roof, 159/115. The doctor says it's not a one-off increase. Nor is it stress, even if I sometimes feel as if I'm going to explode in the middle of everything like a bomb planted by a terrorist who's got the wrong target.

ESSAY

My father found out he had high blood pressure at 35, my current age, and he's taken medication every day since. My grandfather died of a heart attack aged 60; my grandmother Victoria, from a brain haemorrhage. I can't win anymore. The game's turned against me. 3–2. I'm hypertensive. I suffer from stage 1 arterial hypertension. That's all. But hang on a moment, is there any chance the high blood pressure could be a symptom of something worse? How much worse? Something horrible, probably, because the doctor looks at the tip of his shoe. 'The test will tell us,' he concludes. Although we still have to wait for that. Suspense.

Chronic arterial hypertension is called 'the silent plague of the West' and is the principal cause of death in the world, ahead of hunger and cancer and AIDS. It's called this because it acts silently, affecting the blood flow, and is a risk factor for cardiovascular or renal diseases. The cause is unknown in 90 per cent of cases, but almost always has to do with genetics and poor habits. Bingo!

No one would say I'm a fat person, but equally no one would say I'm a healthy person. And this is a condition I have borne with pride all this time, which makes me feel alive and lively, the complete opposite of being dead: I drink, I smoke, I go out, I get drunk once a week and once a week I die of a hangover, sometimes I take drugs, I eat junk food, I hate most vegetables, I'm a mother, I'm not baptised, I work in an office, I hate the human race, I'm someone's wife, I stream TV series until three in the morning, I don't exercise, I don't have domestic help, I spend ten hours a day in front of a screen and the only part of my body that gets any exercise are my fingers hitting the keyboard, like now. It's a miracle my arse isn't the size of Brazil. I'm a journalist who specialises in putting herself in extreme situations and writing in the first person about those experiences. Oh, and I'm almost forgetting the most important thing: I love salt. Coarse–grain salt especially, those tiny diamonds on a good piece of steak, and dips and sauces so salty my eyes roll with excitement. When I was a girl, I remember now, my toxic DNA drove me to sneak surreptitiously into the kitchen when my grandmother Victoria stepped away from the stove and sink my index finger into the red salt pot. Once I'd pulled it off, I'd run with my white, shining finger back to the telly. For a long time, sucking my salty finger while I watched my favourite cartoons was a version of happiness.

¶ Things were beautiful, once. Seriously, they were. Hangovers were generally manageable. And devouring hamburgers and fried chicken had no consequence other than pleasure. I can't say exactly when this impunity ended. It was probably when I turned 30. But I didn't take the hint, I decided to carry on being young and foolish, which goes with the territory of being young, and I kept on living in the only way I knew how, that is: believing I was immortal, never reading the labels on products and publicly declaring myself enemy of the fitness world and its devotees. Only every now and again a glitch in the matrix made me think that something might not be right, a slight acceleration in my pulse rate, for example, as if a savage with a drum had snuck into the magnificent chamber orchestra of my chest.

¶ I touch my face and establish that my spots are still there. I run my hand over my stomach, too, and verify that it's still round, like a four-month pregnancy bump I've grown accustomed to. I stopped worrying about my reflection in shop windows some time ago. I stroke my neck and feel my growing double chin. I think about all this, about the poor fit between my body and the mental image I have of it (in which I prefer the real image not to intervene). It's been a long time since I stopped thinking about it, or perhaps I never did.

Back at home, the days following the bad news about my blood pressure are strange. It's no wonder, because I have to start a strict diet in order to become the kind of person I wouldn't bother talking to even if we were stuck in a lift together. I'm not allowed to drink alcohol, maybe a glass of wine or two, but I can't conceive of going to a bar without getting drunk so I stop going out. My girlfriends promise they'll give up lines and gin and tonics for me, that they'll switch to spliffs and white wine, but I can tell they're lying. I start to consider a change of friends. Food without salt, on the other hand, is like not eating at all.

The scenario wouldn't be complete without its dose of pharmaceuticals. Every day, for three months to start with, I have to take two five-milligram tablets of Enalapril. The box of sixty costs a disconcerting twenty cents, and the list of possible side effects takes up half the leaflet. Am I supposed to fill my body with these cheap pills for the rest of my life? One day I meet a friend who tells me he has the same condition, that he spends his days eating garlic and doesn't take blood pressure tablets because 'they kill your sex drive'. Hearing this, another close friend says I'd better top myself. Add to this the harassment and takedowns I've been subjected to now that everyone has something to say about my health, especially my family, who once again take the liberty of overprotecting me. I suffer various episodes of anxiety thinking I could have a heart attack at any moment and, as if that wasn't enough, I'm getting my blood pressure measured so often that I've become really popular in the local pharmacies. One night, like every night, I take off my clothes in front of the mirror and see a slight red mark on my right breast, just beside my nipple. I touch it. It's a lump. Something hard. It wasn't there before, I'm sure of that. Then I scream.

⁂

LIVE YOUR DEATH DIARY
PART ONE

The first part of this piece is written with the ironic distance I almost always assume because I believe I write better from there. Except now I don't want to do that. It wouldn't be fair to the experience or the workshop leaders or the people who were there giving everything and opening themselves up to others. Nor would it be fair to readers or to myself. I'm going to copy an extract from the diary I wrote that weekend so whoever reads this can see me warts and all:

They've taken our mobiles away, so I don't know what time it is. I'm dead tired. We have to go back in an hour. Today we're breathing. The morning was fun. We danced for two hours, electronica, salsa and a ridiculous song called 'My Tantric Boyfriend'. After that we did contact exercises with partners: looking each other in the eye without talking, touching each other, hitting each other. I was with a really hot, muscly guy, his caresses made me tremble. I liked the exercise where you had to talk non-stop while the other person listened without saying a word. I talked about my family, about Jaime and Lena. My partner, a young girl this time, was really sad. She said it made her happy to know I was happy. It made me feel good about my life. She cried and I couldn't say anything to her because I wasn't allowed to. This is part of the double experience: repressing the desire to help the other person because in reality, when the moment comes, no one can help you. We live together, but die alone.

We spent a long time letting ourselves fall backwards onto a mattress, losing our fear and, as they say, 'letting ourselves go'.

What I liked most was the blind person and guide exercise. I was a terrible guide, I almost killed my partner, who was an older man this time. I made him run and bump into things so much that he had to sit down and couldn't carry on. When it was my turn to be blind, my partner was incredibly loving, he took me outside, made me smell and touch the grass, splash myself with water from the fountain, feel the breeze and the warmth of the sun. The workshop's probably having an effect, touching my most sensitive fibres. Every time we do an exercise, somebody cries. After we ate I saw a boy who lives here playing with two dogs. I remembered that the director told us to want something badly. That's what I want, more moments in the sun, a huge garden and dogs that Lena can play with. Strength and patience to bring her up happily. Are my eyes shining like everyone else's? Have I got a pious smile and a desire to hug everyone yet? No, I can't be at peace with myself, it doesn't fit my personality. My position in this workshop isn't the easiest: on the one hand, I feel I've got to be conscious enough to write this story when I get back, a story about whether it's possible to try out death, with at least some critical perspective. Because, let's accept it: you can't try out death, death is a show that goes out live and direct, pure improvisation. And what does it matter, getting closer to it isn't going to immunise us against our fear of the void. On the other hand I feel as if thinking like that, with so little faith, stops me committing to anything, not just to this. I want to try it, I really want to do it. This workshop is full of dysfunctional, lonely, sad people who feel pain and don't know where it comes from. Am I superior to them because I don't take myself seriously or am I the absolute opposite precisely because of that? Am I superior because I think of myself as happy? I can't carry on kidding myself that other people are the crazy and dysfunctional ones so as to keep firing witty phrases into the sky.

LIVE YOUR DEATH DIARY
PART TWO

The session finished at almost two in the morning. Today half of us breathed and tomorrow the other half will have a go. It's my turn tomorrow, so today I was a carer. The brief is not to intervene in the other person's experience even if we see them suffering. We can only act if they ask us to. My dying person was a woman of around 40. You have to be patient and humble to be a carer. I spent long hours by her side wetting her lips, holding a plastic bag to collect her sick. The person doing the breathing lies down, their eyes covered. The person caring watches over their deathbed.

We're in a circle, like in a ritual. In fact, the workshop itself is inspired by shamanic sessions with ayahuasca, the famous entheogenic plant. When we were all in position, the music started. The workshop leader guided the ses-

sion, encouraging us, asking them to be brave to go into the beyond and sometimes playing a drum. The music is key because it makes you travel through
different emotional states, from the most violent to the most peaceful. So, in
a way, the workshop leader is also a kind of DJ. There was everything from
insufferable mystical songs to Wagner's RIDE OF THE VALKYRIES. It touched
me to hear Mercedes Sosa singing 'I'm bread, I'm peace, I'm more: come on,
tell me, tell me all that's happening to you now / because otherwise your soul
weeps when it's alone. / We have to get everything out, like in spring. / Look
each other in the eye as we speak, get out what we can / so that inside new
things grow, grow / grooooow.' The breathing is similar to breathing while
in labour: short, rhythmic inhalations and exhalations. Some people breathed
sitting down, or even standing until, finally, they reached catharsis. When
someone complained about the pain, you could ask the workshop leader to
come over and move them. He would press some muscle or other which made
the person feel a sharp pain and cry out with relief. I saw people laughing and
crying, writhing in pain, shouting as if something had shattered into a thousand pieces inside them, and it's impossible for that not to shake something up
inside you. When my dying woman seemed to be at peace, I covered her with
a sheet. She had gone.

∴

I've rarely been close to death. Perhaps that's why I'm so afraid of it. For
people who see it every day, like funeral directors, death is something ordinary, like sleeping and waking up. My parents always tell the story of when,
as a very little girl, I learned that people die. From that day on, whenever
they mentioned someone to me, I would ask: 'And have they died yet?' Cue
laughter.

    Children see death as something strange and fascinating. I don't know at
what point death stops being a word in a fairy story and becomes a real circumstance. We spend a large part of our lives thinking of death as something
remote and, above all, alien, something that happens to other unfortunate
people, until this misleading idea gives way to the painfully physical perception that one day we too will expire irredeemably. Adult life means continually prodding at Nothingness with the fingers of our imagination. This is the
bad thing about having precarious beliefs, being pessimistic and vaguely in-
telligent. More than the instant of death itself, which is already scary enough,
humans fear the anonymity of disappearing. Philip Larkin puts it best: 'No

rational being / Can fear a thing it will not feel, not seeing / That this is what we fear – no sight, no sound, / No touch or taste or smell, nothing to think with, / Nothing to love or link with, / The anaesthetic from which none come round.'

My first dead person was my grandfather Carlos, the one who had the heart attack. I was 9 years old and my parents told me two days after the funeral. I didn't even see his coffin. I've never gone up to see the body at a requiem mass. I didn't see the bodies of my dogs. I only dared to peek briefly into the room at the funeral parlour where my mother was dressing my grandmother Elena and I saw her foot, dropping to one side in the same comfortable position it used to be in when she was listening to the radio in bed. It was like seeing her alive. I didn't see the body of my grandmother Victoria either because when she finally died I was already in Spain. The only coffin I dared snoop in was my grandfather Máximo's, and only because I hardly knew him.

I've never seen the dead face of anyone I love. This is something else that ranks highly in my list of terrifying things.

I've been scared I'll die countless times, especially on aeroplanes, but only once did I say goodbye to everyone, to my family. A furious wave from the Pacific Ocean tumbled me over on the shore and amidst this whirlpool of foam, with my eyes open, I thought I was going to die, but I came to the surface. During the Civil War years in Peru I was more afraid of death than ever. I thought that at any moment a car bomb would blow up in my face or that terrorists and the army would come to our house and cut off our heads. My father's a journalist and I clearly remember the night someone woke him up to tell him eight colleagues had been murdered in a village called Uchuraccay, in Ayacucho. He immediately travelled there and I saw him on TV surrounded by the black bags containing the bodies. I went to the huge funeral procession in Lima and shouted 'justice'. I was 6 years old and that year in Peru was the most violent in its history. Ever since I've had a daughter I'm afraid I'll die of almost anything. In fact I'm so afraid that I don't walk under scaffolding on buildings or cranes lifting cement and I don't cross on red lights. I try to make sure there's not a psychopath behind me on the metro who might want to push me. If a neo-Nazi insults me, I no longer say anything back.

❡ Dinner at our friends' house. Her father is dying of cancer. 'It's hard to be next to someone who's dying, they go from one terrible mood to another in a matter of minutes,' she says. A few days later a friend's mother dies. Another aggressive cancer. My father and his brother, my uncle, both overcame bowel cancer a few years ago. In other words, my genes don't just have the T in hypertension, but also the C for cancer. Not forgetting the D for diabetes. I have the sneaking suspicion that a crow has landed on my tree. 'The white girl,' as they call her in Mexico, must have lost something around here. It's no coincidence that I just killed my sister in a story. And I haven't made a will, I don't have a dying wish and I can't imagine how my life will be without me.

Sometimes I wonder if I'm not externalising my frenzied consumption of five seasons of SIX FEET UNDER. I haven't watched anything else in the last two months and I feel alienated, as if I've put myself in the series or I'm going to die tomorrow. Someone dies at the beginning of every episode; in other words, over the course of five seasons we see some sixty ways to die: from an accident, disease, murder or old age; peacefully, prematurely, violently... In the final episode, flashforwards show us how each of the characters will die in scenes that only last a few seconds and end with their names and dates of death. It's the first time I've thought about the date of the year I'll die. If I live out my whole life and die naturally at an average age, I could die in the year 2050. My grandfather is 93 years old and in perfect health, so if I've been lucky enough to inherit his genes I might stretch it out until 2060. But no longer. I won't see 2070, or 2100. According to the website *theday-ofyourdeath.com* I'll die aged 62. 'You have 9,907 days, 00 hours, 14 minutes and 56 seconds left,' it warns me. *Yourfears.com* says I'll commit suicide on 30 December 2040 after losing everything. On *mydeath.com*, it says I'll die in 2024 in a paragliding accident. According to *beingdead.com*, my husband will beat me to death within two years. There are lots of videos on the internet of people talking to themselves and saying how they think they'll die. They're fun. I watch a 20-year-old girl say she's going to die of breast cancer aged 30, and that she's known this since she was a girl, although for the moment she's completely healthy. Death is more here than there.

In SWIMMING IN A SEA OF DEATH, David Rieff writes about the illness and death of his mother, Susan Sontag, and about her deep fear of death after suffering cancer three times throughout her life. He quotes a phrase from her diary: 'Death is unbearable unless you can get beyond the I.' Rieff assures us that, unlike other people, Sontag didn't manage that, partly due to the 'poisoned chalice of hope'. For example, the last poems Bertolt Brecht wrote from his deathbed, says Rieff, discuss the artist's reconciliation with the fact of death, like in the poem where he sees a bird sitting in a tree, whose beautiful song he thinks is even more beautiful knowing that when he dies the bird will still be singing. 'Now I managed to enjoy the song of every blackbird after me too,' he wrote.

Sontag, meanwhile, wounded by mortality, left us this phrase: 'In the valley of sorrow, spread your wings.'

¶ My scream startles my husband. Jaime runs to the bedroom and finds me crying with anxiety, clutching my breast.

'It's massive! Why didn't you notice it before?'

'Why didn't *you* notice it before? It's red, can you see?'

'Yes, it's red.'

First thing tomorrow we'll go to the hospital. I look at myself in the mirror again and again. I'm scared to touch it. It wasn't there a few days ago, I would have noticed it. Jaime tells me that if it is a tumour, and we're not sure it is, it'll be treatable. I remember the scene in Rieff's book when he describes how they remove Sontag's breast, an incredibly violent operation which, to get rid of all the diseased cells, has to gouge out a large part of her chest muscle.

I see myself through the looking glass and close my eyes.

I'm tired. It's exhausting being an adult, having to take care of everything and, for that reason, I've often wanted to get ill so people will look after me and I won't have to do anything. I'd be so happy if I could stay in bed watching TV series all the time and sucking liquid food through a straw! I've repeated this dangerous mantra so many times that I ask myself if this unmentionable desire has anything to do with my recent find in the mirror.

That night, unlike others, Jaime and I won't play with the idea of dying, we won't talk about who'll die first, in which ocean we'll scatter the other's ashes and who we'd choose to remarry in case of being widowed. It's not funny anymore. We say nothing and wait for dawn.

¶ Gynaecological emergencies share a waiting room with the labour ward. I watch the husbands pacing and the doctors busy bringing life into the world. At last it's my turn. The nurse asks me to go in alone. I hear a baby cry. The doctor examines me. She feels my breasts: 'I can see it,' she says, 'I can feel it.' I nearly faint.

While she touches my boob I try to cling to something. Something that isn't the word I don't want to pronounce and which, nevertheless, is in the head of every woman having a breast lump checked by a gynaecologist. All I can think about is another book I'm reading at the time, ironically: OTHER LIVES BUT MINE by Emmanuel Carrère, a true story of two events that shocked the author in a few months: the death of a child for her parents and the death of a woman for her children and husband. There I find a reference to the spectac- ular book *Mars* by Fritz Zorn, a bestseller that the Swiss writer delivered *in extremis* to his publishers days before dying. In the book he sticks a finger in the wound of the relationship between an insipid life and cancer. The book's opening pulls no punches: 'I'm young and rich and educated, and I'm unhap- py, neurotic and alone. I come from one of the best families on the east shore of Lake Zurich, the shore that people call the Gold Coast. My upbringing has been middle-class, and I have been a model of good behaviour all my life... And of course I have cancer. That follows logically enough from what I have just said about myself... [Cancer] is a psychic disorder and I can only regard its onset in an acute physical form as a great stroke of luck.'

Jaime is waiting for me outside. I go out and smile at him. He smiles back. I sit on his knee. I hug him. He hugs me back. We stay like that for a few long minutes. I've only got non-puerperal mastitis (one that doesn't occur when breastfeeding), an inflammatory lesion of the breast.

¶ My tomb is this mattress on which I'm going to travel. My eyes are covered. My carer promises she'll be watching. I breathe deeply, I breathe and I breathe and I breathe, but all I can think about is being there, about the faces of the others. I don't think they like me. Is it possible that I feel like I'm a really nice person but nobody in this workshop realises? The ideas that pop into my head make me think I'm light-years away from being reconciled with myself. Or maybe it's a survival instinct, which won't let me go over to the other side. But I carry on, I try, I breathe increasingly rhythmically. This is hard, when it would be so easy to take LSD or drink a bit of ayahuasca and save ourselves a whole lot of work. The *Star Wars* theme tune helps me concentrate. It's ridiculous, I know, but it reminds me of Jaime and Lena. I picture them. I hear some of the others shouting, having started their journeys. I feel almost cathartic now. My back starts hurting and I ask the workshop leader to ma- nipulate me. He comes and twists my shoulder blade. The pain is intense. He says in my ear: 'Shout, Gabriela, shout, what would you say to your mother?' I don't know where he got that about my mother, maybe from my drawing or the values test. The only thing I know is that it works. I cry like a little girl, like I did on nights that were too dark, a scream that comes from being alone and afraid: 'Mum, mum, muuuum!' I cry like a wretch. I cry like I haven't done for years. I cry in stereo. I cry so much that I think I've come here to get depressed. I cry and go through all my sad topics. I cry and ask myself if one day I'll be able to stop crying like a little girl. I cry and remember that I'm not the little girl anymore, there's another little girl now and I have to look after her. I cry because I'm everyone's daughter: my mother's, my husband's, my daughter's. I cry because I'm scared I'll fail as a mother. I say sorry to my little one for being the infantile person I am. I promise I'll be solid, patient and happy for her. Then I give myself over to the most absolute darkness, I allow it to come, to wrap me as if I'm being embraced by an enormous animal that swallows me and spits out my bones. Now I'm part of its shining pelt. The darkness is warm for the first time, like a black sun; my mind expands inside it. Crying is a way to empty out my contents. I'm empty now, as usual I've cried more than I should have, but I'm not sad because I haven't lost anything. I'm going with everything I am. In the final judgement – this experience tells me – the judge and the accused are the same person. And now I see the beautiful landscape and the blessed light at the end of the tunnel – the cultural fantasy of resurrection and the intuition of mystery – the path to the suspension of all pain, of all fear. I smile to myself. If this is what death is like I don't mind dying tomorrow. I feel someone covering me with a sheet. I've gone.

¶ The good news is that you do come round from this anaesthesia. The following day, in the final meeting where we describe our experiences, the workshop leader suggests an exercise for me: I should go into a corner and write a list of the things that do me good and another of the things that do me harm.

Things that do me harm: being connected to the internet all day, checking Facebook, bills, KFC, alcohol, drugs, not being with my daughter, my infantilism, the literary world, the pressure of having to write, people's contempt, frivolity, injustice, not being in Lima, salt, not doing exercise, judging others, judging myself.

Things that do me good: sex, Lena's love, Jaime's love, giving love, being loved, cooking, writing, sleeping, going out and seeing the sun, watching TV series with Jaime, laughing, doing absolutely nothing, doing something well, tenderness, not being in Lima, crying, eating healthily without salt.

The survival instinct is moralistic.

It's time to leave the workshop and apply its teachings in daily life. The participants are best friends all of a sudden, they exchange emails, make plans, tell each other about new workshops where they can meet again and carry on trying to find their place in the universe.

It hasn't been one of the most important experiences of my life, as that girl promised, but I feel good, in harmony, so much so that I carry on letting go and head out to walk alone and fulfilled in the countryside; I follow a path that goes into the woods, I walk and walk without looking back, I go a long way without realising and, all of a sudden, I stop still and, looking around me, in the midst of that natural solitude, I become myself again: in other words, I'm afraid an animal will come out and eat me, I remember that I have to go home, to the only place where I feel safe.

¶ I'm getting rid of Lena's nits while she watches TV with her friend Gael. She caught nits at school again. I drag one out with the comb and kill it. Lena is watching *ASHA'S INCREDIBLE ADVENTURE*. Asha's fish dies in this episode. A friend explains to her that after death there are three possible paths: you disappear, you go to heaven or you're reincarnated.

'What would you come back as?' I ask Lena, but she doesn't answer.

'What would you come back as, Gael? I'd come back as a tree, for example...'

'I'd be a lion.'

'And what about you, Lena?' I press her. 'Go on, say what you'd come back as. A flower? A butterfly? A princess?'

'As me, end of.'

The blood tests showed no problem with cholesterol, kidney function or blood sugar. I'm absolutely fine except for my blood pressure. My diet is pretty boring and I've managed to lose plenty of weight. They'll check my blood pressure again in three months, and if it carries on like it is now, they'll probably increase my dose of Enalapril and I'll keep taking it for life. Beyond that, everything is unpredictable.

I don't know yet where I want my ashes to be scattered. A good place would be in the Nanay river, which goes past Manacamiri, a small village near Iquitos in the Peruvian Amazon, where Jaime and I were really happy. Or perhaps, so as to not suffer from exoticism, in the Mar de Grau, in Lima, where I hope to return one day, or in the Mediterranean, if I don't go back. In the years I've got left, which I hope will be many, I can't write it off, I might find another significant place to spread my wings in this valley of sadness and joy.

On my imaginary headstone, death is still a blank space to be filled. And rain makes the weeds grow.

A VICIOUS CYCLE
BY EVAN LAVENDER-SMITH

I HAVE SEEN THE BUMPER STICKERS ON THE BUMPER OF
YOUR TOYOTA PRIUS therefore I have induced that you believe you
are working here to make the world greener. You should know I voted for
President George W. Bush twice and I would have voted for him a third time
if they had let me. At present there are major differences between you and I.
Normally I do not like people like you. If you were anybody else we would
have major personal issues between us which I would not let you forget and I
would consistently be doing things to irritate you and get under your skin and
I would probably be handing you your ass on a regular basis. I do not believe
global warming has been caused by humans nor do I believe we are going to
run out of oil any time soon. I have three Daughters who are in elementary
school. Maya is in the first grade. Halley is in the third grade. Celeste is in
the fifth grade. I love my Daughters in a fierce and animalistic way which
I cannot describe using words so I am not even going to try for that in this
letter. My Daughters have been indoctrinated to believe that global warming
has been caused by humans pumping carbon dioxide into the atmosphere and
that we are going to run out of fossil fuels sometime next week. I allow them
to continue believing in these falsities because I am a hero to them for working at a Recycling Plant. I have visited their classes on the days when Fathers
are asked to come in and talk about their jobs and when I say I work at a
Recycling Plant the teacher and the students look upon me with supreme awe
and reverence. I will admit I like my girls thinking what I do is crucial to the
welfare of the planet. I will admit I like people thinking of me as a real hero
and yes I am going to keep it that way. However the fact is it would make not a
lick of difference to me if I were the guy whose job it is to steer oil tankers into
icebergs in order to drive up the price of gasoline if it paid better than what I
make here. One of the first things you are going to need to learn is we are not
here to save the world. You are going to need to get that saving the world crap
out of your head ASAP. What you are going to need to learn to understand
is that the only reason you are here is to sort through Recyclables as fast as
possible because if you lag on the belt or if you lag on the lot that is going to
fuck the rest of us up which means we will have to stay late with no overtime.
If you are not busting your ass out there like the rest of us then you will get
that same ass handed back to you. I do not care who your Grampappy is.

   Now as you may not know the man who works glass on the belt is named
Ricardo. The first piece of truly important advice I will impart to you is Do
Not Fuck With That Particular Mexican. Do not talk to him or look him in the
eyes even when he has his face mask on. Ricardo was incarcerated for seven-

teen years prior to his employment here for a reason that if I were to divulge it to you I am 100 per cent certain you would quit immediately and then I would find myself in a world of shit with Miss Heather. Ricardo has what are called anger issues and you will be able to tell exactly how careful you need to be around him based on his behaviour on the belt on any given day. If Ricardo is up there deliberately smashing bottles and allowing the shards of glass to pass onto the shredder that means you have to be extremely careful and sensitive toward him at all times. For example if you see Ricardo smashing bottles on the belt the first thing you have to be sure to never do is touch a glass bottle which comes out of the feeder. You are going to be working right in front of him so this is very critical to you. After you climb up your ladder and get to your station if you see Ricardo up there smashing bottles all over the place then you must not touch an unbroken glass bottle under any circumstances. Say you are working your #1's and say you see a crushed three-litre bottle of Mountain Dew which happens to be underneath or perhaps merely touching a glass bottle. Just let that Mountain Dew pass you by. It is not worth the risk. Of course Danny is going to be pissed if a crapload of #1's start coming his way and yes you will feel that pain. Danny works clean-up which means he is at the end of the belt. Danny is the one of us who has to deal with all the Recyclables we miss in order to prevent any and all Recyclables from going into the shredder. So say Ricardo is smashing bottles and say the feeder drops a crapload of glass and a crapload of #1's on the belt at the same time. What are you going to do? You are going to let those #1's pass you by. You cannot risk it. Say you reach for a #1 at the same time Ricardo is reaching for a glass bottle to smash and your hand gets in the way or by picking up your #1 you knock the glass bottle away from where Ricardo was reaching for it. If that happens Ricardo is going to grab another glass bottle and smash it on your hard hat or smash it on your face mask or most likely smash it on your hand. The glass will hopefully not penetrate your glove but your hand is going to hurt like hell no matter what and that is going to fuck your performance level up which means it is going to fuck the rest of our performance levels up. The belt is not going to stop just because you cannot move one of your hands. So you are going to need to go ahead and let those #1's pass you by which of course is going to fuck everything up too. What is going to happen is Danny is going to have to deal with all the #1's coming his way. Remember the bin for the #1's is behind you and also that you are on the opposite side of the belt from Danny which means Danny is going to have all these #1's coming his way and he is going to try to throw them across the belt down into the #1 bin

behind you. That is not easy. And if Danny starts missing and #1's start rico-
cheting off the sides of your bin and falling down onto the lot then the Illegals
working newspaper or cardboard down there are going to have to pick up the
#1's and toss them up into the bin in order to sort through all the Recyclables
they have to sort through. Now if Miss Heather looks out the window and
sees a pack of Illegals doing jump shots with #1's we are all fucked. Also
remember there is a good chance that if you have to let a crapload of #1's go
by in order to save yourself from the wrath of Ricardo then a lot of the #1's
which Danny has to deal with and try to throw past you are going to end up
hitting you in the face mask or hitting you in the chest and they will often
bounce off you and land back on the belt and head back toward Danny again
because generally when something hits you up there you do not have time to
react. So now that same #1 you let pass the first time is going to end up going
back to Danny again and Danny is going to throw it back your way again to
try and land it in your bin and of course there is a good chance that same #1 is
going to hit you and fall back on the belt again and head back toward Danny
again and he is going to throw it back at you again and all the while other #1's
will start passing you by because you will be distracted by Danny throwing
#1's your way which means more #1's will be coming his way and therefore
more #1's will be thrown your way and therefore even more #1's will get by
you. This is what we call a vicious cycle. A vicious cycle fucks everybody up
and everybody is going to want to hand you your ass and yes somebody will.
But trust me when I say the ass handing pursuant to a vicious cycle will not
be as painful as if Ricardo smashes a bottle on your hand. If and when one
of us hands you your ass on account of a vicious cycle we will hand it to you
only up to a point. All of us understand that vicious cycles are sometimes un-
avoidable. Thus there will be difficult decisions which you are going to have
to make up there on a daily basis. They will not be easy because for example
you are weighing the certainty of getting your ass handed to you on account
of a vicious cycle versus the uncertainty of Ricardo seriously injuring your
hand and maybe also getting your ass handed to you. If the glass penetrates
your glove and there is blood you will have another difficult decision on your
hands. You will then need to weigh going down to the trailer for stitches and
the certain ass handing you will later receive from one of us for fucking our
performance levels up by leaving us in the lurch versus the health risks associated with the amount of blood you will lose if you stay up on the belt with
a gash on your hand.

I can tell you are a smart kid despite your socialist political leanings which

I believe are an act of treason punishable by death but then again I am no judge. So I am sure from what I have stated above you can induce that if Ricardo were out of the equation things would not be so stressful up on the belt. But the fact of the matter is nobody will ever rat out Ricardo for his psychotic behaviour on the belt because everybody knows what Ricardo did to receive those seventeen years of incarceration and everybody up there has families and nobody is willing to take that risk. Not even Jimbo who could reach over and crush Ricardo's skull with his bare hands in two seconds flat. Or as many of us often fantasise Jimbo could reach over and push Ricardo backwards out of his station which would result in Ricardo falling thirty-five feet hopefully to his death and we could make it look like an accident. But Jimbo has got four Daughters ranging from 2 to 9 years of age and he will not take that risk. Lately Jimbo's Daughters have been over at my place being watched by my wife because Jimbo's wife Carla is once again despite eight months of sobriety back to huffing and Jimbo being the caring Father that he is knows his girls cannot be around that kind of shit under any circumstances. Carla is a beautiful woman. Carla is a beautiful soul and a good Mother too but that woman has a terrible disease called substance abuse which makes her look like shit and act like shit and makes her 100 per cent unfit to be a Mother. But here is the thing you need to realise. The thing you need to realise is all of us belt workers are part of a family. As you may not know everybody who works on the belt except for you and Ricardo are part of an amazing family which sticks together not only through the very best of times but also through the very most fucked up of times. If you want to become a part of this family then you are going to have to earn our trust. I am willing to give you the benefit of the doubt but right now none of the rest of us trust you. Right now there are a couple of us who still believe you are a spy. I do not personally believe you are a spy. I would not be sticking my neck out like this for you if I believed you were a spy because a lot of the shit I am telling you would fuck us all up if it got back to Miss Heather or your Grampappy. I do not know why you are here exactly but if you are planning to stick around and this is not just some summer gig where you think you are going to dip your big toe in real life for a minute then split the first thing I would suggest is you sell that alien ship car and use the money to buy yourself a brand new Chevrolet truck. Most of us think I am nuts to be taking any sort of interest in you and I have taken no small amount of shit for my interest in reaching a hand out to you like this but the fact is I was once 17 years old and I was equally misguided and I could have used some words of wisdom and a good family like this one to go to for support when I needed it. So I guess I am doing this out of the goodness of my heart even though there are certain things about you which make me want to kill you. I will not lie when I say that on Monday there was a moment on the belt when you threw a #2 over your shoulder and I had to do everything in my power to stop myself from pulling you out of your station and pinning you down on the belt and letting the shredder have its way with you. That is how Dale died. As you may not know Dale is the name of the man you are replacing on #1's. But the difference is Dale going through the shredder was an accident and I am talking about pushing you down into the shredder on purpose.

I will return to my discussion of the interpersonal human dynamics of the belt in a minute but before I forget I need to remind you that the temperature on the lot regularly reaches 140 degrees Fahrenheit and the temperature on the belt even though there is the canopy and there are finally misters thanks to the political manoeuvrings of yours truly runs to around 120 degrees Fahrenheit. Now there is a big difference in those 20 degrees. It is like the difference between being on the surface of Mercury without any liquid cooling in your space suit versus being in a mild climate with a cool ocean breeze swirling all around your naked chest. It is a difference which you will come to understand quite well if you have not done so already. Now all of us prefer the belt to the lot because of those 20 degrees even though the belt constitutes a much more hazardous work environment than the lot. Most of us are going to want to work the belt as much as possible and for the time being that means you are probably going to have to work the lot more than you would like even though you are not an Illegal. The Illegals spend 100 per cent of their time working the lot because they are willing to do anything for a buck and they do not really understand the difference anyhow. Also you have to speak English to work the belt. That is a regulation put in place for safety reasons even though no one talks up there because there is also a regulation which states that everybody must wear ear plugs at all times on the belt and therefore we cannot hear any English which we might want to speak. Some of the Illegals probably speak enough English to work the belt but we do not let them unless one of us is out sick in which case Marcus will go to the lot and ask, 'Which of you Illegals speaks English?' and all of them will raise their hands until Marcus asks a more specific question like, 'What is the opposite of hot?' and only a few of them will be able to answer it. Marcus will then choose from one of the Illegals who said, 'Cold.' I am sure it is going to be hard for someone like you who comes from a privileged liberal upbringing and believes everyone deserves the same rights and the same respect but you are going to need to learn to think of the Illegals as basically animals and you cannot concern yourself about whether they get seriously injured in the workplace. There is at least one serious injury on the lot every day. There is usually one serious injury on the belt per week. By serious injury on the belt I mean an injury which results in the worker needing to go to Miss Heather's trailer for medical attention or needing to go for offsite care. If you work the numbers you will understand the belt is more dangerous given that there are only seven of us up there whereas there are about forty Illegals working the lot plus most of the accidents which happen to the Illegals on the lot would not happen to you or I because we possess human reason. When one of the Illegals sustains a serious injury he is fired on the spot. That might seem unfair to you but the fact of the matter is that son of a bitch was lucky to have that job in the first place. We are all our brother's keeper is something I believe in down to the very deepest most recesses of my soul but what you are going to need to learn to understand is that Christian doctrines do not apply to the Illegals and if one of us sees you treating them with respect or mingling with them like you were doing yesterday then one of us will most certainly be handing you your ass later that same day.

You will get your ass handed to you if you sustain a serious injury unless it is so serious you have to go for offsite care. If you have to go for offsite care and you end up in the hospital you will be visited by our Wives who will bring chocolates and flowers and such things to you. If it looks like you are not going to make it then I would not be surprised if you were visited by two or three of us belt workers ourselves even if something like that happened to you this week which it absolutely will if you do not heed the advice being presented herein. If you stick around and end up becoming one of us then all five of us brothers will be there by your side from the minute we get off work until the minute we hit the bar. Believe it or not even Ricardo showed up at the hospital where they took Dale after the accident. Ricardo came into the waiting room with an empty Heineken bottle in his hand and we all went to cover the heads of our Wives and Daughters but then Ricardo gently placed the bottle down on the bedside table next to some flowers. I do not know what kind of get well present an empty Heineken bottle represents. That sort of thing only emphasises Ricardo's psychotic nature but we all had to admit at least it was something which was why Billy and Marcus and I stopped plotting to kill Ricardo every day over lunch. Now listen up. Dale worked the #1 station on the belt for nine years. Those are some very big shoes you are going to have to fill. I guess you would say Dale was our equivalent of a genius. I remember for example coming in late on a Monday morning last year because the girls missed the bus and Debra was down with the flu and I was walking through the lot toward the belt whereupon I found myself bearing witness to two perfect streams of #1's flowing forth from above Dale's shoulders. I am talking about two perfect parabolas of #1's spinning end over end which would rise from Dale's shoulders high into the sky and then begin to fall and finally land smack dab in the middle of the #1 bin. It was like something out of one of Maya's cartoons. Or it was like something you get to see maybe once in your life like Halley's Comet or an act of superhuman ability like somebody lifting a two-ton Chevy under which one of his Daughters got pinned. That is the kind of amazing I am talking about and that is the kind of amazing you are going to have to become if you want to become a member of a truly amazing family such as this.

There is some other stuff you need to know. You have been here now for almost a month therefore I will induce that you have noticed all of us belt workers wear pink bandannas under our hard hats and there is a reason for this which is not that any of us are homosexuals. We have noticed you alternate between wearing a blue bandanna and a green bandanna. If you do not change to wearing pink bandannas exclusively then you will be putting your human welfare at serious risk and here is why. As you may not know Billy is the name of the man who works aluminium next to me on the belt and he is also one of the Bobcat and front loader operators on the lot. Billy is a truly racist individual and he has it out for the Illegals in a way which none of us really understand but Billy is who he is and there is nothing to be done about that. On the lot none of us ever wear our hard hats even though it is technically against regulation but Miss Heather does not say anything because the Illegals are not provided with hard hats and therefore that regulation is not enforced. When Billy is operating the Bobcat or the front loader it is these pink bandannas we wear which serve to distinguish us from the Illegals none of which ever wear pink bandannas because I am sure in Mexico just like in the USA pink bandannas are the code word for homosexual. As I saw on the Discovery Channel while watching a nature documentary for one of Celeste's biology homework assignments homosexuality rears its sinful head among all species alike. Now I am not a racist but I am also not stupid. You may have been taught racism and stupidity go hand in hand but that is 100 per cent incorrect because Billy is indeed racist but he is not at all stupid. Billy went to two years of community college plus a year of regular college and if Billy has an opportunity to seriously injure an Illegal with the Bobcat or the front loader without getting caught then oftentimes depending on what is going on in his head at that moment he is absolutely going to do it. He will not ever do it out in the open in front of all the others but say if a couple of them happen to head off alone to collect some newspaper which the wind has blown over near the freight containers then you bet your ass if Billy is driving the front loader and sees them he will punch the gas and follow them out there either to screw with them or to seriously injure them or both. But now here is the thing so listen up. All of us love it out there by the freight containers because there is so much shade and that is where we go to take a nap or relax if we happened to find a good magazine on the lot that day. This is something else I am going to have to tell you about because there is a system in place for determining who gets to take which magazines home and you must respect that system even if you feel you are being short changed because maintaining trust amongst one another depends in large part on everybody following the rules of the system we have set up for the allocation of the magazines which get found nearly every day amongst the newspaper and the cardboard. For example if you ever find an astronomy magazine or a science magazine that has something to do with outer space you have to hand it over to me with no questions asked because the universe is a serious hobby of mine. Likewise if you find any fishing magazines or any magazines regarding mature nude models then you have to hand those over to Jimbo. But if you go back there by the freight containers to read your magazine there is a chance especially if he is blasted that Billy might follow you and crush you against the wall with the front loader or run you over with the Bobcat but if you are wearing a pink bandanna he will not do so no matter how drunk or psychotic he happens to be at that moment because not only does Billy believe passionately in the eradication of all peoples who are not of Aryan lineage he believes with equal passion in the preservation of all Aryan peoples of which you are one. When Billy sees that pink bandanna on your head his racist passion will override his drunken psychotic rage and you will be OK.

All of us except Ricardo rotate showing up early before Miss Heather gets in to deposit a twenty-pound bag of ice and seventy-two cans of Miller in the big blue cooler we have stashed behind one of the freight containers and we have to drink those beers pretty fast during lunch which is why the majority of serious injuries occur between one o'clock and two o'clock in the afternoon which was when Dale suffered the serious injury which resulted in his death. If you become a part of us and your turn comes to bring the beer and you forget to bring it or if you forget the ice or if you buy anything except for Miller then you will receive an ass handing the manner of which is inconceivable to you at present given what I imagine to be the privileged conditions of your liberal upbringing. And let me say now before I forget that if those bumper stickers are not removed from your vehicle by tomorrow I will do it myself. I have worked here for eleven years so I know what I am talking about when I say a lot of shit about you is going to have to change very soon or else there will be no future for you here.

I am coming to the end of this but there are a couple other things you need to know. You need to know all of us belt workers have only Daughters except for you because you are only 17 years old and you have not started a family quite yet. I have three Daughters. Jimbo has four Daughters. Billy has a Daughter and another Daughter in the oven. Marcus has two Daughters who are twins. Danny has a Daughter. Dale had a Daughter. Even Ricardo has two step-Daughters if you can believe it. That makes fifteen total Daughters. Sometimes we talk about the fact that we all have only Daughters. All of us wanted only Sons but I think now we are mostly fine having only Daughters. For the past couple of years on one Sunday a month we all get together with all of our Daughters while our Wives go off together to see a movie. You might be wondering what a bunch of guys like us do with a bunch of little Daughters running around all over the place. Well of course we drink beer but we cannot get blasted because we are solely responsible for the welfare of our Daughters during those three hours our Wives are at the movies and we take that responsibility very seriously but also because our Wives leave us with a strict ration of beer. I know you are only 17 years old but if you really do want to become a part of us then you are going to have to start drinking a lot of beer and you are probably also going to have to have yourself a Daughter. Dale has been dead for over six months so maybe I should introduce you to Jolene. You and her might end up getting hitched and then you can help raise Tiffany and you can come over and be with us on Sunday afternoons if you start to change your ways. One of the other things we do on Sundays is play hopscotch on the driveway but I am not going to get into that here. You look at these guys on the belt and you try to imagine them on their knees drawing hopscotch lines in all the colours of the rainbow and then hopping around the driveway with a bunch of beautiful little Daughters. The other day I snuck up on Jimbo by the freight containers to find him jacking off to nudey photographs of 80-year-olds. Last week at lunch I saw Marcus break a Miller bottle over his bare head for no reason whatsoever. Try to watch in your head

Billy chasing down an Illegal with the front loader and then try to see him hopping his way across the grass of my backyard with his feet and the skinny legs of all these amazing Daughters of ours tied up in potato sacks. That might seem like a paradox to you right now but if and when you become one of us I guarantee you will soon learn to see it is all in perfect accordance with the universal rules of human logic.

There are many other things you need to know but I do not have time to get into all of them so I will conclude by telling you what happened to Dale so you know whose shoes you will be filling and then you are just going to have to pick up the rest as you go along.

Like I said Dale's accident occurred between one o'clock and two o'clock which means that we were 100 per cent blasted. Dale usually does not imbibe as much beer over lunch as the rest of us. Usually Dale only drinks six or seven beers but on this particular day he drank ten or eleven beers. Dale and Jolene had a big fight the previous night and that is why he drank more than usual which is completely understandable. I remember all through lunch as he was drinking those beers he could not stop talking about what an asshole he had been to Jolene the previous night and how much he regretted this thing he said and that thing he said and all of us tried to console him by telling him we were 100 per cent sure Jolene deserved whatever terrible things he had said to her. At one point he started crying and I will tell you in my eleven years working here I have never seen a man cry at this Recycling Plant even during the most brutal of ass handings. When we got back to the belt everything seemed to be going smoothly. Dale was tossing #1's over his shoulders like the true Olympian athlete I will always remember him as but then all of a sudden he decided to stop I guess on account of a sudden re-emergence of those sore feelings about what occurred between Jolene and him the previous night and he starting letting all the #1's pass him by. Danny was not expecting a vicious cycle because Ricardo was not breaking bottles that day but a vicious cycle is exactly what Danny got and when you are blasted a vicious cycle becomes vicious to the second power. Danny started throwing #1's in the direction of Dale and trying to land them in the #1 bin but most of them ended up back on the belt and of course all that time more and more #1's were coming out of the feeder and pretty soon it seemed like all there was up there was #1's. It was like a river of #1's maybe three or four feet deep and so at that point all of us even Ricardo started double-shifting on #1's because we knew Dale was out of the game and we knew if one of us hit our Emergency Kill Button just because of a vicious cycle we would be in a universe of shit with Miss Heather. I turned to look at Dale and saw him standing in his station with his arms at his sides and his head down and I think I saw those tears again but it is hard to say because of how many #1's were bouncing off his face mask and his hard hat at the time. I remember I looked over to the shredder and I saw some legs and jeans being twisted up together like some braids of hair and at the time I did not believe that what I saw could actually be what I thought I saw by which I mean it did not register in my brain that those could in fact be the legs and jeans of Dale. One minute he was standing there in his station and then another minute he was not there anymore. Try to think of something you are always used to seeing where it is like Polaris commonly known as the North Star and then one night you look and it is not there anymore because it went supernova. To you it is just something out there far away that is gone but up close there was a whole world there or even many worlds if it had orbiting planets and even more worlds if those planets themselves had moons. That is how I think of the passing of Dale by which I mean some worlds disappeared that day including the ones created by him and I when we would engage in our lengthy conversations at the end of the bar in which we shared together our theories concerning all the physical properties of the universe.

Danny later told us he saw a pair of boots amongst the river of #1's headed down into the shredder but he thought nothing of it because stuff like old boots is exactly the sort of trash Danny often lets pass through because liberals will mix stuff like old boots in with their Recyclables because they do not understand the difference between charity and sustainability. Liberals just close their eyes and grab blindly at ways to save the world. And it is good folks like Dale and the rest of us here who end up suffering the consequences. I have worked here for eleven years and not once in all that time have I ever personally recycled a Recyclable. At my house we have a bin designated Garbage and a bin designated Recyclables and the girls love to come ask me whether this piece of plastic or that piece of plastic is a Recyclable and I tell them the truth and then watch as they toss it in the appropriate bin. Once per week they help me load the Recyclables bin in the Chevy and on my drive to work I make a detour to the dumpster behind the Big K and dump all the Recyclables in the trash. That is another thing. If we ever catch you recycling a Recyclable outside of the Recycling Plant your ass will be handed to you and when you look down at your ass it will appear to you as if your ass itself has been recycled. Now there is one I am sure even your Grampappy would appreciate.

You must think carefully about everything I have told you and ask yourself if you believe you have the strength and courage of character to join us in a very serious way. If you think you do then I will keep sticking my neck out for you and eventually you will become part of us because these guys look up to me. I am their moral leader because I am the one who convinced Miss Heather to let us run water to the belt and install the misters which was a very big deal around here. If you think you do not possess the required character traits or if you are not willing to do the hard work to learn them then let me know and I will aid you in your departure by which I mean your ass and my foot will have a brief but highly productive meeting.

Now go back and read this whole thing over a few times and then once you have it memorised you will need to burn these pages to a crisp with the matches I have included and then come see me first thing tomorrow with your answer. We will be waiting for you out behind the freight containers. I cannot speak for the others but at least one of us will be hoping you make the decision to join us and that is all it takes. Like it says on your bumper sticker which will soon be removed either by your hand or by my hand holding a tool which was not designed for the removal of bumper stickers One Voice Can Change The World.

LISTENING TO YOURSELF
BY
LAWRENCE ABU HAMDAN

IN THE EARLY 2000s, Belgium, Germany, Holland, Sweden, Switzerland, the United Kingdom, New Zealand and Australia began implementing a screening technique for asylum seekers and undocumented migrants called 'Language Analysis for the Determination of Origin' (LADO). This attempts to determine if the accent of an undocumented migrant corroborates their claim of national identity. For example, the authorities aim to determine – based on accent alone – whether a Somali is from Mogadishu (a legitimate place from which to claim asylum) or in fact from northern Somalia (considered a safe place to live and thus to be deported back to). The tender to carry out these tests was mostly won by two private Swedish companies, Sprakab and Verified. These companies conducted phone interviews with asylum applicants in the target countries, using Sweden's largely unemployed former refugee population as a resource of informants to listen in on calls and conduct interviews. These informants' non-scientific assertions on where they thought people 'really' came from were then reworked by linguists, who bolstered the claims with international phonetic symbols and turned them into forensic reports for use in court in the target countries.

When academic linguists throughout the world were alerted to this flawed screening process, they began to contest its ideology of monolingualism. Linguists insisted that the voice is not a bureaucratic document, but rather a biography, and an index of everyone you have ever spoken to. The itinerant lives of refugees meant that their voices in particular should not be used as a national identifier. They argued that while the informants conducting the interviews may speak the same language as the applicant, they frequently were not from the same place. This could affect the dialogue and the quality of the data. After hundreds of wrongful deportations, governments finally began to listen to these campaigning linguists. Yet rather than scrap LADO, they insidiously incorporated the critiques, deciding that since dialogue was rendering the tests unscientific, they would use monologues instead. Now, rather than soliciting speech in an interview, asylum seekers were expected to simply speak for fifteen minutes non-stop. They were free to say anything they wanted, because nothing they said had any relevance. Only their accents mattered. One of these accounts is reproduced over the following pages: the words this time emptied of their voice. What seems at first like an anxious stream of consciousness is in fact a precise account of the weaponisation of freedom of speech, which is reaching its nightmare conclusion in today's liberal democracies.

ESSAY

AUDITOR: Off you go.

ASYLUM SPEAKER: Umm... Good morning. I am a married woman. I have two children, [breathes in] that is I have two daughters, very pretty [breathes in]. One of them is 15 years old, the eldest, [breathes in] and the youngest is still 12 years old. My daughters I feel are the most precious thing in my life. [Sharp intake of breath] Umm... I feel that happiness and the whole world come from them. [Breathes in] How much I love them I cannot possibly describe to anyone at all, because they are the soul and spirit inside of me and my body. I wish for God Almighty to keep them for me and that I be destined to be able to raise them as best I can so they are productive in society. [Breathes in] I would like to talk a little, I am remembering now, and often remember, my school. How I used to go to school when I was little, how they used to treat us in school. [Breathes in] Maybe there are some very nice things that one can remember, but there are also some very painful things. I studied and learned and was very good at school, I always liked going to school. Even if I was sick, nothing mattered [breathes in], whatever it was. I used to always go to school, even if I was tired and sick. Although I went through some very difficult experiences [large sigh], I experienced some difficult health issues, I was very distressed as I had to undergo surgeries [breathes in], but in spite of that, to me school was always the core of my life. [Breathes in] And I was very studious, I never missed a class. Umm... one time, and I can never forget this... One time I was at school and I was in tenth grade, [breathes in] I was a little late one morning. In order to make it on time and not be very late, I started running. I ran and ran [stretches word] from my parents' home until I reached school. I went in, our first class was Arabic language [breathes in]. I entered, I got there and I entered, I knocked on the door and I entered. Our teacher was there, and she had started giving the class. So she looked at my face and said [imitates a stern tone], 'What's up with you? Where were you?' I told her [imitates an innocent tone], 'I am very sorry teacher, I apologise, but I am late because the alarm didn't ring at home.' She looked at me and started berating me, using nasty words, I can't repeat them because when I remember them and repeat them, I feel a lot of pain and a lot of pressure that I don't need in my life. [Breathes in] Anyway the important part of the story is that she said, 'So you are late to school and you have make-up on?' I told her, 'I am not wearing make-up teacher,' because my mum and dad were very strict about this, [raises the pitch of her voice] 'It's shameful for a girl to wear make-up, a girl should not dress this way, a girl should not speak this way.' [Breathes in] So all the time, thank God, they had raised us in the best way. I swore to her by the Qur'an that I hadn't done anything, that I wasn't wearing make-up on my face, that I had never used any [*breathes in*]. She opened her bag and took out a Kleenex tissue, and the colour of the tissue, I remember, was white. [*Breathes in*] And she started rubbing and rubbing [*stretches word*] and rubbing my face, and my face was getting redder and redder. She'd rub and look at the tissue and see that it was clean, there was nothing on it, nothing that indicated that I had make-up on my face. But because my skin is white, and I'd been running, and I felt very hot from running, my face and cheeks turned very red [*breathes in*]. She looked at me and said, 'Go [*short pause*], get out of my face and sit in your place' [*breathes in*]. Although I was one of the best students in her class, [*swallows*] but what she thought at the time, I have no idea [*breathes in*]. Unfortunately some memories are painful [*discreetly clears throat, swallows*], but nevertheless, some experiences that a person goes through are very difficult to forget [*fingers tapping on table*]. [*Breathes in*] Another thing, also one time at school [*exhales*], umm... the teacher responsible for discipline at school. I came to school, and my mother had forgotten to wash my trousers the day before, my school trousers, the uniform that we all wore. So I had to wear other trousers. And I went to school. The teacher saw me, or the supervisor. She said to me, 'Come here you why aren't you wearing the complete uniform?' [*Fingers tapping on table resumes*] I told her my mother didn't have time to wash it, what could I do I had to wear whatever trousers I had...

TYPIST: [*Whispers something inaudible to the auditor*]

ASYLUM SPEAKER: [*Breathes in, catches breath*], or different colour trousers [*resumes breathing in*]. In order to punish me, she made me take off my shoes...

TYPIST: [*Whispers to the auditor, louder this time but still hard to make out*]

ASYLUM SPEAKER: ...and stand in a pool of water, and the water was very very cold, it was ice cold, I remember that very well, because I was in the ninth grade then [*breathes in*]. It was very cold, and she made me take off my shoes, as well as my socks, everything, and to stand in the pool. When I got very cold and I felt that I could no longer stand there with my feet in the cold water, I started shouting and crying. When I shouted and cried, she took me out of the pool. Then, and as a result of this, I had renal colic because I was suffering from a kidney stone. If I caught the cold, I would have an episode,

the pain wouldn't stop until I was admitted to the hospital and given tran-
quiliser and painkiller shots [*sighs*]. Of course the director came out because
of the sound and noise we made in the schoolyard. She said, 'What's wrong
with you?' [*Voice hardens*] I told her, 'I have a pain in my kidney, [*raises pitch of
voice*] I can't take the pain anymore, I need medicine. Call my dad so he can
come and take me to the hospital.' Of course the school director knew my
father well and had a very good relationship with him. And she used to visit
us at home sometimes. [*Breathes in*] When she saw me like this she told her,
'Couldn't you find another student than this one to punish?' She spoke to the
teacher, 'She's one of the very polite students in school this one, [*breathes in*]
she doesn't neglect her duties, she's well raised by her parents, why did you do
this to her today?' The supervisor told her [*imitates a belligerent tone*], 'Because
she has changed her trousers, she's wearing different trousers.' She thought of
course that I had liked to embellish and beautify myself and that sort of thing,
but I didn't have that intention or thought at all. It was just that I didn't find
other trousers to wear because the other ones were dirty [*discreetly clears
throat, breathes in*]. Anyhow she took me to the administration, to the administration room [*breathes in*], the director, she sat me down there for a bit, she
brought me a hot cup of tea, and gave me a pill, a painkiller from her drawer.
And she called my dad. Of course my dad came and took me from there in the
car to the hospital. As a result, I spent the night at the hospital, and they had
to do a surgical operation. [*Foot tapping on floor*] Now I'd like to speak a little
about my childhood memories. [*In the background, the sound of a key turning in
a lock*] I was living happily, I remember, with my parents, my sisters and
brothers. [*Breathes in*] We are, praise God, a large family, may the evil eye be
shamed. I had many girlfriends at school, and also in the area I was living in
[*swallows*], but the dearest one to my heart and best friend, she's my lifelong
friend, her name was Serene. May God ease her way and give her happiness
wherever she goes. She was someone a person could really trust [*breathes in*],
a person who deserves all my appreciation and respect. [*Breathes in*] Because
she is someone who stood by me through many difficulties and through life's
trials, that one naturally goes through. Of course life is full of them, and
every person has certainly gone through a lot, and yet, this person I would
always feel standing by me. I remember, even in 1980, when I had my operation, how she stood by me, how she cried [*pronounces word emphatically*], when
they took me to the operating room, how when I came out and woke up from
the anesthesia, I felt her standing beside me, waiting for me to open my eyes.
She felt with my pain, and laughed with my laughter. She used to be with me

the whole time, we went to the same school, the same class, even the same bus [*catches breath*] where we sat together. A wonderful person, I can't describe her. But I also had another friend, we used to be together all the time the three of us, our parents used to call us 'the merry trio'. [*Breathes in*] We used to hang out together, we slept over at each other's house sometimes. Once, she and I, on New Year's Eve, I told my parents that I would like to spend it at her house [*breathes in*], to hang out just the two of us. Her parents weren't home, they were going out somewhere [*breathes in*]. We sat together, she had prepared food, she had made *mulukhiyyeh* and other delicious dishes that we liked, we stayed up late just the two of us, there was nobody else there at all at all [*swallows*]. We stayed up almost until the next morning [*breathes in*], we didn't sleep until maybe after six o'clock in the morning [*breathes in*]. [*Chair leg scrapes on the linoleum floor*] We would talk about how our school day went, what our childhood was like, we talked about our shared memories, the bitter and the sweet, and sometimes laughed at each other. Anyhow, we spent the whole night drinking juice and drinking tea, and smoking also of course, smoking was forbidden, it was shameful for a girl to smoke, but maybe to me it was something new, and I felt like trying it. But now that I'm grown up, I feel that my parents were right, they used to always tell me, [*imitating strict tone*] 'Don't smoke, it's shameful.' Maybe they said it was shameful for a girl to smoke, but at the same time, they shouldn't have just said it is shameful, they should have explained to me why it was shameful, maybe they could have said that it is dangerous for the health, maybe I could have been more convinced, but just that it's shameful, that I shouldn't do it because it's shameful, why not tell me from the beginning that it is dangerous, healthwise, that it hurts the lungs, that it harms a person's health, even fitness decreases with time because of it, with the years and with age, you can no longer breathe normally, it causes constriction in the arteries, it could lead to heart attacks God forbid, it could cause many health problems. [*Breathes in sharply*] But unfortunately this health education was not at all available to any of our parents. Maybe, when they forbade us to do certain things, they thought, first and foremost, that it was shameful, because society said it was shameful, because it is shameful for a girl to go out, it is shameful for a girl to come in, it is shameful for a girl to smoke, it is shameful for a girl for example, to do this or that. At least explain to us, you're supposed to raise some kind of awareness in us, [*breathes in*] something that I used to read about a lot in books, and it was a hobby of mine, reading, I liked books. [*Breathes in*] I read many books. Until now, the story that I can never forget as long as I live [*breathes in*] is THE MOTHER, by Maxim

Gorky. I liked his novels a lot. I also read, with my friend that I am speaking about, Serene, I read a lot of books by al-Manfaluti. Until now I remember one of the stories, it was called 'Majdaline', it was very beautiful. Praise God books were always accessible to me [*breathes in*], I loved reading, I liked, what I liked most of all was to sit on the couch and just read. [*Breathes in*] I wasn't that much into watching television, because I always felt like: so what are all these programmes? [*Breathes in*] They are just entertainment, but not useful mentally, there's no culture in them, no educational value, whether in terms of health awareness or any other kind [*breathes in*]. So I wasn't too interested in sitting and watching TV series, very rarely, although I felt that the rest of the family was. And maybe that's the time that we as a family would sit together, we'd sit, eat together, and watch television together [*breathes in*]. Especially during the evenings of Ramadan, may God allow it many returns, always in prosperity and good health for all. It was a month that brought together the family. Our customs during Ramadan were very enjoyable, we used to prepare a variety of dishes, [*swallows*] my mum used to always cook *sayyadiyyeh*, which the whole family [*breathes in*] loves. We'd sit, gather together and eat, she used to like making tabbouleh, and we liked it a lot, especially when we were little, and I still love it and prepare it for my children, and my girls like it very very much. They always tell me, 'Mum cook for us, make us *umlukhiyyeh*, make us tabbouleh, make us fattoush', the dishes that they like and enjoy very much. I try as much as I can to make the food that they like, always. [*Breathes in*] Anyway the nights of Ramadan were the most beautiful nights of the year, especially on the night of Eid when the Takbir for the feast would begin, it was a very very beautiful thing. We would sit and make the *kaak* biscuits together, the *kaak* for Eid, we'd get together with the neighbours [*breathes in*]. These were the beautiful moments and occasions. [*Sharp intake of breath*]

AUDITOR: OK, thank you, that is enough.

A SAMURAI WATCHES THE SUN RISE IN ACAPULCO BY ÁLVARO ENRIGUE

tr. RAHUL BERY

TO MIQUEL

I possess my death. She is in my hands and within the spirals of my inner ears.
She is in the balls of my eyes because she is my eyes. If you are having a bad day,
my eyes are also your death. My death creeps carefully around the spiral of your
inner ear and pushes out buds through the branches of your fingers.

He met Misaki Konishi in his living room. When he entered Misaki was
squatting down, reading. The servant barely cleared his throat before an-
nouncing the visitor's name: Itakura no Goro. The old man raised his face
and made a slight movement of the head in the direction of his guest. He responded martially. Ask my wife to prepare the tea. The servant disappeared
behind the sliding door. Misaki tried to stand up. Aren't you going to help
me? he said. The samurai hurried to do so, looking away so as not to humili-
ate him. Now standing, the old man placed a hand on his lower back and gave
a bow, possibly ironic, to which Itakura once again responded in earnest.
The old man smiled: I see that your heart remains in Kyushu; you are from
Kyushu, no? From Nagoya. You are among friends. The old man purposefully looked towards his stick, which had been left on the floor. The samurai
stepped forward to pick it up, and held it out to him. A beautiful city, Nagoya;
I'm from a fishing village; they call me Misaki because that's where I'm from;
the name with which I was born is Ogata, Ogata Konishi. Itakura nodded,
barely closing his eyes, which made the old man smile again. I tell you, you're
among friends, he said. Leaning on his stick, he indicated the panel which
opened to the garden, at the back of the living room.

To Itakura it seemed that, more than being old, Misaki represented age
itself. Did you leave any family behind in Nagoya? he asked. A wife, and two
male children. They'll have opportunities in the city, they won't be forced
to do as I did. They didn't stay in Nagoya, they went to Hara, said Itakura.
A flash of consternation took hold of Misaki's face for a second. His inter-
locutor noticed it, but did not want to bother the old man with a personal
question, and instead showed interest in the *kakemonos* that hung on the walls.
They were my father's, replied Misaki, he bought and sold drawings between
one war and another and ended up with a collection; that's where my liking
for business must have come from. Itakura nodded discreetly. He was both
things, a driver of men, but also someone who knew how to enjoy the benefits
of a bit of money, I'm the same; you are a *ronin*, aren't you? Itakura responded
negatively: I work for the *daimyo*. Kumigashira? The samurai replied: *Mono-*

rashira, but I have a very small division, twenty men. From *Nihon*? Just one, the rest are Negroes, Indians, mulattoes, Filipinos. That's more than enough for the task I wish to entrust to you, said the old man. He sighed, then continued: I too was a soldier. Itakura straightened his back, or made a gesture which revealed that it was totally rigid. With all due respect, he said, I know who Ogata Konishi is: you were a general. *Sodaisho*, the old man finished, and for the first time in the conversation it was evident from how energetic his vowels were that he was a man who had commanded multitudes. But I fell into disgrace, for the same reasons as you, and now I am an old and foolish trader who can no longer defend his own merchandise; I am going to pay you very well so that you may carry out the task as I myself would have done it. Itakura lowered his head.

Before drawing back the sliding door that gave onto the garden, Misaki halted. You'll have to excuse my wife during the tea ceremony, she has not got the hang of it. Itakura looked at him with curiosity. And she did not let me educate my sons as drivers of men, and therefore I have to resort to strangers – no offence intended. Itakura shook his head almost imperceptibly. Her name is Josefa, said the old man, looking him in the eye. He noted with satisfaction that Itakura showed no surprise whatsoever. She's Spanish, he continued; my sons are called Esteban and Bernabé Misaki, just imagine: the sons of Ogata Konishi. He shook his head in a somewhat comical resignation as he said it. At least they are with you, Itakura replied. He made an extra effort so that his words would not transmit the compassion the old man inspired in him or the sadness of his own case. Misaki fixed his gaze on the roof of his living room and said in good humour: What times we have been chosen to see, Itakura, a *sodaisho* whose sons couldn't slice a melon with a *katana*; a *monorashira* who gives orders to mulatto samurais. Itakura smiled. They are well trained, he said, but they are not samurais; they are no more than mulattoes with swords. Likewise, I know who Itakura no Goro is, said Misaki; I know what your men have done for this *han*. He opened the door. Behind the corridor, the garden was bursting with the liquid exuberance of the tropics. A servant approached Misaki. Don Diego, he said to him in Spanish, Doña Josefa says can you hurry, the tea is getting cold. The old man gave Itakura a look that pleaded patience. Don Diego? It's my name here in Veracruz, replied Misaki, Don Diego de la Barranca. They advanced through castor plants towards the teahouse. My servant will collect you, he said, to close the conversation. Make sure you stay wherever he found you; it will be worth your while.

The death I possess is my death. Only if I entrust her do I continue to live.
Someone approaches and sees nothing more than death. It burns him.

I begin this letter in a city called Orizaba, in the *ban* of New Spain, an immense country in an empire a thousand times bigger than the *mikado*. I am writing at night, while my battalion sleeps. I write because I have been thinking about you.

Although the gluttonous, pampered life of the Mexicans has not changed me, I have had to adapt so much that you would not recognise me. I wear boots, I do not ride an armoured horse, I have no helmet, I wear my hair tied in a ponytail at the back of my head and not on the crown, I wear black trousers, black shirts. The only aspect I have kept from how I dressed when I left *Nibon* is the *sotei-no-o* because I cannot get used to carrying the *katana* on my waist, pushed into a leather belt, as the Spaniards do. This habit of using iron is good for showing off, but hopelessly clumsy for everything else.

I arrived in New Spain in charge of a squadron of our soldiers. In Manila they had contracted us to defend a port over here called *Akupuruko*, and to protect the merchandise which must cross the country, from one ocean to another, on its way to Europe. As time passed and we were not able to return to *Nibon*, my samurais began to disperse: they married and set up dwellings in the horrible, pestilent cities in which the Mexicans live, or they grew tired of the chaos and went to seek their fortunes elsewhere. Many died in combat. As the white men in this country only accept orders from those who are more fair-haired and blue-eyed than they are, I substituted the soldiers I lost with the cantankerous men whom I encountered on my travels, the majority of whom had been slaves or whose parents had been slaves. In my platoon, they are permitted to bear arms and go on horseback, no matter where they are from or what colour they are. In *Nibon*, we would not be able to defend a city from a band of squirrels, but over here my army of half-breeds, my *pardos*, can halt the air in the trees. I am proud of them and they are loyal although they do not have the slightest notion of what honour is. The *daimyo* has not once paid what it owes us for defending it, but we are permitted to pay ourselves discreetly, and we do just that.

I also have two officials. Sabu is a samurai, although he was born in Puebla. He is a little younger than you, but he is learning fast. I promised his father, who was pierced in an ambush by many swords, that I would look after him as if he were my son. Do not be jealous. I am sure that in *Nibon* someone is doing the same for you. The other is called Cherian Zacarías

Mampilly and he comes from the kingdom of Cochín, in Kerala. He is a giant, half-Portuguese and half-Indian; the Spaniards think he is a Negro and the Negroes think he is a Spaniard. He can close the fingers of his enormous hands around a grapefruit without crushing it, he can crush a head with his fingers as if it were a grapefruit. For the time being, they are my family.

My death does not think, she does not grow, she does not go anywhere.
She is my death, the death that awaits those who wish to speak with her.

Itakura found Zacarías and Sabu seated on the same stone on which he had left them. They were outside the town hall stables, looking straight ahead. They didn't ask any questions when he sat down next to them. They waited like this for hours, no one saying a word. Misaki's retainer arrived when night was falling. He was accompanied by a man whom he introduced as Don Pablo, who said he was a herder. None of the three men believed him because he was white and most probably Spanish; he had blond, receding hair and light eyes; his horse was magnificent. When he took off his hat to greet them, he kept it at chest height, as the *tercios* did. He held his hand out with a smile, from which a great number of teeth were missing. None of the three extended their hand to reciprocate the greeting. We don't need a herder, said the samurai in Japanese, looking at Misaki's servant. And the merchandise? said Zacarías, to finish off. It's in a hold at the docks. The Spaniard watched them without showing any distress at the fact that he didn't understand their words. How will we recognise it? continued Zacarías. Don Pablo will take you, said the retainer, and bent his spine by way of saying goodbye. The three men got up from the stone. And what do we do with this imbecile? asked Zacarías, pointing quite openly at the bogus herder. I'll go ahead with him to the port, said Itakura. You two go and get the battalion. Don't cross through the city, get to the docks outside the wall, I don't want any scandals. The last order was only thought, not spoken, but his lieutenant understood all the same.

To Itakura, Veracruz had always seemed more of a calamity than a port. The street that led from the town hall to the customs office also served as a gutter for the city during rainy periods – which, in his opinion, was always – and so to get to the port in a direct way it was necessary to walk with your boots sinking in a river of mud and shit through which everything found its way to the sea, including the already swollen corpses of dogs, goats, cows, and luckless men.

They went through the alleys, but there was such commotion in the streets and such a din emanating from this commotion that they did the journey on foot, pulling their horses along by their bridles. It was the time of day at which the residents of Veracruz went out onto the streets *en masse*, in order to keep doing what they had been doing all day inside their houses: nothing. Itakura noticed, as he advanced by Don Pablo's side − both men in front of their horses − that people were opening the way for them: evidently the foreman was more important than he was making out to be. He didn't try to make conversation with him, partly because he didn't like spies and partly because he knew that when he spoke, he imposed tonalities onto the flat language of the Castilians which in Japanese sounded aristocratic and martial, but were completely mangled in Spanish: nobody understood a word he said. Soon they reached the city walls and went through the gate to the port. The guards not only let them pass without looking at their documents, they also gave a martial salute to Don Pablo, who ignored them.

The docks were always in a good state: the health of its commerce mattered more to the empire than that of its subjects.

If anyone comes for me, he must know that it was my death that brought him.
My death is your death.

Zacarías, Sabu and the rest of the troop arrived at the storehouse later than Itakura would have wished, if Itakura had been capable of wishing anything. When he saw them approaching, the samurai realised that sending them around the city had been a foolish waste of time: twenty horses with twenty Indian, Black, Filipino and Chinese horsemen, armed to the teeth, would be ostentatious wherever they went in New Spain. He was in a black mood as he waited for them outside the hold, next to his horse. Don Pablo remained by his side.

What's wrong, Zacarías asked his commander in Japanese. The samurai indicated the inside of the storehouse with the wings of his nostrils − a gesture that no one else would have noticed. Zacarías put the troop at ease, and ordered them to dismount. A Filipino, one of the most alert, whose main flaw was the fact that he was called Maimónides, came up close to ask him if the herder who was with Itakura was actually a soldier disguised as a foreman. A mulatto called Serapio, who was something of a joker, added: He's not from Veracruz. Zacarías didn't bother to answer. He went over with Sabu to see what it was that had troubled his boss at the storehouse.

Inside, other herders too white to be herders and too disciplined not to be *tercios* were loading the backs of what appeared to him to be too many mules. The load was packed into regular boxes of a comfortable size which, nevertheless, made the animals buckle when they tied them onto their backs in pairs. At the back of the hold, two operators, also white, were packing Spanish fabrics into the last of the boxes, squeezing them in with a press.

What are they loading in those boxes? Zacarías asked Itakura when they were back outside. You saw, he replied, fabrics. But did you see how they made the animals buckle? And also, white stevedores, he added, when have you ever seen that? Itakura blinked for a little longer than usual. Couldn't Misaki rent a better fed pack of mules? The samurai didn't raise his shoulders, but Zacarías understood that, deep down, that was what he was doing. Sabu pointed out that perhaps the boxes were made of ironwood and that was why they weighed so much. It doesn't make sense, said the giant: Why would you pack fabrics in ironwood; I'd like to see how we're going to go up and down two mountain ranges with these mules. Caressing the handle of his sword, the samurai used the part behind his eyeball to indicate the bogus foreman of the bogus storehouse stevedores. Zacarías understood that he had to talk to him.

The giant took a bunch of San Andrés cigars which he had bought that afternoon in the city centre from his bag and lit one with the hold's outside lantern – it was high up, the perfect height for him – and approached the foreman. With a gesture he considered refined, he offered him tobacco, but even so the man was startled. Not now, said the Spaniard, taking a step back. Zacarías drew in the smoke from his cigar and made his best attempt to appear diplomatic: he began to speak, swaying his head around, as if saying yes and no at the same time might make him appear inoffensive.

So you will be our hostage until we depart from Veracruz? he asked diplomatically, or so he thought. The Spaniard gave him a sinister smile. Actually, I am going to escort you to Acapulco, he said, we don't trust chinamen around here. Zacarías stayed quiet, took a puff from his cigar and extended his index finger with the intention of driving it into the Spaniard's windpipe and pulling it out through the hole, until it broke away from the lungs – one of his favourite tricks. He felt Itakura take him by the elbow and reprimand him: he began to sway his head around again. The lads from the storehouse are soldiers of the king, am I right? *Tercios* assigned to the port, responded Don Pablo. The samurai said, in Spanish, that it was an honour to be aided by the *tercios reales* of Spain, so as to make it clear that it was not a good idea to kill a soldier of rank in plain view. The foreman didn't understand a word, but asked: Are you really Itakura no Goro? The samurai nodded his head in a way that seemed pompous to Zacarías. Then it's true. With his medulla oblongata, Itakura ordered his lieutenant to ask him what was true. Don Pablo responded: That he exists. Who? Itakura no Goro. He continued: They say that you are masterful with the sword; let's see if you can teach me some tricks on the journey. The samurai thought to himself that if the Japanese ever ventured forth from their islands, they would conquer the Spanish Empire between one full moon and the next.

The *tercio* soldiers were not efficient, but they were more formal and disciplined than Itakura's. As they worked, Serapio fell asleep. The rest sat down to play a terrifying game of cards: they bet their wives. As always, a group of Chinese, who played in a team, won. Dominga Curiel, an iron Bantu, whom a priest in San Lorenzo had played a cruel trick on by baptising him with a woman's name, promised, as ever, that he was going to kill them.

When the loading was finished, they counted twenty-three mules, each one with two crates, forty-six in total. Misaki's servant arrived before dawn. Zacarías asked him to accompany him to the dock for a minute, and once they were away from everyone, lifted him up by the neck and asked him exactly what kind of herder had been assigned to them. He squeezed. He's a captain from the port detachment, he said. That much is clear, replied the giant. He's Doña Josefa's cousin, responded the other man, half asphyxiated; she asked Misaki to let him accompany you to *Akapuruko* and we couldn't get rid of him. Itakura approached them. Put him down, he ordered. We haven't discussed money, he said to the retainer. In *Akapuruko* they are only expecting twenty-two mules and forty-four crates; you take what's in the last two as payment. Itakura consented, closing his eyes. The servant continued to repeat the instructions he had memorised. When you get to *Akapuruko*, unload at a free dock, a Dutchman called Luc de Rooy will meet you. And, looking at the samurai, he said: You must have made a very good impression on my master, for he told me to tell you that you can negotiate your return journey to *Nibon* with de Rooy. Itakura stifled the muddle of feelings of hope that rose up in his stomach before it could be seen in his eyes, but Zacarías could feel how it filled his breast. You would be responsible for paying for your journey.

They left the city without any incidents, accompanied as they went by the captain of the *tercios* of the port. They had barely crossed the wall when Zacarías went up to Itakura and asked him in Japanese: Shall we kill him once and for all? As was the custom, he received no reply, but they hadn't even reached Mandinga before Don Pablo had got involved in a quarrel with one of the dark-skinned men. The *señor* won't take anything, said the Filipino Lucrecio Lobato, after which Itakura had reprimanded him by thrashing him with a sheathed sword. When the captain announced that Lucrecio Lobato would be arrested as soon as they arrived in Puebla, Zacarías half shut his eyelids. He knew, as did everyone but Don Pablo, that to get to Acapulco it was necessary to leave the *camino real* after the Metlac ravine, that once in Orizaba one had to take a detour toward Atlixco and Cuautla, that they wouldn't pass through Puebla.

I possess my death. Sometimes, I am death. My eyes are death.
Things only happen through death. I can cut a seagull down from the air.

Do you remember me? I was born a retainer of Nabeshima Nahoro in Nagoya. My father served his family without anybody minding that he was a Christian. He distinguished himself on the battlefield in times of war and was a principled and serene amanuensis in times of peace. I myself defended the *han* when it was necessary and made up a part of its bureaucracy as a superintendent in the military schools when the service of arms held no rewards. It was on one of my journeys to a training camp that I met your mother. We married: she was also a Christian. You had a lord's upbringing; you must remember it as a golden age. Your brother was also born in Nagoya, but he won't remember anything: he was two years old when the persecution began.

We fled with the authorisation and the help of Nabeshima. We travelled to Hara, walking by night and sleeping during the day. I don't know if you could have rounded up enough samurais in Hara to defend a Christian province, but we certainly thought it was feasible, and we were in the best spirits to achieve it. We had the help of outside empires. In the first days, Hara was the *ronin's* utopia: there were no masters, honour and hope reigned; we had no desire to go to war, but we were getting stronger and stronger.

They were not the best years in which to be a boy, this much is true: founding a world demands sacrifices. Hara was growing beyond its capacity to receive refugees. We had to accommodate peasants who arrived at the camps with nothing, there were epidemics, food was rationed even for us, money ran out. That's why I accepted the work I was offered in the Japanese colony of Dilao, in Manila: the Spaniards could not defend their merchandise from Chinese pirates and they needed swords to keep up their business. I went: they paid very well.

FICTION

One day, the ship owner with whom I sent back what I earned told me that *Nibon* had closed. I asked for more news in the Spanish captaincy and a functionary told me that the Christians had taken on the mikado's forces in Shimabara, that as a reprisal the emperor had prohibited any contact whatsoever with the European powers, and that no one had been able to come in or go out since then.

It was in this captaincy, through which I passed when I could to ask for news from Hara, that I found out about a job in the remote and mysterious *ban* of New Spain. They needed squadrons of samurais to protect the goods sent by the Manila traders between their disembarkation at the quays in the Pacific port in Acapulco and their re-embarkation for the journey to Seville, in the gulf port of Veracruz. I signed up: perhaps from there I would be able to find my way back to *Nibon*.

That's how I ceased to be a *ronin* and became a driver of men, the *monorashira* of a bunch of *pardos* who serve a *daimyo* they call the viceroy, whom nobody ever sees and who never has any money with which to pay, but who allows all to become rich beyond their wildest dreams. If my fate had been different, if I had taken you all to the Philippines with me, and brought you with me to New Spain, I would be rich. I would have left the path of war.

Many things can be said that can make one feel in awe of death. But my death is only death: nothing disturbs it. There are haggard old witches who cure ills for which not even the Chinese doctors have a solution. With time and wisdom, one can temper a sword which cuts through all other swords. I have seen a woman writhing with pleasure, howling with pleasure, begging me not to cause her any more pleasure. The veil of the mysteries of the world can be cast open. Not the veil of death: it is the only riddle with no solution. Death, and a child's mind.

They spent the first night in Orizaba. After removing the loads to let the mules rest, Zacarías and Sabu overwhelmed Don Pablo. They tied him up and gagged him. That following morning they lifted him onto the hind quarters of Zacarías's horse, his head to one side and his legs to the other. The *pardos* put the loads back onto the mules.

The battalion reorganised at the Maltrata diversion: the point at which the path rasps into silvery abysses through the fog of the peaks. Zacarías addressed his men, the captain bouncing on the horse's haunch. We will advance in single file, Itakura at the front, to sniff out the trail, and Sabu and I behind, to repel any attacks. Each one of you is responsible for one mule and a half: three crates. If any get lost, it is I, not Itakura, who will be in charge of bringing you to justice, so you should expect to die like a dog between these hands, indicating them as he spoke.

I see nothing more than my death watching over me, but as we crossed the river Metlac I noted something colossal and unsettling, something I had never seen before. The trees bursting with orchids, the radiance of the birds, the smoke rising from the mud, the voluminous clouds. The mountains, that way the mountains in this country have of looking like the mountains in which the world began.

At the top of the peaks, Itakura halted the band's onward march. He waited for Zacarías to gallop up to him from the rear guard. Where did you leave Don Pablo, he asked when he saw that he was no longer on the horse's haunch. On a mule, said Zacarías, slightly pained: he was moving a lot. Bring him here. They were in a place where the track grew thin between a stone wall and a rift. Zacai could hardly turn his horse. The cloak of fog meant that one couldn't see the end of the drop. The giant returned promptly.

Itakura unloaded the hostage and tore off his gag. The captain continued to say what he had been saying when they silenced him. They took no notice as they waited for him to finish. Then the samurai mumbled something in his lieutenant's ear and he asked the hostage in Spanish: He wants to know what Misaki offered you? Misaki trusts you, he didn't offer me anything; Doña Josefa told me that they are only expecting twenty-two mules in Acapulco, that it didn't matter who gave them over. Again Itakura mumbled something in Zacarías's ear. He wants to know why Misaki contracted us. He doesn't trust his sons, he replied. There must be something in the crates or he wouldn't have called us. The fabric must be very valuable: my men packed them before your eyes. Something doesn't add up: why did they send you? Josefa wants one of the crates, she told me the other one would be mine, and that I wouldn't regret it. And why is she stealing from her husband? She wants to go back to Spain: he is an old man and she's still nice and young. Zacarías looked Itakura in the eyes, and the samurai confirmed with his optic nerve that she was indeed a fine specimen. I think he's telling the truth, the giant concluded in Japanese. Itakura sighed and scratched his head. He mumbled a last question, which was also imparted by Zacarías: Has the government ever paid you for your work? Never, but they look the other way when I pay myself.

Itakura drew his *katana* and gave him a single slash. Don Pablo, admiring the swiftness with which he was ending his life, thought that, effectively, the samurai was like a scorpion, and then that this was his last thought and that it seemed a worthy one. He moved his hand to where he thought the wound was, and saw that he had been set free. Itakura sheathed his sword and nodded very slightly. With the left hemisphere of his brain, he gave the order to advance. Zacarías understood him. When Sabu, who had stayed watching the rear guard, arrived to find the Spaniard free and smoking a San Andrés cigar, his eyes opened wide. The boss is getting sentimental, said the giant as he took his place in the mule train, it's a miracle he didn't offer him work.

The stones, the chasms, the pines, the fog. Zacai is nervous and he's right.
Beauty is the assassin of death, of my death.

I'm writing to you because I think about you all the time and because I don't know if I will get back. Ever since I found out that this road, which I have taken so many times, may end in a vessel that would take me back to *Nihon*, I entertain foolish thoughts, I shun the sword, I cannot focus. Besides, the journey is ill-fated: we are carrying merchandise which is clearly worth more than it cares to admit, I'm almost certain we are being followed, the Spanish authorities are in on the deal, but I don't know how. If you are reading this, it means I didn't make it to *Akapuruko* alive. Zacai, my Keralan brother in arms, delivered what you are reading. Honour him: it's as if he were I.

One does not consider death, nor cultivate her. Death is pure.
You are death, you are not death. To cease to embody death is to hasten it.

The first ambush occurred as they passed Atlixco. They were advancing in a fairly relaxed formation through a trail that led between two reed beds when a group of men surprised them from the fields. The battalion put off punishing the bandits until Sabu and Zacarías came up from the rear guard to finish the job.

In the end, they counted eleven dead men. As always, they left one of the attackers alive so that he could testify that Itakura no Goro's *pardos* continued to be invincible. Zacarías was holding him by the neck, the jaw squeezed between his breast and his left biceps, when he said to Sabu: You have greatly improved. The giant then inserted two fingers into the prisoner's eyes. He shook, furiously and in vain, bellowing like a bull being castrated. Those cuts are superb, Sabu, Zacarías continued; clean and below the stomach, the mark of a professional. He sank his fingers in until he could feel that he was scraping the man's skull. What are you doing? asked Sabu. Preparing the delivery. Sabu put his sword away. It's disgusting, he said. A good and very humane thing to do, replied Zacai: they can shake his head when he gets home; his eyes will come out again and they might still be of some use to him. They threw him onto the side of the road, so that the mules would not finish him off as they passed. None of the *pardos* paid the slightest heed to his cries.

Zacarías took stock of the battalion without detaining the convoy. Dominga Curiel, a Filipino called Menelao Laspelotas and a mulatto by the name of Justo Comercio had been left with scratches and bruises, for they had withstood the attacks as they protected the load whilst he and Sabu dealt with the aggressors. They had carried out their massacre with ease, but they noted the absence of Itakura's sword; he did not even turn to contemplate the skirmish from afar.

They didn't stop to rest their animals until Temixco. There, Zacarías summed up the courage to tell his boss that he was worried: You left us alone. Itakura was cleaning the mud off his boots. You didn't need me, he replied. We had three men wounded. Flesh wounds. Now openly indignant, Zacarías showed his shirt: it had a tiny thread loose. This would not have happened if you had got involved. I couldn't take my eyes off the load. But the witness will say that he didn't see you fighting, that you're not what you once were. Not what I once was? I was there when the servant told you that you could return to *Nibon* after this job is over. The samurai remained silent for a long while. I'm writing a letter, he said, still attending to his footwear. The worst part of the journey is yet to come, replied Zacarías, you can't act as if we don't exist. Itakura didn't betray any emotion at this rebuff. If my time comes you are going to have to leave this business for a period; you will have to go with the Dutchman, look for a way to find my son, deliver it to him. Zacarías looked him in the eye. He said that of course he would do it, but that it seemed difficult to believe anyone could kill Itakura no Goro because he was the toughest son of a bitch who had ever lived, and that if Itakura no Goro did go it would be because someone had got the better of Cherian Zacai Mampilly and that person had not yet been born. Do I have your word that you will deliver the letter? You have my word that you will get to *Akapuruko*. And if I don't? I'll rise from the dead to deliver it.

In Jojutla and Puente de Ixtla they repelled attacks, each better organised than the last. In both cases, the bandits fled as soon as the *pardos* went on the offensive, leaving less casualties behind. Both times Itakura let Zacarías take charge, but he took a more active role in organising the fencing off of the

mules. He did it as a – rather theatrical – gesture to his lieutenant. Did you
notice how well they retreat? Zacarías asked the samurai one night. Itakura
kept on with what he was doing, but his friend understood that he was saying
yes. They're soldiers, said the giant.

At the crossroads in the Western Sierra Madre shrublands, which were
even more tortuous, no one tried anything, nor were there any incidents between Iguala and Chilpancingo, but further on, on the road to El Ocotito,
they encountered a barricade. When he saw the heap of mud and trees which
blocked their way, Itakura drew the air fully into the ravines of his nostrils
and, for the first time since the assaults had started, drew his *katana*. He rode
up to the rear guard, using his sword to order them to double up and surround
the mules with their backs to where the path was interrupted. Then he organised a double defensive line. He remained at the front with Sabu and his
lieutenant, each one of them holding their sword in both hands, their horses
disciplined by the rigour of boots in stirrups. The silence while they were
waiting was so profound that they could hear the Indian Demócrito Xicalaca
whispering prayers to the gods of his ancestors.

With the fire of the harquebuses the attackers announced that they were
coming fearlessly down upon them and that their weapons came directly
from the crown. They were manifold, and they fell on them in waves, so that
they had no rest. They came out of the scrub in small bands with branches
sewn on to their peasant jackets, charging from all sides. At one moment
during the fight Zacarías said to Itakura: Ah, Brother Death, how I'd missed
you. Itakura did not respond; he did not listen, dedicated as he was to the
harvesting of heads, shredded fragments of heads, mutilated bellies.

> *I possess my death*, he thought, *I have her in my hands and in the spiral of my
> inner ear; I have her in the balls of my eyes because my eyes are death.*

I do remember you. I can't forget your fingers, so thin, stretching out towards
me when I left Hara. Your mother's hands on your hips to stop you running
off after me. We spoke about it, we had spoken about it. Perhaps I might have
brought you, you'd be Sabu's companion. She saw times of strife coming and
didn't want to stay without a man to protect her, to care for your brother even
if, back then, you would have struggled to qualify as a man: you were 12 years
old.

When we made the decision that I would go to work in Manila, we told
you. Your mother asked me to explain it to you although I was never able to

explain anything. I'm going tomorrow, I told you, a samurai cannot live on charity. You were a strong boy, we had raised you to be level-headed and you had seen things which many do not see until they are older: being a fugitive is both a gift and a bottomless pit. You crumpled. You said nothing, but I could see how it broke you. You were kneeling next to your mother on the carpet we used as a communal dining area.

I remember how your body shook that afternoon, how your fingers shook the following morning as I mounted my horse. I see your eyes, so far apart that when you were born, my friends used to say that I had had a fish and not a child. I see your mouth wide open, your hair which grew in every direction, but I cannot put it all together. There is no longer a face.

Your brother must not remember me at all. He was sitting on the earth when we said goodbye. He didn't take any notice: he was playing with the stones from the river that your mother heated to boil the water. I lifted his face up – with you shouting in the background – and he smiled with the assurance of someone who knows that daddy's going to return the next day with a plum in his sash just for him. He lowered his head to continue playing.

Everything we do always seems like a slight variation on what we did the previous day. Even the most extreme actions seem normal when we are actually doing them. It didn't seem to me that anything could change permanently, and I was consoled by the idea that I was living in accordance with a truth. As I rode towards the port, I thought to myself that difficult days would come for everyone, and nothing more. If I had known that what I was doing was opening up a ravine, I still would have done it: the way of the samurai is death.

I am your death.

Itakura decided not to return to Chilpancingo because there was a regiment there – perhaps the same one they had just repelled – and war had already been declared. They advanced in disorderly fashion, carrying the wounded as best they could. In total, they lost two mulattoes, a Filipino, two Chinese and an Indian. The forty-six crates were intact, but four mules had died and the horses that found themselves without masters had never had to carry anything other than mercenaries. The next time they're going to be waiting for us with cannons, Zacarías had said, and Itakura had not denied it.

They set up camp in an orchard that was some distance from the city, the property of the widow of a samurai who had remained in Iguala when the campaigns against the pirates of the Pacific had ended. They mixed up the mules amongst the stables and the bullpens and hid the crates in the sugar-cane mill. They put the wounded in a grain store. When everything was in its place, Itakura asked Zacarías for one of his San Andrés cigars. He went over to a rock to smoke alone.

He returned when the night had spread itself out over the ranch, and found his lieutenant and Sabu in the mill, with one of the crates uncovered. It's just fabric, said the apprentice, I don't understand. How many useful men do we have, asked the samurai. Eight, and us three, replied Zacarías. Send them in pairs to the towns, to San Isidro, to San Antonio. Have we got any Indians left? Two. They should go to Chilpancingo, all unarmed so that they can't be identified; they should bring some wagons, we need three, four; send them right now, so that they can steal them by night and we can begin to load them before dawn. We're going to transport the goods in wagons? asked the lieu-tenant. The samurai didn't bother to answer.

The following morning the carts were on the patio of the ranch as the day dawned. Seeing them, Sabu imagined himself riding one instead of his horse and thought to himself that, after the battle of El Ocotito, they had gone from being a band of mercenaries to an association of grandmothers.

Itakura ordered half of his men to begin dismantling the planks which made up the main body of the wagons until they were down to their skele-tons: axles, wheels and the driver's seat. Meanwhile, another group, super-vised by Itakura himself, would take apart the merchandise trunks, using the six panels which made up each trunk to reconstruct the wagons; he made it clear that the work should be done as if they were building carts of glass.

When the carts had been rebuilt, he ordered them to make new crates with the planks that had been left as waste from the wagons. They stuffed them with as many fabrics as they could. There were no presses in the ranch, so they left the widow with a considerable pile of leftovers from which she could get some money. They packed up the new wagons with the new boxes, tied four mules to each one, loaded up the wounded and went on their way.

They had not even got to Xaltianguis when they found themselves face to face with a complete squad of *tercios* from the port of Acapulco. No Goro, who went at the front as always, gave the order to halt and got down from his horse. He awaited the arrival of the Spaniards on foot, with Sabu and Za-carías on both sides. He shouted the order: Don't do anything to make them think our *katanas* could come out. Zacarías raised his eyebrows considerably: Itakura was so tense that he had forgotten to give the orders by telepathy.

We are Itakura no Goro's troop of *pardos*, said Zacai in Spanish, when they finally found themselves standing before a Spanish official. We are going to Acapulco to deliver merchandise from Don Diego de la Barranca, and we have the viceroy's consent to carry arms. The official ordered the wagons to be inspected and acknowledged the legitimacy of the papers Zacarías had handed to him. It is an honour to meet you, he said to Itakura, holding out his hand. The samurai bowed his head. We need to get to Acapulco, said Zacarías, we have wounded men. We will escort you, replied the official. Itakura showed his consent with a movement of the head that was scandalously perceptible.

They made the journey down to the coast in silence, crushed by heat, fatigue and the embers of the last battle. With the walls of Acapulco in view, the official reminded them that they had to stop at the custom houses, so that the merchandise could be checked and they could be given passage through to the port. Zacarías confirmed that there was no problem, that it was ever thus.

At the checkpoint they drew back the canvas that was covering the boxes. The inspectors were opening the first ones when Don Pablo crossed the doors of the fort, dressed as an official and heading a second group of soldiers. Itakura's face didn't move a muscle when the captain greeted him with his dead man's smile. Don no Goro, he said. Don Parrot, Zacarías answered. I have the authority to confiscate your merchandise, he added, shaking some papers which could have said anything because all that mattered here was that the *pardos* had no way out. Ask him if they're going to detain us, said Itakura to Zacarías, without touching his *katana*. He put his hand on his chest to touch the letter he had written to his son. Don Pablo answered in Japanese: I also have honour and memory; all I want is the crates. Can we rest in the port? Itakura asked in his language: my men need relief, we are wounded, we haven't eaten in days. If I grant this, will we be square? Itakura agreed. The captain asked the customs officers to unload the crates and give out the permits. Do whatever you like, he said to the samurai, but never return to Veracruz: I don't want you in my territory.

The bands of the sea wheel around the spiral of my inner ears as they
try to scale the cliff, uncrowned. A cricket bends a blade of grass.

They entertained themselves in the city until night-time, and then they took the wagons to the end of a remote, empty dock. They dismantled them, threw the wheels and the axles into the sea and piled up the panels into two towers, which ended up having quite a considerable height. They put aside the twelve which belonged to the *pardos*: the two boxes with which Misaki had said he was going to pay them. Itakura kept three – one plank for him and another for each of his lieutenants – and he gave the nine that remained to his men. He asked Zacarías to tell them to take the mules, and divide the planks amongst the wounded men in the widow's ranch before they dispersed. Zacai will look for you if he is given another job in the future, he said, by way of a goodbye. The *pardos* had never received such an unusual reward, but the boss was so deadly serious that they didn't make any jokes. They loaded the panels onto the mules and went, certain that this time Itakura had swindled them.

Zacarías and Sabu stayed with him. In the middle of the night a barge, with no flag or lamplight, approached the dock. There was a group of very fair-haired men on the prow, men of a size which, although it did not threaten Zacarías, certainly piqued his interest. Itakura? said one of them. With a martial blessing, he confirmed his identity. I'm Luc de Rooy, an associate of Ogata. The samurai gestured towards the heap of panels. He says to count them, his lieutenant pointed out. The captain's eyes almost popped out of his head. I can't believe you've brought so much, he said. So much what? Sabu mumbled to Zacarías, who shrugged his shoulders. Between them they carried the load onto the boat.

Ogata's contact was adamant that we had to transport one of you to Giapan, said de Rooy, when they had finished the operation. That's me, responded Itakura. You'll have to be patient, for first we must take the merchandise to Katay. The samurai mumbled something in Zacarías's ear. He says he has already waited for six years and one hundred and thirty-two days. You will also need lots of money to be allowed to enter; there have been instances of people getting through, but they are rare. Itakura's *katana* split his panel into two. A river of silver coins covered their boots. There you go, said Sabu to Zacai, contraband *pesos*, destined for China.

The samurai turned toward his companions and nodded with the faintest expression. It seems you won't have to deliver the letter, he said to Zacarías. He was almost smiling as he said it. Where are you going, asked the Dutchman. Hara. The smuggler puffed before saying: Hara hasn't existed for years. For a moment, even the water ceased to splash on the pontoon. He continued: General Hosokawa overcame the city and laid waste to the castle; they killed everyone, including women and children; they threw the stones into the sea. Everyone? asked Sabu, his mouth dry. Not a Christian left in all Giapan.

I possess death in my eyes and my death watches the stars draw pictures on the sky. When I am in my death, in the most decisive point of my death, I see them falling. Another samurai sees them rising up in the mikado. Then the ball of the world breaks, and the first to see my death is the partition that separates the sky from the sea.

BASIC NEEDS
BY EVAN HARRIS

I KNOW THE DATE the bankers visited the children because I recorded it in an email to a friend. It was 3 December 2012, two months after I'd started working at the primary school in Leytonstone; three before I'd quit. During the previous summer I'd exhausted my overdraft and stamina for job application forms. Like many young graduates, I took work as a teaching assistant through a temp agency because it required no experience and there were positions available.[1]

Miss E. had prepared the class, pitching her voice above the clatter and shriek of thirty children clearing their desks.

'Some very important people are generously giving you their time,' she said. 'I'm expecting your best behaviour.'

She aimed her finger at my primary charge, Faaruq.

'I don't want a squeak out of you,' she said. 'Sir will be watching you like a hawk, won't you sir?'

I raised my eyebrows, as if in assent.

The group from Barclays bank examined the colourful wall displays, their hands folded across their chests or holstered in their smart-casual pockets.[2] One politely asked if I could make for the children sufficient copies of the worksheet they had brought to structure their informal lesson. They had come to impart financial prudence to the children, community outreach as part of the bank's 'corporate citizenship' programme, and seemed enamoured with the children's volubility, if at first a little awkward managing it. As they fielded questions from the students about their careers and the banking system, the bankers exchanged with each other the kind of glances you give to close friends to discreetly communicate surprise, shock or pleasure. I imagined them later returning home on the tube, resting their heads on the

---

1. I earned £290 net a week. The temp agency took a cut and employed what is called an umbrella company to administer their payroll to temps, through which you hold travel and food costs against income tax — again for a service fee. Using this company was non-negotiable. That is, the state paid me to work in a state school, and two private companies took a cut of my wages — and one of these companies was employed so that I wouldn't pay any tax back to the state. Temps don't get holiday pay; there are eleven weeks of mandatory holiday in the school year.

2. Between 2000 and 2011 Barclays' tax avoidance division generated £9.5bn in revenue. A member of the parliamentary commission on banking standards accused the bank of 'industrial scale tax avoidance'.

window-glass, eyes narrowed as they contemplated their encounter in the school, and later reporting to the community outreach coordinator that they had learned as much from the experience as the children had.

In class, the most loaded glance between the bankers came when the confidently smart but contrary child Duane, illicitly pivoting on the hind legs of his chair, raised a hand for permission to speak. 'Is the banks a safe place to put our money, then? My dad says there was a crash or something. Says it's like gambling.'

Miss E. winced and gave him her own glance, but smiles appeared in series across the bankers' faces. One leaned forward on his child-sized chair and said, 'There are lots of rules now. The government gives you a kind of promise. Perfectly safe.'

A quick exit poll of the children as they sped out of the classroom for break suggested not all had been impressed by the prospect of a career in finance. Some, clutching their coats under their arms and trying to shake me off, said yes they would like to be a banker when they grow up because they make lots of money and are powerful. Faaruq asked if the bankers made enough money to buy iPhones. I told them that they did and more, and he was sold. Others were unchanged: their aim, they said, remained to be a footballer or a pop star like Rihanna. To a greater or lesser extent, regardless of the professions to which the children aspired, inherent to their aspirations was the accumulation of material wealth. When I was 9, I wanted to be a marine biologist, as a teenager, a musician, though I sometimes enjoyed the fantasy of wearing a suit to a steel and glass office and being very, very rich. Each of my youthful projections assumed what I now understand to be an above average disposable income, and I presume that I am not unusual in this regard.[3] The thought embarrasses me now, but sometimes I imagined being invited back to my school to impart my wisdom to the children, though mainly to flaunt my wealth in the faces of teachers who said I would amount to very little, the way I was going. And here I was, back in the classroom.

¶ I first drafted this essay from a different class, sixteen months hence: I was awarded a scholarship to study creative writing in the US, for which

---

3. In 2014, UK median income for full-time employees was £27,195. Newly qualified teachers begin around £22,000, but with her experience Miss E. would be nearer £30,000. If you are fortunate enough to be a contracted teaching assistant you might get £17,000; if you're not contracted it's more like £12,000.

applications I composed a short story based on my experiences at the school. It adhered pretty closely to real events, though it didn't occur to me to include the visit from the bankers. In a fiction it would have seemed implausible, I think now, a facile allegory that attributed to the bankers the greatest responsibility for the limitations of the children's lives, obscuring with a popular bogey(wo)man the systemic inequities of the school and elsewhere.

The story did not succeed: in changed circumstances the sublimation of past labour was painful, and fiction seemed inadequate to the complexity of experience and the imperative to record it. Unable to evade the consequence of the work, I later wrote this essay of recensions to exhibit and recontextualise my relationships to three children as staged in the story. The intention was to examine at one remove both my wage labour and the process of literary composition to better understand my discomfort with both.

I.

In class, David sits between Tayden and Faaruq at the 'Air Table'. Tables are named after Presocratic elements; Miss E. has named this one for its low academic ability. David is a buffer between the boys, two sincere 9-year-olds who, Miss E. insists, would kill each other if left unattended. David doubts this prediction. Mostly, Tayden is placid, mouth agape, perfect teeth displayed like an advert for toothpaste, a substance often encrusted at the corners of his lips. His thoughts and sensations seem dulled by a fog, and David often wonders if he is sedated.

Sedation is what Miss E. wishes for Faaruq; she sometimes suggests, in jest, that they spike his water bottle. The boy is an elastic-limbed fidget, excited by everything in the class but the work. Pencils are his favourite, but anything to hand will do. Except when sad, Faaruq overflows with energy and David takes the shocks. It displeases him, but it pays his rent and distracts him from his sadness the way a stubbed toe momentarily obscures toothache.

¶ Both boys had arrived to the UK as very young children, though neither could recall for me anything of their countries of birth (the Democratic Republic of Congo and Somalia). Their recall was limited to mobile phones, videogames, football. Occasionally the boys would do some work and seek my praise for it; occasionally my praise delighted them. When, for example, examining Faaruq's work I would affirm that he had grasped, at least for the last thirty minutes (he would not remember it the next day), the mathematical concept of long division, he would perform the same bombastic jig with which he celebrated his football goals at break time. Then Miss E., hands planted on hips — sometimes offering me a comradely glance or wink — would shout at Faaruq for being silly and disruptive.

I was well-behaved in primary school. I remember the force of the teacher's raised voice and emphatic gestures, but I don't recall fearing them; they weren't for good boys like me. I remember watching in horror as Jeremy, one of the kids in Mr James's class, shrugged off such force, and Mr James with Jeremy's collar bunched in his fist howling and sneering insults in Jeremy's face. It's improbable that I can recall it with such clarity, but, visualising it now, Mr James's face is puce and Jeremy's the kind of ill red you get with dangerous fever or a tantrum protracted to the point of exhaustion. Mr James was my favourite teacher. Watching him intimidate Jeremy I experienced a kind of thrilled awe at the intransigence of adult justice. I knew what to do, it made me feel safe. I was a good kid and Jeremy was bad, that's what everyone was told, that's what I believed and was rewarded for.

Every day, watching small children get similarly shamed and intimidated by teachers, memories like this re-emerged, and I watched with detached impotence, this time invested with that power to administer adult justice to children but not to other adults, my material needs dependent on a closed system that valorised this kind of punishment. I was overwhelmed with my own shame until I learned to distract myself by counting my wage in hourly increments until it reached the figure of my weekly rent.

In my experience of working in schools, unless they had a particular enthusiasm for it, teaching assistants enjoyed the privilege of diminished responsibility for classroom order. That is, though I was expected to support the teacher's system of discipline, the responsibility ultimately lay with the teacher — I could just attend to the small group I had been assigned.[4] Though I did resort to threats, and raised my voice, I tried to be patient and take the children's interests seriously, spoke to them as if they were adults, and politely

---

4. I had briefly worked at another school with a similar demographic intake as the one in Leytonstone. It had a policy of less threatening discipline that used a complex system of charts the children were expected to administer themselves — the children policing and shaming each other. The teachers were discouraged from raising their voices and rarely did. Its more insidious method still disturbed me, but it at least created a more pleasant atmosphere, and in it children of all abilities seemed more productive. I remember being awed that a 9-year-old was reading *DAVID COPPERFIELD* of his own volition and could tell me all about it. I wanted to tell him that Dickens had become a common reference again for conditions in contemporary London.

took interest in their enthusiasm for football or phones. Faaruq had a basic model Blackberry. He told me he was going to upgrade soon; his dad was always going to take him to the phone shop at the weekend to arrange it. He pestered me for weeks to see what phone I had, and I deferred: the school had a 'no phones in class' policy, which I didn't want to embarrass myself by breaking, and the boys were likely to be agitated by me showing it. One day I bargained with them a look at my phone for half a page of geometry, and pulled from my pocket the scuffed basic smartphone and laid it on the table. I don't think he could help it, the way you can't because you're uninhibited and having fun.

'That's a shit phone, sir, that is.'

Faaruq clamped his hands to his mouth as if he were a cartoon character in error, given added effect by eyes that anyway naturally protruded. You can sense it bodily when someone is genuinely frightened; if you spend enough time with kids you know the difference between the act and the real thing. Faaruq was genuinely frightened. 9 years old, he had sworn at a teacher. I thought he was wonderful; Miss E. gave him a verbal hammering worthy of Mr James. As encouragement to improve himself, at high volume to Faaruq's face she told him he was a failure, a lost cause. He was sent to the head teacher for more of the same, and a letter followed him home that evening. They made him deliver me a spoken and written apology the next day. I could sense that it was genuine.

¶ Tayden and Faaruq had a thing for pencils. They took pencils from students, from the table's central stationery container, they took pencils from each other. They took pencils surreptitiously and they snatched. They put pencils in their pockets, on their laps, kept pencils under their bums like hens do eggs. When told to stand and move their laminated name tag to the red zone of the discipline wall chart, I would hear turn across the textured plastic of the standardised school chair the wood–timbre patter of hexagonal pencils. With a little force a sharp nib punctures easily the soft epidermis of a child's too-slow hand. The boys used pencils in play and in anger.

This boy, Faaruq, is at the end of a row of children, as far from Miss E. as he can sit. In his lap he has a collection of yellow-and-black striped pencils, the domed red ends woody with tooth-chew. He takes one of the pencils, pointed nib facing out, and slowly raises it to the neck of the girl that sits before him. His eyes are wide, his mouth an O of anticipation. David watches Faaruq inch the pencil forward. The school operates a colour-coded warning system. Faaruq is already on yellow. If David intervenes, Miss E. will move Faaruq to red. If Faaruq is on red at the day's end, he will be sent to the deputy headmaster, who will ask Faaruq's parents to enact retribution. It is true that every time this justice is performed Faaruq is much quieter, much better behaved the next day; his eyes are unfocused, his restless energy is absent; each time an adult addresses him, he flinches against his chair.

What can David do? However he acts, the result will be the same. If he reprimands Faaruq, Miss E. will move his name to red. If he does nothing, then the girl in front of Faaruq will feel the point of a pencil in her neck, will cry out to Miss E., who will then reprimand Faaruq and move his name to red. And this, of course, is what happens: Faaruq's name is again a red name, again he is a bad boy.

¶ In the story, the pencil serves as a continuous metaphor for violence — the way structural violence (systemic, impersonal) is resisted or protested with direct physical violence. A pencil sharpened by David and given to Faaruq as an instrument to write with is used instead as a dangerous prop in a play of resistance. The fiction climaxes when Faaruq is excluded from mainstream education for stabbing Tayden with a pencil. In reality, Faaruq did get Tayden in the hand. He wasn't excluded but the word was increasingly used in teachers' repertoires of threats, along with predictions of a dismal future.

Miss E. had two sons, and I think it's fair to say she was a proud mother — proud both of her sons and her maternal practice. To emphasise the qualitative difference in parental care between that which her sons received and that which, say, Faaruq received, she would boast about the limits she set on her sons' gaming time and how high her sons' reading levels were. Nearing Christmas, she took me aside and described for me the difference between the resources allocated for the Christmas play in this school compared to that in her sons'. 'They have theatre lights,' she said. 'They've been rehearsing for two months already.'

Miss E. lived in Archway but sent her boys to school in Highgate; had moved to the former so that she would be in the catchment area of the latter, where it's unlikely she would have been able to afford a property on her teacher's salary. Like some of her colleagues, she was critical of the Leytonstone school's management, but attributed most of its difficulties to the children and their families, without acknowledging, to me at least, that the children's families didn't have the resources for the kind of aspirational move she had achieved. Instead, Miss E. contrasted her students' and her sons' differences in privilege in meritocratic and moral measures — that is, by the organising reason of the classroom.

So that my treatment of the children would be well-informed, she sometimes took me aside to narrate their backgrounds: incarcerated siblings, absent fathers, benefit claimants, and so on. She would reel off in disgust how many kids by how many fathers an unemployed single mother had, childcare administered by plasma widescreen. This attitude, that students' social and academic limits are set before they enter school, and that a student's deviation from school norms is a confirmation of delinquency as opposed to an expression of need, was shared by many of the staff of the five schools I worked in over a year. This cynicism affirms and reinscribes a fact of predetermined lives: depending on the analysis, UK social mobility since 1970 has been either static or in decline. That means there is a diminished possibility that these children will ever earn more than their parents do. Their parents don't earn much. There are 326 administrative boroughs in England; this school is in Waltham Forest, which is the fifteenth most deprived. That's determined by the measurement of seven domains: income deprivation; employment deprivation; health deprivation and disability; education, skills and training deprivation; barriers to housing and services; living environment deprivation; crime. The usual metric for students' poverty in a school is their entitlement to free school meals; in this school almost half were entitled, more than double the borough average. Faaruq and Tayden were entitled. In as blasé a tone as if only predicting their maths grades, Miss E. had marked the pair out for unemployment or prison. Both boys were enthusiastic about violent games like CALL OF DUTY and FAR CRY; they told me they aspired to become soldiers.

II.

For a month David has been phone-checking for messages when the girl takes his hand in the school yard. She leads him away from the fence he leans on. Beneath one of the school's silver birches she pauses to speak.

Her language is unfamiliar. David grasps at the sounds to stitch them into sentences but they shape-shift and vanish like smoke. She's pointing somewhere and he looks and it makes no sense. A cacophony whirls and howls around them, the enormous aggregate of 400 voices, 400 children with half an hour to play. The girl frowns below the elasticated hem of her black hijab. He balls his hands and blows on them. The girl takes his hands and exaggeratedly puffs, her cheeks inflated and her lips pushed out. She squeals, delighted by the coils of clouded vapour and the rude noises that ripple from her lips. He smiles: for a moment she has distracted him. The bell rings. Break time is over.

❡ Hani was 8; she spoke no English. Three months earlier she had arrived in London from Gambia, and she had two favourite games. One was sneaking from the rear of and onto the bench I sat alone on, leaping onto my back, and clamping herself to my body with surprisingly powerful limbs as I applied evasive manoeuvres and tried to peel her off. The other was pulling me up from my seat, and, palms against my belly, pushing me backward until I collided with a tree or post or the fence that delineated the school football pitch's perimeter. I would see through my eyelashes her dental arcs in a mouth agape with anticipation. As I struck a solid upright she stamped around in comic delight while I feigned confusion and shock.

In the fiction Hani is a kind of platonic substitute for David's ex-lover. They keep each other company at break time and get pleasure from play. She is an opportunity for David to invest his care in someone receptive to it; he sees the investigation of Hani's life as an opportunity for redeeming his disintegrated relationship. He imagines telling his ex a narrative composed of African stereotype and cliché.

David has solved the mystery, he is a stream of sympathetic knowledge. Gambian scrubland, relatives executed in the doorways of their homes, a brave family in the back of a lurching truck. He has taught her English and she is making friends at school, but she always comes to visit him on the bench. She is complex: though she is wide-eyed excitement itself, she has frequent moments of contemplation, insights that only early trauma can nurture. He knows she will grow to be a sophisticated and socially conscious adult, a human rights activist or community leader.

And the teacher's privilege: knowing that in some way he contributed to her success.

❡ I knew nothing of Hani's life, couldn't have. Neither she nor her parents spoke English and I only managed to teach her a few English nouns at break time; understandably she just wanted to play. She was not unusual: in the school, the number of children whose first language was not English was well above the national average; thirty-eight different languages were spoken in total. The number of children who were learning English from scratch was also well above average, and there were very few additional resources provided for them — they had to participate in lessons with the fluently communicating children.[5] Hani once led me by the hand into her classroom to show me her workbook — it contained simple drawings and addition, nothing tailored to an English learner.

My and David's motivations for investigating Hani's background were different, or I withheld from the fiction a congruity that would necessitate greater exploration of character. I did not imagine the articulation of Hani's story as leverage in a relationship, but perhaps I could have imagined it as a kind of intellectual currency to spend amongst my politically concerned friends, redeeming the drudgery with a little exotic trivia; on reflection, comparable to the way I imagined the bankers would circulate in conversation their own edifying experiences with the children. Today I learned something, at least. Yet while it provided the fiction with a little plot, it was in reality appealing to learn about Hani's life — I fleetingly pretended that the information I found would improve her school experience. But most of all it alleviated the boredom.

My investigations yielded very little. When I asked her teacher what language Hani spoke, so that I could use Google Translate to teach her nouns, the teacher suggested Gambian. There is no Gambian language: the country is composed of many ethnic groups, each with its own language or dialect. The official state language is English.

David sits on the bench, and she wriggles her body onto his lap. He slides her off onto the bench, beside him. Look, he says, pointing at his phone, Gambia. She pulls his hand and smears hers across the screen. Gambia, she says. Wait, he says, look. He zooms in on the list of languages, speaks each name in turn: Mandinka, Fula, Wolof, Serer, Jola, Serahule. Hani says: Serahule! David points at Hani. Serahule, he says. Serahule! she repeats. He sees that Serahule make only 9 per cent of the population. Why has her family come here? Hani grasps the phone again, presses a button, takes a photo of David's knees. She laughs, climbs onto the bench, smothers his back and squeals with delight.

¶ Depending on the source, female genital mutilation (FGM) is widespread or universal in Serahule culture, and is not uncommon in the UK: an estimated

5. The head-teacher purchased for the school thirty iPads and a charging station the size of a family refrigerator. Under supervision, the children could use the iPads once a week to do the same basic IT work they used to do on PCs. The staff agreed that this wasn't the most appropriate use of a very limited school budget.

137,000 girls have had it done to them in this country, with another 24,000 at risk annually. I deployed this in the fiction as an extreme test of David's passivity, introduced through a character who can easily seem constructed to give the fiction weight: an energetic smiling young girl who cannot communicate, who can neither confirm nor reject David's assumption of abuse.

My assumption. When I raised it in the staffroom at lunchtime, a veteran and contracted teaching assistant casually added that there were lots of girls entering the nursery who had had it done, and 'it's a mess when you take them to the loo'. The other staff nodded in acknowledgement or tutted, returned to their phones, spooning into their mouths reheated leftovers from Tupperware containers.

In the fiction, David tentatively goes to broach the issue with the head teacher and finds Faaruq crying on the carpet outside her office. The head teacher impatiently — her own lunch has been disrupted — tells Faaruq that she doesn't want boys like him in the school, and asks David to agree. David doesn't mention FGM. I didn't even go to her office.

In 2014, the year after I worked in the school, following an advocacy campaign by NGOs and the *GUARDIAN*, the Minister for Education wrote to schools to remind them of their responsibilities to girls regarding FGM, and the government announced programmes and guidelines to prevent its occurrence. I do not know to what extent they have been implemented. I do know Hani's teacher never determined what language she spoke.

Hani and I interacted less and less in the five months I worked at the school. I tired of the repetition of push and clamber and my inability to interpret anything from her speech; Hani seemed dejected by my diminished enthusiasm for imaginative play. She sometimes found company in other social outliers and mimicked the dance routines they performed behind the football goal. Sometimes she walked the perimeter fence alone.

III.
As part of his daily routine, David hunches on a child's chair, sharpening pencils after class. One hundred pencils; 3.3 pencils per child in class 5D. His phone is on the table; he reads news articles as he works wood. Also it's near in case it should ring. Turning hands carve away the seconds, he hears them fall from the clock. He tries to calculate how many hours, how much total carved from how much total life. He strokes his phone screen. The classroom is empty. Outside it's dusk but in class it's clinically bright.

¶ The headmistress didn't want me to leave the job. I was a good worker, she said, and I had a rapport with the children. I sold all my saleable possessions except my laptop and phone and moved to Budapest, because there were jobs available with sufficient disparity between income and rent that I could save a thousand dollars for graduate school applications. I wrote the story in the afternoon breaks of thirteen-hour workdays teaching call centre managers, accountants and IT workers who administered the trunk systems of banks. They were learning English to better their career prospects; some wanted to move to London. I applied to ten funded creative writing programmes and was accepted at the only one I did not send this story to.

¶ The group from Barclays were here to deliver the children a short informal lesson about managing personal finances. They asked the children rowed on the carpet to raise their hands to suggest things that they, the children, needed in their lives. We got clothes, food, phones, Playstation, books, cinema trips, ice-skating (some with their parents had visited the Winter Wonderland rink in West London). The bankers then asked the children to suggest a country that isn't as rich as England. Someone suggested Africa; the bankers exchanged one of those impressed glances and used Africa as their example.[6]

'So, do people in Africa need the same things as you or different?'

'Different!'

'OK, great. Wow. Well, what do they need then?'

The children wobbled on their knees or bums, waving arms in the air — some supported with a hand the bicep of the waving arm as if they might raise it higher, off their shoulder.

'Water!'

'Good.'

'Oooh, oooh, I know! Food!'

'Excellent.'

The bankers continued to elicit suggestions until they had filled the whiteboard with basic needs. They used a triangle to illustrate that personal finances should be arranged by a hierarchy of needs, with these basic needs in the lowest stratum of the hierarchy. The takeaway message was: when you have money you take care of these needs first. When the children were split

6. About a third of the class were either born in Africa or their family was born in Africa, which is, famously, a continent not a country. A financial manager's average base salary is £52,000/year before bonuses and such.

into groups to negotiate priorities amongst themselves using a hypothetical monthly budget, a triangle diagram and symbols that represented needs and responsibilities, I had a hard time convincing Faaruq and Tayden to prioritise the gas bill over a new videogame.

'What about heating when it's cold in the winter?'

'Put my coat on!'

'But your hands will be too cold to use the controller.'

'Sir, I've got gloves!'

¶ At the end of the session, the bankers distributed to the children blue HB pencils bearing an embossed Barclays logo. They told the kids to work hard, dream hard, and waved as they departed to give their presentation and branded stationery to Miss M.'s class, next door.

5D were unusually animated. They excitedly exchanged facts they had retained from the talk; some waved aloft their Barclays pencils as if they were enchanted wands and struck each other with extemporised curses. Miss E. yelled at them to calm down. They would never be bankers, she said and gave me a glance, if they didn't behave themselves. Faaruq effervesced amongst the standardised furniture, his eyes more cartoonish than usual. He tracked and disappeared the unattended pencils, pursing his lips the way some kids do when they think they're getting away with it. To distract him from imminent punishment, I asked if he would like to be a banker. He asked if they made enough money to buy iPhones; I told him they did and more. I made my disappointed face and shook my head to deter him from his next victim. Tayden glazedly looked out of the window, his lips as always glossy and unlatched. He clutched tight to his chest the unexpected pencil — then squirmed away from Faaruq's creeping hand.

DEBT BY
NATASHA SOOBRAMANIEN
& LUKE WILLIAMS

This is the story of our book.

¶ Edinburgh, June 2014. The sluggishness of early afternoon. The sky clouding over, a slight chill in the air. *The same uninterrupted sadness*, a kind of listlessness that went with everything we did. We'd made it to the Meadows. It had taken him a while to get her out of bed but he'd persisted, offering to buy her a coffee and one of those cardamom buns she likes so much if she would come to the library. He noticed how those passing noticed her. She was thinner now than in London, skirt slipping down on her hips, constantly tugging at the waistband. We slowed our pace. Before the Meadows there was the chance she might change her mind. We were still talking about the morning as if something out of the ordinary had happened when really we'd spent it the way we spent every morning, him coming to her room with coffee, her accusing him of switching the heating off, him denying this. He'd told her, We really must get up earlier. It won't help to stay in bed. In the kitchen she lit up a tube, picked the raisins out of his cereal, milk still unpoured, put them with the other raisins extracted from other breakfasts. Currency she said, They'll see us through The Emergency. She ate. We stared at opened screens. We argued about whether or not to cycle to the library, but when we looked out of the window the sky seemed unsettled and unusually close from up where we were, on the sixth floor. We decided to walk. The billboard above ScotMid still read 'Straight Talking Money. Wonga'.

In the Meadows, some kind of fair. Tabletop stalls and food tents. Let's mill she said. He began to look for something – a set of *ENCYCLOPAEDIA BRITANNICA* 1911 – he's always looking for a set of *ENCYCLOPAEDIA BRITANNICA* 1911. By the time we met again the rain was falling. She took him to a stall and said, Can you buy me this dress? Is that a dress? he said. Then, Yes. He paid and she disappeared with it and when she came back she had it on over her jeans and raincoat. Just imagine there are whole loads of famous people who were never photographed she said. He thought about this. He looks like a young Nosferatu. Max Schreck. He would not know which screen star to liken me to because he's ignorant about these things. A fine rain. Dim light through the cherry trees. We walked away from the fair not speaking and when we reached the part of the Meadows that opens onto the tennis courts, just before the University library, we turned up onto Middle Meadow Walk. Ignoring the unbroken row of posters – comedy acts appearing next month at the Festival – not ready to stop – not ready for a coffee or a bun or the library – we took flight at the traffic lights and cut through Bristo Square, after that letting ourselves be carried by chance. *And the sadness opened out.*

❡ The city is built on several hills. There are valleys and there are bridges and there are stairwells that connect the two. In those days we would stop on one or another of the bridges and lean over to observe the streets. Sometimes we watched the gardens or the rail tracks. It was thrilling to come upon these sudden and dramatic views, which made us think of the postcards sold everywhere on the Royal Mile and all over the city for that matter. The Old Town and the Grassmarket, Cowgate at Night, Princes Street Gardens, Princes Street Looking West. We would stand there looking down and she would say, We're too fuckin scared to jump.

Because, when we walked, we failed to take in our surroundings, and because when we stopped walking we usually stopped on one of the bridges and looked down, we always had the sense of living above the city, of looking down – dizzy – on its many faces. We watched people flushing past like debris on a flood the same faces staring at their screens. Knowing the city this way, from above, having arrived recently in it, we didn't feel part of it and were nervous and irritable. This seemed to increase our togetherness. It gave us – only us together, not individually, never when we regard ourselves alone – a place in the world that we have not had before, not in London. Together we wandered the streets unwelcome leaning miserably into the wind or drinking ourselves stupid in a pub. And all of this under the ugly, haar–obscured sky that we didn't realise we'd invented ourselves.

❡ The first time she saw him he was in a photograph on a website about books. She thought he looked odd and his book sounded odd. She couldn't find a copy anywhere but found his email address. He could not send her a book because he had bought the entire stock of remaindered books and shredded them at the vulgar, pseudo–political, faux-Dada readings/performances he had given for a while at various art schools and gonzo bookshops – though he didn't tell her any of this. The first time we met she said, I hope you've brought money and he said, I have. She showed him a photo of V. S. Naipaul and said, This is my dad. Later when we ate he ate like a rat let loose in a grainstore, even finishing the leftovers on a nearby plate. It was sad but in the end it didn't matter all that much. The first time we went to a party together it was in a library. The party was honouring a famous English writer – one of those realists who writes like a politician – whom she approached saying, Do you want my autograph? The second party we went to together was a few months after that. We happened to be in Edinburgh at the same time. We found ourselves in a basement bar. We talked beautifully! about Can Xue, Elfriede Jelinek, Robert Walser, all the while drinking ourselves stupid. At one point he came back from the bar with two shots of vodka spiced with hot chillies, we chimed the glasses and drank the vodka down and he said, Hang on. He ran downstairs to the toilet and boaked into the bowl. Meanwhile she'd gone and got talking to a dangerous-looking character who could not look or step or speak without a sparking flow of words conveying his poor stupid thoughts and spilling into the smoky room. By the time he returned from the toilet she and the character were on their way out. She said, Come on come on, we're going to a party. We left the bar and hailed a taxi. We drove through town. We looked out the windows at the passers-by, many were dressed as policemen, or perhaps they were policemen, dressed as themselves, and many more were dressed in kilts, and we burst out laughing because we remembered it was New Year. The party was at Restalrig, then it wasn't, so we drove on further out of town.

Our character was subterranean, his style of conversation mineral, the way the headlights of the passing cars slanted across her breasts seemed to dazzle him. London she said when the character asked. He handed round the tubes. She said, Can we and the character said, This is Scotland and opened his mouth wide to swallow the tube while his sparking words continued to flow. Can I have some of your water she said. Without stemming the sparking he reached into his jacket pocket. With his left hand he passed her the water with his right an Apple Mac, she drank it down (eyes expanding like cameras chasing mirages in a desert). Would you mind not talking so much he said to the character. Jesus, OK, but the sparking

We heard the party before we saw it. Felt the speakers in our chests. It was in a field somewhere on the coast, on a small promontory. Red 2 was playing as we got out the cab. The character threw his head back and yelled, grabbed her hand, pulled her to the stage. He found them pressed up against the wall of speakers, dancing. The character reached out to encircle her with his arms (she didn't move away) while the sparking flowed into her ear. She stood without moving, shivering slightly. Then the sparking was in his ear and he moved away, back through the crowd then suddenly needed to boak and he went off to look for somewhere & she started to dance in front of the man where is he I want to talk to him she took another Apple Mac and the sparking When we came together again it was among a group sitting on the edge of the promontory. From there we could see the oily black water and the white surf, the moon, the character gone. A girl with plaits was playing the guitar and another girl was singing. A boy with dreads was peeing off the promontory. There were seagulls we couldn't hear above the noise of the music and the sound of the waves where is she I want to talk to her. Then we were next to each other and she was saying something in his ear. What? Do you know. What? he said. Do you know the German word for. What? he said. The German for. What? The German for promontory is half-island.

He forgot *Halbinsel* but remembered it almost ten years later, the day we met the sad man.[1]

¶ Standing on North Bridge, the station roof like a hothouse roof. The rain gone, the afternoon swelling with warmth. *The sadness – amplified by something with an edge that felt like hunger.* Some kids were throwing bottles onto the mess of broken panes. Now is a dumb lie. Her screen flashed, 'Unknown number'. She didn't answer. Since coming to Scotland she almost always kept her screen powered down. She was afraid that RBS, with their clever moves to try to recover the substantial sum she owed them, would find out she was in Edinburgh right under their noses. She was also afraid but defiant of DCA Mabbots, the debt collection agency EDF had sold her less onerous but not insignificant debt onto after two years of failing to recover it themselves. He said, Why don't you just answer. She said, Why don't you stop giving advice. He had given his screen away several months ago, off the train from London, to the first guy who'd asked for change. Now he didn't have a screen of his own. He wasn't on Facebook, Instagram, Twitter, Tumblr, etc. for the same reason: The Emergency. She respected his viewpoint and listened with grave concern to his theories concerning asset bubbles, derivatives, guns and whisky and hollowed-out Bibles, total surveillance, TEOTWAWKI, the precariat, Charles Ponzi, Robert Allen Stanford, the totally administered society, the Pharmacopornographic era, structural adjustment, Bitcoin, gold, hunger, debt – personal, civic, regional, national, federal, continental, intercontinental, transnational, global, universal, dark pools of – but she could not bring herself to respond in any particular focused way. Even so, she did not want them watching him. He did not want them watching her. He did not want them watching us. We did not want them watching us. She did not mind them watching her because she didn't believe in them, not really, not

1. What Day? This day. The day we're writing about now.

when it came down to it.

The kids smashed another pane on the station roof, all of the panes dazzling in the sun, now the broken bottle too. She took off the dress from the fair and threw it onto the roof and we watched it being dragged here and there by the wind, which wasn't so much wind as a kind of constant agitation of *stuff*, the kind that collects around those sites of perpetual transition such as railway stations, docks, border crossings, motorway service stations, car parks, etc. She took off her raincoat and put it in our bag. She leant her elbows on the bridge, rested her chin in her hands. He took a deep breath feeling really shit. Allowing the *sadness* to overwhelm him he closed his eyes and rested his head on her shoulder. She smoked a tube. He started to doze. Her/his shoulder/neck felt warm against his/her neck/shoulder. We stayed there resting on top of the bridge, while she, not taking her eyes off the station roof, tried to remember a dream she only now realised that she'd had. It had left her feeling lost. She was trying to find her way back into the memory of it, to the almost pleasurable sadness it had left her with, searching for the point where it had begun. But then her ringing screen had pulled her back, and then him starting with his moaning about her not answering. He had been in the dream too. The blue honey of the Mediterranean, that's what Fitzgerald said he'd said.

It was the kind of thing he would say, the quoting of a writer. At least it was the kind of thing he used to say. Since we'd come to Scotland she could not remember him doing it once, this previously constant quoting thing. But he'd never have quoted an American, having this quasi-rational fear/hatred/fascination/repulsion for all things US (not American – US – he'd say). Unlike most white men who liked to quote writers he would quote as many black writers as he did white. Dambudzo Marechera:

> Whatever insects of thought buzzed about inside the tin can of one's head as one squatted astride the pit-latrine of it, the sun still climbed as swiftly as ever and darkness fell upon the land as quickly as in the years that had gone.

But all men. Always, always men. She had had to teach him to read women, and now he read mostly women, and had stopped quoting.

She shook him and without knowing she was going to say it, said, I'm hungry. Do you have any cash? He lifted his head off her shoulder feeling really shit, almost violent saying, Yes, but we should go to the library. She said, I need spaghetti vongole, they have it at Marcello's. But not wanting to feel violent. She took out a tube and lit it to take the edge off her hunger. I don't think they have it at Marcello's he said. We stood in silence while she smoked, looking down at the station roof. The dress was still there. Why did I throw the dress away? The kids had gone, leaving smashed panes and the dazzling. When she'd nearly finished her tube she said, Let's eat, then go to the library. OK he said, but I'm not hungry. You can't share mine she said and took a fresh tube from the pack and lit it with the still live butt of the first.

It was at the moment of ignition, we think, that we first set eyes on the sad man.

❡ He was standing on the opposite side of the road, visible in flashes between passing cars, bent over a heap of bags. He seemed to be looking for somewhere to sit down why doesn't he just sit down on his bags? Or maybe he did not want to sit down at all but just gave the appearance of wanting to sit down. We watched his hands, first thrust into the pockets of his jeans then pulled out abruptly, the left now running through his hair, the right stuck on the back of his neck he probably doesn't know where else to put it. We watched him because he looked like he was about to do something. He seemed nervous. No – more than nervous he seemed afraid, though when we learnt where he was from we would come to call him 'sad' – his fear telegraphed by every jerky and deliberate movement and by his body which he held as if about to break off down the street, away from the heap of bags.

What's he doing? she said. There's something in the man's expression, something I recognise in the way he's looking at that heap of bags. He's probably just waiting for someone he said. The neon numbers above Argos showed 14:10. He felt his face break out in a sweat. You're right she said, Let's go. We started walking along the bridge, in the direction of Marcello's. The noise of the trains, the electric sound of the track, the roof shaking in the sunshine. We could do him a favour he said. Like what? Show him around or something. Does he look like a tourist? He has bags. Too many she said, and nowhere to put them, anyway I'm hungry. It would give us something to do he said. I thought you wanted to go to the library. We carried on walking along the bridge toward the High Street. Every now and then we turned to look back at the man. A bus with an ad for Wonga – 'Tired of waiting? Money in your account in 15 minutes. Wonga' – stopped in front of us blocking our view. We waited for it to move. Some school kids got off, they were carrying screens which gave out music. The bus drove off and he said, I'm going to speak to him. He lit a tube and started back & there's something in the way he's holding his tube down by his thigh there's something about the way his back suddenly looks a bit less collapsed as he got closer to the man he examined his face, it was younger than we'd thought, more like early 30s & she watched how he – back straighter still – gesticulated forcefully, tube in air, then tossed it to the ground and stamped on it carelessly. The man was wary at first but was soon smiling and nodding, taking out a pack of tubes, hanging one from his lip then patting his pockets & saying, Wait a minute, I don't have my lighter, saying it in a strong accent which sounded Indian, French, maybe French-African he thought. When he frowns he looks older and when he smiles he looks younger. My friend has a lighter he said and turned and jogged across the road to her. Can I have your lighter? I'm going to give it to that man. You want to give our lighter away? Yes he said. Moron she said handing him the lighter. Yes he said, we both are. He turned and crossed the road, almost bounding across the road.

❡ She asked him what they'd talked about but he didn't say, just that when he heard the man's accent – a French accent, possibly French-African, though a bit Indian – he had asked him where he was from and the man had said, Mauritius. Why didn't you tell me! she said, I could have come over there and spoken to him. You can do that tonight, we're meeting him this evening. I said we'd go for a drink with him. On our way to Marcello's we passed a second-hand bookshop. He wanted to go in. She didn't. In this mood she could not be persuaded to do anything unless it involved food or the promise of food, so he offered to pay for lunch if she would just come to the bookshop. Spaghetti vongole she said. The bookshop sold mostly novels. Some of the novels were old and some were new and were written in a slightly different style from the old, which now read exactly like the new. We browsed the novels then went to the back room where the shelves were labelled History, Social Science, Philosophy, Literary Biography, Botany, Psychology, Science, Popular Science, Reference a set of ENCYCLOPAEDIA BRITANNICA 1933 but it's incomplete and Film. We hung around by the Philosophy section where there was an armchair. She sat down. He happened to pick up MINIMA MORALIA by Theodor W. Adorno. He happened to sit down on the arm of her chair and flick through it and stop on page 42. The section was called 'Articles may not be exchanged'. Honest giving is impossible in these inhuman times, Adorno wrote. We read:

Instead we have charity, administered beneficence, the planned plastering-over of society's visible sores. In its organised operations there is no longer room for human impulses, indeed, the gift is necessarily accompanied by humiliation through its distribution, its just allocation, in short through treatment of the recipient as an object. Even private giving of presents has degenerated to a social function exercised with rational bad grace, careful adherence to the prescribed budget, sceptical appraisal of the other and the least possible effort. Real giving had its joy in imagining the joy of the receiver. It means choosing, expending time, going out of one's way, thinking of the other as a subject: the opposite of distraction.

He folded the corner of the page. This made her angry. She reached across to unfold it scolding him because it wasn't yet our book. Also because the corner folding suggested he was getting interested and might read on and she was hungry. Let's go she said. He didn't answer. It was hard to concentrate especially when she was looming over his shoulder like she was and he could hear her breathing and even see the page lifting slightly, but he thought he'd understood the gist of Adorno's argument a moment of lightness. It was hard to concentrate when she felt as hungry as she did but she'd been moved by what she thought was the gist of the argument, despite her hunger and its present insatiability books books books and not a fuckin thing to eat. Ten minutes you said she said. Don't you think this is amazing he said. She was too hungry to understand and this was making her angry. The point about object and subject was clear enough. What was hard to grasp was the last bit. What does Adorno mean by distraction? What about my spaghetti vongole? He said, Let's finish this paragraph, then we'll go, I promise. Which made her even angrier. Which made her even hungrier, that dangerous spiral known as *hanger*. He began to read aloud:

Beside the greater abundance of goods within reach even of the poor, the decline of present-giving might seem immaterial, reflection on it sentimental. However, even if amidst superfluity the gift were superfluous people who no longer gave would still be in need of giving. In them wither the irreplaceable faculties which cannot flourish in the isolated cell of pure inwardness, but only in live contact with the warmth of things. A chill descends on all they do, the kind word that remains unspoken, the consideration unexercised. This chill finally recoils on those from whom it emanates. Every undistorted relationship, perhaps indeed the conciliation that is part of organic life itself, is a gift. He who through consequential logic becomes incapable of it, makes himself a thing and freezes.

He thought this was one of the most brilliant things he had ever read. She thought it might be brilliant but her hanger was preventing her having any kind of nuanced understanding. Each word evaporated before she'd fully registered its meaning. Soon, we knew, her hanger would prevent her not only from understanding this or any other argument in MINIMA MORALIA but pretty much anything at all – whether philosophical argument, moral argument, negative dialectics, logical expression, the workings of chance, directions to the Grassmarket, how DCA Mabbots got her screen details, why the green man was never green when we came to the lights – the condition of hanger being something like debt during The Emergency in that its growth factor is exponential, the greater one's hanger the more difficult and specific its assuagement becomes, which meant at this moment – as we left the bookshop and headed at pace across the Meadows – it was no longer enough just to eat spaghetti vongole from Marcello's, the spaghetti vongole from Marcello's had to satisfy a particular set of requirements which became increasingly precise as her hanger raged unchecked, e.g. it was important that the dish be *hot enough* when served, without being *so hot* that she could not immediately eat a mouthful and begin to arrest the hanger. We passed the fair, it was busy. He said, We're nearly there once again it's almost three and we're still not at the library. She said, I want a Coke with my spaghetti vongole can you move please can you move please can you fuckin just move THANK YOU. He said, OK conceiving of forms of giving which might be possible when The Emergency is over. We reached the edge of the Meadows and spotted Marcello's Emergency: the rule and mode of existence hence never over. He tried to say something about giving and The Emergency. Don't talk to me she said. It was no longer enough that the spaghetti vongole *be hot enough* without being *so hot*, now it had to have the correct ratio of sauce to pasta and vongole to sauce, fresh not dried parsley, and if the sauce appeared with the tell-tale bubbles of microwave convection

But there was no spaghetti vongole. She swore at Marcello. She tried to fling the napkin holder at Marcello but he caught her wrist in time and pulled her away. She was almost in tears saying, Fuck this just get me a pie. Back across the Meadows. The sun now hot. Choochters in our way. Progress slow, the people, peopling paths, the grass, everywhere, moving in all directions. The exasperation. She waited outside while he bought a chicken pie, a cup of tomato soup and a can of Coke. We took her lunch to Greyfriars Kirkyard, pushed through the tourists. Our usual bench near the entrance, near that long list of buried bodies not one a woman. She sat down and tore open the bag, tearing off pieces of pie with her teeth, muttering to him – now sat down next to her – with a mouthful of pie, Don't talk to me. Distorted relationship. Suddenly she stood up half-sobbing and flung the pie across the yard. It hit a gravestone, disintegrated. Lumps of white sauce on the stone, chunks of pink meat sliding. He said, Why did you do that? Then when she didn't answer, Drink your Coke, please? He walked over to the gravestone. Bent to wipe it with his napkin, then turned back laughing. You hit Greyfriars Bobby. She shrugged. Greyfriars Bobby, the dog he said. I know who he is. My pie was cold. Well he said, You did a good thing. Dogs love pies. Right she said, dogs *are* greedy bastards.

¶ *They is the THEY.* That's what Marechera said she said.

¶ A bench outside the pub we always went to, though it was not our favourite pub. The sky clear and bright and the sun hot but not too hot. *The sadness as always* but the listlessness abated just a bit. He'd bought a new lighter, a pack of tubes, two pints and now we were sitting and smoking. The pub was dead inside, through the window yellow with dust and reflections we could see the barman with his mongrel who was sleeping. The picnic bench where we were sitting was dry. None of the slats were missing like on some benches outside pubs sometimes and it was stable on its legs too. She helped herself to a third tube – she normally chain-smoked while drinking – and he did not object. He was too excited to care. His big nose like a beak poking in his bag, a mumbling coming from the bag which could have been *Leave me alone* or *I feel great*. He re-emerged. Flexed his shoulders. Then he took two tubes and tossed one to her. She lit it and held it between her knuckles then lay her arms flat on the table and leant forward, resting her cheek on one arm and letting the tube just burn. She said, What's wrong with you? He said, I'm thinking. About what? I don't know he said. Yes you do. You're thinking about Adorno. No, I'm not thinking about anything. She lifted her head and took a drag of her tube, looked at him directly. I demand you tell me what you're thinking about. Then when he didn't answer she said, You're looking quite beaky these days. A motorbike drove by noisily. A sort of tearing sound. Once, walking through Regents Park in winter, passing the zoo, hearing a tiger roar – a tree being torn up. She lifted her head from her hands and said, Look at me. Do this with your mouth. As the noise of the motorbike receded we looked at one another, she opened her mouth wide as if she were afraid – he didn't move his mouth – she smiled with her teeth showing, she closed her lips and furrowed her brow. We continued to look at one another but he didn't move his mouth or change his expression in any way. You know what? she said, It's not just your nose, it's those stupid glasses. It accentuates the beakiness of your nose. He reached inside his bag and took out *MINIMA MORALIA* and began to read. Did you buy that? It was a present. He said this without looking up from the page. Who from? He didn't say anything but carried on reading for several minutes. All clear now but not like he'd thought. The argument about giving and capital. She leaned her arms on the table and rested her cheek on one arm. After a minute he looked up from *MINIMA MORALIA* saying, It was stupid of me to give the sad man your lighter. She didn't move or say anything just let the tube burn itself out. He looked at her hand then returned to the page. Her tube burned completely out and she sat up and threw it under the table. She said, That was Scottish giving. What? He looked up from *MINIMA MORALIA*. Scottish giving. It's when you give something away that belongs to someone else. Huh? You know, like Indian giving. You call someone an 'Indian giver' when they give something then take it back. Some kind of historic misunderstanding between settlers and Native Americans she said. You being Scottish. But I gave you that lighter in the first place he said, and I took it to give it to someone else – someone who needed it. Needed? We stopped talking and sipped our pints. He put *MINIMA MORALIA* on the table and thought about The Emergency, then he looked at her, at her beady eyes, and he thought about how clever her eyes looked especially with her green raincoat. Hey and what about the book? she said, That's a kind of giving. You're right. The shop gave me the book. I suppose she said, but I was thinking more about the writing of the book. Didn't Adorno write it for his friend's birthday? German giving, she said, a gift that places a burden of reciprocation on the giver. After a while, smiling at her, he said, Mauritian giving: when you give something with a flourish in a show of great generosity when it's something you owe anyway. Like Diego Garcia, she said. That's what the British would say. But really, Mauritius owns Diego Garcia and the US *owes* it. Then she said, Mauritian giving is when you give something great to someone who doesn't really deserve it. Well Scottish giving is when the gift is so much greater than the recipient deserves that it dignifies the receiver. Sounds like Adorno she said. Not exactly he said, Adorno says... I was kidding, you moron. Then, No, sorry, tell me, I want to hear. He thought for a moment. I don't want to talk about it right now. She finished her pint. She stretched her arms out in a curious way then rubbed the back of her neck. He lit a tube and said, So what about US giving? Oh that's when you give something with a huge flourish and lots of pomp but the gift is shit. Or lethal. He finished his pint and went inside to order more from the barman who was trying to attract the attention of his decrepit dog. He left the barman pouring the pints and took a piss then splashed water on his face & she picked up MINIMA MORALIA and read the page he'd been reading, a section called 'Doctor, that is kind of you' which she thought very good & he made a murmuring noise in front of the bathroom mirror and closed his eyes tightly like he'd been staring at a bright light & she put MINIMA MORALIA down and examined the composition of the rubbish below the table, empty packets of Walkers, Snickers, an empty green bottle – glass with the label peeled off, some tube stubs, all the same brand judging from the identical colour of the filters <u>American Tan</u>, the wrapping of a Subway sandwich, a till receipt from Starbucks & he thought of the comics whose faces lined the Meadows and thought how unfunny or even tragic they looked collectively & she thought about the sad man and his jeans and how that particular kind of stonewash has come to look exotic since you only ever see it on the most foreign looking – which is probably to say, the poorest looking – of immigrants & he dried his face continuing to look into the mirror his eyelids now stinging, wide open and the water still cold on his skin and he decided he knew nothing and that this was the constant, the only thing that changed was how he felt about knowing nothing & she thought about whether it was bad or good his habit of stealing bad books from chains to leave on the shelves of shops that sold good books so he could steal good books of equivalent financial value from them, the five finger discount she thought, and then she thought about how 'discount' can mean, 'not to consider' & he moved his eyes slowly from the bathroom mirror to the bathroom window because he'd seen a group of tourists, he could see them now looking up towards the top of a building, and he could see that they were laughing, and their guide was laughing, and fuck it the sky was laughing too, and so were the open windows of the building and he tried to think how he could tell her this, tell her it was OK & she thought that she should have brought a book or bought one from the shop but she couldn't bring herself to read another one after the one she'd just finished WOMEN AND LOVE by Elfriede Jelinek whose hairstyle kind of reminded her of Hitler's girlfriend's & he thought it wasn't OK but then he remembered MINIMA MORALIA and how everything had become clear to him earlier suddenly but not the way he expected, his hatred of capitalism, how it being the very thing preventing him from doing anything whatsoever – no, no giving – not having to just hate but love it too, the two at the same time & she thought about an idea for a story or maybe not maybe an essay but more fictional and why not a kind of fictive criticism? or maybe it was just a good title, 'Factory Girls', an essay comparing Bolaño's dead girls from the *maquiladoras* and Jelinek's poor bitches in the bra factory and she thought about the job she had had in the turkey processing plant one summer when she could never rid herself of the smell of fat and became vegetarian for five weeks & he thought how it was a double bind but anyway that was better than the fuckin... this massive amount of hatred blinding him so that its effects whether on himself or everything had been a done deal & she wondered if she would give him the German gift of a book she had written just for him – he always mocked her for dedicating her first and only published novel to her parents, while she mocked him for dedicating his first and only novel to her – and she thought about the book she once bought him for Christmas, a 'celebration of writerly friendship' which he had taken back to the shop and exchanged for a Hamsun book, it wasn't *Hunger* but she couldn't remember the title and his present to her had been a jumper with holes under each arm & deciding he'd better get back he turned from the mirror and walked out of the bathroom with a tenner in his hand to pay for the pints, but when he got to the bar he saw the barman had fallen asleep on his stool with his head on the bar & and she thought what she would give him was music as he didn't know jackshit about music in the most dumb and basic way and she remembered playing him 'Hallogallo' by Neu! and him nodding his head more birdlike than ever, as though he was pecking at the ground, saying it was good music to write to and writing to it as he said it and she lit another tube and gagged which was a sign she had drunk too much too fast and smoked too many tubes and she thought maybe The VU, he only knows the obvious ones, the sweet tinselly ones but she detected in him of late a taste for *Gelassenheit* and wondered if this was her influence which made her laugh out loud a honking sort of laugh to think how outraged he'd be & he turned from the barman to the dog who was whining but louder now he was moving towards it & what is that noise she thought & as he got close to the dog it began to tear at the webbing on the underside of the barman's stool, but despite this the barman didn't wake up, so he put the tenner on the bar, knelt down beside the dog and made a sucking sound with his teeth and rubbed his thumb and forefinger together until he got its full attention & it was true that he'd love 'The Murder Mystery' specifically the simultaneous recitations of competing lyrics and contrasting choruses, he'd find it very *contemporary* she thought & then it occurred to him that the mongrel had the wiry long hair of a lurcher but the flabby flanks of an ageing lab & she thought of the very first time that she knowingly heard The VU which was also the very first time she had tasted espresso which was in the bedsit of a busker ten years older than her who she'd followed home – that beautiful long-haired man with a broken smile who had looked at her sad then proud when describing how, inspired by The VU, he had once been a heroin addict and how some months later when she had forgotten all about this man he had rung her up from a phone box asking for help of some kind and how she had made an excuse for why she could not see him thinking, What does he want from me, I'm only 16 and how that first song, the one that had prompted her to ask, What is this? was called 'The Gift' & he thought what an unproductive mix that was, lurcher and labrador – he had a peculiar love of dogs, not strange when you consider his vegetarianism, but perhaps strange when you consider what bitterness he had at times for all things living except perhaps for her – he stroked the dog's head until he'd calmed it and gently led it away from the bar and towards its bed, then he went to the bar, picked up the tenner and the pints and returned outside to the bench and put the pints on the table then sat down opposite. We looked at one another as if all the strangeness of the day was not a new experience. After all we often got sidetracked from the library and not infrequently ended up at the pub. But the day *did* feel strange and, in being strange, felt surprising, an instance of insanity or hunger, insanity-hunger, what Marechera called the *House of Hunger – where every morsel of sanity was snatched from you the way some kinds of bird snatch food from the very mouths of babes.* Seagulls in Cornwall. We picked our pints up and lit two tubes and after a short pause he looked at her and said, Tell me about English giving. It's when you give something to someone that really you want for yourself... *you* English-give all the time. What do you mean? Well for example every book you've ever given me you've wanted to read yourself. OK he said after a while, that's true. No! What about that, oh who was it by? One of those transnational ones, you know – one of those *My Grandmother's Rice Bowl* ones. Remember, at the airport? I remember she said, but you didn't give that to me. You bought it for me because I didn't have any money. You never have any money he said, how come you never have any money? How come you always have money? How come you read such shit books? We heard a scratching sound and looked up. The blind mongrel was trying to get out of the pub. Let the poor thing out she said. He got up, opened the door then returned to the bench. She reached out and gently stroked its temple. The dog followed then began blindly sniffing at the rubbish below the table, sticking its muzzle into the bright packets and licking the sugary or salty stuff inside. Get outta here she said and nudged the dog with her toe. The dog moved off and lay down outside the door of the pub. We sipped our pints. What were we saying? I can't remember he said. There was a pause. Come on, you do know. What? I really don't! You don't? No! he said. You do, yes you do she said I want to know. He didn't say anything. Tell me! He pretended to rummage in his bag before finding the packet of tubes on the table then lighting another. She looked at his hand. The way his fingers move ever so slightly the way the smoke rises without it seeming to rise. She looked directly at him but he just looked at her as if confused and smoked his tube. *If pressed to say why I love him I'd reply, because it was him, because it was me.* OK she said, in that case I'll tell *you*. We were talking about how come you have money and I don't. It's because my credit rating is better than yours. That's not hard she said and slumped on the table. I thought we were having a nice time. She took the screen from her pocket, turned it on. It flashed – *dca mabbots don't answer.* He said, They'll never find you here. She turned the screen off and put it in her pocket. We put our elbows on the table and our heads in our hands our faces close together. If it makes you feel better he said, I have less money than you, I mean when you count how much I owe. Tell me, she said. Will it make you feel better? She nodded. He thought for a while. I don't know. I know *who* I owe money to though. I have an overdraft from HSBC and another one from Co-op, a handful of student loans, a bank loan I took out when we couldn't pay the rent last year, credit card debt I pass from one card to another whenever they send me an offer. What else? A bike to work scheme loan. But you lost your job and your bike got stolen! Yes he said, but I still owe the money. He drank down half his pint. So as well as what I already told you, let me see, I owe working tax credit because I signed the form too late, and there's money I owe T-Mobile because I didn't finish my contract before I gave away my screen. You moron she said. Then, That is strange. What's strange he said. What else but money can you have less than none of? I owe even more he said there's PayPal and the library, two libraries! Some of the debt was for books I borrowed for *you* and – wait – I haven't included the public debt I'm paying back, I mean all of us, every poor fucker. Ah yes that billboard ticker thing in New York. *The National Debt Clock.* The numbers constantly ticking up, I can't remember how much it was when I saw it but it was a lot, it was... I don't know, it was fuckin... it was a massive amount of dollars, and then below the National Debt Clock another set of numbers also ticking up but more slowly and next to these it said *Your Family Share $.*

¶ Bankocracy consists in circulating debt to make money solely from money and time. The primary relationship between a creditor and a borrower is not important. Everything is arranged in order to multiply the number of people involved in the chain; debt must circulate to the point that the debtors no longer know to whom they owe money. A state that wants to offer reassurance regarding its solvency need only increase its penetrability. In reality, it is of little importance if it will be able to repay what it owes. The objective is not for debt to be settled but for it to circulate in order to produce profit. Strictly speaking, 'what one owes' is not to return the money but to continue playing the game. The imperative is less to keep a promise than to make the structural adjustments so that promises can multiply. What is important is not the initial promise but further surplus-promises, the game of simulacrum and its bluffs.[2]

¶ The sad man was standing beside his bags at the library entrance, blocking the pavement. We each picked up a bag, the sad man took the rest and we walked to Sandy Bells on Forest Road. Inside it was hard to hear because there was a fiddler playing, but we talked anyway. We talked about the weather we talked about the city we talked about statistics in literature. We wanted to talk about Mauritius but we didn't. *We* talked and the sad man listened and nodded his head. We talked sometimes in English and sometimes in French and once she tried to talk in Mauritian Creole. We leaned back on the bench and exhaled. We watched our reflections in the window and drank our pints. We talked about boats we talked about cancer. We exited to smoke tubes, first she and the sad man with him guarding the bags, then him. The sad man said little but when we started to talk about tubes he told us about the packs he'd brought over en route from Mauritius. They're called Horseman and they're strong and foul-smelling. His favourite brand is Sportsman. Another suitcase is full of these. Do we want to buy some? OK we say, we love the name but we don't know the brand. The brand? We decide to look it up on YouTube, on the sad man's glary screen. We watch the best goals of the season we watch the National Debt Clock live we watch piglets being kicked across a pig farm in Kentucky why am I not vegetarian we watch Stromae singing 'Formidable' he looks like a marionette but nothing is as good as the ad for Sportsman tubes. We laugh. We buy more pints and we drink them. We watch our reflections in the brass trim of the bar. When we run out of money we sell several packs

2. Maria Kakogianni & Marie Cuillerai, 'Bankocracy: Greek money and the new idea of Europe', in *Radical Philosophy*, 186, 2004.

of Horseman to the fiddler and buy more pints. The sad man points to his bags and tells us what's in each. Tubes. Shit plastic toys. Codeine. Saris. He talks for ten minutes about the Armani until he gets tired of it then moves on to a black suitcase tied around the middle with a belt. We drink our pints we scowl at the fiddler we talk with our feet resting on the barstools. We exit to smoke tubes. She says she wishes Arsene Wenger was her dad. Fuck Wenger says the sad man, he lacks the killer instinct. We take codeine. He can no longer feel his feet. He doesn't know whether this is because of the codeine or his vegetarian shoes. The sad man says to the fiddler, I'm watching you and we exit Sandy Bells. Let's get out of here she says. He is the only one who has not spoken these last minutes. He cannot stand straight. He buys a Coke from a cornershop and when he returns she and the sad man are gone. Shit he says. He drinks the Coke, thinks he should eat something, then goes to buy another Coke. He feels like having sex with a stranger. He doesn't feel like but anyway contemplates jumping from a bridge. He explains to himself that really it is best if he goes home. He starts walking & she and the sad man are holding hands in the toilet of Sandy Bells. Let's get out of here she says and they dump the bags in the cubicle, locking it from the inside, then exit Sandy Bells and head on foot to the Grassmarket & he is walking too, he can't feel his feet, the world is colourful, things go on and on & she's thinking that's what's *so sad about anything* and how he'd said nothing's worth anything in the end and how she'd said that's not true there's got to be something worth something and how he'd said do you have a point here at all? do you? do you?

THE PIOUS AND
THE POMMERY
BY ROSANNA MCLAUGHLIN

I.

WHERE IS THE CHAMPAGNE? On second thoughts this is not
entirely the right question. The champagne is in the ice trough, on top of
the elegantly-worn Eames table behind the partition wall. The woman with
a pom-pom on her head milling around beneath the late Frank Stellas has
a glass of the stuff, as do the men in overcooked salmon slacks, the eternal
palette du jour for collectors' trousers, but it doesn't seem likely that any of it is
going to make it out of the booth they're standing in, at least not into my hand.
Given the circumstances, *Who do I have to be to get a glass of champagne?* might
well be the better question.

   'Of course if it was up to us, and a lot of people we work with, you know, it
would just be open to everyone the whole time,' Matthew Slotover, co-founder
of Frieze Art Fair, had told me some weeks prior, a little unconvincingly.
Because at 7 p.m. on 14 October, 2015, standing in the aisle of London's
most lucrative contemporary art fair on the opening night, the meticulously
planned tiering system is as clear as the shoreline under the Saint-Tropez
sun. Slotover has given me a 5 p.m. VIP pass, which in the Frieze running
order makes me a fourth-class citizen. Above me are the VVIPs, who can
access the tent from 2 p.m.; above them are the VVVIPs, free to mill around
from midday; and above them are the VVVVIPs, persons of paramount
importance who can enter the tent from 11 a.m., and are furnished upon
arrival with a complimentary bag of beauty products. The 5 p.m. VIP pass,
then, is for persons of distinctly ordinary importance.

   But not to despair, because although I am only fourth on the ladder there are
many more beneath me. There are the eager groups of art students sneaking
in on the ticket of an art world friend, only to realise, once zapped through
the guarded bag check, that Princess Eugenie is back in her castle, Benedict
Cumberbatch has left the tent, and the champagne, that damn champagne, is
anything but forthcoming. And then there are the 80 per cent of visitors to the
fair who actually *pay* to get in, visitors who are also subjected to the rigours of
tiering. *Be the first to see Frieze!* The website rather disingenuously advertises
the Premium ticket, available at an extra cost on Wednesday when the fair
first opens to the great and uninvited. By Saturday the collectors have cleared
out their luggage from the cloakroom and departed the tent entirely, en route
to Dubai or Moscow, having enjoyed the benefits of their 'non-domiciled'
status, a boon to the city's high-rolling international residents that makes
splashing out at the fair particularly appealing. Or off to Paris's Grand Palais
for the opening of FIAC, the next fair in the calendar, where many of the

galleries at Frieze London will once again lay out their wares, before moving on to Cologne, Miami, New York, Hong Kong... or back across the park to the mansion houses of Primrose Hill for that matter, making way for the hoi polloi of London's culture-curious on Regent's Park's lawns.

If on Tuesday the fair is a chin-tuck in Dior brogues, by the weekend it's a schoolgirl with a Winsor & Newton sketchbook, diligently cross-hatching her way through a sculpture in the booth opposite, without noticing that seen from behind it is not, in fact, the sincere mid-century meditation on the union of landscape and female form she thinks it is, but a gigantic bronze penis, penetrating itself through its own, Henry Moore-esque orifice; if only she had taken the time to walk around the thing, but she was put off by that rather stiff-looking Parisian gallerist in a tailored suit and trainer shoes, the one doing his utmost to appear as if he were alone with his MacBook in the 6th arrondissement, waiting for a collector to arrive for a *vue intime*. Perspective, alas, is not something one learns from still-life lessons alone...

Art fairs have a habit of showing everyone present in an unsympathetic light. Because, of course, the gallerist is not there to offer free tours to school children but to sell art, and has stumped up a five-figure sum for a booth in a prime location, money that will not be repaid by acts of benevolent pedagogy. And that girl studying the bronze, has she not in fact arrived with the rather commendable notion that one might learn something from art, and was she not also enticed to the tent by Frieze itself, which publicises the fair as a place to buy art, yes, but also as a glittering pin thumbed into the map of the cultural landscape? 'Experience moments of immersion and interaction,' says the press material, 'encounter impressive outdoor works,' 'explore Frieze Projects, the fair's non-profit programme of artists' commissions.' *Experience, encounter, discover, explore*, words tailored to an altogether different audience than *buy, sell, network* and *speculate*.

Herein lies the crux of Frieze London. It is everything all at once, trade fair and cultural institution, commercial and non-profit, a fair that commissions artists at the same time that it is paid by galleries to show them. Frieze is a microcosm of the art world from the fringes to the moneyed core, and reveals all its dazzling paradoxes. These were paradoxes, I decided, that I should like to get to the bottom of. And so, in the run-up to the 2015 edition of Frieze London, I spoke to three people who have been involved in the fair from its inception – the former Young British Artist Jake Chapman, super-collector Candida Gertler, and the co-founder of Frieze Art Fair, Matthew Slotover – as well as a number of newcomers and casualties, in order to track the various beliefs and investments that follow artworks as they pass through the heart of the market.

II.

'When I go to Frieze I think a lot about the idea that if there was an overnight virus and everyone died, and the Martians came down and started trying to catalogue what the fuck people were up to, you know, there would be certain things they could say *yep, yep, absolutely, we get that.*' Jake Chapman breaks off from his story, one of many he would tell me over the course of an afternoon at his gated studio complex in Hackney Wick, and picks up the glass in front of him as an example. 'But there'd be certain things they'd be looking at saying *what the fuck is this?*' I ask whether the aliens would approve of the artworks he makes with his older brother and collaborator, Dinos. 'It wouldn't last. Ours wouldn't, no!' Would the aliens not understand, I enquire, the artworks they produced? 'I think they would understand them, they'd think children made them! Weird children, very disturbed children.'

Jake Chapman is a big man. His face is peppered with stubble, where his head is not bald it is shaved close to the skull, and his arms are covered in scrappy homemade tattoos. When we meet he is dressed in a camouflage T-shirt, jeans and heavy leather boots. But despite his imposing figure, there is something disarmingly innocent about him. His eyebrows point upwards in the middle in an expression of mild and pleasant surprise, he is prone to debilitating bouts of giggles, and while his rampant verbosity might be unbearable in someone else, even the most convoluted of tales are turned sweet on Chapman's lips, tales which he delivers with the freedom and gaiety of a bird singing in a tree. These qualities combine in him, so that whatever the argument he is busy extolling, whether Armageddon or the existential crisis of the artwork at an art fair, he gives the impression that his spirit, for all the world, is as light as cotton candy. Here is a man able to be at once deadly serious and completely infantile, and who has built a career out of this particular capacity.

'I remember Matthew Slotover and Tom Gidley coming up to me years and years and years ago, and they gave me a little piece of paper, a little photocopy,' Chapman tells me, breaking into a very silly voice. 'And they came up and they said, we're gonna do a... they were really little, you know... *we're gonna do this magazine, it's gonna be called* FRIEZE, *and we're wondering if you'd like to write for it.* And I remember thinking, ah, that's sweet. And look at it now.'

The Frieze empire began with *FRIEZE* magazine – founded by Slotover, Amanda Sharp and artist Tom Gidley in 1991 – and rose to prominence with the Young British Artists – a group whose swaggering, shock-baiting antics featured heavily in the early editions, and who now command vast sums on the international market. The Chapman brothers are among those associated with the YBA moniker who went on to become household names, along with the galleries and dealers who made them. Jay Jopling, owner of White Cube gallery, continues to represent the Chapmans to their mutual benefit; he also launched the careers of Damien Hirst and Tracey Emin. Jopling was never a poor man – the son of a Conservative Baron, he was educated at Eton – but his estimated fortune of £100 million has certainly been bolstered by White Cube's commercial success. 'I always liked to collide the establishment with the avant-garde,' he said of his *modus operandi* in an interview with the *FINANCIAL TIMES*' art critic Jackie Wullschlager. 'In art world terms,' Wullschlager explains, Jopling '*is* the establishment.'

Chapman tells me that he wrote for *FRIEZE* magazine on a number of occasions, but stopped after deciding that the magazine was too 'humane' and 'confessional'. One of Damien Hirst's now trademark butterfly pictures featured on the cover of the first edition – a staple-bound magazine with a flimsy, callow charm. By the time that the 174th edition came out in October 2015, the magazine had a print readership of 320,000, and three of the world's most prominent art fairs had opened under the Frieze umbrella: Frieze London, Frieze Masters, which joins the original fair on the lawns of Regent's Park, and Frieze New York.

Shortly before the opening of Frieze London 2015, I visit Matthew Slotover at Frieze HQ, on the top floor of a converted Victorian poor school in Shoreditch. The door to his glass-walled office opens, and Slotover rises with a slow, broad smile. He looks good, a trim figure with dark, close-cropped hair who shows little evidence of approaching 50. To the right of his desk is a lounge area of mid-century furniture in black leather and dark hardwood. A rubberised pannier bag unclipped from Slotover's bicycle is propped against the wall, and strapped to his wrist, catching the light as it cascades through the Victorian window panes, is the blank, glossy face of the latest Apple smart watch.

The initial idea for *FRIEZE*, he says, was to 'promote young artists and sell their work directly through the magazine', but the plan changed when he was advised that wasn't how the industry worked, 'that you go through the galleries and there's a reason for that', and that it would be 'tacky' to sell art through a publication. A nascent contemporary art magazine, of course, would considerably hamper its chances of success by cutting out galleries, the same art world professionals who form an integral part of FRIEZE's readership, and who shell out upwards of £3,000 for a full page advertisement (advertisements which, in 2015's November edition, account for roughly half of the magazine's content). The initial idea to sell art through the magazine was not so much dropped as recalibrated. Page space and not artworks would be the object in which FRIEZE traded, allowing artists and galleries to become 'friends', as Slotover calls them, rather than direct competitors. 'Doing a magazine', he tells me, 'you get to know artists, you become sympathetic towards them. Of course you're supposed to be critical about them but generally you're on their side. And if something's not interesting, we just don't cover it.'

It would not be until 2003 that Frieze London first pitched its gargantuan white tent on Regent's Park's lawns, but the seeds for the magazine's expansion had been sown some years prior. In 1995, FRIEZE published an article by photographer Collier Schorr titled 'Who is the Fairest of Them All'. 'The art fair', Schorr opens, 'is the most frequented and beleaguered event manufactured by the art world.' Full of moustachioed dealers wearing braces and monk shoes, she suggested they were no place for the future faces of the market. There was, however, an exception – for Schorr, and significantly for the young Matthew Slotover – and it came in the form of UnFair.

UnFair was established in 1992 by a group of galleries who had been denied booths by a dinosaur of the fair circuit, the prestigious and long-running Art Cologne. Unlike Art Cologne, held in the great trade fair halls on the edge of the city, UnFair took place in a disused department store in the centre of town. The stuffy old world had been banished; this fair had renegade status.

Slotover recalls UnFair fondly. 'They had Motown playing over the tannoy,' he tells me, 'and Damien Hirst was at the tiny White Cube stand, and he put twins sitting on the stand next to twin frankfurters in formaldehyde – *because it was in Cologne*,' he says, grinning. It was at UnFair that the YBAs began to shine in the eyes of the international market; it was at UnFair that the market place could, at long last, be cool. Gregor Muir, now the director of London's ICA gallery, remembers UnFair through similarly rebel-tinted spectacles. 'I hitched a ride to Cologne with FRIEZE magazine,' he writes in his memoir *LUCKY KUNST: THE RISE AND FALL OF YOUNG BRITISH ART*, with none other than a young Slotover behind the wheel. After an encounter with an artist pretending to be unpacked from a shipping crate, who 'delivered a thigh-slapping proclamation that he would continue to live in his crate for the duration of the fair', Muir headed to the opening party with Jake Chapman.

'The atmosphere was exhilarating,' Muir continues, 'everyone dancing to the thumping beats that reverberated through the vast interior. I looked up from my triple vodka and tonic and saw Anthony Reynolds, an otherwise reserved London gallerist, boogying on the dance floor.' The night did not end there. At two in the morning, Muir and Chapman returned to the fair, arriving the picture of rebellion, 'utterly inebriated' and covered in crumbs 'from the collection of cakes we'd stuffed in our mouths after passing a bakery preparing for the day ahead'. Once inside, Muir helped himself to beer from behind the bar, and Chapman began swapping the paintings between booths – that is until Muir intervened, fearing their antics would provoke such grave retribution that the pair would be 'deported'.

UnFair ended after only two years, but it showed that at a fair one really could have it all – boogying gallerists, pickled wieners, performance artists, and no end of minor rebellions. Best of all, like an anarchist fancy-dress party in a hedge-fund office, was the potential to have all this while making vast sums of money. 'We would go to the art fairs in Cologne', Slotover tells me, 'and Basel and Paris and Madrid, and think, "Wow, these are great". And we would go there as art critics to try and find out about the art, and meet the dealers, and see what artists were doing. So we always thought art fairs were great places, not thinking at all about the buying and selling of it, just as a way of communicating.' The first Frieze fair was unveiled in 2003, with 124 galleries from across the world participating. By the end of the week, £20 million of sales had taken place within the tent, with Frieze making just shy of £1 million from renting out floor space alone.

III.

The Chapman brothers have been frequent exhibitors at Frieze Art Fair since its inception, showing in the blue-chip section at the front of the tent. If access to the fair is subject to a strict tiering process, so too is the tent's topography, with galleries organised alphabetically into zones from front to back according to status. Up the ramp at the entrance, drop off your luggage, through security, locate your zone... Universal Studio, the firm who designed the tent, are masters in the art of transforming corporate non-space into a luxury destination. Also on their résumé: the Fortnum & Mason Champagne Bar at Heathrow's Terminal 5.

The bulk of exhibitors – commercially established galleries working with commercially established artists – are in the Main Stand, with the bluechippers in the A zone by the entrance where the cost of floor space enters five figures. Such outlays can be recuperated in a single sale: at White Cube's stand in 2015, Damien Hirst's painting HOLBEIN (ARTIST'S WATERCOLOURS) (2015) sold for just shy of a million before lunchtime on the opening day. At the back of the tent, bringing up the rear in zones G and H, is the Focus section for younger galleries. Here careers are less established, business more precarious, floor space is cheaper and there is pressure, particularly on debutante galleries, to show artworks of a less straightforwardly commercial nature. 'If you want to get in the club', artist Samara Scott tells me, having embedded a pond of fizzy drinks, shampoo and various perishable matter directly into the floor of the tent for the maiden voyage at Frieze of the gallery that represents her, South London's Sunday Painter, 'you have to do a difficult initiation act.' Once the hazing is over, a gallery can pull out the plinths, hang the paintings, and take the easier route to making sales. But 'it would be distasteful', Scott says, 'for a young, upcoming gallery to do something so – oh my god! transparently commercial, how disgusting!'

One of the Chapmans' most memorable outings at Frieze London was PAINTING FOR PLEASURE AND PROFIT in 2006, for which they set up shop in White Cube's booth painting half an hour portraits for £4,500 a pop. 'I could see what Dinos was doing,' Chapman says of this venture, 'he could see what I was doing, but the people sitting couldn't see, so we'd do two people at the same time, and it was the funniest. He did the most beautiful, really beautiful, exquisite painting of this demure Spanish woman who sat down, paid her money – and it was not an insubstantial amount – and he painted her and she had this lovely necklace and beautiful silk dress, and he painted this. And then he painted this severed neck!' Chapman's face concertinas in giggles; evidently he is immensely pleased by the memory of the decapitated subject. 'Just the idea of sitting down and not getting your portrait done!'

The demure Spanish woman in the silk dress would have been disappointed, of course, if the Chapmans hadn't come up with something suitably puckish. The pair thrive on playing the court jester, of presenting the apparently unpresentable to their audience. Among their biggest feats to date are buying a set of Francisco Goya's DISASTERS OF WAR etchings from the early nineteenth century and defacing them for an exhibition at White Cube in 1999, and adding rainbows and love hearts to watercolours painted by Adolf Hitler – at least ostensibly, the pair have form when it comes to the art world hoax – for their exhibition IF HITLER HAD BEEN A HIPPY HOW WOULD WE BE at White Cube in 2008. Gruesome portraits to order, by their standards, are relatively tame fare. At 2007's fair they were back at White Cube offering to deface £20 and £50 notes for fairgoers, free of charge – an exhibit that Candida Gertler, art collector and founder of philanthropic organisation Outset, described as among her favourite exhibits to date.

I met Gertler at the Greenberry Café in Primrose Hill to find out more about the tightly entwined genesis of Outset and Frieze London, as well as the curious attraction of the super-rich to the 'non-profit' sides of the art world. With her ringed fingers sparkling in the North-West London sun, Gertler eased into an origin story of how she, Sharp and Slotover had concocted the plan while out for dinner one night 'in a little Korean restaurant' in 2002. The details of this story were evidently important, as if the smallness of the restaurant and the fact that it was Korean displayed not only the intimate relationship she had with Sharp and Slotover, but a subtler form of sophistication. When one could very well eat every meal at the Ritz, it is those things which not only have to be paid for but discovered that are the mark of the truly cultivated. They hatched a plan: to create a fund of money – £150,000, made up of individual pledges from private donors in Gertler's network of friends and associates – with which artworks would be bought at Frieze London and donated directly to the national collection at Tate. One of the artworks on Outset's shopping list for 2004's fair, Roman Ondák's *GOOD FEELINGS IN GOOD TIMES* (2003), would become the first work of performance art ever owned by the Tate. Ondák's piece consisted of performers instructed to line up in queues between seven and fourteen strong, reading papers, twiddling their thumbs, in areas of the fair where one might not expect a queue to form.

GOOD FEELINGS IN GOOD TIMES was exhibited as a part of the non-profit Frieze Projects, a section of the fair Gertler describes as showing '*less obviously commercially viable*' artworks. Unlike the majority of artists participating in the fair, whose work is displayed in booths paid for by the galleries that represent them, artists showing as part of Frieze Projects are commissioned by in-house curators to produce site-specific work. Dotted around the tent as a series of theatrical and participatory interludes, the Projects bring to the fair something missing from the rows of paintings and objects on plinths which – typically having little to no conceptual relationship with the tent, the artworks they are displayed alongside or the fair itself – appear ready to be packed up and shipped on. The Projects take seriously the fair's ambition to be a space of curatorial as well as financial value; they make Frieze appear less like a bazaar and more like an exhibition.

'There was no price tag to it,' Gertler tells me, recounting the purchase of Ondák's work, 'and I remember standing in the corridor with Jessica Morgan' – then the Curator of Contemporary Art at Tate Modern – 'who was at the time part of our team, and Roman said "I don't have a price for it," and then they disappeared, and you know, there was two minutes of conversation, and they came back with "£8,000". OK! £8,000!'

Gertler's excitement at having bought an artwork without a price tag was palpable. But in reality, buying a performance work from the non-profit section of the fair is like asking a shopkeeper if you can buy the jacket on the mannequin in the window. It might not be the obvious choice, it might be, as Gertler so aptly put it, less obviously commercially viable, but it is a request that is hardly likely to be denied. A shop is a shop, a market is a market, a fair is a fair, and for the right price everything is for sale.

There is evidently an appeal in aligning oneself with artworks that have a less explicit relationship with commerce. Like that *little Korean restaurant*, such artworks offer something that the big names of the art market do not. When having the bank balance of a multi-millionaire is qualification enough to hang a spot painting by Damien Hirst in the stateroom of your superyacht, buying the ostensibly un-buyable is an especially piquant pleasure. By this logic, it is perhaps unsurprising that when Gertler lists her favourite exhibits at Frieze to date, the list should include three exhibits that are *less obviously commercially viable*, and which all also involved waiting in line – an experience of thrilling mundanity, one can only assume, for those unacquainted with Lidl on a Sunday afternoon. In addition to Ondák's queue and the Chapmans' defaced bank notes, topping Gertler's list is rolling down a grass slope as part of Paola Pivi's installation for the Projects section in 2003, a popular attraction that required a brief spell of the much enjoyed hanging around.

IV.

The Chapman brothers have been granted the keys to Frieze City, and in his studio, Jake Chapman runs me through a number of convoluted and improbable suggestions they have floated concerning their participation. 'We wanted to do a booth where you could go and buy someone else's work from somewhere else and bring it to us and we'd change it.' The flaw in this proposal, alas, was 'the unpredictability of people's egos'. Another idea involved offering 'free money' to homeless people at the fair. For this, he tells me, 'we'd need to have an ATM, we'd have us drawing, and what people would have to do is take out £20, give homeless people £10 and we'd draw.'

But the mother of all proposals, also including the unsuspecting homeless, was one suggested to Miuccia Prada, head of the luxury goods dynasty, a major patron of the arts.

'We had another idea to do a show in Milan at the Prada Foundation, and I just remember sitting and talking to Miuccia Prada and suggesting this as a possible idea. It was called TRAMPS ON ICE. We wanted to build a big ice rink – because Milan is full of smackheads and a terrible sort of drug population, sub-population – and we'd say if you come there you'd get some money and a free dinner. But you have to ice-skate for an hour. I mean it's hugely fascistic but the idea was that when they arrive, they skate for an hour, and then they have a shower, then when they come out we take their clothes, we put them on a hanger and put Prada labels in their clothes, they get Prada clothes, they get a meal and then they leave. So the show's on for three months, the clothes would get less and less worn because the same people would be coming and bringing back Prada clothes and getting fresh Prada clothes. We'd bottle the shower water and call it Eau de Tramp, and the by-product is that these drug addicts would end up being brilliant ice-skaters. Win win! Obviously they didn't really go for that.' There was, however, 'lots of laughing'. And that, of course, is precisely the point. Neither Frieze nor the Prada Foundation – a cultural organisation with a permanent exhibition space in Milan, in a building designed by Rem Koolhaas, one part of which is clad in 24-carat gold leaf – were going to entertain ideas that poke such extensive fun at the conspicuous wealth behind their operations. Not to mention allowing the homeless through their doors, which at Frieze would require extending the fair for at least another week, in order to make space for all the rungs on the social ladder between the VVVVIPs and the destitute – but both were no doubt pleased to be in on the merriment, just as the demure Spanish lady would have been pleased with her severed head. This is the particular appeal of the Chapman brothers. Not only do they have license to mock the cultural aristocracy, but the aristocracy actively enjoy it – it adds a little *frisson* to proceedings.

V.

In large part, the Chapmans' prolonged success is down to having mastered a defining characteristic of the contemporary art industry: the fine art of double-tracking. To double-track is to be both: counter-cultural and establishment, uptown and downtown, an exotic addition to the dinner table who still knows how to find their way around the silverware. The exemplary double-tracker, wrote Tom Wolfe in THE PAINTED WORD in 1975, arrives at a private view at MoMA in a dinner jacket and paint spattered Levis, exclaiming '*I'm still a virgin!* (Where's the champagne?)'

Art is a decidedly social industry, where business doubles up as pleasure; an industry in which clients are friends. Accordingly, collectors don't just want the clay or the paint or pound shop dreck transformed into cultural gold, they often want a relationship with the alchemist too. And so, as much as artists ply their trade in the studio, they must also ply it on the social circuit, enabling the rich to journey vicariously to the exotic lands of the (relatively speaking) poor, without ever mentioning the arms or the oil or the property portfolios that bankroll such boutique vacations, or the promise of money that explains why the artist is present in the situation at all. 'I feel at times like a weird escort,' Samara Scott told me shortly after the 2015 fair, smarting from the pressure of having to socialise with potential business interests. 'I mean you don't have to sleep with them, but there's an exchange that you have to give.' Frieze London's own flair for double-tracking reached its zenith at 2015's talks programme, organised by the Lucky Kunst himself, Gregor Muir. The talks covered a range of subjects from the social impact of museums to the imprisonment of art activists and the legacy of punk. But the stand-out event was a panel discussion, titled 'Off-Centre: Can Artists Still Afford to Live in London?' The event was so popular that tickets had to be reserved in advance, and attendees were advised to arrive twenty minutes early. Behind me as I waited in line a young man in a fur hat and a brocaded coat so long that it tickled his ankles knocked back a mid-afternoon glass of champagne. By this point the entire queue ought to have known, in fact should have known already, why the talk we were yet to see was flawed. For there may be many artists struggling to afford the cost of London living, and many non-artists for that matter who cannot afford the rise in rent ushered in by the influx of artists, who set up studios in poorer areas of the city, shortly to be followed by coffee shops and craft breweries and property developers, but not one of those people was to be found among the fur hats and the £36 entrance tickets. Nevertheless, such a dose of political engagement makes for a bracing digestif, following those Serrano ham croquettes in the VIP lounge.

Double-tracking is not only a pious mask to cover the whims of the wealthy. It is the thing that allows us all to appreciate the painting on the gallery wall without being deluged by the thought of the machinations and the millions that led to it hanging there. It is what enables us to engage with the world not in its unsavoury entirety, but as an artist presents it to us, and as we ourselves would like to see it. Without it, it is questionable whether there could be any art appreciation at all. What distinguishes double-tracking from its less discerning relatives – the flip-floppers and the U-turners and the outright conmen – is that it cannot be easily faked or fudged. For the gallery, for the artist, for the middlemen and for the viewer alike, double-tracking requires dedication, and most importantly of all, it requires *belief*.

As a sign of the significance of this faith, it must be upheld even in the most explicitly commercial contexts. It is something that Frieze insists be carried out throughout the fair, right down to the selection process. Following 2015's fair I spoke with Barnie Page, director of the London gallery Limoncello. Page told me he knew a number of figures on the London commercial scene who had applied repeatedly to get into Frieze London, but were routinely rejected. The reason, he told me, was that they were seen as 'dealers' and not 'gallerists'. While a gallerist is both a businessperson and a pious servant of the arts – a gallerist must be able to vouch for the quality, and not just the marketability, of the artworks they promote – to be branded a 'dealer' is to be tarnished by purely avaricious interests. It is to adhere, and fatally, to only a single track.

VI.

In 2010, Matthew Slotover took part in a debate at the Saatchi Gallery. The motion: 'Art Fairs Are About Money Not Art'. Slotover, in the 'no' camp along with artist Richard Wentworth and critic Norman Rosenthal, was pitched against Louisa Buck of THE ART NEWSPAPER, artist and writer Matthew Collings, and a then-painter named Jasper Joffe. Joffe was present because he had set up The Free Art Fair, a short lived, alternative model of fair at which artworks were not sold but given away at the end via an elaborate raffle. 'For once', reads the now obsolete press material, 'instead of art going to the highest bidder or those who can afford it, someone who really loves an artwork will be able to have it for free.' The Free Art Fair had some limited success: of its three incarnations, one was held at the Barbican Centre, and it attracted a number of well-known artists, including Bob and Roberta Smith and Joffe's sister, the painter Chantal Joffe.

At the debate focus inevitably shifted to Frieze, and Joffe – the least known of the group and evidently the least proficient in the etiquette of debating – lost his cool. Anger tuned his voice, his ample curls were furiously smoothed against his skull, and his cheeks flushed crimson. His main gripes: Frieze exhibits more men than it does women, the selection process is run by a cartel of gallerists, and that by pandering to the tastes of the rich, Frieze does a disservice to the majority of underpaid artists. Slotover responded coolly, adhering to rule number one of debating: that showing one's emotions is a mistake on par with a fox offering its bottom to the hounds to sniff.

He began by pointing out the history of unequal representation at Joffe's own fair, listing the disproportionate number of male participants from The Free Art Fair's press material, before reminding the audience that 80 per cent of visitors to Frieze Art Fair come to spectate and not to buy. Hardly, he argued, a statistic befitting an avaricious cartel. Later that same year, an artwork of Joffe's was removed from Frieze London.

London radio station Resonance FM had been invited to participate in Frieze Projects, and planned to use their booth to hold an auction as a fundraiser. One of the intended lots was a painting by Joffe of a po-faced Nicholas Serota, director of Tate, with the words 'Cheer Up Love' painted in the background amid a sea of polka dots. Frieze removed the painting before the auction began, citing the fair's 'strict policy of selection'. 'I presume', said Joffe at the time to the *INDEPENDENT* newspaper, doing his best to at least go down in flames, 'it is because I was recently in a debate at the Saatchi Gallery with Matthew Slotover, and he seemed quite upset and angry that I criticised Frieze.'

I mention to Slotover that I had seen this debate. Joffe, he tells me, had made a 'big deal' about their confrontation afterwards. He 'edited my Wikipedia page to make it really big, and stuff like that. It's all been a bit... *stalkery.*' And, as a final nail in poor Joffe's coffin, 'not being selected, I think, was his main problem.' This seems a rather cruel dispatching of the subject, cruel, because it was no doubt true. *If something's not interesting we just don't cover it*, Slotover said of the magazine's selection policy, and at the fair, as it is at the magazine, not being selected is a judgement that offers little room for reply.

'Facts', wrote Aldous Huxley, 'do not cease to exist because they are ignored.' The same cannot be said for careers in the arts. A week prior to meeting Matthew Slotover, I had breakfast with Joffe. At his suggestion we met in a co-operative café in Hackney, the day before it was due to shut down. Over rye bread toast and fair-trade coffee Joffe spent an hour expounding on the evils of the art world, revealing that he has subsequently quit art altogether, setting up in publishing instead. The narrative of being a dangerous agitator excluded from the market, a Guevara to Slotover's Kennedy, disarmed of his aggravating spotty canvases, evidently suited him well – just as it suited Slotover to write Joffe off as 'stalkery'. 'I would question people who feel they're excluded from Frieze. Are they excluded from other fairs as well, that have nothing to do with us?' Slotover reasons, considering from the apex of the golden ladder the man who has slipped down a snake to the bottom of the board. 'Unfortunately, a lot of the time you come to the same conclusions. And not through any collusions because it's not in anyone's interest. So, you know, it's competitive. But life is competitive!'

VII.

Slotover's fondness for broadcasting that 80 per cent of Frieze Art Fair's visitors come as spectators and not buyers is a masterstroke of double-tracking, which does much to reframe the fair as something other than a trading floor. It is a statistic that can be found repeated in numerous publications. The NEW YORK TIMES have it, the SPECTATOR too. It is even cited, no less, in the first lines of Frieze Art Fair's Wikipedia page. And come the non-buying spectatorship do, for there is nowhere better to see a comprehensive who's who of the commercial art world. The fair provides an annual survey of the artists and artistic trends at the forefront of the international market. It also provides an opportunity to witness gallerists and collectors in action, those agents of the commercial art world so often invisible to the gallery-going public, and so often just out of reach for aspiring artists.

What was not listed on Frieze's Wikipedia page was the pleasure of arriving at the fair as one of the 20 per cent, with the sole purpose of spending large sums of money. And so at Frieze HQ, I ask Slotover perhaps the most obvious question of all. Why is buying an artwork better than simply looking at it? 'Well, like you I never used to own it, partly because I couldn't afford it – but you know there are editions and things that one can buy that are not expensive,' he says, graciously empathising with my financial status, before taking the opportunity to advertise the cheaper end of the market. 'When you go to a fair it takes on a different atmosphere when it's like, "OK, I'm gonna buy something." There's an excitement about it, and you're looking at art with that view, so it's like, "OK, what do we like, how much is it, is it available?" And you kind of have a motive, you know, a mission. And then you buy it and the dealer's really happy and the artist's really happy, and then you get it shipped home or you take it home, and you find somewhere in your house for it, and you look at it every day. And then a year later you might move it around, brighten up a room that was a bit dull or boring before, and it's amazing.'

The dealer's happy, the artist's happy, the new owner's happy – the art fair, according to this description, is at least a peaceable kingdom.

The suckling child may well be playing on the hole of the asp, or have his hand in the cockatrice's den for that matter, but only, one suspects, because he has learnt to tolerate the poison. Slotover's vision of the fair is a far cry from that of British artist Jesse Wine, who first showed at Frieze Art Fair in 2013 with his London gallery Limoncello, and who entered the proceedings by way of a baptism of fire. In order to secure their place in the Focus section of the tent, dedicated to younger galleries, Limoncello proposed that the three young men they were exhibiting would be present in the booth alongside their work for the entire duration of the week.

It is highly unusual for an artist to man their own booth. After overseeing the installation of their work, if indeed their oversight is required, artists appear tentatively in the tent – at the private view, to meet with collectors or journalists at the request of their gallery, or to take a furtive, midweek glance at what else is on display. (A case in point. When I ask Jake Chapman if he will be participating in 2015's fair, he replies with the sort of nonchalance that is the sole preserve of the firmly established: 'I think Jay will probably drag something down there.') Unless an artist is in a position of power so considerable that they are able to demand complete control over the manner in which their work enters into circulation, they keep their presence to a minimum and for good reason. 'Artists don't make art to make sales,' Wine tells me, but at Frieze, the boundary that distinguishes an artwork from a commodity, and for that matter an artist from an escort, is in serious danger of dissolving.

This, then, was a masterstroke for a young gallery: to say to the beast how beautiful it is, what a pleasure its company. Abercrombie & Fitch may employ the services of shirtless, six-packing gym bunnies to entice customers into their stores, but they've got nothing on the appeal of three fresh-faced colts at an art fair, instructed to be as available as possible and no doubt rendered desperate by the task at hand. For six days Wine stood in the booth, enticing the passing crowds to stop for a while, to take a seat with him on one of the chairs provided with such *tête-à-têtes* in mind. 'I just sort of thought,' he says of the experience, 'if I look the devil in the eye a little bit with this art fair stuff, and am present and see exactly how it works, and see the emotional transaction and the financial transaction take place, then I won't be able to be disturbed by it.'

VIII.

Speak to any artist who has exhibited at an art fair, and they will likely tell you that while the conditions for display are far from ideal, participating is necessary if you intend to make a living. Speak to any gallerist, and they will likely tell you their business depends upon it. 'The one thing that I would say that really makes sense,' Wine says of mounting a commercially successful booth at Frieze, 'is to be consistent in your display. Because it's the same as when you go to a shoe shop. You don't see a pair of stilettos next to a pair of Timberlands next to a pair of flip-flops. You don't see that. You see four different colours of Timberlands. Because then you've got a choice, but within a confined environment. And I think that's how the fair operates, that's why the people with the display which turns over the most cash – and that is obviously the goal of it – are the ones that fucking treat it as a normal commercial environment.'

London gallery Stuart Shave Modern Art is no stranger to the logic of the shoe shop. In 2015 it was declared winner of the Pommery Champagne Stand Prize, receiving as its reward £10,000 and a bottle of Pommery the size of a small child. On the walls of its booth were five works by artist Mark Flood, identically sized and evenly spaced in a range of colours, each a pixellated image of a Mark Rothko painting. Here, surely, is that *choice within a confined environment*, a reproduction of a popular product for sale in bubblegum pinks and greens, as well as deep purple and midnight blue for the more soberly inclined. And on the floor of the booth, a line of sculptures by Yngve Holen – seven washing machines, each topped with a warped sheet of plexiglass, and model aeroplanes pointing in various directions. The masterful control of minor differences – the choice between an aeroplane pointing East or West, of plexiglass bent upwards or plexiglass bent down – and of course the domestic scale they offered to Flood's Rothkos – useful as an indication of how they might fit in back home – ensured the stand was triumphant. No mention of the 'different-colours-of-Timberland-boots' approach was made by the judging panel, who praised instead the 'intellectual and formal dialogue', but one can only assume it had been tacitly acknowledged. With the financial stakes so high for artists and galleries alike, and with certain types of artwork proving bankable, it does not take a huge leap of the imagination to see how the art fair has begun to dictate the nature of artworks being produced. This idea was given short shrift at Frieze HQ. 'Look,' Slotover tells me, 'I think it's your duty as an artist to make the best work you possibly can. And to follow your interests and your dreams and whatever.' But, 'if the gallery is exerting pressure on you as an artist to make work that you don't think is good, well, there's no gun to your head. It's your decision. If a gallery says, "Oh, I quite like that piece but can you make it smaller, and in pink, because we could sell it?" you've got a choice. Either you say "Great, I'd love some money this month, and if you think so, I'll do one in pink." Or you can say "How dare you tell me what to make. I'm off, I'm going with another who's not going to do that." Eventually, it's down to the artist. And all artists have to think about it. "Am I interested in selling stuff, do I want the market to follow me or me to follow it?"'

I ask Jake Chapman about the experience of exhibiting at an art fair, and he replies with characteristic merriment. 'When you go to Frieze and you see the scale of things, and you see the works in such a homogenised environment – in a sense you get to see how hopeless a work of art is, as a thing which can actually fulfil all of the things you want it to do when you're in the process of making the thing. And that's easier to have when objects can gang up on the viewer, when there are enough objects or enough paintings that can build some kind of cosmology of meaning based on their context. But when it's one thing, then another thing, then another thing, it's like watching the existential crisis of the work of art, not being able to actually get away with what it's supposed to do.'

Shorn of any affinity with their surroundings bar commerce, Chapman concludes, all artworks can be at the fair are 'little punctuation marks in someone's journey through this screaming forest of little existential objects which are just so totally orphaned, because their meaning is attached to context'. I recount this rather bleak appraisal to Matthew Slotover, who replies with an act of double-tracking *par excellence*. 'That's very good,' he says. 'Did he write that or did he come out with that?' When I tell him it came straight out of Chapman's mouth, he is evidently extremely pleased. 'Really? That's excellent!'

UNCLE HARRY: A LYRIC
LECTURE WITH CHORUS
BY ANNE CARSON

SET:

Some tall piles of folded sheets which a person (or two) is shaking out, folding, refolding upstage centre... Comfortable armchair upstage L. Lectern with
reading lamp and microphone midstage R. Row of chairs midstage centre.

CAST:

LECTURER

CHORUS: Four seated Gertrude Steins who resemble Picasso's portrait of her.
Each holds up a Gertrude Stein mask on a stick that gets snapped up and
down (once in unison) when indicated. CHORUS 4 has a voice 'like a beefsteak'
as Mabel Dodge said of GS. CHORUS 1,2,3 may use lighter pitches.

[enter LECTURER to lectern]

CHORUS 1:

Anyone looking at us sees we are Gertrude Stein

CHORUS 2:

We are a chorus

CHORUS 3:

A chorus of four

CHORUS 4:

Four is better than one

CHORUS 1, 2, 3, 4:

Now to begin

[all snap masks]

LECTURER:

THE VIEW

He was someone surrounded by having his distance very near as Gertrude
Stein said of hills.

    First he was not my Uncle Harry but my father's. I was a child when I
knew him. He was already old with hair a white haystack and moustache
a horizontal wire brush. He had a way of standing with both hands in the

front pockets of his pants and both arms braced against a wind always bearing down on the front of him. He had a way of talking sideways over a pipe that stuck straight out the side of his mouth and clacked on his teeth. He was a champion scyther. It was one of the things he had perfected a 360 degree overhead scything technique that amazed all who saw it. All who saw it were not many. Uncle Harry was a kind of hermit.

Now although he never heard of her and might have disagreed with most things she said in her life Uncle Harry was born the same year as Gertrude Stein. I like a view but I prefer to have my back to it said Gertrude Stein. Evenings Uncle Harry would stand in the hay and look down towards the lake for a long time. He stood so still you would call him a person listening except he was deaf. The lake at that hour was like a detail of an old painting with black-green parts and chunks of blue and thick gold. The setting sun burnt a path across it. You might hear a loon call and as its call echoed down the lake all time disappeared into this. Evening held itself. Evening released and it was night. They say there is a moment at life's end when the soul leaves the body. I don't know if it has a sound. Or a sort of duration that is the sound of sound cocking itself.

CHORUS 3, 4:
He was a full one living

CHORUS 2:
Quite an old codger

CHORUS 3, 4:
No he don't want a lodger

CHORUS 2:
Did the family enjoy themselves

CHORUS 1:
I would say so

CHORUS 2, 3, 4:
Can you repeat that

CHORUS I:

I love a poetical history

[all snap masks]

LECTURER:

THE LONELINESS

Was he lonely. I don't know. Nine months of the year he lived alone on a farm in the north of Ontario. A near town was five miles away a near neighbour uncertain. Most land around the lake had been parcelled out in cottage lots years ago. Cottagers are seasonal. Some come for Christmas or a weekend in winter. Most board up their cottages on the last day of August and reappear in June. It was a deep long winter Harry had by himself with his dog and his two horses and his subscription to the NATIONAL GEOGRAPHIC SOCIETY MAG-AZINE. Snow drifted up to the eaves. His hay wagon got him to town every two weeks for supplies. He ate tins of corned beef hash and green peas and coffee. He liked now and then an O'Henry chocolate bar. Until probably the middle of May he lived in two rooms of the farmhouse namely the kitchen (which had the stove) and the bedroom directly above it (which had the stovepipe). Other rooms whispered with ice.

And then three months in summer Harry's world filled suddenly up. The cottagers came back and so did we. Who's we. Harry was the brother of my father's mother Ethel. Ethel had four children including my father and they all had children and the children all had friends. Week after week in summer these people arrived in groups of three to ten. The idea was to 'help Harry bring in the hay' this was the phrase they used and enjoy a vacation at the lake. The idea was not Harry's. I never heard him comment on it. He did comment on the inability of my father and my uncles to master scything technique. Harry could scythe 100 square meters of hay in three and a half minutes leaving a patch as level as his moustache with fallen stalks unbruised. There was frustration and a redfaced man in the hayfield many an afternoon. Harry remained unfailingly polite to everyone. So did the dog (whose name was Shep although it was a succession of dogs) so did the horses (Prince and Florence who were immortal at that time).

CHORUS I:

The horses were apparently immortal

CHORUS 2:

The horses were usually immortal

CHORUS 3:

The horses were to some extent immortal

CHORUS 4:

And the fur smelled of violence

CHORUS I, 2:

Very old winter violence

CHORUS 3, 4:

Now worn by young girls

CHORUS I, 2, 3, 4:

Explain why this matters

CHORUS I, 2:

Trembling oh the bells

CHORUS I:

Oh the bells that were stirring were not the same

CHORUS 2:

Why the bells were the bells were

CHORUS I, 2, 3, 4:

Not the same

CHORUS I:

Explain bells

CHORUS 2:

Explain girls

CHORUS I, 2, 3, 4:

Explain very old trembling

> CHORUS 1:
> Were girls the same

> CHORUS 1, 2, 3, 4:
> Oh very

> CHORUS 1:
> Were horses

> CHORUS 1, 2, 3, 4:
> Oh very

> CHORUS 1:
> Were bells oh the bells Oh the bells that were trembling were not the same

> [all snap masks]

LECTURER:
THE GEOGRAPHIC
When Harry died in a psychiatric hospital at the age of 94 my father went to clear out the farmhouse. All the rooms except the kitchen were packed floor to ceiling with issues of the *National Geographic*.

> CHORUS 1, 2, 3, 4:
> How many natural phenomena are there

LECTURER:
From the door to the bed in Harry's bedroom a narrow channel had been left open and another around the stovepipe. The smell you can imagine.

> CHORUS 1, 2:
> Volcano and say so
> As often and say so

LECTURER:
Now if you had ever met Harry the one thing you would say is that he was someone who knew a lot of things about a lot of things. He knew about haying and horses and weather but also the history of violins or where to build a

canal or volcanoes in Papua New Guinea. How he got this way was a mystery
as he left school at age 15 the year he went deaf.

CHORUS 3, 4:
He is easily curious
He exactly remembers

LECTURER:
He had few books in his house and no public library anywhere around there.
Certainly he read the *NATIONAL GEOGRAPHIC* from cover to cover.

CHORUS 1, 2, 3, 4:
There is no use whatsoever all winter long

LECTURER:
His mind gave excitement to everything he read and it entered into his will
to live.

CHORUS 1, 2, 3:
No noise no potato

CHORUS 4:
However a volcano

LECTURER:
Living for Harry was knowing how things work. This was the happiest he
could be.

CHORUS 1, 2:
Repeat potato

CHORUS 3, 4:
Repeat volcano

CHORUS 4:
Repeat the happiest he could be

CHORUS 1, 2, 3, 4:
The happiest he could be

[all snap masks]

LECTURER:
ETHEL
Ethel was big. Ethel was six feet tall. Bony. Rigorous. Her husband had a heart attack in a department store on a Toronto day in 1932. There were four young children. Ethel went to work cleaning other people's houses. I remember her huge hands and the smell of Noxzema on her skin. Every day a clean housedress a clean apron. There is one photograph of her standing by the lake with Harry just after the war in trousers and sunlight. She has a barrette in her hair and an expression bounding forth like joy but it is untypical.

CHORUS 1, 2, 3, 4:
How many natural phenomena are there

CHORUS 1, 2:
Volcano and say so
No noise no potato

CHORUS 3, 4:
He is easily curious
He exactly remembers

CHORUS 1, 2, 3, 4:
There is no use whatsoever all winter long

CHORUS 1, 2:
Repeat potato

CHORUS 3, 4:
Repeat volcano

CHORUS 2:
Repeat the happiest he could be

CHORUS 1, 2, 3, 4:
The happiest he could be

[all snap masks]

LECTURER:
As Harry's elder sister Ethel felt responsible for seeing him through the summer when his world got complicated. She stayed from June to September.
There was a reordering of Harry's life. Three meals a day. Clean underwear.
No cursing. There were points on which they agreed to disagree like Harry's
admiration for starting the day with a tot of whiskey. He had his little low
shelf behind the chair where he always sat at the head of the kitchen table.
A dusty bit of old green leather tacked over it for privacy. Harry rose at five
in the morning to light the stove. Ethel slept till five-thirty. He usually got
his whiskey. But she absolutely forbad him to eat peas off his knife. Another
skill he had perfected. I remember sitting with cousins uncles aunts around
the kitchen table on a sweltering summer noon. Bowls steamed on the red
plaid oilcloth. Meat mashed potatoes carrots green peas. A good hot lunch
Ethel said. Up at his end of the table Harry sat peacefully lining up peas on
his knife. He filled the length of the blade with single-file peas and raised it
to his open mouth and shot it with a motion like a sword swallower. Never a
pea was spilled. *Harry!* flew from Ethel's end of the table. Then Harry tipped
the peas off his knife and sat quietly. Or reached up with one hand removed
the hearing aid from his ear laid it by his plate. Went back to lining up peas
on his knife.

CHORUS 1:
When they go he will be different

CHORUS 2:
And it was promised that all the arrangement

CHORUS 3:
Might move from right to left

CHORUS 4:
That all the arrangement afterward

CHORUS 1, 2, 3, 4:
Promise it they say

CHORUS 4:
Remembering the cold

CHORUS 1:
When they go he will be different

CHORUS 2:
Afterward they say

CHORUS 4:
Was he right

CHORUS 3:
Was he left

CHORUS 2, 3, 4:
Was he after all

CHORUS 1:
Out in the cold

[all snap masks]

LECTURER:
THE ODD QUESTION
Was he vain about being a hermit asked my friend Ben and I thought *What an odd question* – it made me laugh. Uncle Harry being the least vain person I ever met and hermit not a word he would use. He liked being alone. He had one good suit a black suit that he wore annually to visit the Canadian National Exhibition in Toronto at the end of August. He went alone by train. He viewed all the exhibits tried all the samples and came back the same night. He was buried in the black suit.

CHORUS 1:
Vanity is no defence

CHORUS 2:
A lake is a defence

CHORUS 3:
A laugh is a defence

CHORUS 4:
They did not defend him nor did I

[all snap masks]

LECTURER:
THE LAUGH
He had a rough square laugh like characters in comics who say HAAR
HAAR HAAR. Laughs came out his face sideways over his pipe somehow
this adding to the hilariousness as if his whole being had slipped out on a jag
– 'sudden glory' as Hobbes says of laughter.

CHORUS 1:
Vanity is no defence

CHORUS 2:
A lake is a defence

CHORUS 3:
A laugh is a defence

CHORUS 4:
They did not defend him nor did I

CHORUS 1:
Meanwhile snow came at an angle

CHORUS 2:
It was more than a pleasure to go

CHORUS 3:
To go on with my life a state apart

CHORUS 1, 2, 3:

And to whom would there be an obligation

CHORUS 4:

To whom would the commas feel like cattle brands

[all snap masks]

Lecturer:

THE LAKE

The lake was a masterpiece. I loved it like a person. It had birch trees slipping themselves silver in the wind along the shore silver in itself and situations of water lilies both sides of the dock tangling to a swimmer. I swam all day. We all swam whenever we weren't having to do anything else. Harry didn't swim. He had lost his hearing by diving fast and deep into the lake when he was fifteen rupturing an eardrum. On very hot afternoons he would come down from the barn and sit on the shore to take the breeze a while.

There is something else to tell about this lake that I thought of as Uncle Harry's lake although on maps it had the name Paint. Once I had surgery. Afterwards things went awry what doctors call complications. I lay for some days and nights in a hospital cloud of pain. Then there was a fifth night and something rose up. I can't call it a dream it didn't seem to me I was asleep. I can call it a visitation from the devil. The devil took this form. A sequence of TV screens came forward one after another behind my closed eyes. As one came another disappeared as another came. Each screen had some bright fast story gibbering and grabbing itself along so TV does and we are accustomed to this but each story had also a quality I can only describe as evil I mean an entire human coldness a cruelty like an essence of torture. I call it a devil. Each TV glowed out at me a consciousness that wanted to suck me into its evil. It Was Black, Black Took says Gertrude Stein somewhere and black in the sense of a life-or-death contest going on. The only action I could put against the pull of this was to insert myself into Uncle Harry's lake and swim continually backwards and out backwards and out away from each screen as it approached away from that suck of death worst where I swam hour after hour placing myself into the red stalks of the water lilies shifting their weight in the vast silence of underwater here to there here to there placing myself pushing myself back away from the devil and the stench of death pouring out of TV screens filling every molecule of the night except for swimming.

At some point it ended or I awoke it was like being washed out of hell. This account sounds melodramatic to you I imagine. However I am also sure that in the grit and dregs at the bottom of the psyche where pain has its kitchen there are only extremes there is no mildness there is no mercy. Mercy is from a lake or from an uncle. Having no sense of time at the time I later calculated the night in the lake to be a Wednesday.

Wednesday made me think again about Uncle Harry and loneliness. It was not pleasant to think about before. It was not pleasant to be specific. Now the parts change. I see him a Wednesday night in his kitchen looking out the back window on black January black silence black snow. I see him turn and go to the stove and take off the stove lid and stir the embers with an old poker that hangs on a hook on the side of the stove and his face gets hot. He stares down into the fire. He is at the centre of a reasonable kingdom. He does not often think about another. Another what. Exactly.

CHORUS 1:
If the week had one Wednesday

CHORUS 2:
If the month had four Wednesdays

CHORUS 3;
If the year had fifty-two Wednesdays

CHORUS 4:
If TV had 10,000 Wednesdays

CHORUS 1, 2, 3, 4:
And they all came on the same night

CHORUS 4:
You might prefer to be shot dead

CHORUS 3:
What good's your uncle to you now they said

CHORUS 2:
You need something to smoke and something to chew better already

CHORUS 1:

I'd suggest taking off that red scarf with a very little example

CHORUS 3:

It's a very little example

CHORUS 1, 2, 3, 4:

Exactly they said

[all snap masks]

Lecturer:

THE ICE

The most impressive tools that Uncle Harry owned − surpassing even his scythe which in the hands of someone who knows how to use it is an instrument of almost supernatural grace and clarity as you may know if you've ever seen anyone scything − were his ice tongs. A pair of tongs as big as himself that hung sideways on a hook outside the ice house. Harry needed a small income. Part of it came from selling lots to cottagers. Part of it came from building them cottages. After that he started his ice business. Ice is a staple of summer life. Nobody bothers with a refrigerator at the lake − you could never get one delivered that far up north anyway fridges take too much electricity. Most people had an icebox in the cellar. An icebox needs a block of ice every so often. In late April Harry went out on the lake with Prince and Florence and cut one-metre square blocks out of it. Using his tongs he hoisted them onto the hay wagon. Prince and Florence hauled it up the path to the ice house. Harry tonged the blocks off the wagon into the ice house wrapped in dry gold sawdust and straw and didn't they look grand. All summer he delivered blocks of ice up and down the road. Odd he had no icebox of his own. Every day just before noon I was sent out to the creek behind the house to pull up a bottle of milk from between two rocks where water got deep and rushed along. I must have tried to bite the glass one day because it is a memory I have in my teeth and lips and hands the glasshard chill of it.

Another thing about ice. This came after his death. During his life I was never at the farm in April so I did not hear what must have been an annual event for Harry although as a deaf man he would have processed it differently than I do − have you ever gone to a Stevie Wonder concert and watched deaf children in the front row lay their heads and arms on the stage to get the sound – by means of what is called infrasonic vibrations. When the ice goes out there is a gigantic pluck as if a bowstring stretched deep under the ice from end to end of the lake had some vast finger pluck it once. A vibration shoots across from shore to shore. If you are standing anywhere near you vibrate too. It feels low and long and strange like an animal stare.

CHORUS 1:
Do you like the word infrasonic

CHORUS 2:
Let's evolve it

CHORUS 3:
Become Gertrude Stein on sabbatical

CHORUS 1, 2,4:
Now you are infragrammatical

CHORUS 3:
If you're Harry's scythe shaped like a harp

CHORUS 2:
You'll be infrasharp

CHORUS 3:
If you're one of Harry's nephews from the city

CHORUS 2, 4:
You'll infrahuff and infrapuff your way through the hayfield arousing pity

CHORUS 1:
Become Harry's knife

CHORUS 2:
Infra green peas and strife

CHORUS 3:
Become James Joyce (go on be brazen)

CHORUS 4:

You'll find yourself inventing the word infrahuman

CHORUS I, 2:

Become Prince and Florence

CHORUS 3, 4:

But there I can't go

CHORUS I:

It's nice to imagine that we can imagine our way into anything living and real

CHORUS I, 2, 3, 4

But No

CHORUS I:

It just isn't so

[all snap masks]

LECTURER:

THE REPAIR

Uncle Harry was good at repair rethinking rearrangement. His eyeglasses held together with tape at the corners and wads of paper under the pads that press either side of the nose leaving a red mark. His socks overalls truck the pump beside the kitchen sink had each been refashioned were each by now a collection. I can't see when I move through the rooms of the farmhouse in memory anything there that was new and shiny. The objects he used had no indolence in them none of that lazy disregarding storebought glow. They were heavy with work and always clean. Later an era of neglect set in. Harry got old. Nobody spent their vacation at the farm anymore because of dirt and his moods came on sudden. Prince and Florence died. The barn was unsafe. My father went up north in winter and came back angry and sad. *He has to leave that farm* he would say. *Nobody can tell Harry anything* he would say. Finally Harry got gangrene in his leg. There was a family consultation of everybody not Harry. Everybody not Harry decided. My father and his two brothers went up north and took Harry out of the farmhouse into hospital.

The gangrene healed but Harry's dementia impressed the doctors. He was transferred to a psychiatric ward and never went home again.

I remember visiting him at the hospital with my father. The psychiatric ward was separated from the rest of the building by solid walls of steel mesh and a difference of lighting. Uncle Harry stood in a total fury. I don't recall anything else. I don't believe he spoke. We left him in his bright room. My father vanished into the warden's office while I waited on a chair. Years later after both Harry and my father were dead I found in my father's desk a folder of letters from this warden. Each contained an itemized bill for sheets and blankets. Whenever sheets and blankets had been given to Harry he tore them apart with his hands.

Natural phenomena make it difficult not to look says Gertrude Stein but can we not look. Can we change the sentence.

CHORUS 3:
A sentence says you know what I mean

[all snap masks]

LECTURER:
Can we go back to a moment when he was living and clean and there still were things in the world he thought he could repair. The following happened one autumn. Harry was at the beginning of getting old. One of my father's brothers whose name was Ken decided Harry would be better off to leave the farm and come live in suburbia. Ken had a ranch-style house with a guestroom 400 or so miles away from Harry's farm. How Ken persuaded Harry into the car no one knew.

CHORUS 3:
A sentence says

CHORUS 4:
A sentence says

CHORUS 3,4:
A sentence says you know what I mean

FICTION

CHORUS 2:
Suppose a lone man

LECTURER:
Maybe he said it was just a visit. They drove south. Soon Harry was standing in the guestroom looking out on Ken's back patio with its barbecue and
clipped cedar hedge. He didn't sleep. Some days and nights went by.

CHORUS 1,3,4:
A sentence says you know what I mean

CHORUS 2:
How are you at grinding

CHORUS 3:
How are you at hours

CHORUS 1, 2, 4:
How are you at that door

LECTURER:
At midnight he dressed in his black suit a clean white shirt a tie. He let himself out the patio door and stood on the lawn a while. He took in the night its
sway its way of cocking. He got his bearings. He set off north crossing back-
yards peony beds other people's sleep. He walked in the direction of the lake.

[person folding sheets upstage goes downstage centre with sheet and begins
ripping sheet slowly in pieces, continuing to end]

CHORUS 1:
Did we neglect persecution

CHORUS 2:
Glass makes ground glass

CHORUS 1:
Suppose a family

CHORUS 4:
Keep away from that door dear

CHORUS 2:
There follows a question which is not a question

CHORUS 1:
A family has useful knowledge

CHORUS 4:
Keep away from that door dear

CHORUS 2:
How are you at hours

CHORUS 3:
A sentence says you know what I mean

CHORUS 1, 2, 3, 4:
Suppose you don't

CHORUS 2:
Suppose a family

CHORUS 1, 2, 3
Suppose a lone man broke forests and had an extra sun

CHORUS 4:
Keep away from that door dear

CHORUS 1, 2, 3:
Keep away from that door dear

CHORUS 1, 2, 3, 4:
How are you at keeping away from that door

CHORUS 3:
And to whom would the commas feel like cattle brands

FICTION

[all snap masks]

LECTURER:
Do we need a finale
Everyone needs a finale
The finale

CHORUS 2, 3, 4:
He was a full one living

CHORUS 2:
He seized it when he saw it

CHORUS 3:
A most beautiful sound

CHORUS 2, 3, 4:
Is the sound of what happens

CHORUS 1:
Can you repeat that

CHORUS 2, 3, 4:
I am going to do so

CHORUS 3:
Explain why this matters

CHORUS 3:
I am going to do so

CHORUS 4:
There is an intensity of movement

CHORUS 2, 3, 4:
Combined with not seeming to be getting anywhere

CHORUS 1:
Can you repeat that

CHORUS 2, 3, 4:
No. This is the end.

CHORUS 1:
There is not such an end.

[person ripping sheet drops pieces and bows to audience from the waist,
deeply, once and during brief blackout exits]

APPENDIX

Claire-Louise Bennett is the author of *POND*, published by Fitzcarraldo Editions. 'The Lady of the House' appeared in *THE WHITE REVIEW NO. 8*.

Rahul Bery, a secondary school teacher and translator from Spanish and Portuguese, is based in Cardiff. He has translated essays and stories by Daniel Galera, Cesar Aíra and Enrique Vila-Matas, all for *THE WHITE REVIEW*.

Anne Carson was born in Canada and teaches Ancient Greek for a living. 'Uncle Harry' appeared in *THE WHITE REVIEW NO. 15*.

Alexander Christie-Miller is a freelance writer and journalist, based between Oxford and Istanbul. He was Turkey correspondent for the *TIMES* of London from 2010 to 2016 and has also written for Newsweek, the *CHRISTIAN SCIENCE MONITOR* and the *ATLANTIC*, among other places. 'Forgotten Sea' appeared in *THE WHITE REVIEW NO. 11*.

Jack Cox has a master's degree from the University of Sydney and lives in Paris. His first novel, *DODGE ROSE*, was published in 2016 by Dalkey Archive Press. 'The Fishermen' appeared in *THE WHITE REVIEW NO. 6*.

Lauren Elkin is a contributing editor to *THE WHITE REVIEW* and the author of *FLÂNEUSE: WOMEN WALK THE CITY* (Chatto & Windus, 2016). She is Lecturer in English and co-director of the Centre for New and International Writing at the University of Liverpool. 'Barking from the Margins' appeared in *THE WHITE REVIEW NO. 8*.

JH Engström is a Swedish photographer. His work is held in collections both in Europe and USA. He lives and works in Skåne, in the south of Sweden. His work appeared in *THE WHITE REVIEW NO. 2*.

Álvaro Enrigue is a Mexican author based in New York. His novel *SUDDEN DEATH* is published in the UK by Harvill Secker in Natasha Wimmer's translation. 'A Samurai Watches the Sun Rise in Acapulco' appeared in *THE WHITE REVIEW NO. 12*.

Lucy Greaves translates from Spanish, Portuguese and French. She won the 2013 Harvill Secker Young Translators' Prize and in 2014 was Translator in Residence at the Free Word Centre in London. Her work has appeared in *GRANTA* and the *GUARDIAN*, among others, and her translation of Maria Angélica Bosco's *DEATH GOING DOWN* was published by Pushkin Press in 2017. She lives in Bristol.

Lawrence Abu Hamdan has made projects in the form of audiovisual installations, performances, graphic works, photography, Islamic sermons, cassette tape compositions, potato chip packets, essays, and lectures. In 2013 his audio documentary 'The Freedom of Speech Itself' was submitted as evidence at the UK asylum tribunal and the artist called to testify as an expert witness. His works are part of collections at MoMA New York, Van Abbe Museum Eindhoven and the Arts Council, England. 'Listening to Yourself' appeared in *THE WHITE REVIEW NO. 16*.

Evan Harris is a writer based in London.

Camille Henrot is a French artist who lives and works in New York. She was awarded the Silver Lion at the 55th Venice Biennale for her film Grosse Fatigue. She has had solo exhibitions at the Palais de Tokyo, Paris; New Museum, New York; Schinkel Pavilion, Berlin; New Orleans Museum of Art; Musée du Jeu de Paume, Paris. Her work has been included in group shows at MoMA, New York; Centre Pompidou, Paris; Astrup Fearnley Museet, Oslo; Stedelijk Museum, Amsterdam; and SculptureCenter, New York; as well as the 2015 Lyon Biennial and the 2016 Berlin Biennial. She is the recipient of the 2014 Nam June Paik Award and the Edvard Munch Art Award 2015. Her Ikebana series appeared in *THE WHITE REVIEW NO. 5*, and she was interviewed in *THE WHITE REVIEW NO. 10*.

Jennifer Hodgson has written about books for the *GUARDIAN*, *THE WHITE REVIEW*, the *REVIEW OF CONTEMPORARY FICTION*, *MUSIC AND LITERATURE* and others. She has edited a collection of Ann Quin's unpublished stories, published in 2018 by And Other Stories, and is working on a book about Quin's life and work. 'On the Decline in British Fiction' appeared in *THE WHITE REVIEW NO. 7*.

Lars Iyer teaches creative writing at Newcastle University, and is the author of the novels *SPURIOUS*, *DOGMA*, and *EXODUS*, which was shortlisted for the 2013 Goldsmiths Prize. His latest novel is *WITTGENSTEIN JR* (2014). 'Nude in

Your Hot Tub' appeared in *THE WHITE REVIEW* online in November 2011.

Chris Kraus is the author of four novels, *I LOVE DICK* (1997), *ALIENS &
ANOREXIA* (2000), *TORPOR* (2006) and *SUMMER OF HATE* (2012), two books
of cultural criticism, *VIDEO GREEN* (2004) and *WHERE ART BELONGS* (2011),
and a biography of the avant-garde writer Kathy Acker, *AFTER KATHY
ACKER* (2017). She was born in New York and raised in New Zealand. She
teaches creative writing at The European Graduate School in Switzerland.
She lives in LA. 'Resistance' appeared in *THE WHITE REVIEW NO. 10.*

Brendan Lanctot is Assistant Professor of Hispanic Studies at University
of Puget Sound. He is the author of *BEYOND CIVILIZATION AND BARBARISM:
CULTURE AND POLITICS IN POST-REVOLUTIONARY ARGENTINA* and articles on
contemporary Argentine film and literature.

Patrick Langley is a writer and producer based in London. His work has
appeared in *THE WHITE REVIEW*, the *TLS*, the Lisbon Triennale, *ARC
MAGAZINE*, *ARENA HOMME+* online, Radio 4, Radio 3, Resonance FM,
the South London Gallery and elsewhere. His debut novel, *ARKADY*, is
published by Fitzcarraldo Editions in March 2018. 'Ordinary Voids'
appeared in *THE WHITE REVIEW NO. 9.*

Evan Lavender-Smith is the author of *FROM OLD NOTEBOOKS* and *AVATAR*.
His writing has recently appeared in *BOMB*, *THE WHITE REVIEW*, *HOBART*,
THE TOAST, *ARTS & LETTERS*, *LITRO*, and *THE GOOD MEN PROJECT*. He
is an assistant professor of English at Virginia Tech. 'A Vicious Cycle'
appeared in *THE WHITE REVIEW NO. 11.*

Deborah Levy is a British playwright, novelist and poet. She is the author
of the novels *BEAUTIFUL MUTANTS* (1986), *SWALLOWING GEOGRAPHY* (1993),
THE UNLOVED (1994), *BILLY & GIRL* (1996), *SWIMMING HOME* (2011), which
was shortlisted for the 2012 Man Booker prize, and *HOT MILK*, which was
shortlisted for the 2016 Man Booker Prize. She is also the author of a collection of short stories, *BLACK VODKA* (2013), which was shortlisted for the BBC
International Short Story Award and the Frank O'Connor International
Short Story Award. She has written for the Royal Shakespeare Company
and the BBC. 'Weeping Machines' appeared in *THE WHITE REVIEW NO. 4*,
and subsequently appeared in part one of Levy's Living Autobiography,

THINGS I DON'T WANT TO KNOW (Penguin). The sequel, *THE COST OF LIVING*, will be published in 2018 by Hamish Hamilton.

Jesse Loncraine was born and grew up in London. He studied English Literature at Bristol, and Violence, Conflict and Development at SOAS. Since then he has worked on documentaries, written and taught about the International Criminal Court, worked as a landscape gardener in New York, and in a bowling alley bar. His first novel *IN THE FIELD* was published in 2017 by Blue Mark Books. 'Topsoil' appeared in *THE WHITE REVIEW NO. 7*.

Rosanna Mclaughlin is a writer and curator based in London. 'The Pious and the Pommery' appeared in *THE WHITE REVIEW NO. 18*.

China Miéville lives and works in London. He is three-time winner of the prestigious Arthur C. Clarke Award and has also won the British Fantasy Award twice. 'Estate' appeared in *THE WHITE REVIEW NO. 8*.

Samanta Schweblin was born in Buenos Aires in 1978. In 2001, she was awarded first prize by both the National Fund for the Arts and the Haroldo Conti National Competition for her debut, *EL NUCLEO DEL DISTURBIO*. In 2008, she won the Casa de las Américas prize for her second collection of stories, *PAJAROS EN LA BOCA*. Two years later, she was listed among the Best of Young Spanish Writers by *GRANTA* magazine. Her novel *FEVER DREAM* (translated by Megan McDowell) was shortlisted for the 2017 Man Booker International Prize. 'To Kill a Dog' appeared in *THE WHITE REVIEW* online in January 2014 .

'Debt', which appeared in *THE WHITE REVIEW NO. 12*, is the first chapter from *DIEGO GARCIA*, a novel-in-instalments by Natasha Soobramanien and Luke Williams. Chapter 2, 'Individualism', was published in *BOMB MAGAZINE* (Winter 2015) and chapter 3, 'Emergency', will appear in issue number 5 of Semiotext(e)'s occasional journal, *ANIMAL SHELTER* (Autumn 2017). Previously, Soobramanien wrote *GENIE AND PAUL* (Myriad Editions, 2012) and Williams, *THE ECHO CHAMBER* (Hamish Hamilton, 2011). She lives in Brussels, he, in London.

Patricia Waugh is a professor of English at Durham University. Her first book was *METAFICTION: THE THEORY AND PRACTICE OF SELF-CONSCIOUS*

FICTION (1984); since then she has written numerous books and essays on modernism and postmodernism, intellectual history and aesthetics. 'On the Decline in British Fiction' appeared in *THE WHITE REVIEW NO. 7*.

Gabriela Wiener (Lima, 1975) is author of the collections of crónicas *LLAMADA PERDIDA*, *SEXOGRAFÍAS*, *NUEVE LUNAS* and *MOZART, LA IGUANA CON PRIAPISMO Y OTRAS HISTORIAS*. Her work also includes the poetry collection *EJERCICIOS PARA EL ENDURECIMIENTO DEL ESPÍRITU*. Her Crónicas have been translated into English, Italian and French. She has lived in Madrid since 2011, where she continues to write for some of the most important magazines and newspapers in America and Europe. 'A Weekend with my Own Death' appeared in *THE WHITE REVIEW NO. 14*.

ACKNOWLEDGEMENTS

To name everyone who contributed to the success of *THE WHITE REVIEW*
over its first seven years would require the publication of a separate volume,
but the editors would like to thank some of those without whom it could not
have existed. These include our first supporters who showed faith in the
enterprise when few would have, and those, like Sophie Lewis, who advised
us in the early days when we didn't know what we were doing. Special
thanks to Tom Morrison-Bell, now a member of the board, to Michael
Amherst for his early encouragement, and to everyone who has subscribed
over the years.

The magazine has been shaped by the many who have worked with us
before moving onto better (and better remunerated) things: Esme Anderson,
Isabel Blake, Cassie Davies, James Draney, Louisa Dunnigan, Lucie Elven,
Ellen Evans, Helen Graham, Mary Hannity, Cosima Hibbert, Octavia
Lamb, Carla Manfredino, Bella Marrin, Hannah Phillips, Izabella Scott,
Oliver Taylor, J. S. Tennant, Harry Thorne, Gabriella Voyias, Lowenna
Waters and Scott Wilson. We're fortunate to have enjoyed the support
of wonderful contributing editors, who relay ideas to us from around the
country and the world: Jacob Bromberg (the very first), Lauren Elkin,
Emmie Francis, Orit Gat, Patrick Langley, Sam Solnick, Emily Stokes and
Kishani Widyaratna.

Special thanks also to Daniel Medin, whose annual translation issue
has been a highlight of the magazine's publication schedule since 2013, and
to whom we owe the inclusion of Samanta Schweblin in this anthology.
Thanks are also due to the current *WHITE REVIEW* staff: Francesca Wade,
Tyler Curtis, Cecilia Tricker, Shoshana Kessler, Rose Alana Frith, Ralf
Webb, Berry Patten. Thanks to Chris Burman for dealing with web crises
from silent meditation retreats in France. Thanks, as ever, to art director
Ray O'Meara and designer Thom Swann for making us look good.

Most of all we are grateful to the artists and writers with whom we have
worked, upon whose talent *THE WHITE REVIEW* has been built.

Cover and title page:
Camille Henrot
Untitled, ('Tropics of Love' series), 2010
Ink on paper
21 cm × 29.7 cm